The FATE of TOMORROW

*A Tale of the Annigan Cycle
in Three Acts*

BOOK ONE

R.W. MARCUS

LAUGHING BIRD PUBLISHING
SAINT PETERSBURG, FL, USA

Copyright © 2018 by Jeff Morris

All rights reserved under the Pan-American and International Copyright Conventions. No part of this publication may be reproduced, distributed, or transmitted in any form or by any means, including photocopying, recording, or other electronic or mechanical methods, without the prior written permission of the publisher, except in the case of brief quotations embodied in critical reviews and certain other noncommercial uses permitted by copyright law.

Published by Laughing Bird Publications, St. Petersburg, Florida

Visit us on the web!
https://AnniganCycle.com

Front and back cover design by SelfPubBookCovers
https://SelfPubBookCovers.com

Laughing Bird Publications® is a registered trademark of Mark Phillips

Manufactured in the United States of America
10 9 8 7 6 5 4

First Printing, 2018
Second Printing, 2020
Third Printing, 2021
Revised Fourth Printing, 2023

ISBN 978-1-7320211-8-1

*Dedicated to
Edgar Rice Burroughs,
with a wink and a nod to
Philip José Farmer,
and Quentin Tarantino.*

CONTENTS

CONTENTS iv
ACKNOWLEDGMENTS i
PREFACE ii
Welcome to the Annigan…... iii
ACT ONE The Makatooa Incident 1
ACT TWO The Zorian Quandary 122
ACT THREE The Amarenian Legacy 278
GLOSSARY 384
MAPS 422
ABOUT THE AUTHOR 428

ACKNOWLEDGMENTS

The number one instrumental force in the writing of this book was a place and not a person. I sat on the porch, at Dog Island, Florida, watching ghost crabs scurrying along the dunes and asked myself the fateful question, *I wonder what sentient aquatic life would be like?*

Thank you…

To my Partner in Crime, Cheryl Pepper, for making that moment, her support and being the first to see this work.

To Mark Phillips, for his constant, unwavering support, creativity and being the best sounding board ever. He also pushed me to expand on and add new original content for this revised version of my first novel.

To the original gaming group which honed this world while in development as a Role-Playing Game: Valentino Pine; Geoff Nelson; Sally Phillips-Withrow; Pat Toohey; Joe Kelly; Jon Anderson; Alan Rosenthal; Wes Ganote; and Michael Hutchins.

And, of course, a big shout-out to my Beta Readers: Pat Boyer; Tom Lancraft; Lynn Marie Firehammer; Dave Holman; Marge Skaggs; Tristan Shuler; Lare Watson Hailey; Misti Kehoe; and Stephen Culbreath.

Special thanks to Yrik-Max Valentonis for taking the time to critique all aspects of the story, and to Rosy Hall. They both doubled down with the initial editing duties.

As this third edition rolls off the press, I would be remiss if I didn't acknowledge the team at Laughing Bird Publishing who grabbed the baton and ran with it. It was their constant support and belief in this twisted little endeavor which saw things through.

Last, but certainly not least, is the amazing artwork by Raven and Black.

PREFACE

I literally completed this book in a hurricane. While Hurricane Irma slashed across my city, I penned the last words watching the trees dance outside my window. A fitting and rather Hemingway-style conclusion I imagined, to a writing project born with the demise of my Role-Playing Game Campaign.

Initially, the first act of this work was to be a standalone module, to be played in coordination with the main game. The problem started when I became totally enamored with the characters. These, I decided, were too compelling to turn over to gamers and their whims.

Another reason to take my world from the gaming table to the printed page was the copious amount of back story and world building in every game that went undiscovered. Players would often go in completely different directions.

Finally, I discovered that writing this novel was very therapeutic. In my hectic, very stressful life, where control is limited, here was a world I could command. A rather pleasant bonus that was because this is fantasy, I didn't have to worry about the usual constraints of science and reality.

In other words, this manuscript has allowed me to feed my inner control freak.

Welcome to the Annigan...

...this mostly aquatic planet travels in a geosynchronous orbit around a small yellow sun. It's set far enough back in the solar system's Goldilocks Zone it maintains an atmosphere conducive to a wide variety of life.

Sentient creatures, terrestrial, marine or amphibious, share a hyper-fertility devoid of genetic boundaries. Any sentient creature may mate with any other and produce offspring.

Lumina basks in perpetual sunlight on one side of the Annigan. Humans dwell alongside many other sentient races thriving across its various continents and island chains. The fertility enriching rays of the sun, and the warmth of the Shallow Sea, support a vibrant and rich ecosystem.

Although life is abundant there, Lumina is hardly a serene place as you will see. Millennia of feuds, ruthless ambition and individual hatreds forged a fragile peace, barely sustained under the rule of the Great Houses.

Because of the incredible diversity of sentient creatures, all races, genders and hybrids in Lumina enjoy social equality, judging each as an individual based upon their own merits. Beneath the veneer of peace, however, dwells a hotbed of totalitarian torture, raider uprisings and a constant escalating cold war between the Great Houses.

Nocturn, languishes in constant darkness on the other side of the Annigan. Only moonlight, starlight and bioluminescence illuminate the land of endless night. Without the warming rays of the sun, Nocturn's oceans froze over, but constant geothermal activity heats the land masses, creating a temperate and misty terrain teeming with exotic and predatory sentient races.

Imperialistic cat people rule aboveground and hive nations of humanoid mantises swarm beneath the surface. In the Ocean Deep, a race of sentient octopoids dwell in vast underwater cities worshiping the ancient ones of the abyss. You are predator or prey in Nocturn's despotic societies.

The Twilight Lands reside at the fringes of the Annigan and remain in a constant gloaming. Here, warm and cold air currents clash, generating a perpetually stormy climate.

Ruled by the amphibian Bailian race, the Twilight Lands serve as a neutral zone for cultures from every corner of the Annigan. Many encountering the other races for the first time, and like the weather, their clashes can prove tempestuous.

Only the sun of Lumina keeps back the nocturnal predators of the dark side. Legends tell of a prophesied great eclipse stripping away all boundaries and igniting an apocalyptic war. Until then…

…these are the tales from the Annigan Cycle.

The Annigan cycles through the void.
Moon and fog, blood, and flame
the sentient cycle, the cycle of man
All flow into tomorrow, with fate unknown.

ACT ONE

The Makatooa Incident

"This damnable fog is ruining the collar on my new jacket," Shom Eldor grumbled. Sweeping a bang of straight blonde hair off his smooth babyface, he scowled and pulled the knee-length, Kel skin coat tighter against the dampness.
Captain Maluria de Scoth stood next to him on the bow of her ship, the *Regis*. Her honey brown skin and white blouse vibrantly contrasted against the fog surrounding her.

"This is why I left your whiny ass grands ago," she said with a sideways glance. "If I hadn't seen you fight with my own eyes, I'd swear you were a Morasian Puff Boy."

Shom narrowed his eyes but let the jab pass.

"I just assumed you made your rather *sudden* departure because another unpleasant slice of your colorful past came calling. I mean, with the skeletons in *your* closet, Maluria, you can only imagine how shocked I was to find you still sailing *any* ship, much less this thing."

Mal's shoulder-length black hair swayed as she spun on her heels and placed her hands on her hips, defiantly. Her green eyes flashed, glaring at her former partner and lover. It had been four grands since she fell for the youngest royal of House Eldor. Their scandalous affair was torrid, tumultuous, and brief. He was decent with a blade and in bed, but she always knew she'd have to cut him loose.

"As I recall, *this thing* got our asses out of many tight situations," she snapped.

"I must admit, she's fast, and she *did* get us into some rather remote locals."

"Yeah, like this one. Remember, you are the reason we're sneaking around this way... so keep your fucking voice down. Sound travels over water."

Mal peered back off the bow, raised her hand and pointed starboard. The helmsman up on the quarterdeck acknowledged the captain's direction and adjusted course around a low outcropping of mangroves. The dense aquatic tree's thick, tangled roots appeared out of the murky haze.

"Look, I understand keeping a low profile," Shom said, "but traveling *this* far in the backwaters in the middle of the Kan..."

"Look, Shommy, *I'm* in charge of this tub. I don't know what the fuck we're carrying, but you paid me a lot of money to get your package to Zor. And..." she stretched the word out, ignoring his impish grin when she mentioned his package, "I've got my own special cargo and no desire to run into a quartermaster's Interceptor. So, we're doing it my way, even if it fucking means creeping along the coast to Honia."

Shom's lips tightened. "Don't call me Shommy."

"That's because, *Shommy,* if we take our time, they'll just be shaking off the Kan when we get there, and when their boats hit the water, we get lost in the crowd."

"Fine. Whatever it takes, just get us there. I don't know or even care what's in the damn box. I just know delivering it might be my last chance to redeem myself in my father's eyes."

"I don't know about that, Shommy, once a prodigal always a prodigal. Besides, this package can't be *that* fucking important, or they wouldn't have given it to the family fool to deliver…"

Shom cleared his throat and postured to protest, but Mal pressed on, "…but clearly, they want you *and* your package out of sight. So, we keep to the coast."

Shom sighed and stared into the eerie, milky white fog of mid Kan, the traditional time of rest in the Goyan Islands. According to his childhood tutors, Mount Goya's volcanic activity creates subaqueous geysers erupting like clockwork, mid cycle, boiling up the massive cloud banks of moisture. This dense fog rolls in off the Shallow Sea and over the islands, providing relief from Lumina's endless sunshine.

The Kan seemed to cast a primal spell over the islanders and lulls most to sleep. The very name Kan came from, Kanay, a word for sleep in the ancient proto-human language, Yassett.

Even now, Shom needed strong teas and short naps to fight back the conditioned drowsiness. Not that he hadn't spent many a Kan carousing in taverns and whorehouses—the only thriving industry during those hours—but the majority of Goya shut down and returned to their homes to rest.

Because the fog's denseness made travel too difficult for most, raiders, brigands and smugglers used the Kan to cover their crimes. Mal, being a Spice Rat, clearly felt far too at home smuggling in it, but for Shom being out in it carried a sense of unnaturalness and dread. He'd discovered that the absence of light brought out the worst in others.

He remembered bedtime stories his nannies told about Nocturn—the land of perpetual night on the dark side of the world. Their tales of unspeakable monsters thriving in the everlasting night haunted his childhood dreams.

Shom shuddered gazing through the mist at the jungle's foreboding silhouettes just five feet off the port side. His eyes played tricks with the shadows and he reminded himself Lumina had its own share of evil.

"Aren't you worried about anyone onshore?" he asked.

"I'll take my chances with the locals," Mal impatiently replied. "Just keep the quartermasters off my ass."

Shom nervously eyed the thick vegetation.

"Check… quartermasters… nasty lot …"

Mal shook her head in remembrance. "By the time they strike their colors, the EEtahs are already in the water and you are going to be boarded. Have you ever *seen* an EEtah Shommy?"

"Of course, I have! Those vulgar, foul-smelling Man-sharks are everywhere."

"Have you ever seen an EEtah *angry*?"

Shom opened his mouth to speak, but Mal stopped him. "Angry *at you,* Shommy?"

He sighed, acknowledging defeat. "I asked you not to call me that."

She pouted mockingly and brushed her palm against his cheek.

"Aww, with all we've been through, I figure I've earned the right to call you anything I want."

"I would rather you no…"

The sudden heaving of the ship propelled Mal into Shom's chest, cutting his sentence short. He instinctively reached out to steady her, when a tree branch ripped across his shoulders pushing them face to face. Instinctively, Mal quickly shoved Shom off her.

"Dammit Shommy, shut the fuck up and stop distracting me!"

Shom didn't hear her over his own tirade of obscenities upon discovering the tear in the back of his jacket. Yanking it off, he examined the large gash in the Kel skin and threw it onto the deck in a fit of rage. Mal scowled angrily at Shom before grabbing him, covering his mouth, and growling in his ear.

"I told you to shut the fuck up!"

The Fate of Tomorrow

The mangroves rustled and they felt the bump of something heavy dropping onto the deck of the ship. Turning they saw a bone white face with dark, ominous accents around the eyes and mouth. It howled fiercely before disappearing in the mist. It was quickly followed by the death cry of a crewmember and a haze of gore spraying across the deck.

Mal and Shom drew their swords while blood pooled around their feet. They heard three more thumps and more shipmates screaming. Both now swung blindly into the mist, but the invaders seemed to fade in and out of the Kan evading their blows.

Shom stumbled over his jacket on the deck and swept it up with his free hand. Waving it over his head cleared a bank of fog around him.

Through the parting gloom he could make out four stout warrior women—bare-chested, barefoot, and wearing coarse, loose-fitting, cropped pants—crouching on the main deck. The ghostly warriors brandished short swords and they looked around for more victims.

Mal was astonished to see that the old sea stories were true. Their exposed bodies were covered with thick white powder, highlighted by black streaks, which camouflaged them in the Kan, creating the uncanny effect of fading in and out of visibility. The accents to their faces gave the appearance of skulls, supporting the illusion they were otherworldly fiends.

Two more invaders dropped on the deck from the low-hanging branches above. One drew her sword from a scabbard strapped across her back, mid-leap, and plunged the blade through the top of the first mate's head. The momentum drove the steel to the hilt. Red mist sprayed the snow-white chest of the wild-eyed attacker and she let out a bloodcurdling war scream. The others joined in like a howling pack.

Before Shom or Mal could react, a low, swooshing sound drew their attention and they watched in horror when a grappling hook swung from the trees, impaling the helmsman. He toppled to the starboard side, spinning the ship wheel with his momentum.

They lurched violently toward open water, sending Shom and Mal over the side and into the murky waters of the Shallow Sea.

The two surfaced and began treading water in time to see the *Regis* slip into the fog. Mal continued to stare where her ship disappeared, her face masked with pure rage. She could still hear the clash of fighting ringing from the decks and echoing across the water.

"So much for the locals," Shom quipped, spitting out a mouthful of water.

"Those weren't locals," she said, shaking her head. "Those were Kan Ghosts… fucking Amarenian raiders!"

"What in the name of the Gods are they doing this far west?"

"How the fuck do I know? But mark my words, those quims will fucking pay and pay dearly for this."

"Well, until that payday," Shom said, "we best start swimming for shore and hope the sharks don't notice."

Fia, captain of the raider ship, *Voola,* stood on the poop deck of the captured *Regis* and surveyed her prize. She untied her thick reddish-brown hair and shook it free; it fell just shy of her shoulders. She stood six feet tall in her bare feet, with broad shoulders and big bones. Rayth tribal style tattoos ran the length of her body, encircled her breasts and framed the bone-bead pearling around their areolas. War stripes crossed her face from right to left, like the claw marks of a Deard Cat. The Amarenian raider never felt more alive than when she heard the lamentation of men. Her nipples stood so erect they ached.

She'd ordered her crew to capture as many prisoners as possible, and they hadn't disappointed. The sheep like peoples of the Goyan Islands had grown so soft under the rule of the Great Houses. Eighteen of the twenty-three crew members of the *Regis* surrendered under the threat of her fierce Rayth raiders.

The mariners easily overpowered those brave enough to fight back. They gutted them with their cutlasses, flamboyantly showing off their martial skills, before leaving their steaming remains in a heap on the deck.

They separated the human males from the other captives. Her crew lined the remaining two human females and one Picean male up against the starboard side of the ship. They tied their hands in front of them and bound their ankles in heavy rope. Armed mariners held blades to their throats and Captain Fia walked up to the Picean.

"Are you their translator?" Fia asked the tall, humanoid fish-man in Amarenian.

"I... I am," the Picean stammered in her language.

"Translate for *me*," she said, "or I'll cut your throat where you stand, and you'll never speak again. What say you?"

"I w... w... would be honored to serve you, Captain," the Picean said, the dorsal fin on top of its head leaning submissively to the left.

"I accept your offer, translator," Captain Fia proclaimed. Fia nodded and the two mariners released him from his bindings. "Your services start now."

She turned to the first human female. "You have an important choice to make."

The Picean hurriedly repeated the statement in Common. The Amarenian captain pushed nose to nose with the trembling female. Her hands slid under the captive's shirt and groped her small breasts.

"Not much here to work with," Fia said, circling the nipples with her fingertips, "but you are a woman and Amarenian custom demands I offer you this choice. You either can swear yourself to my crew or I push you into the cold wet embrace of the Sea Goddess Charen. How do you choose?"

Fia pulled her hands from the shirt and waited for the translator to finish.

The captive listened and then turned away from the pirate captain's gaze. Her mouth opened to speak, but she could only whimper.

The Amarenian captain grabbed the woman's chin and tilted her head up, forcing eye contact.

"Is that a yes or a no?"

"No, no, no," the captive began repeating, her eyes wide with panic.

"So be it, *cock lover*," Fia said with a sneer.

The captain withdrew her cutlass and cut the rope binding the woman's hands in a manner which sliced open her inner arms and wrists so the blood would attract sharks. Fia then kicked against the hostage's chest and propelled her backwards. Blood sprayed from her flailing arms when she fell over the taffrail. Her brief scream died with a loud splash.

Captain Fia then approached the next prisoner. Before she could even speak, the woman frantically nodded her head.

"I'm in!" she yelled. "I swear myself! I swear to you! I'll join you! I'll join your crew!"

Fia smiled knowingly at the prisoner with the Picean's translation.

"Oh, so you'll *join* my crew?" she asked incredulously. "You're not joining. You're swearing yourself *to* my crew.

Then, if you first prove yourself worthy, we may talk of you *joining* my crew. Amarenians rose from slavery, and so must you. Now, do you still so swear?"

Fia grabbed the woman's ponytail and pulled her head back, so they faced each other. The captive swallowed back the pain with a gasp but continued to nod against the captain's grip.

"I do," she confirmed. "I swear."

Fia gestured for the mariners to untie her. Once they released her, they kept their hands firmly on her shoulders and forced her to keep facing the captain.

The crew had bound the human male captives in a row, wrist to wrist and ankle to ankle, showing off the finest in Amarenian bondage knots.

As was Rayth raider custom, she'd ordered them stripped naked. They then secured the entire line of hostages to the mast rigging in a manner, so they suspended them across the center of the deck, arms and legs vulnerably pulled apart. While they hung exposed, Fia stood before them.

"Not that long ago," she began, "men just like you, hailing from the so called 'noble' House Whitmar..."

Her crew jeered and hissed in hatred so loudly at the name Whitmar it forced the translator to yell over the din. The agitated crew shook the ropes tied to the rigging and forced the hostages to rock back and forth violently. Captain Fia gestured for them to calm down before continuing.

"Those *men*..." she extended the word, grimacing with distaste, "...of House Whitmar took our foremothers as slaves and sold them into whoredom. But the blood of Tanil pirates flowed through their veins, and they rose against their overlords. No man will ever despoil us again."

She turned to face a mariner, even taller and more muscular than the captain. "Hill Sister, check these miserable dags for worthy breeders."

Fia moved aside for the burly Amarenian. The Hill Sister approached the first hostage. She examined his hair, teeth, and the whites of his eyes. Then she knelt before him, focusing her attention between his legs. The outline of a large, partially erect penis bulging inside her cropped pants confused the prisoner.

Large, rough hands clutched his testicles and squeezed them.

The Hill Sister then stood up, shook her head no and walked behind the prisoner. She placed the tip of her cutlass between his ass cheeks.

"As our defilers penetrated us," Captain Fia proclaimed, "you have been deemed unworthy and so you shall be."

The hostage howled in pain when the blade ripped into his bowels. The Hill Sister then repeated the process with each prisoner.

With everyone's attention focused on their bloodlust, the Picean translator slowly backed towards the taffrail. The last male prisoner's shrieks of agony covered the sound of the Picean's dive overboard, and she made her escape undetected.

Unfortunately, she landed in the middle of the swarming shark's feeding frenzy. Even though Picean's are incredible swimmers, she wasn't fast enough to escape the sharks of the Shallow Sea.

His name was Madzos and, like his friend Ruffin, he was born in the same nameless fishing hamlet on the eastern side of Paden Island. The two friends had fished the waters of the Shallow Sea together almost every day for the last fifty grands. Everyone laughingly claimed it was to get away from their wives.

The Fate of Tomorrow

When they were younger and stronger, they fished the western side of the island where they found the biggest fish. Because of the powerful crossing currents sweeping up from the Zerian Reef to the west, it took skill and stamina to navigate those waters in their tiny fishing boat. Now they stayed to the quieter, eastern side of the island. The fishing was still decent, just not as dangerous, which suited the old fishers just fine.

This trip proved different, however. They stayed out too late, chasing a school of Paota fish, and the Kan rolled in, forcing them to make camp. The sound of a seaborne battle just offshore awoke them. As a precaution, they broke camp early to return home before the fog lifted. They doused the campfire and began loading the boat.

"Do you think it was pirates?" Ruffin nervously asked.

"Who knows," Madzos replied. "Once the navy pulls out, everything always goes to shit."

Ruffin chuckled and tossed his sack into the boat. The sound of splashing drew his attention to Shom and Mal walking out of the Shallow Sea and into camp.

"We don't have any money," Ruffin stated meekly, bowing his head.

"Yes... yes," added Madzos. "But we will gladly share our catch with you, if you are hungry."

"Hello," Shom began, stepping forward with a broad smile. "My name is... well, my name really isn't important. What is important, is the fact my friend and I require immediate transportation on your boat."

The two fishers exchanged nervous glances.

Shom grimaced to stress his earnestness. "It is *rather* urgent."

"W-w-well," Madzos timidly stammered. "We were heading home and..."

The old man stopped in mid-sentence at the sound of Mal noisily drawing her sword from its sheath.

"Splendid, we'll tag along then!" Shom proclaimed.

He leaned into them, placed a hand on the side of his mouth, in an exaggerated whisper.

"She really *can* be quite insistent."

As luck would have it, tracking the stolen ship wasn't difficult. The Kan fog quickly lifted, and the old men were deceptively strong rowers. The procession of bodies and debris in the water left an obvious trail, beginning with the corpses of her helmsman and first mate.

Mal stared down at their lifeless forms floating by, and a low growl came from the back of her throat. The raiders didn't just kill her men. They stripped them naked from the waist down to emasculate them in standard Amarenian Rayth fashion.

She had never previously dealt with the infamous Kan Ghosts. They tended to prey on the shipping of the eastern agricultural islands instead of the western spice islands. However, sailors liked to talk, and the tales of torture and sexual enslavement whispered over late-night tankards were horrific.

"I actually liked that crew," she murmured.

She watched various deck flotsam float by, shaking her head and running her hand over the hilt of her sword nervously, thinking, *it's all gone—my crew, my ship, and cargo… but not for long.*

They finally caught sight of the *Regis* in the straits, with the rest of the outgoing fishing boats. She listed badly while making the crossing from Padan to Galin Island.

"What the fuck did they do to my ship?!" Mal yelled when she first caught sight of her.

Shom joined his friend on the bow, staring in disbelief. An Amarenian raider ship sailed beside the *Regis*, with colors stowed so as not to attract attention. Their vessel was about the same size as the *Regis*, with two masts and a medium-to-low draft for navigating shallow waters. No wonder the raider could hide among the mangroves.

"Every single one of those quims is going to die slowly, and I will savor every centi of their anguish," Mal swore.

"May I remind you my dear," Shom noted, "there are only two of us?"

"She won't make it very far damaged like that," Mal assessed.

"You would have thought they'd have just taken the cargo and burned the ship," Shom offered.

"Not Amarenians," she countered. "They need every ship they can steal. They'll have to stop in Makatooa for repairs and, at that point, their asses belong to me!"

"I imagine you have friends there?"

"In my business, you really don't have friends, Shommy, just associates and customers."

"Well, that certainly explains us," he resolutely noted.

"But, yes, I've got a *very* influential contact in Makatooa."

They escorted the *Regis* along the northern coast of Galin Island and headed west. Madzos' fishing boat easily followed without being noticed, lost among the volume of fishers on the channel near the busy seaport.

A lack of Caldani ships in the area struck Mal as odd, since this was their primary area of operation. Not that she minded their absence—she operated illegally as a Spice Rat and Calden Privateers worked hand in hand with every smuggler's main nemesis, the quartermasters.

However, since House Calden, favored harassing House Aramos charters, Mal carried shipping charters from both Aramos and Calden. An expensive initial investment which had saved many a cargo from confiscation.

Two miles from the Makatooa Inlet, the Amarenian raider ship peeled off from the *Regis* and set anchor close to shore, hidden in a stand of mangroves. The injured ship continued its crippled pace toward the seaport.

After a sleepless Kan breaking in her new Goyan Island cabin girl, Captain Fia warily eyed the docks ahead. The entrance to Makatooa Harbor made for an impressive sight. They built the sprawling seaport nestled securely in a deep mountain inlet surrounded by a dense, tropical rainforest extending to the sea.

She also noted they built the entrance to the harbor narrow enough to be easily defensible. Its strategic location put it in proximity to the Zerian Reef, the Outer Zerian Chain, and, ultimately, House Aramos, which controlled the territory.

Fia put First Mate Betha in command of the hidden raider ship, *Voola*, along with five mariners. Her remaining crew of eleven stayed on the *Regis* to quickly secure repairs and liquidate the cargo. She supervised Mariner Neaux, a short, stocky brunette with a plump face and chest, struggling with controlling the ship's damaged wheel.

"Steady, just a little further," Fia encouraged, still surveying the inlet.

Mariner Suu, a tall, slender brunette, bounded up the stairs to the bridge and approached the captain.

"Captain," she reported, "we've completed inventory of the hold."

"And what did we find?" she asked, keeping her eyes on the bustle of maritime activity.

The Fate of Tomorrow

"There's been a problem."

This broke Fia out of her trancelike assessment of the harbor.

"What?"

"Mariner Keann attempted to identify the liquid in a small cask..."

"And?"

The mariner's head bowed.

"She's dead."

"What?!?"

Without waiting, she set off down the stairs, with Suu right behind her.

"We tried smelling it first," Suu explained, trying to keep up with the captain. "It had no odor, so Keann dipped a finger in and touched it to her tongue."

Fia scrambled down the stairs and around obstacles. Wary mariners saw her coming and, noting the expression on her face, quickly got out of the way.

Down in the hold, two mariners knelt over the prone body while three others stood in shock. The captain pushed them out of the way and stood over her dead crew member. The mariner's skin had turned a grayish purple. Blood oozed from her eyes, nose, and ears. Her bloated, black tongue protruded completely from her mouth. The corpse's eyes were wide open, as if in awe. Fia shook her head in grim recognition.

"Noma," she muttered.

"What?" Suu asked, leaning closer.

"Venom of the Noma Viper," the captain explained. "A snake common to these islands, every bit as deadly as our Seet Adder."

The crew gasped and murmured amongst themselves. By now, even the deck hands peered curiously into the hold.

"With a very important difference," Fia added.

All went silent.

"If you process Noma venom correctly and inhale the right amount, it allows temporary travel into the Middle Realms, making it priceless for collectors and mages. Breath in too much, however, and you'll never leave those realms again. Under no condition is it *ever* touched, much less tasted."

The captain slowly rose from the corpse.

"Full immersion with honors," she ordered.

Fia walked away but saw the crew continuing to gaze down at their fallen comrade in shock.

"Get back to work!" she bellowed. "We dock soon and I want us ready!"

The deckhands scrambled away from the hold. Fia turned back to Suu.

"Get her body ready for Immersion and then..."

The body of Mariner Keann twitched and then convulsed. They stepped back in shock when the animated corpse of their former crew mate rose to its knees, reached out and tried to speak. The bloated tongue prevented anything but gibberish and bubbles of black bile to escape.

Captain Fia drew her cutlass and, in one powerful arc, cleaved Keann in half from skull to groin. The horrific stench forced all but the captain to recoil in revulsion. Rotting, gray body parts and putrid blood greased the deck. Fia calmly reached down, wiped her blade off on Keann's right pant leg and sheathed it.

"She travels the Middle Realms now," she said flatly. "My order still stands. Prepare her for immersion with full honors."

Suu nodded solemnly. Fia placed her hand upon Suu's shoulder and held her head up speaking at the open hold and her eavesdropping crew.

"We *will* pay proper tribute to our fallen sister, then we must repair the newest ship in our fleet and safely be on our way."

"Well, that was unexpected," Shom noted, clearly amused.

"What, Shommy?"

Mal came to an abrupt stop, ignoring the noisy commotion of the docks. Shom also quickly stopped to avoid running into her.

"It's... It's just..."

"What?!" she demanded, shoving herself inches from him, face to face.

"I mean, you *paid* them! That was from your emergency stash."

"So?"

"You wouldn't possibly be going soft on me, would you Maluria?"

She stood silently, staring. Shom swallowed nervously under her intense gaze.

"I don't steal from people poorer than me!" she declared.

Nodding confidently, Mal pushed on through the noisy crowd. Shom scratched his head in confusion and followed.

"I have someone I need to talk to," she said over the din.

Alto de Gom felt proud, stepping onto the docks of Makatooa and into a new life. At the age of thirty, he would be the youngest Rohina Takii swordmaster to ever open his own school. The school's location might not be on his home island of Gom just down the chain, as he had hoped, but with the size of this city, his master's decision made sense.

Taking in the bustling seaport, he adjusted his backpack and swept shoulder-length brown hair from his face. At first glance, there was nothing which would single him out from a crowd, nothing betraying his deadly occupation. His thin almost six-foot frame and olive complexion matched most men of the Goyan Islands. Upon closer examination, the matching long sword, short sword, and boot knife might give pause to anyone paying attention; or perhaps they might notice his graceful walk, like a cat gliding.

With a deep, contented sigh, Alto stepped into the crowds. He was contemplating the size of the Gull station when a very determined Mal walked directly into his path. The Spice Rat kept as brisk a pace as possible, given the activity around her, and nearly collided with the swordmaster.

"I beg your pardon, Mz," he apologized with a slight bow.

Mal ignored him, almost pushing him out of the way. Shom, a step behind, paused for a moment.

"Please forgive my friend," he implored. "Her ill-tempered mood perfectly complements her complete lack of social graces."

Both men chuckled. Then they eyed each other up and down, focusing on the other's weapons.

"Takii?" Shom asked, his eyes narrowing.

Alto gave a sly smile and nodded.

"Zorian?" Alto asked back.

Now it was Shom's turn to nod. "Briefly. Apparently, I had discipline issues."

Alto smiled at the self-deprecation and gave a little shrug.

"You do realize," the swordmaster said, "by all rights, we should be arranging a duel right now?"

A brief, tense moment passed between them.

"However, I just arrived," Alto said, breaking the silence.

"As did I," Shom added, "and... I'm not from here, nor do I have any plans to stay. I'm just keeping my friend out of trouble. So, I guess this is good day sir. Perhaps we shall meet again."

"Perhaps," Alto agreed.

With that the young royal was off trying to catch up with Mal.

Alto smiled and stroked his neatly trimmed goatee.

An interesting welcome indeed, he thought. *First things first however: lodging, a meal, some drink, and then a whore.*

The dockyards of any Goyan seaport could overwhelm the senses. Mal struggled to ignore the cacophony of noise, babbling languages, filth and food. In the larger cities, such as Makatooa, the waterfront can appear like complete chaos. Fishers and merchants turned aggressive barkers, selling wares spread across the docks and competing for prospective buyers.

She navigated around the congestion of an Otick pearl vendor. Three of the large, humanoid crabs displayed tubs of low-grade pearls they harvested from their vast oyster beds just offshore. They negotiated a price with a human artisan apparently seeking the pearls for decoration. A Picean, whose cranial dorsal fin stood erect in attention, facilitated the negotiations. The Piceans were the second most prevalent race on the docks next to humans. The Oticks waved their claws about accentuating the bargaining. The Picean's gills fluttered over his ears when its membrane translated the Otick's high squeaks to the human.

Mal continued down the docks with a determined stride, tersely brushing off the overzealous merchants and almost getting into a fist fight with one. She finally stopped before a Nelayan fish merchant who set his catch up next to the *Regis*. While standing expectantly over the seemingly uncaring deep diving fisher, Mal discreetly counted the Amarenian guards surrounding her damaged ship.

The Nelayan's vibrant blue-green skin and long, curly red hair shimmered in the sun. It perched upon a long shipping box, reclining against a pylon with his two large folded, dorsal fins cushioning his back. A huge, brimmed hat hid his face and shielded his naked body from the constant daylight. His barbed fishing spear, taller than the vendor, rested beside him with its rope lanyard coiled against the dock mooring.

Lying beside him were only two fish. However, they were different in color and size than the others being offered up and down the wharf. Mal recognized them for being a delicacy, and impossible to catch by line or net, because of their ability to navigate the deep Zerian Reef. Both would fetch a handsome price.

Mal stood, looming before him. He appeared oblivious to her presence, clearly the only vendor who evidently didn't care about making a sale.

"By the gods," Shom admonished, just catching up with her, "did you intend to make an enemy of everyone on these docks? Must I point out, once again, there are only two of us?"

Mal ignored him, staring down at the seated Nelayan, who still hadn't acknowledged her presence.

"What happened to your ship, Mal?" the Nelayan asked with a high-pitched voice from below the hat. "And who are your new friends?"

He glanced up from under his hat and smiled. His large nose, ears, and lips, studded with piercings, complimented a mouth full of sharpened black teeth.

"I've missed you too, Kuut," Mal said.

"They pulled in three deci ago," Kuut offered, nodding toward the *Regis*. "Their guards set up a perimeter, allowing no one on. Their captain met with the harbormaster, over there, on the main gangplank."

"You wouldn't have overheard anything?" Mal probed.

"Perhaps...?" he hissed.

In a quick, fluid motion, undetectable to anyone else on the docks, she flicked a silver coin into his lap.

"They told the harbormaster they found it drifting abandoned and claimed salvage rights," Kuut whispered. "Brought it in for repairs, invoking the Maritime Acquisition Clause."

Mal sneered, her fist tightening around the hilt of her sword. She surreptitiously tossed him another coin.

"And...?"

"From his body language, I don't think they convinced the harbormaster," Kuut added. "Once he left, the captain headed for town carrying a small box."

Mal and Shom exchanged nervous glances. Shom dropped a secor, an Imperial gold ingot, into the Nelayan's lap.

"I trust you'll keep a sharp eye on our current situation?" the prodigal asked, nodding toward the *Regis*.

Kuut's face lit up as he palmed the single most valuable coin in the Goyan Islands. He flashed another smile before pulling the brim of his hat back over his face.

"I always look out for my friends," he said, "especially ones who pay."

Mariners Suu and Zoe watched the repair crew from the long main boardwalk of the wharf. The dozen carpenters and shipwrights moved about the ship with ballet-like grace and precision which impressed them. An elderly man on the dock reviewed schematics unrolled over a low table, pointing at the diagrams and then the ship. Occasionally, he would address a younger man beside him who nodded in agreement.

"These are the men we seek," Suu declared, and motioned toward the old man, "and *that* is their leader."

Zoe nodded in agreement and the pair made their way through the laborers. Suu caught Zoe wincing at the pungent body odor from the sweating male workers around them.

"Remember Mariner," Suu advised softly in Sister Speak, "we must appear friendly. I know you're uncomfortable, but this is important."

"Dags!" she spat, using the derogatory Amarenian term for male slaves.

"Don't speak our language so loudly," Suu admonished. "Use the Common tongue. And look on the bright side, Zoe, at least they're not Whitmars."

Zoe nodded begrudgingly and the two approached the old man in time to overhear him berating his assistant.

"You better remind those carpenters working on the rudder," he warned, in a deep, craggy voice. "I expect it complete before the Kan or I'll dock their pay!"

The young man nodded furiously.

"Go!" he impatiently ordered.

The assistant quickly turned and scurried off. Zoe seized the opportunity and stepped up to the table.

"We require your immediate assistance," she demanded in a mercurial tone.

The old man ignored her and focused on the schematics.

"I said, we require your immediate assistance!" Zoe repeated, raising her voice and stepping forward.

"I heard what you said," the old man replied without looking up.

A few tense moments passed.

"Well?!?" she asked indignantly.

Zoe instinctively gripped the hilt of her short sword. Suu placed her hand on the mariner's shoulder, turned her around, and gently pulled her away.

"*Friendly*," Suu whispered in Sister Speak.

"I *was* being friendly!"

"Better let me handle this."

"Be my guest."

Suu nodded and stepped around Zoe to face the elderly man.

"Master Shipwright," she cheerfully hailed, "my comrades and I would beg to hire you. Our ship is damaged, and we have a schedule to keep."

"We all have schedules," he said, still not raising his head.

"We will compensate you handsomely for your troubles."

"Young lady, do you see that ship out there?" the old shipwright asked, finally meeting her eyes. "It's costing the owner one hundred secors for a refitting, and we won't finish for at least two more cycles. That's if I can get those lazy bastards working up there to pick up the pace! I've got three more jobs right behind that one. If you wish, you can get in line, and I might get to it by next quinte."

Suu silently retrieved two small, round objects from her pockets and placed them on the table before him. The old man's eyes widened in recognition at two Veros pearls glistening in the sunlight. These were the highest grade Otick pearl, exceedingly rare, and of such quality, one could imbue them with magic. They were easily worth one hundred secors each, more than doubling his asking price.

Slowly, he directed his attention back to the Amarenians.

"Where did you get these?"

"Good sir," Suu answered, "I would much rather you focus your abilities on repairing ships than dwelling on such unimportant issues."

He hesitated, briefly contemplating the deal.

"Done!"

He snatched up the pearls and the women shared grins.

"However," he added. "I must finish the current job. My reputation demands it."

Zoe went to protest, but Suu touched her arm.

"Very well," she conceded, "two cycles. Our ship is…"

"I know which one is yours," he said, cutting her off. "Now, the sooner you allow me to get on with my work, the sooner I can start on yours."

As the Kan crept over the wharf and into the narrow streets—snaking past artisan shops, pubs and brothels—the turine tidal clock in the harbor rang out twelve bells. Vendors closed booths, fishers packed their wares, and the seaport wound down. Though the streets remained moderately busy, once the thick fog rolled in, most citizens found refuge indoors.

For Captain Fia, like most predators, the Kan wasn't a time to rest, but a time to hunt. She crept along with the mist, moving in the shadows, hyperaware of her surroundings. Under her left arm she held an oblong wooden box.

She approached an unobtrusive, single-room hovel located deep within central Makatooa. The shack's simple door, constructed from plain wooden planks, didn't appear to have a visible handle. After making sure she wasn't being watched, Fia pushed a knot in the wood of a doorframe plank. The knot receded under pressure and unlatched the door, which creaked open revealing an empty room with a wooden table in the center.

Diffused sunlight filtered through the fog creating strange shadows against the wall when she stepped inside and closed the door behind her. The captain unceremoniously placed the box on the table and spun around nervously inspecting the bare room. She produced her dagger, scrawled a few lines into the top of the box and quickly exited the shack.

Fia stopped and once again made sure no one was watching, before she placed a small piece of blue fabric in the jamb and closed the door on it. She depressed in the receded plank knot again and relatched the door.

The population on the streets had thinned considerably in the brief period since she stepped inside, but a sudden commotion rose behind her through the fog.

"You know I can make you scream," came a rumbling boast, answered by a woman's laughter.

An EEtah of the Outer Clans staggered down the street with a young human prostitute. Even though the humanoid shark was small for an EEtah, he towered over her diminutive frame. Drunk, he swayed and almost toppled over twice. It took all the weight of her half-naked body to keep him propped upward and moving forward. His slurring ramble kept switching between EEtah and the Common tongue. Every time he growled in his native language, she giggled and rubbed his member through the pants. The massive bulge in his pantaloons demonstrated his lust.

Thankfully, neither of the amorous sentients noticed Fia. *That kid is in for one rough ride tonight*, she mused. In a voyeuristic moment, she even considered following them. Rolling her eyes, she reconsidered. There was cargo to sell and The Stormwatch Pub was on the way to the ship.

"This is without a doubt, the best idea you've had on this entire dreadful endeavor," Shom rejoiced, stepping out of the fog and into the bustling welcome of Hanno's Tavern.

"We're here for information Shommy," Mal chided, "not to get drunk."

Shom laughed. "Perhaps *you're* not, but *I'm* having a drink."

They made their way through the tavern to the back bar. It sat next to a hearth with a crackling fire casting a warm glow about the room. Noisy patrons filled a dozen tables running from the aisle to the bar. Most of the regulars were human, but Mal noticed a Bailian couple at a corner table.

The Bailian's slightly elongated heads, pale blue skin and strikingly beautiful eyes stood out in this mostly working-class, human seaport tavern. Half-naked prostitutes made their way from table to table soliciting drinks, dance or sex from inebriated patrons. When one approached the Bailian couple, they smiled and politely refused.

"They're a long way from home," Mal remarked.

"Gods be damned, they're beautiful," Shom swooned. "I think I want to fuck them both! Maybe I can buy them a drink."

Mal's hand landed on his shoulder, blocking his attempt to approach them.

"Not tonight," she growled in his ear.

"Oh, alright, but I'm getting that drink."

Mal ignored him and they approached the bar. A rotund, balding barkeep held an animated conversation with several patrons, punctuated by frequent bouts of boisterous laughter. The bartender's face went ashen upon noticing Mal and he fell silent.

"You don't seem happy to see me Hanno," Mal mentioned, forcing a pout.

She bellied up to the bar, nudging aside several of the incredulous patrons who scowled at the interruption of their nightly conversation.

"I was hoping we could talk, Hanno," she said to the now sweating owner.

"And I would adore a drink!" Shom chimed in loudly from behind her.

"I'm a little busy," Hanno weakly complained.

"It'll only take a centi," she assured.

Reaching across the bar, Mal gently cupped her hands over the barkeep's drumming fingers. Shom pushed in next to her and cleared his throat loudly. She snapped a dirty glance at him, before turning back to the barkeep with a defeated sigh and shook her head.

"Will you please, for the love of the Goddess, give this man a drink, so he will shut the fuck up!"

Hanno gazed warily over at Shom. The prodigal's face lit up when he gained his attention.

"I've not been to these parts," Shom conceded. "What's your best, most powerful drink?"

The barkeep silently reached onto a shelf behind him and, without looking, pulled an unlabeled bottle from the assortment. With his other hand, he grabbed a glass. In a fluid motion, he poured it a third full. Shom examined the quantity and frowned, then looked back at Hanno. Sighing and rolling his eyes, the owner filled the glass to the top. Shom smiled contently and set several silver coins on the bar.

Hanno swept them up and turned back to Mal. With a nod of his head, he motioned her to follow him to the end of the bar.

Shom, now alone, savored his drink, seemingly oblivious to an antagonistic group of men surrounding him. Slowly, but deliberately, the ill-tempered patrons closed in on the prodigal. A towering human to his right, much taller than Shom and with the physique of a laborer, glowered leaning in close to the thin, well-dressed connoisseur.

"You're a fancy-boy aren't ya?" he goaded.

Shom tilted his head back, sipping the liquor with rapturous joy, completely ignoring the taunt.

"You know what we do to fancy-boys around these parts?" he threatened.

The small blade was out of Shom's ruffled sleeve and at the man's throat before anyone could react. The dockworker's eyes grew wide and he froze.

His friends reached to draw their weapons, only to realize what Shom already knew—the quarters were much too close for swords.

Shom pressed the dagger's tip just above the lump in the antagonist's throat. He ignored the surrounding group, kept the blade firmly in place, and gently set his drink on the bar.

The royal calmly stared at the man formerly threatening him, who now fought back panic.

"As I said," Shom began, never breaking eye contact. "I'm not from around here. Now, I *could* cut your throat, but that would make a mess. It would also be bad for business for my new friend Hanno over there."

Shom calmly retrieved his drink and took a sip, all the while not releasing the blade or breaking his stare. With a thin smile, he nodded toward the malevolent group surrounding him.

"Then your friends are going to want to kill me, and they, of course, will also have to die. I would seek to avoid that."

At the end of the bar, Mal leaned into Hanno. "Have you seen Soshi lately?"

The tavern owner glanced down the bar and nodded at the situation Shom found himself in.

A quick glance preceded a nod of the head.

"Yeah, he's okay," Mal reassured.

Hanno lifted his hand to shield his mouth. "She makes her rounds just about now."

"The usual route?"

"More or less."

The clinking of a gold coin on the counter was all the thanks Hanno needed. He plucked the money off the bar mid-bounce and swept it into his pocket in a single motion.

Shom downed the last of his drink. His eyes cautiously remained locked with the sweating antagonist. Setting the glass on the bar, he steadied himself for the inevitable brawl.

"Now, if we can all act like…"

Mal stepped up and grabbed him by the arm, interrupting his monologue.

"Come on, let's go," she demanded.

Shom grinned and withdrew the blade from the man's neck.

Six pairs of eyes narrowed to angry slits when she pulled him away, clearly enraged at being bested by a "fancy-boy."

"Alas, I must go," he said to the dumbfounded mob, "Apparently, duty calls. I hope this unfortunate minor incident hasn't in any way ruined what…"

Mal grabbed the verbose prodigal by the sleeve and began dragging him towards the door.

They had only made it a few steps before two scowling burley dockworkers blocked the exit.

"Oh, for the love of the gods," Shom groaned. "This crowd really is as stupid as they look."

"Where do ya think *you're* going?" one growled.

"Anywhere with a better clientele than here," Shom said sounding bored, sensing the others coming up behind him.

Mal smirked and stepped over to the bar, leaving Shom to face the indignant crowd.

"You got yourself into this one," she said, attracting the bartender's attention. "Hanno, I think I *will* have that drink."

One of the men barring the door stepped aggressively forward. "You're a little prissy smart ass."

"Immensely preferable to being a dim-witted brute," Shom replied, lashing out with a front kick to the groin.

The assailant cried out and dropped to his knees with both hands covering his crotch.

The eyes on the man next to him went wide with shock and he lashed out with a powerful roundhouse punch. Shom easily sidestepped the crude blow. He reached out with the flat of his hand and gently guided the man's fist into the bar railing beside Mal, who calmly sipped her drink. The blow landed with the sound of bones cracking just before the man's screams filled the air.

Shom then took control of the assailant's elbow and yanked him backwards, off balance and into the three coming up from behind. All four tumbled into a table full of customers with the attacker clutching his broken hand.

While they untangled themselves from the other patrons Shom calmly stepped over to the closest one and kicked him in the head, while he struggled to regain his footing. The would-be aggressor dropped silently to the floor beside the one nursing his wounded appendage.

"Do you really intend to continue this preposterous exercise?" Shom asked, watching the remaining two scramble to their feet.

One just screamed in defiance and lunged forward with outstretched arms in a tackling maneuver.

"Well, I guess so," the noble answered himself, avoiding a badly timed grapple.

Shom seized the back of the man's shirt and assisted his vault, plunging him headfirst into the side of the bar with a loud thump. He toppled to the floor, lying motionless at Mal's feet.

The prodigal then straightened the cuffs of his shirt while assessing the last aggressor.

"Well, so what will it be old boy?"

Uncertainty had replaced the rage on the man's ruddy face. He held his hands out meekly in front of him, before bolting for the door.

"Are you *quite* finished?" Mal asked.

Shom looked around at the four broken men on the floor. "I believe so."

"Good," she said, downing the remainder of her drink and placing extra coinage on the bar, "because your dick measuring is costing me."

❂ ❂ ❂

To anyone else passing on the unnamed street, a piece of blue fabric stuck in the door appeared innocently caught and torn from some unknown passerby.

For Soshi it was a beacon.

Her eyes widened in concern. They didn't use this signal lightly. They needed her. She nonchalantly strolled across the street; her body covered by a hooded, floor-length cloak. Only long wisps of brown hair betrayed the feminine beauty beneath.

Soshi had just crawled from beneath a mid-level city bureaucrat and felt exhausted, not because of the man's sexual virility or lack thereof—he climaxed in less than a moment after entering her—but as a side effect of coming down from recently ingested Oldust. She glanced fondly at the missing fingernail on her left hand, shuddering as she remembered the exquisite high.

To the people of the streets, Soshi was a renowned Ol'daEE, a mage who cast sexual spells to order while under the influence of Oldust. She'd even fashioned the valuable dust into false fingernails to travel with and avoid theft.

Unbeknownst to the citizenry of Makatooa, the unusually fair skinned woman was an Amarenian spy. Her mission was operating under deep cover to report ship movements for the Rayth raiders.

Soshi's primary ability, among others, was orgasmic memory extraction. Under the guise of prostitution, she built a client list around second-tier government officials and businesspeople who knew most everything their superiors knew. This allowed her to keep a low profile in her dangerous occupation.

Over the years, she'd perfected her control of the drug and could cum as quickly as her patrons, but each orgasm linked Soshi to their memories, from the mundane to the critical. The more they came the more she knew, and Soshi made them release until they collapsed in ecstasy.

This established her on the streets as one of the most powerful information brokers. Her clients trusted her implicitly, because she never asked prying questions and they never failed to bring her to authentic orgasms, feeding their fantasy of sexual prowess and the illusion of her vulnerability.

Checking up and down the foggy street and seeing no one, she pressed the knob and opened the door. The blue cloth fell to the ground. She retrieved it and entered the room.

❊ ❊ ❊

As soon as the Kan set in, the Amarenian crew set about bringing the cargo up onto the deck for asset liquidation. They knew they must act quickly and carefully. If the Quartermasters Guild caught wind of cargo being sold without the proper tariffs being paid, they could very well lose the ship and their lives.

Mariner Suu nervously surveyed the fog-shrouded docks. With Captain Fia away, organizing the crew fell to her and she'd assigned the sisters guarding the gangplank to keep an eye out for City Guards to track their patrols.

They didn't notice the humanoid rodent, about three times the size of a city rat, sitting in the shadows. The Cul-Ta picked his teeth with a thin, dried fishbone and watched. Once the crew began unloading cargo onto the deck, it grinned, tossed the bone into the water and scurried off.

❊ ❊ ❊

Alto sat up in bed and watched the prostitute slip the sheer red dress back over her naked body. She'd cost one whole gold piece but proved well worth it.

So far, this city had treated him well. The inn's meals were simple yet filling, and his room was relatively clean and comfortable. Next door, Hanno's Tavern provided an excellent respite for refreshment and female companionship. Yet, despite the fullness of this cycle, the Kan found him restless.

The girl leaned down and gave him a quick kiss goodbye.

"Anytime luv," she cooed.

Alto sighed watching her leave, before swinging himself up out of bed to dress.

Perhaps a walk, he mused.

The city was still deep in the Kan. Its streets would be less congested. Fog would allow him some anonymity while he got to know the lay of the streets.

He passed quietly through the dark dining room downstairs. A single light burned in a small room down the hall next to the front door. Unlocking the latch betrayed his exit with a loud click and an elderly woman popped her head out of the room.

"Oh no, mister Alto, you should not go out in the Kan," she warned. "It not safe!"

Her concern genuinely touched the swordmaster.

"I'm just going out for a short walk, Widow Tomlan," he assured her.

"I say a prayer to the Goddess for you," she offered, seeing her advice going unheeded.

Alto gave a slight bow of thanks and stepped out into the mist.

✸ ✸ ✸

The door closed silently behind Soshi, enveloping everything around her in darkness. She pulled a stone from the sash around her waist and, cupping it in her hand, struck it against the wall. A small piece chipped off and started glowing. It bathed the room in a warm orange light.

The Ol'daEE suspiciously examined the nondescript wooden box Captain Fia had left on the solitary table. There didn't appear to be any official markings or apparent booby-traps. After reading Fia's brief message, noting the theft and where they stole it, she produced a bejeweled dagger from under her cloak and cautiously pried open the top. The pins creaked in protest when the wooden lid gave way without incident. She let out a sigh of relief seeing no traps.

Soshi reached inside, parted the copious amount of straw padding, searching until her hand touched something smooth and metal. She carefully withdrew a brass tube the length of her forearm from its housing. She had seen enough diplomatic courier containers to recognize one, but the craftsmanship of the fine metal with its inset of semiprecious jewels suggested the importance of the contents.

Her eyes narrowed when she recognized the red wax signet of House Eldor sealing the cap at the end. She reread the captain's message to make sure she'd understood it correctly.

How did a royal container of *this* significance end up on a Spice Rat's ship sneaking through *these* waters?

Soshi meticulously inspected the container again. Once satisfied there were no traps, she twisted the cap off and broke the seal. The inside of the container housed a rolled document which easily slid out into her hand. She unrolled the scroll and ran her fingers across it, appreciating the texture of the fine paper. Unfortunately, she didn't recognize the language, but scanned the paper for clues.

Upon closer examination, it appeared to be a combination of two documents. The top of the page contained the official imperial accounting numbers and the Royal Seal of Eldor—leaving no doubt as to the document's importance—but the bottom half, considerably shorter, contained fewer numbers and bore the Royal Seal of House Aramos.

With the bloody history between those two houses, these two seals would normally never share the same page. Something huge must be in the works.

Soshi rolled the document back up and returned it to its container. She silently chastised herself for her inability to read it, but she knew someone who could.

❇ ❇ ❇

The warm blush of fine liquor rapidly wore off when the dampness of the fog permeated Shom's clothing and mood.

"Just what *exactly* are we looking for?" He asked impatiently, gazing around in boredom.

They stood at a crossroads, off a main street in central Makatooa, with a view of six smaller crossroads. Despite the hour, a slow stream of drunken sailors, prostitutes, and other denizens of the Kan kept the streets busy.

"Not what," Mal responded, not taking her eyes off the street. "Who."

Shom sighed heavily. "Very well, *who* are we looking for then?"

"I told you," Mal said, amused by his frustration, "I have an influential contact here."

Moments passed and Mal remained vigilant. Shom stared off into space, lost in a fugue of self-pity and fidgeting in the chill. Then, across the street, Mal recognized Soshi from the glow of a street vendor's fire. She exited a side street, apparently in a hurry. Quickly checking her surroundings, Soshi pulled her hood back over her head and disappeared down an alley.

Mal could tell Soshi didn't care about the three sailors leering at her when she passed them. The Ol'daEE prostitute had long ago numbed to the obvious attentions of lustful men. When she headed into the darkness of the alley, all three exchanged conspiratorial glances. They wiped the greasy food from their mouths onto their sleeves and followed her.

Mal's eyes narrowed and she shook her head. "Poor dumb bastards."

"What?" Shom asked, yanked back into the present. "Is she your…?"

"Come on," Mal ordered.

With Mal in the lead, they crossed the intersection toward the alley.

❄ ❄ ❄

Alto kept a leisurely yet robust pace along the main road leading east from the city center to the Makatooa Outlands. He was simply too excited to sleep. So many places to explore. So many things to consider. It would take quite a few cycles to determine the best location for his school.

His stomach growled when he smelled meat cooking over an open fire. He thought his hunger odd, considering he ate a full meal earlier this Kan, but then remembered the prostitute.

"Ah yes," he said aloud.

After-dinner sex often led to a late-Kan appetite he recounted when his nose guided him to the chow vendor. Rounding the corner his mouth watered witnessing the cook serving meat on a skewer to a handful of patrons. He then caught sight of Shom and Mal, just beyond the vendor's stall, rushing into the alley. Curiosity piqued, he pushed aside his hunger and followed them down the backstreet.

❈ ❈ ❈

The Rayth dock sentries monitored the patrol of the city guards as ordered, counting the time between rounds. With each encounter, the guards eyed Mariners Treesh and Wanda with contempt and both sides traded mutual sneers.

"I swear," Wanda said, watching them moving out of sight into the dense fog, "I just want to castrate them, shove their worthless cocks in their mouths, then laugh and drink as they bleed out before me."

Treesh chuckled at her shipmate. Wanda was such a poet. Before she could respond, the sound of a carriage rapidly approaching drew their attention. Both mariners readied their spears when a small carriage, pulled by a large, six-legged lizard, appeared out of the mist suddenly and rolled to a halt before the sentries. The commotion caused all the Amarenians on deck to stop moving cargo and line the ship's railing with weapons ready.

A Cul-Ta stood in the passenger side of the carriage and bowed ceremoniously. Beside him, a slightly larger Cul-Ta held the reins and stared ahead at the docks.

"Hello," the Cul-Ta greeted them with an enthusiastic squeaky voice in Common. "I would beg to speak with your captain."

Mariner Treesh eyed them with disdain. Their filthy kind infested every city of the Annigan. Usually low-level thieves and criminals, they proved to be little more than a nuisance, but they always worked for someone bigger. No matter where you encountered them, you couldn't trust the little fuckers.

"The captain's not here," Treesh defiantly declared. "Now fuck off!"

"This is unfortunate," the Cul-Ta lamented, affecting a theatrically sad demeanor. "My Friend Asad has important business to discuss with her."

"Are you deaf?" Treesh said, stepping forward, spearhead leading.

"No, no," he begged, cowering. "My Friend Asad has a quick and equitable solution to your problem. Perhaps the first mate in command?"

The Cul-Ta meekly extended both his small arms and hands outward, palms up. Both sentries stopped and stared at each other.

"Better get Suu," Wanda advised.

"That won't be necessary." Captain Fia said purposefully stepping out of the fog and approaching the carriage.

The Cul-Ta bowed, sputtering, "Oh… Oh… Your captainship, I…"

"Shut the fuck up and move over," Fia ordered with a jerk of her thumb.

The Cul-Ta quickly complied, recoiling to the edge of the cab. In a single, fluid motion, Fia bounded into the carriage and took a seat beside the driver.

"Sisters, you performed your duty well!" she called out. "Now get back to work. I want this hold emptied before we shake off the Kan."

The deck hands beamed with her approval and quickly got back to moving cargo.

"Well," she said with resignation, "I guess we're off to meet…"

"My Friend Asad," the Cul-Ta offered cautiously.

"We'll see what happens," she answered.

Fia glanced over at the expressionless driver rat, who shook the reins. The lizard, which had been straining against its bridle, broke into a gallop. The carriage raced off with wheels screeching and disappeared into the fog.

❁ ❁ ❁

"Well, looky, looky what we got here," a deep, gravelly voice called out from the mist behind her.

Soshi stopped and warily turned around. Peering into the fog, she made out two figures rapidly nearing. A boot scuffle behind her drew her attention and confirmed her worst fears. The shadowy outline of a third figure blocked her escape.

The men surrounded her and leered malevolently. Her eyes grew wide and she raised her hands covering her face, appearing to cringe in horror. The Ol'daEE covertly crushed the nail on her right little finger and inhaled.

❊ ❊ ❊

Mal and Shom hurried past the chow vendor and broke left into the alley. The feasting Kan workers barely took notice, unwilling to embrace the passing drama. Mal halted just inside the alley, causing Shom to run into her and almost topple them both.

They could barely see through the fog cover but could make out three assailants ahead of them surrounding Soshi. Shom started forward, grasping the hilt of his sword. Mal's arm gently blocked him from unsheathing it.

"You say this person is your... friend, contact or whatever, right?" Shom asked in a low voice.

"Yep," Mal confirmed.

"And did we not just run in pursuit of her?" he pressed.

"Uh-huh."

Shom stepped back and gave her an evil smirk.

"This feels a bit dark, even for you Maluria."

Mal just winked at him and focused her attention down the alley.

❊ ❊ ❊

The sailor known as Krogoff reached Soshi first. He swore she'd stank of sex when passing the chow vendor booth and Krogoff knew a whore when he smelled one. From what he glimpsed of her beauty beneath the cloak, he knew she must be an expensive whore, but the captain wouldn't be paying wages until after the Kan. Even then, he still probably couldn't afford her.

He grabbed her and spun her violently against him. The force sent the tube sailing out from under her arm and it clattered across the fog slicked cobblestones of the alley.

Soshi cried out when Krogoff's large and powerful frame engulfed her. He reeked of bilge water, stale sweat, and cheap ale. His calloused hands groped at her and rended her dress up past her waist.

The Ol'daEE noticed Mal standing at the mouth of the alley. Their gaze locked for an instant and Soshi used her eyes to direct Mal's attention to the rolling canister.

❊ ❊ ❊

"By the gods this shall not stand," Alto vowed stepping boldly forward.

He was shocked when he ran into Mal and Shom at the entrance to the alley, watching the rape as if it were a spectacle. He also attempted to draw his sword, but Mal spun and stopped him.

"Shhh," she hushed.

Alto sheathed his blade and leaned back, completely befuddled.

"She's got this," Mal said, nodding emphatically. "Now you and wonder boy here, just watch and you might learn something.

"Wonder boy... really?" Shom asked incredulously.

❊ ❊ ❊

"Krogoff always gets 'em first," Aton stewed, watching his shipmate, pants down, pinning Soshi against the top of a nearby crate.

"Get a load of his pasty ass pumpin' away, Aton," Grunn said. "Don't know what he likes more, gettin' pissed, gettin' plunder or gettin' pussy!"

The shipmates laughed bitterly, but never took their eyes off the lurid act happening before them. They unconsciously licked their lips and nervously wrung their hands, impatiently waiting their turn after Krogoff… as always.

"Alright now, Krog," Aton spoke up, "let's not be all Kan about this!"

"Fuck Off!" Krogoff bellowed.

The rapist's attention returned to what now appeared to be an extremely aroused woman demanding his affections. No longer frightened, she moaned, bucked and begged for him to continue. Krogoff leered proudly down at the slut writhing breathlessly beneath him. Grunn and Aton exchanged excited glances, amazed at their good fortune.

"We found us a lil goer," Aton babbled, lewdly rubbing the swelling in his pants.

Soshi's performance proved to be more than Krogoff could take. She ground herself against him, moaning louder and louder, building with intensity. The sailor's brow furrowed. He grunted and panted, signaling release was imminent. The Ol'daEE orgasmed immediately before him.

His two voyeuristic companions had experienced many brothels and whores, but this was different. They could tell she wasn't faking it. They couldn't contain their excitement watching Soshi convulse, scream and moan beneath the enraptured Krogoff.

Grunn and Aton both felt ready to involuntarily orgasm in their pants, but their ecstasy turned to splitting headaches and aching balls. They immediately lost their erections and winced from discomfort both above and below. Krogoff had weakly climbed off her and staggered about the alley in obvious pain.

Soshi calmly propped herself up on her elbows and casually watched the agony unfold before her. Aton and Grunn screamed when they noticed blood seeping from their noses. Soon all three dropped to their knees, holding their heads and crotches in agony, blood flowing from all orifices.

"I know your secrets," she scolded. "And you've been very bad boys, for a very long time."

She sat up, smoothed her skirt and hopped off the crate. Her face betrayed no emotion watching the three men writhe in fetal positions, wallowing in pools of their own blood.

"You deserve every moment of this."

Soshi then calmly walked away without a lingering glance at the dying sailors and over to where the canister landed. She suspiciously pondered Shom and Alto for a moment, before picking it up.

"My dear Maluria," she said. "I don't know your friends, but we need to talk."

Soshi tucked the canister under her arm and set off down the alley. Mal, Shom and Alto cautiously trailed after her.

"Influential contact indeed," Shom whispered to Mal.

❂ ❂ ❂

"My Friend Asad rules the docks here," the Cul-Ta explained during the ride. "Any and all freight pass through his warehouses. If you need to unload your wares, you pay My Friend Asad. If you need long-term storage, you pay My Friend Asad. One way or the other, everyone pays My Friend Asad.

Once they arrived at Asad's office, the Cul-Tal leapt off the carriage and led Fia to the door. He stopped and gestured for her to lean down to him.

"You lucky Cul-Ta here to help you," he whispered. "Most clients think My Friend Asad just short, jolly business human, but he one of four bosses of the Silent Partner. The streets know him as My Friend Asad, because they think he always happy and friendly, but he can be cruel. Very, very cruel. You lucky we here. My Friend Asad is criminal mastermind. He run the docks for Nallor Cabal. You best be careful."

The rat opened the door and skittered across the floor of the office. He jumped up on Asad's desk and whispered in his ear, gesturing towards Fia. She strode in, flopped down in a seat before the desk, leaned back in the chair, and disrespectfully hiked one leg over its arm.

Asad assessed the brash young woman across from him for a moment, before smiling and folding his hands across his ponderous stomach.

"I understand you have cargo to sell but can't help but get the feeling you're going to be holding something back from me, young lady," he stated.

"What?" Fia spat. "You want to know when I took my last shit?"

The fat mobster rocked with laughter, then caught his breath and met her eyes.

"Although the thought of watching you defecate is rather stimulating," he calmly replied. "No, I do not. Watching you produce a ship's manifest, however, would be a good start."

She turned away, repulsed by the thought of him aroused in such a manner, and then composed herself. There was something unnerving about this self-satisfied little male pig, a danger behind his smile. Castrating him would be so satisfying, but she knew she needed to tread carefully.

"What in the fuck are you talking about?" she asked. "That was a Spice Rat's ship. Do you really think smugglers keep a manifest?"

Asad calmly uncrossed his hands before him and stared at her maintaining his pleasant demeanor.

"My dear, there is always *some* record."

"Well in this case there wasn't shit," she insisted.

"Again, with the shit," he said. "I really don't know why you insist on being antagonistic. Right now, I'm your best friend."

"Yeah?" she asked. "How's that?"

"We do things differently in this part of the Annigan," he explained in a soft but fatherly tone. "Although I must commend you on a bold plan. Your 'salvage,' the *Regis*, is due in Zor today. So how long do you think before the quartermasters get involved when it doesn't make port?"

Fia grew silent pondering the consequences. Recognizing doubt in her eyes, Asad pounced.

"Your shipwright can't finish repairs for at least a few cycles," he explained, "By then you'll be ass-deep in EEtahs and ironmarks. And they don't have far to look, the ironmark stationed in Makatooa is a notoriously cruel fucker."

That last threat had the exact opposite effect on Fia than what Asad intended. She scowled at him, her fury rising. Amarenian Rayth don't back down.

"I don't give a flying fuck," she said, bolting from the chair.

"What you give a fuck about does not concern me," Asad replied calmly. "Time is on my side. It's just that simple. I offer you fifty secors for the cargo, sight unseen."

Fia stopped in her tracks. She really wasn't sure how to react. The disgusting little man was right. Time wasn't their friend, and his offer was a lot of money. Asad's next caveat pushed it over the edge.

"And there's a good chance I can help you keep the ship," he added.

Fia could not conceal her interest.

"That is what you want?" he asked, slowly and deliberately. "Right?"

The Amarenian captain nodded. Asad shrugged.

"So, do we have a deal?"

"Sure," Fia agreed.

She sat back down and Asad, once again, leaned back in the chair.

"I don't suppose I could throw watching you shit into the bargain?" he asked with a wink.

Fia gave a wicked grin and shook her head. *Deep down, men were all the same.* She stood and leaned forward on his desk pressing her chest up and outward. His eyes instinctively fell on her bare breasts.

"You get me that ship," she said, drawing his eyes back to hers, "and I'll shit right on your damn face."

"Deal!" he declared, rising to his feet and extending his hand.

❊ ❊ ❊

Mal caught up with Soshi first, leaving Shom and Alto several steps behind recovering from the shock of what they just witnessed. Shom kept glancing back, wincing at the twisted corpses behind him, their faces frozen in agony and crotches of their pants blackened with blood.

"Who are the two men with you?" Soshi inquired in a low voice.

"One is a… business associate of mine," Mal confessed, "but the other, I just met today."

This puzzled Soshi and she stopped walking. "And you trust them?!"

The Fate of Tomorrow

"Actually yes." Mal quickly answered.

The Spice Rat took note of Soshi's incredulously unconvinced look.

"" Shom, I know," Mal defended. "The other one…I've got a good feeling about him."

"You've got a what?!" Soshi growled in a tense whisper. 'A good feeling?! I'm betting my life on your good feeling?!"

Mal's brow furrowed, and lips tensed. "You don't make it in my line of work as long as I have if you can't size people up fast. Besides, that's the guy who didn't hesitate when you were being attacked back there. He was willing to take on three guys by himself for a total stranger, that would be you!"

Soshi's mood softened. "So why didn't he step in then?"

"I stopped him."

"In the name of the goddess, why?!"

'You had the situation taken care of. Besides, I like watching you work."

"You know, as much as I enjoy strolling the back roads of this rustic city," Shom said unable to mask his annoyance. "I feel compelled to inquire about the nature of our business here. Not to mention my questions about *the nature of* the business with those sailors back there."

Soshi spun around. "I really don't think I like you."

"Don't worry," Mal interjected, stepping between them, "that's normal."

The Ol'daEE turned from a smirking Shom to Alto, who stared curiously but remained silent.

"Now, you needed to talk to me, Soshanna?" Mal said, drawing her attention back.

"Follow me," Soshi ordered.

She spun and continued rapidly down the narrow backstreet. Mal, Alto and Shom exchanged resigned glances and followed. Nearing a small intersection, a little way down the alley, they caught the distinctive odor of something being baked or possibly burned.

"What is that *stench*?!" Shom whispered.

"Namis," Alto whispered back. "It's a seaweed bread native to this region."

Shom nearly choked. "You actually eat this?"

Alto shrugged. "Wheat is expensive and seaweed is plentiful."

Much to Shom's dismay, their path led them straight to the source of the odor. Stopping at the entrance of what appeared to be a tiny bakery, Soshi entered and a short while later returned, gesturing for them to come in.

Two wood-burning ovens built into one wall kept the little kitchen oppressively warm. The opposing wall contained a rack loaded with long loaves of the foul-smelling, green bread. A stout older man wearing a white apron bent over the table in the center of the room. His massive arms wrestled a giant pile of dough into submission over a dusting of granulated rice. He glanced up briefly when they entered, before returning to his kneading.

Soshi led them through to a small backroom containing a single desk and several chair. She placed the canister on the desk beside a simple abacus and confronted Shom the instant the door closed.

"Okay, so *who* exactly are you?" she irritably demanded.

The royal recoiled with an insulted attitude. "I'm not at all sure I like your tone…"

"This is Shom Eldor," Mal answered for him quickly redirecting the rapidly deteriorating conversation. "We're… old friends and sometimes business associates. He's irritating, but trustworthy."

"Eldor," Soshi repeated. "As in *House* Eldor?"

Mal and Shom nodded their heads in unison.

"Precisely," Shom confirmed in a superior tone.

"Well, well, well," she exclaimed, "I just may have some questions for you too."

She then turned to Alto, who stood silently by the door.

"And *you*?"

The swordmaster formally bowed. "Alto de Gom, at your service madam."

"The last thing I need right now is servicing," Soshi snapped. "Exactly how do you know Mal and... Shom?"

"Actually, I just met them today," Alto offered, to Soshi's exasperation.

"However," Shom interjected, "if he is who I think he is, trust is not the problem... inferior sword technique, however, that's a problem."

Shom grinned at his own cleverness. Time seemed to stop. Alto stared expressionless for what seemed like an eternity, before slowly returning the smile.

Then, simultaneously, their hands grabbed their hilts with blinding speed drawing their swords a quarter of the way out of their scabbards. Their movements mirrored each other. Eyes twinkled, and they nodded in mutual respect, sheathing their blades.

"Great," Soshi said sarcastically. "If we ever need a fancy circle jerk, you boys got that covered."

Mal shook her head in disbelief.

"Now if you idiots are finished measuring your dicks," she said, "I'd like to hear what the lady has to say!"

Soshi picked up the canister and handed it to the Spice Rat. "They salvaged this diplomatic courier container from *your* ship Maluria."

Shom and Mal exchanged knowing glances.

"Well, at least now we know what was in the damn box," Shom acknowledged.

"Did you look inside?" Mal probed, fully knowing the answer.

Soshi silently nodded confirmation, watching Mal opening the container and sliding out the document. A quizzical expression crossed the smuggler captain's face.

"What does it say?" Mal asked.

"The top part has a bunch of what I think *might be*, royal accounting numbers on it," Soshi speculated. "Otherwise, I can't read the language at the bottom either, it's not one I recognize."

She then pointed out the different royal seals at the top and bottom of the document. Mal raised an eyebrow upon closer examination.

"Then we have the fact that *both* House Eldor and House Aramos have slapped their official seals on it," Soshi exclaimed. "Something, to my knowledge, unprecedented in recent history, if at all."

"Yassett," Shom interjected.

"What?" Mal replied.

"It's written in Yassett," he added, "the ancient language of the First Men, before the coming of the houses. It's considered a dead tongue. Now it is used to code official court documents."

"Can you read it?" Mal inquired hopefully.

"Afraid not," Shom admitted, with a shake of his head.

"You are royalty, and you can't read court language?" Soshi asked incredulously.

"I believe I was getting laid the day that was being taught," Shom retorted. "And, excluding this brief exception, the other experience has served me much better in life."

The two women glared at Shom, obviously unamused. Alto lowered his head and snickered, drawing Soshi's unwelcome attention.

"And why are you along for the ride?" Soshi asked.

Alto shrugged. "At this particular moment, Morbid curiosity."

Silent, piercing stares caused the seasoned fighter to fidget nervously. He shook his head and shuffled his feet.

"My instructor, Master Taxton of Rohina Takii," he began. "Awarded me a charter and gave his blessing to open a school here. Now, I am not a fool. I realize skill only takes you so far. One does not open and run a successful sword school in a foreign city without a reputation, and I, unfortunately have no such reputation, and I doubt if I can acquire one sitting back in my room at the inn."

"May I, please, make a suggestion?" Shom asked.

"What?!" the women demanded loudly, turning their heads in unison.

"Get rid of the fucking thing as soon as possible," he said. "Forget we ever saw it and blame the Amarenians for everything."

He waited a moment for the idea to sink in, but the others stared blankly.

"Because dear lady," Shom continued, addressing Soshi directly, "when you broke that seal you signed all our death warrants. Well, maybe not *all* of us. My family, more especially my father, will completely disown me as the supreme fuck-up that I am. They'll probably take away my allowance and I'll have to resort to conducting dark deeds for the rest of my life to survive. You all, on the other hand, can expect to be hunted down relentlessly and meet death in a slow, horrific fashion."

A disturbing silence fell over the room, finally broken when Alto cleared his throat.

"Well," he said, resting his hand on his sword hilt, "if I survive this, it definitely sounds like a worthy way to earn a reputation."

❋ ❋ ❋

Captain Fia returned as suddenly as she left. The lizard-drawn buggy sped up to the dock and screeched to a stop at the gangplank. Fia hopped out and made her way onto the deck. Mariner Suu joined her there and together they walked around the various crates and barrels making up the contents of the hold.

"Is the hold empty?" Fia asked.

"Yes, Captain," Suu replied. "Except for the cask of Noma venom."

"Excellent work," she nodded, peering around at the already sold loot.

"But captain, how do we get these off the ship?" Suu asked. "There isn't enough time between the city watch patrols."

"My Friend Asad assured me the patrols won't be an issue," the captain stated confidently.

"Captain?"

"Assemble the crew on deck," Fia ordered.

Suu nodded and rushed off. Fia approached the deck sentries standing watch by the gangplank.

"How soon before the next patrol?" she asked quietly.

"Within the next ten centis, Captain," a sentry answered.

Fia nodded and returned to the crates. The crew arrived on deck and quickly gathered around her.

"When the next patrol passes, we'll have to move quickly," she explained. "Be ready for my word and then just start hauling cargo down that gangplank."

The crew exchanged puzzled glances. Without further explanation, the captain turned and joined the sentry by the railing. Within moments they heard the clack of patrol boots coming down the dock to their right through the fog. She could just make out the sentries marching into sight through the Kan mist.

"Any time now," Fia muttered, impatiently tapping her foot.

Sudden movement to the left drew her attention. Two Cul-Ta thieves loudly attempted prying open the locked gate of a fishmonger's stand across the dock. The city watch patrol just began their leering contest with the Rayth deck sentries when they spotted the noisy Cul-Ta bandits.

The Fate of Tomorrow

"Hey, *stop right there* you little rat fucks!" a patrolman yelled.

The Cul-Ta thieves screeched in mock surprise and scampered away. The patrol quickly took off after them. Fia smiled and watched them disappear into the fog.

"Go," she ordered calmly.

The crew started lugging cargo down the plank, but before they even could reach the dock, two large wagons pulled up to the ship. Without missing a step, the sisters loaded the contents of the hold directly onto the wagons.

Captain Fia walked calmly down the plank and approached the hooded driver of the second wagon. He silently handed her a large, heavy bag, before snapping the reins and driving his team of lizards into the fog.

All eyes were on Captain Fia sauntering up the gangplank and into the ship. Suu stared in awe when she passed. Fia beamed and winked, while pinching Suu's left nipple, the Amarenian version of a back pat.

"Courtesy of My Friend Asad," she announced, raising the bag over her head in victory. "Let's get our shares!"

The crew cheered and crowded around their captain.

❂ ❂ ❂

Slowly the fog bank receded back into the ocean waking Makatooa back to life. Soshi moved along the dock while the turine rang twenty-two times, officially breaking the Kan.

The others still slept. They had stayed up late debating what to do. She had to hurry, Cavell the baker would need his office when he opened for business.

She moved past the *Regis* and its Rayth sentries, and past Kuut, who sat beside two large fish freshly caught from the reef. The entire area hummed with activity. Fishers arranged their catches for potential buyers. The royal cooks, up early as usual, moved amongst the fishmongers scanning for the best of the sea's bounty.

Just beyond the morning activity, in the area between where fishers and passenger ships docked, an elderly blind man sat cross-legged on a simple mat next to a long perch of noisily squawking seagulls. Their droppings whitewashed the perch and the area surrounding it.

Soshi approached and stood silently before the old man. He peered up, his toothless mouth and milky-white eyes begging a question. She leaned down and placed a small, rolled-up piece of paper, along with a silver coin, in his hands.

The Gull Master uttered the only word he ever spoke to anyone, "Where?"

Soshi leaned in and whispered. He nodded, listening, and when she stood up, he reached over and snatched a gull from its perch. It gave an initial cry of protest but offered no resistance. Nestling it against his dropping-stained garment with his left hand, he produced a small pouch with his right. He deftly slipped the coin into the pouch while removing a tiny leather band, and, still using only one hand, his long-gnarled fingers secured the note into the band and tied it to the gull's leg. Then, he took the gull in both hands, kissing it on top of its head he whispered its destination and the psychic connection was complete between man and bird. He then tossed the fowl into the air. It circled once and then flew off.

Soshi then headed back at a brisk pace. It would be best if she was there when they awoke.

❈ ❈ ❈

The Fate of Tomorrow

Just another day on the docks in the High Holy City of Zor, Polak de Zor silently lamented. He stared at the empty slip with growing concern. The harbormaster double-checked the docket in his hand and sighed heavily, before marking the *Regis* overdue in his post-Kan report.

Polak, having completed his rounds, entered the quartermaster's headquarters just off the docks. He dreaded reporting the ship overdue, because Quartermaster Kubo was a wholly unpleasant human with a fanatical eye for detail and a tendency toward cruelty.

"Thank the gods the Kan is finally lifting," he said upon entering the mercifully warm moderate sized room.

No one listened. He crossed the room and stood with his back to the open fire in the hearth, shaking off the dampness. The heat felt good and he slowly began to feel normal again.

Kubo sat at his desk on the other side of the office, his thin frame hunched over in his chair intently studying paperwork. Assistant quartermasters stood flanking him on either side, each busy with their own work. Polak hesitantly started across the room.

Kubo's fingers traced the lines of imperial accounting numbers on the documents before him. He paused for a moment and stroked his sharp chin, contemplating an irregularity.

"Double-check the hold of the *Donlevy*," he ordered one of his assistants. "These numbers are just not adding up."

"Yes, Quartermaster," came the obedient reply.

Polak placed the scroll of his report on Kubo's desk.

"The *Regis* is overdue," he nonchalantly said watching for a reaction out of the corner of his eye.

The quartermaster stopped, and his brow furrowed, straining at a remembrance. Reaching over to a stack of papers to his right, he shuffled through them and separated two sheets, one each from the bottom and top. As he examined them, his face grew grim.

"Drop what you are doing," he snapped at his assistants.

The two young quartermasters stopped their work and faced him. He quickly scrawled a message on a small piece of paper, rolled it and handed it to one of them.

"Get this down to the Gull Station immediately," he said. "It goes to the ironmark in Makatooa."

All in the room were taken aback. Calling in the Ironmarks was never taken lightly. The heavy-handed enforcers of the Quartermaster's Guild developed a well-deserved reputation for cruelty and brutality. He distinctly remembered watching a female Ironmark systematically break every bone in a smuggler's body with a thin steel rod, all to the cheers of a bloodthirsty crowd.

"Go!" he barked.

Needing no further encouragement, the young man turned and fled out the door with the message.

On a larger piece of paper, he scrawled a longer note, folded it and handed the paper to the other assistant. "You will deliver this to the head sister of House Nur."

The other assistant nodded and left immediately.

"Ironmark? House Nur?" Polak shook his head.

Kubo held a document up in front of the harbormaster.

"This arrived during the Kan from the Makatooa harbormaster. It states that the *Regis* put in for repairs a cycle ago under suspicious circumstances."

Kubo held up a second document.

"This is the original sailing order."

Polak's eyes grew wide reading the paper. The classified manifest alerted the harbormasters to be aware the *Regis* was transporting a highly sensitive, diplomatic charter from House Eldor.

❋ ❋ ❋

The Fate of Tomorrow

"I would just like to mention one more time, *this is a bad idea*," Shom warned.

Soshi had brought the group back to her single-room, second-story apartment, near the docks of central Makatooa. Shom paced the apartment nervously like a caged animal, repeatedly wandering past the windows, peeking through the curtains and checking the streets below. Alto leaned against the wall by the door, silently observing. Mal sat at a table in the center of the room, prying the gems from the canister with her dagger.

"Dammit Shommy, I don't have deep pockets like you!" she yelled. "I just lost my ship and the entire contents of her hold and I'm down to my last fucking gold piece. So, I would appreciate you shutting the fuck up!"

Shom was about to respond when the door opening drew everyone's attention. Alto spun quickly, with his hand on his sword hilt. He relaxed when Soshi stepped through. Alto smirked over at Shom, for being distracted, while he was at the ready. Shom scowled back.

"Maluria, I am so sorry," Soshi said, her face troubled. "But the Amarenians have liquidated your cargo."

"Fuck!" Mal shouted, plunging her dagger into the table.

The room went silent and she stared off into space while her hand gripped the handle of the dagger until her knuckles turned white. Gradually, she came out of her blinding rage. Her sudden smile made Shom fidget apprehensively.

"That means they collected their pay," she said, with unnerving calm resolve. "And they'll be out celebrating."

She stood and snatched the loose gems from the table.

"Time to pay their dues," she declared. "Don't wait up."

With that, she walked out the door and slammed it behind her. They all exchanged nervous glances. Alto nodded toward the exit.

"Shall I?"

"Not a bad idea," Shom agreed.

Nodding his approval, Alto slipped out the door to follow her.

* * *

Soog, of EEtah House Zed stood on the docks of the port city of Bimor, in the Outer Zerians Island chain, scanning the crowd for his new partner. One would think since most EEtahs stood more than twice as tall as an average human, it would give him an edge in surveying a crowd, but Lumina's throng of unique life forms swarmed the docks in many sizes.

Soog had trouble seeing past the crowd gathering around the docked frigate from Otomoria, flying the Dreeat Standard. Three of the humanoid crocodile crew members had gathered beside the gangplank. They stood almost as tall as EEtahs and could be just as ferocious, but they were a more civilized race. Their principal export of cane sugar confections made them a wealthy one as well.

The smaller of the three Dreeats, a good head taller than the tallest humans, stood before half a dozen baskets full of small brown candies. He barked his sales pitch in Common, while his large green hands sifted through the confections. The two larger ones stood guard by his side, keeping the enthusiastic crowd at a safe distance.

Moving through the crowd of the other races Soog felt a sense of pride as one of the first four sentient races that emerged from the waters of the Shallow Sea. Even though the humans often proved annoying, their employ ended wars lasting millennia.

It was only a few thousand grands ago they established the Great EEtah Compact, making war obsolete on Lumina, but it didn't end all conflict, it just regulated it.

The Alliance Covenant was the pact that bound them. Each male EEtah understood he may work with another of his kind one cycle and have to kill him the next, if hired by rival factions. This single agreement is what unified these contentious warriors into neutral hired soldiers, making EEtahs the perfect mercenaries.

Compacts and covenants didn't end the EEtahs' instinctual need for bloodshed however so, the males of the three great houses instituted war colleges, called Sunals, all highly competitive, all teaching deadly specialized skills.

The female EEtahs formed House Nur to maintain balance, serving as the brains to the male houses' brawn. All scribes, clerics, healers, domesticates and politicians came out of the matriarchs of House Nur. All communications, through every Great House and Sunal, passed through them. They performed all magic. All working positions, Sunal placements and assignments fell within the jurisdiction of this large and powerful company of females.

Soog had graduated with honors from the Morrak Sunal's five grand cycles' training process and specialized in police enforcement. The quartermaster in Zor commissioned him and another EEtah to assist the ironmark in Makatooa. They granted this request immediately and, as per standard procedure, they each arrived from a nearby island chain, to ensure impartiality.

Hearing a commotion in the crowd, Soog saw a giant EEtah moving through the throng toward him. His chest, shoulders and head towered over the next tallest citizen. He munched on a large fish, massive rows of teeth tearing away at it with savage glee. The fisher from whom he had stolen the snack screamed in protest running beside him. Occasionally, the man-shark would glance down at the distraction, but his attention focused on navigating through the masses.

When the huge EEtah noticed Soog across the docks he cried out, pointing at him with the hand holding the fish. The fish's former owner caught up to him, screaming and striking his thighs. Finally tiring of this annoyance, the EEtah whipped his head down to face the fish merchant and roared, baring rows of sharp teeth in a mouth big enough to swallow half the human. The once brazen fisher cowered in fear while shark spit and partially chewed fish sprayed in his face.

Glaring down at the still cringing man, he tossed the half-eaten fish at his feet and grunted in disgust. He then noticed the small, mostly human crowd stopping and gathering around to watch. They pointed and murmured amongst themselves.

"What are you looking at?!" the EEtah roared, dispersing the mob. "That's what I thought."

Walking over to the smaller EEtah, he stopped and thumped his chest.

"Tarrg!" he introduced himself.

"Soog," the smaller one announced, thumping his chest back.

In unison they both then put their fists over their hearts and recited the Alliance Covenant in their native tongue, *"This moment united. Absolution in death!"*

With that Soog reached down and grabbed his duffel bag and Udon harpoon, before heading up the gangplank.

"Makatooa huh?" Tarrg grumbled.

"Uh-huh," Soog agreed. "Now we have to deal with the laughing fool and his infernal wheel."

❈ ❈ ❈

The Fate of Tomorrow

At age fifty-five, Sovereign Patriarch Warbel Eldor of House Eldor, was known for his guile and incredible audacity. His Unification War strategy annexed the Valdurian agricultural lands and brought all the eastern agricultural islands under Eldorian control. Unfortunately, the finishing blow against the Valdurian home island failed, and in the conflict, he'd lost Yurne, his beloved twin brother, and admiral of the navy—both because of a key piece of missing intelligence.

Who knew the Valdurians had airships?

Warbel secretly marveled at the flying crafts even though they were the primary reason his forces were unsuccessful annexing all of House Valdur's territories. Powered by the mysterious Etheria Crystals of Nocturn, these flying vessels put the greatly depleted House Valdur on an even footing with the other great human houses.

Sitting in his private chambers in the royal city of Rophan, the sovereign roughly downed the last of his drink and slammed the tankard in disgust. He stared at the candle in the center of the table and followed the dancing flame while his mind bounced from one unpleasant scenario to another. They would have to resolve this quickly or there would be considerable consequences.

The soft knock at the door broke him from his dark thoughts.

"Come in," he called out, grabbing a nearby pitcher and pouring another tankard of ale.

The door silently opened, and his son Shann Eldor stepped in, closing it gently behind him. He sported long blonde hair and a goatee over classically handsome features bearing a strong family resemblance to Shom. Also like his younger brother, he was an adequate swordsman, but unlike his prodigal sibling, Shann remained entirely devoted to family. It earned him the coveted position of Captain of the Palace Guards. His reputation for cruelty stood in direct contrast to Shom's happy-go-lucky nature.

"You sent for me, father?" he gently probed.

Without invitation, the younger Eldor sat down and leaned in intently. Warbel sighed, sat back, and took a long swig from his tankard.

"It would seem," he began, "your reprobate brother has managed to fuck things up yet again!"

Shann, not one to withhold his disdain for Shom, let out a derisive snort.

"Only this time," Warbel continued, stroking ale out of his long mustache, "it could mean a real predicament for the family."

Shann cocked his head suspiciously.

"I entrusted your brother to deliver a very sensitive document to the Imperial Bank of Zor," the father continued.

"Father!" Shann bolted up in surprise.

Warbel conceded with a nod.

"It couldn't go through regular channels," he explained. "I thought Shom's connections to the underworld would help accomplish it quietly."

"What happened?"

Warbel picked up a piece of paper before him and examined it for a moment, before handing it to his son.

"Apparently, someone hijacked the Spice Rat's frigate he chose," Warbel stated matter-of-factly, lifting his cup once again.

Shann glanced over the paper at his father and scratched his chin. "Makatooa?"

Warbel lowered the tankard and solemnly nodded.

"What can I do to help, Father?" Shann asked.

The good son, the family patriarch comforted himself. He leaned forward and stared intently at his firstborn.

"I need you to *clandestinely* go to Makatooa," he ordered. "If you must, only take two or three of your most trusted men. This already involves the quartermasters and ironmark. Let them do the work. Return or destroy the document. It cannot fall into the wrong hands!"

Shann, knowing better than to ask about the document, nodded and then malevolently sneered.

"And what about my *dear brother*?"

"Deal with him as you see fit," Warbel responded, taking another drink.

❁   ❁   ❁

Mal stepped out onto the busy street and headed toward Makatooa's North End, keeping a determined stride. She traveled several blocks before sensing she was not alone. Spinning around, she caught Alto following discreetly behind, keeping step with her with his hands clasped loosely behind his back as if taking a leisurely stroll. Seeing her turn, he did not try to avoid notice and instead approached her, smiling warmly.

"Marvelous day for a constitutional," he noted, stepping up to her.

"I don't need your help," she insisted.

"I have no doubt as to your abilities," he cajoled with a twinkle in his eye. "But I don't think it's good for any of us to travel alone given our current circumstances."

Mal sighed. "Suit yourself, but this could get messy."

"All the more reason for companionship," Alto persisted.

"Just stay out of my way," she advised, "and wipe that stupid smile off your face."

The two walked abreast through the congested streets. Entering the North End, the character of the city changed almost immediately. The roads grew wider and were lined with better cared for shops with less refuse in the street.

"It appears we have come upon a better part of town," the swordmaster remarked.

"Yeah," Mal responded, "it's not as nice as the Outlands, where the rich live, but the Silent Partner keeps things under control here."

"If you don't mind me asking, what exactly are you trying to accomplish?"

"First, I'm going to sell these gems," she began, "because I'm down to my last gold piece. Then I'm heading down to the docks to try to get some of my money back before those fucking quims spend it all on drink and whores."

"You mean kill them," he said.

Mal chuckled. "If the goddess is kind to me."

Eventually they stood outside a well-fortified building at the end of a dead-end road. Approaching the thick metal door, Mal rapped on it in a prescribed series. A short time later, the door creaked and opened. A well-groomed older man with long gray hair, in an expensive blue tunic, poked his head out. His face lit up when he saw Mal. Throwing the door open, he held out his arms welcoming her.

"Why Maluria," he beamed, "you are as lovely as ever. It has been such a long, long time."

"Yes, it has my friend," she said, leaning into his embrace.

Alto watched them sway warmly in each other's arms for a moment and inwardly doubted Mal's constant insistence that she had no friends. When they broke the embrace, the old man suspiciously eyed the young swordmaster.

"A friend of mine," Mal said noting the old man's demeanor.

Alto came to attention, smiled and bowed.

"Alto de Gom, at your service."

The old man's brow furrowed with bewilderment.

"Does he always talk like this?" he asked.

Mal glanced over at Alto and nodded.

"So far," she noted. "Alto, meet Porgo, jeweler extraordinaire."

Porgo smiled briefly before cautiously glancing over their shoulders. He suddenly realized how vulnerable his shop was with the door open and gestured for them to enter.

"Ah! Where are my manners?" he asked. "Come in, come in."

While Porgo loudly latched the door the moment it closed behind them, Alto saw the reason for the security. Gems in every state and size lined the walls and filled rows of shelves. A large jeweler's worktable sat in the center of the room.

When Alto moved closer to examine a sizeable chunk of raw gemstone, he heard a low growl, but saw nothing but a bare floor. Staring intently, he watched the floor seem to shift until he could make out the shape of an enormous wolf lying beside the table.

"Now now, Bootsy," Porgo gently admonished, "these are friends."

The Shadow Wolf, now fully visible to all, stopped its growling but watched intently. Alto wondered what other surprises this place held. The old jeweler sat down in the only chair in the room at the workbench.

"What can I do for you, my friend?" he asked Mal.

Mal pulled a dozen gems from her pocket.

"I need to sell these."

"Hmm," he muttered, picking up a few in the palm of his hand, while deftly retrieving a magnifying glass from the table.

"These are mid-grade ornamentals," he noted with authority. "They're mostly used for royal adornment on anything less than a symbol of office, like a crown."

He lowered the glass and looked up.

"They're also badly scratched."

"Unavoidable," Mal responded.

"Well, I guess I can polish them up some," he admitted, "but given their condition, I'm afraid all I could offer is fifty gold."

Mal did not argue. Porgo had always treated her fairly.

"I'll take it," she agreed.

The old jeweler nodded, got up and walked over to a nearby shelf. He pulled out a small lockbox and counted out the proper amount of struck gold coins in neat stacks on the table. Mal scooped them up and tucked them in several pockets about her person.

"Well, it's been a pleasure doing business with you," she complimented in a rushed tone. "I would love to visit but we have somewhere to be."

"I understand my dear," Porgo said with a chuckle.

"One more thing," Mal asked, pocketing the last coin. "Can we use your back door?"

"Of course!" he bellowed.

Mal leaned over and kissed him on the cheek, making him blush.

"Thanks, you're a lifesaver," she said, heading out the equally secured rear door.

A sparse wooded area behind the shop butted up against a small road about fifty feet ahead. Mal walked over to a small worn footpath leading through the grove.

"This way," she motioned. "We'll keep a low profile on the way to the docks."

"How do you know you'll find them by the docks?" Alto asked.

"They won't stray far from my ship," she responded, "and they'll only allow them to take shore leave in small groups. So, all I have to do is wait."

"As good a plan as any, I would imagine," he agreed.

The bushes rustled from off to their right and three men, armed with long swords, stepped out in front of them, blocking their path.

Mal suspiciously eyed the three antagonistic men. They smelled awful, which matched their scruffy, disheveled appearance. One stepped forward with his hand on the hilt of his sword. The two behind him watched nervously for city guards.

"Well, here's two folks that suddenly seem richer," the leader growled. "You're coming with us."

"Suppose the lady does not wish your company?" Alto inquired.

The leader leered menacingly and reached for his weapon, but never made it. Alto's sword flew from its scabbard and struck in a movement barely perceivable to the eye, speeding in a deadly arc upwards. The fine Eldorian steel easily severed the man's torso diagonally, from right armpit to left shoulder.

Before the two halves could fall, Alto whirled in a dance-like motion and drew his short sword. He spun to confront the next thief, his long blade in the perfect position for a downward slice, and the man died much the same as his compatriot, but in reverse, from left arm to right armpit.

A third spin placed him directly in front of the last man. His short sword sliced upward, from crotch to neck, with a sickening sound of a blade coursing through butter instead of bones. The last assailant dropped to his knees, desperately trying to hold back his guts from spilling out, all the while staring in shock at the still-smiling master swordsman.

Alto rapidly wiped the blades clean on the man's cloak and sheathed them before the thug toppled over.

Mal surveyed the carnage around her and realized the thieves did not even get the chance to draw their weapons.

"What the fuck was that?" she blurted both shocked and impressed with his ability which, up to this point, she couldn't have guessed at.

Alto shook his head dismissively at the bodies.

"Tasha-O-Nagi, a basic technique."

"Yeah, well we can't stick around here," she announced, pointing at the forearm of one victim. "See those tattoos? Those were Javoko's men."

"Jav… who?"

"Oh, we go way back," she said, walking away, "and not in a good way. Javoko is head of the North End Gang, one of four Silent Partner groups in the city. He won't be happy you carved up three of his men."

"My dear," Alto assured, "if this is the best your Javoko offers, I don't think we have much to worry about."

"Still, I'm getting the fuck out of here." Mal added, picking up her pace.

❂ ❂ ❂

The High Holy City of Zor, operational capital of all the various small continents and island chains making up the Goyan Islands, was deep in the Kan. Esteemed Sister Alosus, the Amarenian ambassador, awoke in the Central Forum to a gentle knocking at her door. Slipping on a wrap, she padded across the rug-strewn room and gazed out the window. She could see the beach and hills below, immersed in deep fog, but not her visitor.

"Who?" she softly asked.

"Sareeta," came the reply.

Alosus opened the door. Sareeta, her seneschal, bodyguard, and sometimes lover, entered the room. Normally these late visits were romantic in nature, but not from the serious expression on her face. She handed Alosus a small roll of paper closed with a wax seal.

"This just arrived from Makatooa."

A Gull delivered message during the Kan? It must be important, any travel during the Kan is perilous. A flick of her thumb broke the seal, and she opened the note. It confirmed her fears. The paper contained only one word:

Avarii.

Sighing heavily, she bowed her head.

"What?" Sareeta implored, gently stroking her arm.

Alosus did not answer. This was an emergency summons from a secret sister, and an untimely distraction. Negotiations were going well with three of the major western houses. House Calden was offering the assistance of their master Brightstar sailors and ships. House Valdur wanted airship ports in her homeland. A future beyond piracy finally seemed achievable for her people.

"Quietly secure a fast boat to Makatooa," she ordered.

"What?" Sareeta pressed.

"We sail at the lifting of the Kan."

The seneschal knew better than to push the subject. She nodded and slipped down the hall. Alosus closed the door and leaned against it, lost in contemplation. Long ago she had served five grand cycles as a secret sister in the Wouvian Islands. She wondered what could be so critical in such a backwash tropical port, as to summon the ambassador and potentially blow their cover.

❖ ❖ ❖

There are approximately twelve taverns in the dock area of Makatooa, ranging from small, private watering holes catering to a few regular patrons, to sprawling drinking establishments, like the Stormwatch Pub, packed with the crews of recently moored ships.

As the Kan set in, light and noise filtered out into the streets, beckoning to those seeking shelter from the penetrating, damp fog. Typical of large pubs in Lumina's port cities, mostly human patrons, along with a few Outer Clan EEtahs, crowded together inside drinking with their shipmates. EEtahs' roaring laughter rose above the din, the volume increasing proportionately to the amount of alcohol consumed. Male and female prostitutes, in various stages of undress, milled about, propositioning clients.

Mariners Saka and Yara stood at the bar, listening to the turine ring twelve. Saka downed her drink in a single gulp and faced her shipmate.

"Okay," she conceded with a slight slur, "let's get back."

"We can't go," Yara protested. "I've still got money to spend."

Saka laughed. "You won't have any if the captain has to come looking for us."

Yara nodded, guzzled the last of her drink and begrudgingly stood up. Saka reached out and tweaked the left nipple of Yara's bare breast. A passing prostitute wearing only a series of delicate gold chains saw the interaction. Misconstruing it, she approached the two.

"Care to make it three?" she purred, nestling her body between the two.

The mariners glanced at each other and grinned lecherously. Yara reached out cupping one of her ample breasts.

"That sounds like…"

"We have to get back to the ship!" Saka interrupted.

"Sorry, next time," Yara said.

Yara's lustful grin fell like the boob slipping away from her hand. Before they had even turned to leave, the near-naked prostitute had already moved on down the bar to her next potential customer. Saka grabbed her shipmate by the arm, led her through the crowd to the front door and out into the fog-shrouded streets.

❈ ❈ ❈

Alto stared up and down the mist filled street one last time, before stepping back into the alley across from the Stormwatch Pub. Mal stood in shadows watching the tavern exit.

"This is a large city Maluria," Alto said, his voice laden with uncertainty. "With many, *many* taverns…"

Mal interrupted him by putting a finger up to his lips and pointing over his shoulder. Alto turned in time to see the two Amarenian mariners exiting the pub.

"Amazing," Alto noted. "How did you know?"

"It's the only pub on the docks big enough to get lost in," Mal replied, not taking her eyes off her targets. "They'd have stood out too much anywhere else."

They stepped out of the alley and remained a few paces behind the Amarenians on the other side of the street. The mariners were lost in conversation and unaware they were being followed.

Mal carefully studied them, devising an attack strategy. Whatever she was going to attempt, it would have to be devastating and by surprise. She doubted if she would get a second chance. Both women were tall and powerfully muscled. Each stood as tall or taller than an average human male. One wore a mohawk with tribal tattoos on the shaved sides of her head and a ponytail down the center of her back. The other had shaved bald to better show off her elaborate ceremonial tattoos and pearling. Both were topless, and even though amply endowed, their chests were particularly muscular.

"Damn, I could have played with those tits for a while." Yara noted enthusiastically while running her hand across the strip of hair on her head.

"If you'd have kept groping her, she probably would have charged you," Saka said, laughing heartily.

When they stopped their amused banter, Saka heard the footsteps behind them and turned back.

Mal saw them start to turn. Quickly spinning to face Alto, she grabbed and kissed him full on the lips. Initially, the swordmaster stiffened in surprise, but quickly accepted the situation. He put his arms around her and returned the kiss. The two slipped deeper into the embrace and Mal accepted his gently probing tongue when it brushed her lips.

The mariners watched the couple kissing for a moment and Yara scoffed loudly.

"Now there's a waste of perfectly good tits," Saka said, before shaking her head in disgust.

The mariners continued walking towards the docks, but the kiss lingered a little too long to be just a diversion. Mal felt slightly lightheaded and her body tingled when their lips slowly separated.

"Well," Alto remarked, "that was..."

"Yeah."

Mal tenderly slid both her forearms between the two of them and gently pushed him away. Alto stepped back and glanced up the street. He cleared his throat and motioned to the mariners disappearing into the mist.

"Oh shit," she muttered, taking off at a brisk pace with Alto beside her. "Okay, I'll get one, you get the other."

"That I cannot do," he stated, shaking his head solemnly.

"What?"

"I took an oath."

"A what?!"

"An oath."

"Are you fucking kidding me?" Mal said, pressing against him defiantly, chest to chest. "I just saw you carve up three armed men like a block of cheese."

"That was different," Alto said, taking a short step back.

"What the fuck are you talking about?"

"I cannot take a life unless I am defending mine or someone who cannot protect themselves," he explained patiently. "To break my oath would mean expulsion from my order."

Mal shook her head in disbelief, but couldn't stay angry however, realizing she admired his principles. She tried to convince herself the kiss had nothing to do with it, but she had to admit, the warm sensation inside and the feel of his lips on hers affected her more than she was accustomed to.

She glanced up the street and then back at Alto, before grabbing him on both sides of his head.

"Tell ya what hotshot, I'll do it myself!"

Abruptly, she gave him a brief but hard kiss on the mouth and then took off after the Amarenians.

❈ ❈ ❈

The mariners were just stepping off the backstreets and onto the main road leading to the docks, when they heard the footsteps rapidly approaching behind them. Both spun to see Mal sprinting out of the fog, her face filled with terror.

"He's going to kill me!" the Spice Rat shrieked, glancing over her shoulder.

Saka recognized her as the woman kissing in the street by the pub and whispered with a chuckle, "See, I told you, a total waste of tits."

"No one's going to kill you," Yara assured Mal. "Least of all any damnable man!"

"You don't know what he's capable of," Mal said, pouring it on.

A carriage buckled against the cobblestone streets behind them and Mal appeared to panic, ducking down an intersecting alley. Buying into the ruse, the two Amarenians followed.

"Here now sweet one," Yara cooed, "we'll protect you…"

Mal suddenly spun and sliced open the mariner's throat in one sweeping motion. Yara's eyes opened wide with shock and she tried to scream but could only gurgle. Her hands instinctively covered the wound, but blood sprayed out between her fingers and poured down her arms.

Saka shrieked in fury and kicked Mal in the stomach with such force, it knocked the wind out of her and catapulted her backward against the alley wall.

The impact knocked the knife from Mal's hand and propelled it well out of reach against the opposite wall. She gasped for air and, before she pulled herself off the ground, Saka drew her short sword.

Mal scrambled across the hard alley floor on her hands and knees, gasping for breath and fumbling for her blade. The Amarenian quickly advanced, sword raised to strike, her face masked in unbridled rage.

Suddenly Saka froze, blinked twice, dropped the sword and fell forward. The hilt of Alto's dagger protruded from the back of her bald head.

The swordmaster stood in the alley's entrance. He walked over to her with a concerned look and offered his hand. She accepted it with a weak smile, and he helped her to her feet.

"Are you alright?" he asked staring lovingly into her pain ridden face.

She nodded silently and they stood there for a moment until Mal caught her breath.

Resting her forehead briefly on his chest she gave out a final exhale before approaching the two bodies.

"Okay, let's see how much of my money they still have left," she said kneeling between them.

She rifled through their blood-stained pants while Alto retrieved his dagger from the skull of the dead Amarenian. He wiped off the blade and slipped it back into his boot while Mal counted her loot.

"Sixty-three gold and ten silvers," she reported.

Glancing back up she caught Alto staring at her with an amused grin.

"What?"

Alto shook his head and shrugged.

Mal gave a mischievous smirk and marched towards him provocatively, putting her face close to his.

"Oh, I suppose you want me to thank you, or some such shit, for saving my life?"

"Actually, I had no choice." Alto coyly admitted. "You were unarmed"

"That code of yours I suppose?" she asked gently cupping his cheek.

Alto nodded his confirmation. "Though I must admit the kiss was very nice, as would be another."

"Asshole," she chided, playfully smacking his cheek. "There's no time for that shit, we need to get back to Shom before he pisses off Soshi enough to kill him."

Mal laughed to herself walking out onto the main street knowing deep down there was probably going to be more kisses in her future.

The swordmaster rubbed his cheek, shook his head and followed.

❇ ❇ ❇

Kuut dragged the Darter fish by its long bill and limped down the dock to his usual spot. He would have had two fish to sell, but blood in the water attracted several sharks. He felt lucky to escape with one fish and only a graze on his right leg.

The wharf already buzzed with the usual pre-morning activity. The Kan would be ending soon and he, along with the other fishmongers, had to set up shop to display their wares. He tossed his wide-brimmed hat on the top of a pylon, slung the flippers off his back and leaned back against the wooden pole to check his wound. After admonishing himself for being careless, he began arranging his meager offering on a display board.

A commotion arose from the far end of the pier catching his attention. The Nelayan could make out through the lifting fog, two large EEtahs climbing out of the waters and onto the dock. Seaweed clung from their head and shoulders, through which the outlines of their harpoons were plainly visible.

A sense of near panic swept down the wharf like a rushing torrent of water. Wide-eyed merchants cowered and nervously mumbled amongst themselves. They knew EEtahs were always trouble, and someone would probably die horrifically.

The behemoths lumbered down the wooden decking ignoring the frightened merchants. They positioned themselves on either side of the archway at the dock's entrance and silently stood like statues.

The high-pitched chanting of children's voices rose in the distance, drawing everyone's attention down the main road into the city. Soon, a deep, rhythmic clunking joined the nearing children's revelry. Murmurs quickly escalated into agitated ramblings. Thorn the Wheel and the Telling Festival were coming.

❁ ❁ ❁

Ambassador Alosus peered out over the bow railing, watching the waters of the Shallow Sea slip quickly past the ship. The Kan fog was receding just ahead of them and they followed it north.

Sareeta stood behind her superior on the poop deck, with her arms folded in front of her, staring straight ahead.

The boat driver, a lithe, wiry man with a long black beard, guided the ship's rudder with virtuosity on the quarterdeck below her.

There were no sails on this rapidly moving craft. This was a Brightstar Nolton boat, constructed of the finest Ukko wood harvested only on the island of Zer. The magical wood made from the limbs of the world tree levitated the hull just above the water. The Ukko rudder also served as a propulsion device, with the depth and direction determining the direction and speed of the ship. Because of this magic wood, these ships no longer needed wind, and the hull's construction made the boat unsinkable.

Alosus couldn't help but wonder if trade with the western houses could result in her sisters reaping the benefits of this wonderous wood.

Now sailing through the smooth waters of dead-calm weather, the driver held the rudder deep for maximum speed. Once they caught the Goyan Current, he estimated their arrival within three deci.

The ambassador wrapped her cloak tight against the spray and took a seat. The sense of impending dread clung like the surrounding dampness and she couldn't help but wonder what peril awaited them in Makatooa.

❈ ❈ ❈

Thorn the Wheel's muscular body towered over most other humans, with ebony skin so black, it shimmered in the sun. His massive physique and stunning appearance however didn't make him the most notorious ironmark. The torture device he designed, later incorporated in his name, set him apart from the other enforcers of the dreaded Quartermasters Guild.

Each ironmark developed their own unique style of torture to forcefully extract payment of taxes, withdraw information, or exact punishment on those who would seek to steal from the guild. Ironmarks preferred to punish publicly so the word would spread. The notoriety of these brutal styles was meant to strike fear in the masses and no ironmark's style terrified the adult islanders more than Thorn the Wheel and the Telling Festival.

Thorn however didn't frighten the children of Makatooa. They loved him, and he returned their adoration. To them, he was a gentle giant and a crowd of street urchins always followed him. He seemed to possess an endless supply of molasses drops for them, but they came for more than just the sweets. The youngsters played a central role in the Telling Festival and today was festival day.

The central avenue in Makatooa came alive after the lifting of the Kan. Thorn walked at the head of a large, jubilant procession lost in unabashed abandon. Children sang and danced all around him. Townspeople followed along banging drums and blowing horns. Shopkeepers waved and cheered from their stalls and open doors.

Two large men trailed behind the crowd who did not share in the festive demeanor. The two trailing laborers pushed what appeared to be a fifteen-foot astrolabe built into a three-dimensional wheel. Rolling down the street, its heavy, rhythmic thumps echoed off the buildings, serving as a metronome for the drums and horns.

Thorn led the parade with two small children riding on either shoulder, until it finally arrived at the archway to the wharf. He nodded at the two, towering shark creatures waiting there for him before moving onto the docks. The EEtahs fell in behind him.

The normal morning traffic of merchants and buyers already congested the waterfront. When the noisy parade came rumbling through, people gathered all along the side docks to get a better view, while those walking the central wharf scrambled to get out of the way.

Children laughed and skipped all around the procession. Several little ones thought it fun to jump on the EEtahs' tails and ride, seeing how long they could hold on. The cranky sentients would finally flip them harmlessly into the crowd which roared with joy. Shortly after one was expelled, another child would take their place.

"I fuckin' hate human children," Tarrg snarled in the EEtah tongue.

"I love them," Soog growled back. "They taste like tuna."

Both laughed in their guttural, staccato fashion, adding to the volume and the diversity of the festivities.

Mariners Ann and Deeta had just assumed their sentry post when the lifting of the Kan revealed the bizarre parade nearing the *Regis*. They grew more nervous when the ruckus drew closer. When it stopped in front of their port, they cast uneasy glances at each other before readying their spears. Mariner Zoe stood on the gangplank and nocked an arrow.

Thorn stood in front of the Amarenians for a prolonged moment, allowing the wild scene to unsettle his targets a bit more. Then, with the simple raising of his hand, the crowd went silent.

The royal enforcer stepped up to the sentries and pushed the hood back from his head, revealing his smooth, dark features. The EEtahs flanked him menacingly. The Amarenian sentries sneered at Thorn and his ominous giants.

"I need to see your captain immediately," Thorn demanded with a grin.

"The captain ain't here," Deeta spat out.

She spoke the truth; the captain had been out all Kan searching for mariners Saka and Yara.

"So why don't you take your freak show and move along!" Ann chimed in.

The mariner's request was met with Tarrg's horrendous roar. This was immediately followed by him bending down and biting her head off with one snap. The crowd gasped in gruesome amusement and a cheer went up. Blood sprayed like a fountain and Ann's decapitated body staggered then fell. The EEtah shook his head furiously and spat the head down the dock.

Deeta heard Soog's Udon harpoon pass through her abdomen and out her ribs with a sickening crack. She didn't feel it until she tasted the blood coursing from her mouth. Toppling over she dropped her unused spear to the deck, face frozen in shock.

Zoe cried out in rage and shot an arrow at Tarrg. It pierced the EEtah's huge, raised forearm. He screamed out in pain and threw his Udon harpoon at the archer. It struck Zoe dead in the chest before she could nock another arrow. The force of the impact launched her back across the deck. The spinning tip completely penetrated her chest cavity and exited out her back.

Tarrg roared in victory. Yanking hard on the lanyard the EEtah pulled her over the railing and into the water. He quickly reeled in his weapon, but because of the coral and sharp rock outcroppings, only pieces of the Amarenian raider remained on it. He shook them off, showering a stunned nearby merchant and his stall with gore.

"Secure the ship," Thorn ordered. "Bring me whoever is in charge."

Soog and Tarrg grunted acknowledgment and advanced up the gangplank while the rabble of remaining Amarenians hurriedly armed themselves.

The Fate of Tomorrow

❊   ❊   ❊

Javoko de Mak's stained work apron and greasy, thick features made him resemble a disheveled baker more than the leader of the Silent Partner's notorious North End Gang. Contrary to his appearance, Javoko gained a reputation of being merciless from the savage beatings and murders of all who crossed him.

His command of the North End Gang established them as the most vicious of the four Silent Partner organizations operating in Makatooa.

If one wanted to do business on the docks, Asad's Warfies were the people to see. The Central Mongers handled finance and loans. Bethia's Uppity Outsiders answered the call for any eccentric hedonistic weirdness. However, for good old-fashioned bone-breaking and killing, the North End Gang reigned supreme.

Javoko headquartered in a series of five connected buildings in the central North End called Javoko's Corner. Along with his office building, Javoko's Corner included a tavern, pawn shop, small inn and brothel—a one-stop shop for commerce.

Javoko was pacing, and everyone knew when Javoko paced, bad things happened. The gang boss' tantrums were infamous. He'd taken his rage out on the messengers of bad tidings on multiple occasions. This fact was not lost on Chu-Chu, the local Cul-Ta leader who cowered behind Javoko and followed. His rat head peaked around the boss' thigh ad his rodent frame and tail were visibly trembling.

"Anyone want to tell me what the fuck happened?" Javoko demanded, stopping in front of his lieutenant.

"We're not sure boss," the lieutenant quietly offered, meekly bowing his head. "The city guards found them when the Kan lifted a little while ago, out back of Porgo's place.

Someone severed Siso and Elek completely in half and opened Tait up from neck to nuts. According to my contact, they didn't even have the chance to draw their swords."

The boss returned to pacing and swearing. Then he suddenly stopped again.

"Did you get a look at them?"

The lieutenant shook his head. "They had already taken them to the Vurr Pyre by the time we found out."

This was bad news. The Clerics of Vurr the Fire God burned their funeral pyres continuously. The magma-hot flames consumed everything, including any personal items, weapons or money. Javoko returned to pacing, this time punctuated by pounding his meaty fist into his palm while working himself into a rage.

"You don't kill my people, on my turf, and get away with it," he roared to his lieutenant. "Get a couple of guys and find out if Porgo saw or knows anything."

The lieutenant set off and nodded for two North End thugs standing outside the tavern to follow. Javoko spun around to face Chu-Chu and nearly stepped on him.

"Sweep the city with your people," he ordered the cringing rat-man. "Someone must have seen something."

Chu-Chu quickly scurried out of the office, escaping the unbearable tension, and disappeared into the sewers.

❈ ❈ ❈

Tarrg majestically appeared on the bow of the *Regis*. With a roar which echoed across the inlet, he victoriously held a raider's severed head up for all to see. The crowd thundered their approval. Raising his other hand in a victory fist, he threw the head into the cheering throng.

The Fate of Tomorrow

It tumbled through space spraying a fine red mist over the jubilant mob. Several hands reached up to catch it and two men ended up in a tugging match over it. The winner then began a game. He tossed it like a ball to see who could catch it. Those who managed hold on to the blood-slicked severed head, passed it on to the next participant. The masses grew more festive with each person who successfully caught the grisly ball.

When Soog marched Mariner Suu down the gangplank, the crowd once again erupted in cheers. Suu walked ahead of the EEtahs with her eyes glazed over in shock. Soog held her arms behind her, but it didn't seem necessary. Having witnessed her shipmates and sisters slaughtered in such a merciless, horrific manner took all the fight out of her.

She had dealt with the EEtahs of the Outer Clans many times, and as deadly as they were, these were Sunal-trained EEtahs. Nothing could have prepared the Amarenians to deal with their size, power and martial mastery.

The crowd grew quiet when the EEtah presented his prisoner to the ironmark. The large, cloaked man beamed down at her.

"Welcome to the festival," he hailed loudly in an elated shout.

The mariner stared blankly forward, acknowledging nothing. Thorn nodded at Soog. The EEtah leaned over and shredded her gray crop pants in a single abrupt motion. The crowd roared at the sight of her nakedness.

Thorn then held his hand aloft and motioned for them to bring the wheel forward. The crowd parted and the laborers slowly rolled it up behind its inventor. The device's two intersecting wooden bands were wide enough in diameter to provide room to accommodate the largest of life-forms. An elaborate restraining harness and pulley system suspended a saddle plank in the center of the macabre astrolabe. Many small holes, forming intricate geometric patterns, riddled the plank. Thorn rotated the wheel until the saddle rested horizontal to the ground.

He motioned to Soog to bring Suu to the wheel. The dazed Amarenian offered no resistance when they strapped her, spread-eagle, into the restraining harness across the saddle. Thorn circled the wheel once he secured her and inspected the dimensions of her body in relation to the geometric patterns on the plank beneath her.

Once satisfied with their positioning, he reached into a pocket on the inside of his cloak and retrieved a folded leather case. Thorn caressed the cover, as if it were a religious artifact, before dramatically opening the long trifold case and revealing a set of long steel needles lining the inside. Thorn ceremoniously pulled out the first needle and held it up to the crowd's roars of sadistic appreciation.

The Ironmark smiled in anticipation before placing the needle in the slot below her left foot. He deftly maneuvered the harness system and lowered the arch of her foot onto the point.

Suu came alive, screaming and writhing at her shackles. Thorn lifted her foot back off the needle.

"You're back with us… good," he announced.

Thorn took out another needle and held the slender shaft in full view of Suu—which she followed, eyes wide in horror, and struggling in vain against the bonds.

He slid it into a slot under the back of her neck until the tip rested within inches of her flesh.

"I really am proud of my design," he beamed, placing another needle between her shoulder blades. "The position of each needle you see, corresponds to specific pain centers in the body."

Thorn theatrically presented each needle placement to Suu and then to the enraptured audience. When his hands left her restricted field of vision, she bucked helplessly against the bindings. Children gathered at the front of the crowd laughing and mocking her movements.

"Of course, all bodies are different," he continued, methodically placing needles along the spine. "So, I had to conduct a considerable amount of experimentation to place the needle slots in just the right position for maximum results."

Finally, Thorn stood back and surveyed the pattern of points spread out beneath her. Nodding his head in approval, he stepped over to the harness system controls.

"Now, tell us where the rest of the crew and cargo is," the ironmark demanded.

The crowd began chanting.

"Tell!"

"Tell!"

"Tell!"

Suu glared back and forth from the chanting mob to her interrogator, struggling to comprehend her situation. Dread consumed her, but she refused to answer.

"Come now," Thorn reasoned, gesturing to the chanting urchins before the mob, "Think of the children. We can't start the festival until you tell us."

Her reserve seemed to freeze time and an awkward hush fell over the crowd. Finally, Thorn shrugged and slowly lowered her onto the needles. Suu's silence turned to screams matching the pitch of the chanting crowd.

"Tell!"

"Tell!"

"Tell!"

❈ ❈ ❈

After procuring a little bread, cheese and ale, Shom, Mal and Alto joined Soshi around her modest kitchen table, eating and debating a plan.

"Perhaps Shom is right," Alto conceded. "Destroying it might be the wisest move."

The prodigal stopped eating and gestured toward Alto while giving the group his I-told-you-so look.

"Not before I know what it is," Soshi declared.

"One cannot help but wonder, why you are so interested in this," Shom inquired skeptically. "And come to think of it, you never really explained how it came into your possession in the first place."

Soshi scowled at the Prodigal. "You know, if I wasn't sure I disliked you before, I'm moving in that direction every time you open your mouth."

"What can I say, it's a skill." Shom sardonically shrugged, betraying no animosity.

Mal was about to get between the two of them again, when there came a soft knock on the door. Shom and Alto stood immediately, readied their weapons and took position at each side of the entrance. Mal placed her ear against the door, listening for movement.

Soshi walked up to the door uttered a word in her native Amarenian tongue. From the other side of the door, a female voice replied with a single word in the same language. Soshi nodded at the others, who relaxed a little but remained vigilant.

The door opened enough for Sareeta to poke her head through and the presence of the others startled her. She gripped her short sword and shot Soshi a questioning glare.

"Friends," the Ol'daEE attested.

Sareeta stood down and cautiously stepped inside, followed by Ambassador Alosus.

The occupants of the room took a moment and sized each other up. The hill sister's proportions clearly shocked Mal, Shom and Alto. She stood every bit as tall and stout as the men. Her modest gray crop pants and leather strappings exposed the muscles striating across her exposed chest, arms and legs.

Ambassador Alosus moved gracefully and held herself with authority beneath the hooded cloak covering her features. She approached Soshi pulling back her hood and Soshi bowed before the ambassador. The two spoke in hushed tones briefly in the same unknown language before Alosus nodded and turned to the others. She maintained a pleasant but serious demeanor while she searched their faces.

"You're Shom Eldor," the ambassador stated, locking eyes with the prodigal.

"I am indeed," Shom confessed. "You have me at a disadvantage madam, as I have not had the pleasure."

"Alto de Gom, at your service," Alto interrupted, nervously bowing.

Alosus raised an eyebrow at the brashness of the young swordmaster while Sareeta fought back a sneer.

"For the time being," the ambassador requested, "I think it best we remain anonymous."

She turned back to Soshi. "Now, why am I here?"

The Amarenian Secret Sister retrieved the mangled canister and handed it over.

"This," she stated.

Alosus examined the scavenged exterior and empty jewel fittings. She shot Soshi a disapproving glance.

"This used to be a royal diplomatic compact," she scolded.

"Yeah… well… we needed the adornments for a more… practical use," Mal defensively offered.

Alosus ignored her and opened the top of the canister.

"The Rayth captain gave it to me," Soshi explained. "She took it off a smuggler's ship."

"Yeah," Mal noted sarcastically, "*my* ship."

"You mean the ship the quartermasters just seized at the docks?" Sareeta asked.

Mal lowered her head and sighed. "Probably."

"My father charged me with delivering the canister to the Imperial Bank of Zor," Shom offered.

The ambassador studied him for a moment before asking warily, "Did you know what you were carrying?"

"My family doesn't entrust me with those kinds of secrets," Shom confessed. "Probably for good reason."

"It's true," Soshi added. "I received it sealed in a box."

"So, *you* broke the seal?" Alosus asked.

Soshi nodded.

"Hence, why I couldn't complete my mission," Shom confided.

"Well..." the ambassador said, "as long as you've gone to all this trouble, let's see what it says."

Alosus slid the parchment out of its container. Soshi cleared the table and they unrolled the large vellum document. The ambassador's expression grew grimmer with each line of text she read. She sighed when she finished and shook her head.

"It would appear your dear father has another invasion in the works," she announced calmly.

All eyes turned as Shom choked and spit out a piece of bread.

"What?!" he exclaimed.

"It would seem that seizing all the Goyan eastern agricultural islands last grand cycle just wasn't enough," she said in an accusatory tone.

Shom put down the partially eaten loaf and stepped forward. Sareeta tensed. Her hand flexed toward her sword. Shom side-eyed the hill sister and smirked, before addressing Alosus.

"Madam," he began, "let me assure you I did *not* understand what I was transporting. So, what has daddy dear cooked up this time?"

"This document is in two parts," the ambassador addressed the group. "The first is a request from House Eldor for a loan of fifty thousand secors to rebuild or commission a proper navy."

"Hardly an unreasonable request," Shom said, furrowing his brow. "Commandeering those islands decimated our navy."

"Yes, but the telling part comes in the breakdown of expenses," Ambassador Alosus explained. "The loan was to be repaid with proceeds from a *forthcoming endeavor*, including a handsome commission, along with seizing rights, to be paid to the operation commander, Prince Serkel de Tor."

At the mention of that name, Soshi and Sareeta let out an involuntary, low growl. Their visceral reaction caught Shom off-guard.

"I've not heard of…" Shom began.

"Amarenian history," Alosus said, interrupting him. "Prince Serkel is our prodigal angel of doom."

"My father is planning to invade your homeland," he acknowledged with slight amusement. "Isn't he, Lady Ambassador?"

"You figure that out all on your own?" Alosus asked.

"Not that hard," Shom answered. "You can read Yassett and you travel with a bodyguard."

Alosus squinted her disapproval and returned to the manuscript. She pointed at a lower section of the document.

"This is a guarantor from House Aramos," she noted.

"Since you picked this up in Aris," Shom added, "they must have wanted it delivered to the Imperial Bank of Zor."

"That makes sense," she said. "This statement of guarantee is signed by none other than the grand patriarch himself, Talon Aramos."

Everything grew silent and they eyed each other nervously. The document was too important and dangerous to ignore.

"We must destroy this document," Ambassador Alosus stated emphatically.

"Thank You!" Shom shouted. "That's what *I* told them. Breaking that seal spelled our deaths!"

"Not just that," Alosus added. "There are diplomatic undertakings… *very private* diplomatic undertakings going on which hopefully will make this document irrelevant. We only need a little more time and forcing House Eldor and House Aramos into renegotiations to draft another proposal might give us just enough."

"Your people want to come clean, don't they?" Shom asked, his eyes brightening with the realization. "Give up the pirate life, as it were?"

"I can comment no further," Alosus said, "but you missed your calling, young Eldor. Politics suits you."

"Yes," Shom said chuckling. "We broached this subject earlier, but it seems drinking and fucking are more suited to my life's calling."

❈ ❈ ❈

Being a master of his terrible art, Thorn knew the extraction of productive information demanded a delicate balance between physical and mental torture. The ironmark had to admit that the Amarenian was tough. He almost had to flip her over and go to work on the front, but fortunately, that wasn't necessary. The front of the body offered a whole new field of pain sensors to exploit, but she had already been through enough. Time was of the essence now, because of loss of blood, but she finally broke—they always did.

"There!" Thorn bellowed at the sobbing figure of Suu. "Now, don't you feel better? Confession is always so good for the soul."

The children moved forward and gathered around the wheel chattering excitedly.

"Now we can start the festival," he decreed.

With that announcement, the children began jumping and squealing with excitement. Reaching inside the wheel, Thorn unbuckled her wrist strap. Suu's face was a mixture of pain and relief knowing the ordeal was over. She began weeping uncontrollably and thanking him over and over.

"Yes, yes..." he said placatingly while he loosened the second strap.

Relief instantly turned to panic when she fell back against the needles. She caught herself by grabbing a small bar near the restraints and shot Thorn a look of panicked confusion.

"Well, we must have something to amuse the adults," he said, pointing to the crowd.

Hands and fingers waved in the air as coins passed back and forth. The crowd was gambling. Suu stared at the smiling ironmark. Thorn answered her unasked question.

"They're wagering on how long you can hold on."

When the realization he wouldn't release her from the wheel set in, Suu started screaming, "No!" repeatedly. Thorn stepped back, and the children began rocking the wheel back and forth. They determined the course by a tugging match and finally all the children pushed in the same direction.

Suu's screams blended with the mob's singing and laughing. The average victim usually couldn't hold on past the dock entrance, and Suu was no exception. Her strength finally failed her and she let go. Her body was dashed against the spikes repeatedly when the wheel rolled onward. A great cheer rose among the adults and money frantically changed hands.

The children rolled the bloody wheel through the streets with the perforated corpse spraying a fine mist of blood over everything. Wherever the macabre parade went, townspeople yielded and even joined in as it passed. The ironmark and EEtahs watched as the Telling Festival moved into the city with the body in the wheel reduced to a wet ball of meat.

"Take ten men and go to where she said they moored their raider," Thorn ordered Tarrg. "If it's there, take it. If not, search the area for it."

The giant EEtah growled in affirmation and moved off. Thorn scanned the city streets and the turine rang out ten bells. Soon the Kan would creep up around his feet from under the boardwalk.

"They're out there somewhere. Find them," he ordered the other EEtah.

Soog nodded and waved at the remaining five men to join him. They set out into town, following the trail of blood-splattered cobblestones. Thorn then made his way off the docks, and headed towards the largest building on the waterfront, Asad's Warfies main warehouse.

I think I shall have a talk with My Friend Asad, he mused.

❈ ❈ ❈

The blow landed with a sickening thud, doubling the man over and lifting him off the ground. Another strike immediately followed, smashing his nose. Blood erupted, flowing down his face and he fell to the floor, cowering. While he lay there writhing in pain, Javoko's boot found his ribs with a savage kick.

"What the fuck do you mean, Asad's Warfies took the money?" Javoko punctuated the question with more kicks.

The man on the floor had now curled into a fetal position and stopped trying to deflect the blows. A knock at the door snapped Javoko out of his blind rage and he motioned for a gang member to attend the alarm. A lieutenant entered, nodding to the man who let him in.

"What ya got, Jonn?" Javoko asked, hands on his hips and slightly out of breath.

"Porgo said a Spice Rat, going by the name of Mal, came by last Kan with some gems to sell," the lieutenant answered. "Porg' went on about them being used for official decoration… or some shit. He also said she traveled with a bodyguard. Young, with very fancy swords."

"Looks like we've found our man," Javoko said confidently. "Find him. I want him for myself."

He then kicked the man on the floor one more time.

"And take this piece of shit with you!"

Jonn nodded and helped the beaten man up. Yet another unfortunate young new runner found disfavor in Javoko's eyes—a rite of passage for all in the North End gang. Once the runner was back on his feet, the mob boss got up in his face and poked him in the chest with his thick fingers.

"Listen here numb nuts," Javoko growled. "Go with him and do what he says. Don't fuck up again. Got it?"

The young man's head quickly bobbed up and down.

"Now get the fuck outta here."

❇ ❇ ❇

Fia was beyond concerned. Two of her mariners hadn't returned at the appointed time and every attempt to locate them had proved unsuccessful. She'd taken her driver, Mariner Neaux, along on the search for them. Neaux's short, stocky build and short-sword skills were perfect for close quarters fighting in the city.

After spending most of the Kan searching bars and brothels across the community, they found neither mariners nor combat to relieve their tension. Fia fought back waves of anger when she was forced to give up the search. The shipwright started work today and she needed to talk to him in person, so they started back to the docks. She just hoped the missing sister's actions hadn't fucked everything up.

Fia heard the rumble and commotion of a crowd heading down one of Makatooa's main streets towards the wharf. They stopped at an intersection to allow the parade to pass, amazed at the number of children singing and laughing. They both found themselves caught up in the spectacle and smiling with the crowd despite the missing mariners. Then they saw the wheel.

They froze in horror when Suu's impaled corpse rolled by them, the centerpiece of the joyous parade. The stark contrast of her corpse riddled by the long needles versus the festive crowd around the gory wheel proved darkly ironic. Fia fought back the urge to throw up. Neaux staggered backward, stunned and terrified.

"They took the ship," Fia softly admitted, breaking the helmswoman out of her trance. "We must get to the *Voola*, NOW!"

❈ ❈ ❈

"Esteemed Sister," Soshi began, staring down at the floor, "it was I who opened the seal. This whole affair is my doing. I will dispose of this accursed item."

"Soshanna, you did not hijack this woman's ship," Ambassador Alosus comforted. "And had you not opened it, we'd be dangerously unaware of a plot against our people."

Alosus walked over and placed both hands on the Secret Sister's shoulders. Soshi raised her head, eyes wide with disappointment.

"You must however return to Zor with us," the ambassador said. "Your position here has been compromised. We must reassign you for your own safety."

Soshi lowered her head, dejected. The Amarenian ambassador reached up and pinched her nipple through her dress and the two traded conciliatory smiles.

"I'll get rid of it," Mal assured. "I know just the person to do it."

Alosus paused, gauging the Spice Rat's sincerity, before picking the container off the table and offering it to her. She briefly held on to it and locked eyes with Mal.

"I entrust the future of my people to you," Alosus stated grimly, releasing the container without breaking her gaze. "For too long they have branded us outlaws in this world. Soon that will change. Raiders no longer hold the majority in our homeland. We are truly poised to enter a new golden era. Please help us."

Why are all politicians such blowhards? Mal wondered.

❊ ❊ ❊

There was still a little bit of time before the Kan fog would rise and Asad was wrapping up some paperwork on his desk, when a knock on the door startled him out of his concentration. His clerk poked his head through with a worried look.

"Yes?" Asad called out, mildly aggravated for being disturbed.

"I tried to tell him we were closed…" the clerk began.

"It's quite alright," came the booming voice as Thorn the Wheel pushed his way into the office. "My Friend Asad has always made time for me."

Asad dismissed the clerk, who closed the door as he left. Without waiting for an invitation, the ironmark took a seat directly across from the gang boss. The adversaries smiled at each other in an uncomfortable moment of silence.

"You know," Thorn began, glancing around the office, "I miss our late-night, in-depth conversations, my friend."

"When did we ever do that?" Asad asked, keeping his diplomatic air.

"Ahh," Thorn assented. "Perhaps just wishful thinking."

"What do you want, Thorn?"

Asad's diplomatic air disappeared and the ironmark's face also turned serious.

"On the last Kan," Thorn explained. "You received the contents from the hold of the *Regis*. Let's talk about that, shall we?"

Asad put down his pen and sat back.

"I'm afraid I don't know what you're referring to," he said, his good nature a little more forced. "As far as I'm aware, the *Regis* set in for repairs two cycles ago. Then, of course, there was that little dust-up a while ago with your people."

"I have it on good authority…" Thorn started, before Asad's laughter interrupted.

"You mean that poor young lady whom you just finished torturing to death?" Asad asked. "Come now, do you take me for a fool? People will say anything to stop torture."

"My friend," Thorn warned, "don't make me return in force and do a complete audit of your warehouses."

"Oh, I doubt if that is going to happen," Asad replied.

The Fate of Tomorrow

"You doubt my resolve?!" Thorn shouted, standing in indignation.

"No, I doubt the *quartermaster's* resolve," Asad responded calmly.

"I speak for the quartermaster!" Thorn proclaimed, pounding his fist on the desk.

"No, you're employed by the quartermaster," Asad retorted. "You're merely a brutal tax collector and child fucker."

That anyone would address him in such a manner left Thorn speechless.

"Tell me, my friend," Asad continued, "how many wealthy merchants offered up their sons and daughters to your lust, hoping to avoid tariffs. More important, how would your quartermaster bosses feel about that?"

The ironmark trembled with anger. Asad returned his attention to the papers on his desk, picked up his pen and continued with his work.

"Goodbye Thorn," he calmly dismissed.

"We're not through here," Thorn warned.

"We are for now," Asad responded.

The ironmark stormed out of the office, quaking with anger and slamming the door behind him.

❖ ❖ ❖

Mal sighed and closed the door behind the Amarenians after their farewells. She sent them off to steal away through back alleys to rendezvous with their awaiting ship.

"I, for one, am famished and in desperate need of a drink," Shom announced. "Perhaps Hanno's Tavern?"

"Uh, I wouldn't go there if I were you," Mal advised.

"Nonsense," Shom argued, "Hanno and I are the best of friends."

"I could eat," Alto agreed.

"There you have it," Shom cheerfully proclaimed, "a bit of refreshment then."

"I'm staying put for a while," Mal announced, "but while you're out, drop by and see our friend Kuut. Throw a little incentive his way, so he won't head out to sea until he sees me."

"Why me?" Shom whined. "He's your friend."

"Because you've got the money," Mal said impatiently, "and the less time your canister is on the street the better."

"Alright," Shom conceded. "Meet us by the dock entrance just after the Kan."

Mal nodded and watched the two swordsmen leave. Once she was sure they had truly gone, the Spice Rat sat back down at the table and rested her chin on crossed forearms. She stared intently at the mangled canister, her eyes betraying internal debate. Suddenly, decision made, she opened the canister and slid the document out. After carefully unrolling it on the tabletop, Mal unsheathed her dagger and began trimming the edges of the manuscript.

❁ ❁ ❁

Makatooa's turine bells rang eleven times. Their tones coursed through the city alerting the residents the fog would soon roll in. Soshi led Alosus and Sareeta down one of the back roads through Midtown toward the docks. Soshi froze in her tracks when they turned the corner to enter the wharf proper. A checkpoint of city guards blocked the entrance to the marina. She quickly turned away to lead them down a side street.

"Hey, you three!" one guard called out, noticing their sudden detour. "Hey, wait right there!"

"Hurry," Soshi urged, picking up the pace.

They had just rounded the corner down another alley, when they heard footsteps running up behind them.

"Halt!"

"Run!" Soshi cried.

❀ ❀ ❀

The Amarenian raider ship *Voola* remained moored just offshore to the west of the Makatooa Inlet, safely hidden within the mangrove trees as ordered. Two cycles had passed, and first mate Betha grew concerned. Although she hadn't seen any naval activity, and only the normal traffic of fishing vessels, the first officer couldn't shake her feeling of dread. The Kan settled in and forced them to remain in hiding for yet another cycle. Food stores were running low and her skeleton crew grew weary and restless.

Betha was watching the last of the day's fishing boats pass through the Kan bank out to sea, when she heard twigs snapping and splashing from the shore. The first officer unsheathed her sword and tapped the deck with the flat of the blade, alerting the rest of the crew below. Mariner Reema drew her bow and aimed toward the commotion.

The call of the Sortr Bird, native only to Amarenia, rose over the breaking waves.

"It's the captain!" she exclaimed and returned the call.

All hands were on deck watching when Fia and Neaux broke through the brush and started wading out to the ship.

"Where are the others?" Mariner Endra wondered aloud. All watching knew the worst had probably happened by the captain's tense body language and taunt face.

The crew silently pulled the two swimmers aboard the *Voola*. The captain was down to business the moment her wet feet touched the deck.

"Make ready for sea," she ordered, "we sail immediately!"

The shocked, but obedient mariners rushed to their stations.

"Captain?" one of the riggers implored. "What happened?"

"All is lost," Fia lamented with a scowl, taking the ship's wheel from her first mate. "We need to leave *now*. I just hope it's not too late."

※ ※ ※

Soshi knew the city well, but so did the guards. She led the way, keeping the ambassador safeguarded in the middle between herself and Sareeta, who brought up the rear. The five guards remained about a block behind. They were closing quickly though, recklessly smashing through angry street merchants, knocking over their tables and wares.

"They're catching up," Sareeta reported.

Soshi veered left down another narrow alley. The constricted street began gently sloping downward, which, burdened by armor and bulky weapons, proved a greater challenge for the guards to navigate.

Unlike their pursuers, the women deftly slipped around and through the surprised vendors. When the narrow road's descent grew steeper, Soshi heard the crashing of armor, shields and swords on the cobblestones and knew it had granted them a little lead.

The Kan fog had already filled the lower streets of the city and Soshi pushed forward into it, reveling in the good fortune of getting lost in the dense mist. When the cobblestones slicked with dew, Alosus slowed to keep her footing, but unaccustomed to such terrain, slipped and twisted her ankle. Sareeta, directly behind the ambassador, abruptly halted, almost colliding with her.

"Esteemed?" Sareeta implored.

"I can make it," Alosus assured.

The ambassador grimaced trying to put weight on her ankle. She haltingly limped a few steps and without hesitation, Sareeta picked her up and swept her over her shoulder.

Soshi waited for them to catch up, but she heard the rabble of swords and boots closing behind them through the mist.

"We're going to have to risk going through the Old City," Soshi stated knowing of the mysterious dangers that lurked below.

A dull thud over their heads drew their attention upward. A crossbow bolt still quivered, embedded in the wall above them.

"Go!" Soshi screamed.

They turned right off the main path and into a partially barricaded alleyway. Doorways blocked by discarded boxes and barrels dotted the walls. They saw no other signs of life, except for scampering rats. A large, ornate wooden gateway sealed off the end of the alley. Fog obscured what lay beyond.

"This way," Soshi directed.

She pushed through the gate and down a wide landing and staircase constructed from the same beautiful, refined wood as the gateway. The steps led down beyond the arch and Intricate carvings covering the walls surrounding the stairwell. The polished wood stairs grew exceptionally slippery in the fog and they cautiously descended the steps into a massive chamber.

Everything appeared carved from a single, gargantuan piece of wood, including additional staircases on the various landings leading to wings of individual rooms. An ethereal orange light glowed from the ceiling, illuminating the thick layer of fog covering the floor.

Alosus, riding on Sareeta's shoulders, reached out and touched the wall. She let her fingers gently trail along its carved surface.

"Ukko," she whispered in awe.

"You there!" a city guard screamed from the top of the stairwell, while the others in pursuit burst onto the landing behind him. "Halt!"

"This way!" Soshi yelled, darting into a chamber to their left.

A crossbow bolt sailed past Sareeta, hitting the floor next to her. It was followed by another, disappearing through the mist ahead. She shifted Alosus out of the line of fire to the other shoulder and hastily followed Soshi into a large empty room with polished Ukko wood walls glowing in the pale orange light. In the far corner, next to a heavy door slightly ajar, stood an altar carved right up from the floor.

"We can't outrun them," Alosus said. "Leave me here. I can invoke diplomatic immunity."

"That's if they even let you speak," Soshi responded. "These are violent men and we have stirred their blood. If they catch any of us, rape is the best we can expect."

"We stay together," Sareeta assured.

Soshi squatted down before the altar and reached inside her cloak. She retrieved a pinch of white powder, brought it to her nose, and inhaled.

"Keep going," she ordered. "I'll catch up."

With that, she bent over and reached for the hem of her garment. Her long straight hair covered her face and she reached up her skirt. A moan grew into a growl and she started masturbating, her hands moving frantically back and forth under her clothing.

Sareeta was growing concerned with the direness of their situation. "Soshanna, I really think…"

"I said, GO!" Soshi roared in a deep voice not her own.

Her head snapped up, hair flipping back to reveal milky-white eyes contorted with rage and lust. Lowering her head again, she continued to rock back and forth, frantically rubbing between her legs, chanting in a moaning cadence.

Sareeta, needing no further encouragement, bolted through the heavy door and entered a small, empty room with a passageway opening into a long hallway on the opposite wall. Sareeta gently set the ambassador down and quickly barred the door behind them.

"What in the Goddess's name was that?" the Hill Sister stammered, leaning her back against the door.

"She's under the effects of the Oldust," Alosus warned, rubbing her swollen ankle. "We don't want to be anywhere near that."

❈ ❈ ❈

Mal wrapped the canister in a large swath of cloth and tucked it lengthwise under her left arm, covering it with her cloak. Walking down the stairs to the street she turned toward the docks. Haste was now needed because the Kan was almost upon them and Kuut would be leaving soon. Upon reaching the end of the block, she noticed Shom and Alto peering around the corner.

"I thought you two were going to eat?" she inquired, approaching from behind.

Shom turned, frowned and nodded in the direction they had been looking. Mal followed his gaze and nearly met eyes with Soog. The EEtah mercenary was leading a brute squad of five large human soldiers in their direction. Ducking back around the corner she exhaled in frustration.

"Yeah, well we still *really* need to get this down to the docks!" she emphatically declared.

"I know, I know!" Shom stressed, "I'm thinking!"

Alto stepped forward, hands folded behind his back and leaned between them.

"You two go," he suggested confidently. "I'll distract them."

"Are you kidding me?" Mal asked. "There's five big guys and an even bigger fish! Do you really believe you can take them head-on and live?"

"I have no intention of meeting anyone 'head-on,'" Alto replied. "And every intention of living."

"You make sure you do," Mal purred, brushing his cheek with the back of her hand.

"Now go," Alto prompted.

Mal headed in the other direction with Shom in tow. When they rounded the next corner, Shom peered over at her with an amusingly perplexed look. "What was that?"

"What?" she asked innocently.

"That, back there."

"I think that's none of your business Shommy!"

"Oh, by the gods, you're fucking him, aren't you?!"

"Why Shommy?" she teased. "Are you jealous?"

"Good gods no," he protested. "I just thought you... well... I just thought you had better taste."

"Why would you ever think that?" she retorted. "I used to fuck *you*, didn't I?"

❈ ❈ ❈

The Fate of Tomorrow

The five city guards ran into the wooden altar room and stumbled over each other, stopping in shock. A solitary woman, one of those they had been chasing, sat alone on the altar, her face obscured by hair, her hands buried between her legs. She paid them no attention and concentrated instead on pleasuring herself. They lowered their swords and approached cautiously; bewilderment etched upon their faces.

"What's she doing?"

"What do you think she's doing you idiot!"

"This Ain't right."

They circled her, but the woman, in the throes of ecstasy, showed no signs of acknowledging them or her surroundings.

"It's a trick!"

"I don't know."

"It's sorcery I tell you!"

"Maybe he's right."

"Run her through, that'll end it!"

Soshi orgasmed in that instant. She threw back her head, whipping the hair off her face, revealing grossly deformed features and bulging white eyes. Her roar was the last thing they heard.

Soshi's roaring cry of release and the massive wave of psychic energy unleashed, shook the walls of the adjoining room. The door buckled and the two Amarenians stared in disbelief when the bending door planks snapped the crossbar in two. It clattered noisily to the floor and the door slowly swung ajar. Sareeta cautiously peeked through the small opening and saw Soshi lying on top of the altar, trying to catch her breath. Not seeing any soldiers, the hill sister rushed to the altar.

"Are you alright?" she asked.

Soshi opened her eyes and gasped for breath.

"Wow, that was a big one!" she panted.

"I know," Sareeta agreed, "you broke the door."

She reached down and helped Soshi up to a sitting position and both watched Ambassador Alosus hobble through the broken door.

"Is she okay?" the ambassador inquired.

Sareeta was about to answer, when she felt something large brushing against her legs beneath the dense fog below her knees. She leaped aside, drawing her sword in a single fluid motion. Horrific sounds of tearing and crunching rose through from the fog, accompanied by the metallic scent of fresh blood.

"By the Goddess!" she screamed and swung her sword through the fog in a panic.

"Stop! Stop!" Soshi screamed.

Sareeta obeyed and backed against the altar, with sword held ready.

Twenty heads slowly rose from the mist. Eventually standing upright, they appeared to be human, but their nakedness revealed shockingly gaunt, hairless bodies. Fresh blood and gore glistened around their mouths, contrasting against pallid skin as white as the fog. Some still gnawed on the remains of the city guards' dismembered extremities.

Sareeta scanned the group nervously, her hands tightening and re-tightening around the handle of her sword when the figures emerged fully from the ground fog. An older male, closest to the altar, stopped feasting on one of the guard's forearms and stepped forward.

"I, and my people, thank you for your offering," he said in a slow, rumbling baritone. "We have gone without food for a long period and now you have brought us a feast."

The macabre group filled Soshi with pity, even though most would consider them abominations. She understood what it felt like to be considered a monster.

Retrieving the knife from her belt, she held up her left hand ceremoniously, and pricked her right forefinger. A small drop of blood pooled at the tip. She extended it gracefully outward.

The ghoul slowly approached, leaned over and extended his tongue. Soshi resisted flinching when she felt its ice-cold tip lick the drop of blood off. She carefully retracted her hand and watched the lead ghoul's face brighten a bit. His tongue slipped back between pale lips and he savored the flavor for a moment, eyes closed with intoxication. When he opened them again, he stared straight at the Amarenian.

"Soshanna," he said to a very surprised Soshi, "we shall know you from this day forward as a friend of the Zoande Clan. Your friends we shall call our friends. Safe passage, friend Soshanna."

It extended its hand and pointed out of the room to the hallway beyond. While they retreated into the hall, Soshi glanced back into the altar room. The fog undulated and swirled from massive activity beneath it. The sounds of teeth gnashing at flesh and bone filled the air again. Soshi closed the door and caught up with the others hurrying down the hall. They had a ship to catch.

❀ ❀ ❀

Soog's men fanned out across the street, stopping anyone appearing the least bit suspicious or carrying anything resembling a canister. They had just stopped to harass a merchant headed home with his cart when Alto stepped out from the alley.

"Gentlemen, I know what you're looking for *and* I know where it is located," he announced, before quickly stepping back into the alley and out of sight.

The brute squad stood there in stunned silence, gawking in disbelief. The merchant took advantage of the distraction and quietly pushed his cart away.

"Well, what are you waiting for?!" Soog bellowed.

All five drew their swords and took off in a dead run for the alley. Soog brought up the rear—his short legs unable to keep up with his human soldiers.

When they reached the entrance, they saw Alto at the other end of the backstreet, smiling with his hands on his hips.

"You're going to have to do better than that," he taunted before bolting down an adjacent narrow access way. The brute squad followed him down the narrow precipice only wide enough for them to proceed single file between the buildings. They struggled to maneuver in such tight quarters and pointed their long swords awkwardly upward, clanging against the walls.

Soog's massive frame proved too big to fit, forcing him to watch from the tight opening.

Alto slowed his pace until they closed in on him and then, suddenly spinning, he charged.

The stunned thugs tried to back up, colliding against each other.

Before they could recover their footing, Alto launched himself in the air and threw his boot knife into the forehead of the last man in line. The soldier fell, blocking their retreat. He screamed, clutching helplessly at the gore-slicked knife handle.

Alto used the momentum of his jump and brought his short sword down on top of the head of the thug in front of the line. It sliced clean through down to his shoulders. The head and throat folded open like the petals of a flower, but his death grip still held his long sword in the air above him.

Alto grabbed his elbow, bent the arm backward and used the thug's own blade to stab the second man in line.

Both victims fell into the third, who scrambled to regain his footing when Alto pierced his throat with a swift lunge and severed his spinal cord.

The final man standing realized his fallen comrades trapped him and tried maneuvering around their corpses in a panicked retreat.

"Fight! Kill him!" Soog roared, echoing off the building walls and through the alleys. "If you back down, I will eat you alive! Now fight!"

The last thug timidly moved forward, licking his lips nervously. Alto stood calmly, watching his half-hearted approach.

Once he was close enough, Alto performed a quick, but obvious feint. The man cried out and fell back, tripping over the body behind him. He lay on his back and watched Alto approach.

Behind him, Soog continued his frustrated bellowing.

The closer Alto came, the more the man scooted away from him, quaking in fear. Standing over the body of the first man he killed, Alto leaned over and retrieved his knife from the man's skull. He met the eyes of the last man while wiping his blade clean.

"What is your name?" Alto inquired softly.

The man stopped crawling.

"G… Griff," he stuttered.

"Griff, today I give you a magnificent gift," the swordmaster stated. "I give you your life."

The frustrated EEtah silently stood framed by the entryway, glaring and seething with rage.

"Do not squander what remains of your time alive working for the likes of him."

Alto tipped his head to the EEtah, saluting with a casual flip of the knife, before turning and disappearing down the alley into the fog.

❀   ❀   ❀

Griff slowly got to his feet, still trembling. He watched the swordmaster fade off out of sight and contemplated his advice. *Perhaps this was a second chance,* he thought, *perhaps...*

A blow cut short his philosophical musings and sent him reeling against the cobblestones. The barbed tip of the EEtah's Udon harpoon protruded from his lower chest. Soog yanked on the lanyard, painfully sinking the barb into flesh, and pulled Griff out of the alley.

"I warned you, weakling," the EEtah growled.

Griff's spent his last conscious moment watching Soog bend over him and bite out his entire abdomen, down to the spine, with one chomp. Soog lifted his head to the sky and growled, gargling the guts. Then, with a scowl of disgust, he spat the gore back onto the lifeless form.

"Huh," he grunted. "Even tasted like a coward."

❀ ❀ ❀

The turine struck twelve when Mal and Shom approached the main avenue leading to the docks. Increased city patrols forced them to keep to the side streets. Shom was stepping onto the avenue, when Mal quickly pulled him back into the alley to avoid a three-man patrol rounding the corner and heading their way.

"How much longer must we endure these insufferable hooligans?" Shom asked, watching the patrol question a merchant breaking down his booth.

"Oh, I'm thinking not much longer," a voice said from behind them.

They spun around to see Shann Eldor step out of a shadowed alcove in the alley with sword drawn.

"You!?" Shom instinctively unsheathed his sword.

"Are you so surprised to see me brother?" Shann mockingly asked.

"Only that you could remove your nose from father's ass long enough to make the voyage."

"You have something that belongs to the family," Shann said, "and I've come to collect it."

"I think not," Shom responded. "Unlike you, I know what it reads. Father has gone mad."

"Go now," Shom whispered to Mal, keeping his eye on his brother.

Shann moved to stop her departure, but Shom stepped between the two, raising his sword. A sinister sneer crossed Shann's face.

"Thank you, brother," he announced. "I've been wanting to do this for a very long time."

Shann attacked furiously, striking such a powerful blow that Shom struggled to parry it, followed by another and another in such rapid succession it drove Shom to one knee against the alley wall.

Mal watched Shann's vicious attack and somehow resisted all her instincts to help. She instead capitalized on the distraction and escaped out of the alley, heading for the docks.

❈ ❈ ❈

The Kan was already enveloping the wharf when Kuut grew tired of waiting. He swung his legs over the dock and put on his large flippers. Stretching his upper torso, he prepared to dive into the water.

"Did you think I wouldn't show?" came a familiar voice from behind.

He turned to see Mal standing there, holding something wrapped in cloth.

"Time to fish," Kuut hissed.

"Just one thing," she implored.

His eyes narrowed when she pulled the canister from under the cloth and handed it to him along with a gold piece.

"Place this in the mangroves west of the inlet," she instructed, "near where they moored the Amarenian raider."

Kuut accepted the canister and then looked confused.

"I want it found," Mal added solemnly.

The Nelayan nodded and silently slipped into the water.

❈ ❈ ❈

Alto heard the clash of swords long before he came upon the alley. Leaving his blades sheathed, he drew closer to glimpse the action.

The sound of combat ended abruptly when he reached the entrance.

Peering into the fog shrouded alley, he made out Shom lying on his back. An open head wound bled across his cheek and his sword lay on the ground just out of reach. Another swordsman, with similar features as the prodigal, stood over him, circling the tip of the blade in his face.

"Such a long time I've waited, little brother," Shann gloated, his voice carried by the fog. "I only wish I could make the sweetness of this centi last."

"To hold such hatred in your heart for so long can poison a man," Alto professed, calmly stepping into view.

Shann turned and sneered. "I suggest you move on! This is no concern of yours."

"Ahh, but he is my friend, so it *is* of some concern to me."

"If he's your friend," Shann added. "You should distance yourself from him and not look back. He's a marked man."

"Alas, in death's eyes we are all marked men," Alto said with a shrug.

Shann had enough of the man's axioms. Raising his sword, he pointed it directly at Alto's face.

"Unless you want your mark called in right now," he warned. "Move on!"

The swordmaster nodded confidently. "Threats without substance are but a brief, foul smell upon the wind."

Shann, sensing the insult, lunged at Alto, who immediately drew and parried.

For several moments they sword-danced around the alley, while Shom weakly crawled to the safety of a nearby corner.

Shann returned to the same hard-form strategy of aggressive attack that worked on his brother, screaming with each blow. Alto easily deflected each strike with smooth precision.

"I must say," Alto calmly critiqued. "Your skills are more impressive than most I have encountered."

This insolence enraged Shann. "I *will* kill you!"

"Do you say that to convince me, or yourself?"

Shann roared and struck several more times, but Alto's superior technique rendered each blow harmless.

Shann's eyes burned with rage and he charged swinging wildly. Alto deftly sidestepped and, as the uncontrolled sword wielder rushed past, he swept his blade low, slicing the back of Shann's knee, severing muscles and tendons.

Shann stumbled forward but kept his footing by using his weapon as a cane.

The man was technically still armed and Alto swung his sword around in a wide arc which sent the blade crashing down across the back of Shann's neck. The Eldor's head separated from his body in one clean sweep. The decapitated torso hovered, holding onto the makeshift sword cane, pumping blood across the walls of the alley before toppling over.

"Well, now you've gone and done it," Shom admonished sarcastically.

The surviving Eldor sat against the wall, futilely trying to slow the bleeding with his hand. Alto sheathed his sword and bowed slightly to his friend. "You're welcome."

Shom struggled to rise to his feet, but fell back against the wall, dizzy from his head wound.

"Do you realize you just killed the only male heir to House Eldor?" he asked.

Alto walked over to Shann's body, pulled out his knife and cut the sash from around the corpse's waist before helping Shom up.

"What about you, are you not in the royal succession?"

"Are you kidding? Father would burn it all down rather than see me running things," Shom answered. "I was born to be a prodigal."

Alto examined the wound, before tying the sash remnant around Shom's head as a makeshift bandage. He felt a wave of comradery and respect at this young man who was willing to turn his back on a life of wealth and privilege to follow his calling no matter how libertine.

"Nothing serious," Alto assured. "But you lost a lot of blood though. Just enough damage for an interesting scar and the story to go with it."

"Good thing women like scars," Shom said, rubbing the wound through the cloth. "You do understand this means our deaths."

"I thought we were *already* dead men?" Alto quizzed.

Shom snickered and then winced in pain.

"Well, there's dead and then there's dead."

"Come on," Alto said, propping up the prodigal. "Let's see if we can find someone to tend to that wound."

Shom nodded in agreement, and they were about to step out of the alley when four men blocked their exit.

"Well, if it isn't Mister Fancy Swords," Javoko taunted, stepping between his men. "I've been looking for you."

"And now you have found me," Alto replied.

"I don't know you," Javoko said stepping up to Shom. "Get the fuck out of here."

Shom slumped back against the wall and glanced over at Alto, who nodded.

"You go, get that cut taken care of," the swordmaster said. "I'll be along soon."

"I wouldn't count on it," Javoko threatened.

Shom stumbled past the four men and disappeared into the street. The gang members advanced, pushing Alto farther back into the alley.

"Like I said," Javoko repeated, "you have a debt to settle with me."

Alto appeared bored staring down the gang leader.

"Fine, how many men are you prepared to lose?"

This show of bravado caused Javoko to laugh.

"You are one cocky bastard, I'll give you that," he said. "Take him!"

Alto's blade sang through the air, slicing off the sword arm of the closest man before any could react. Spinning on his heel, and keeping his blade at mid-level, he disemboweled the next. The third partially unsheathed his blade when Alto's sword arced upward, slicing his face open from chin to forehead. The fourth managed to draw most of his two-handed sword when Alto's blade cut off both of his hands at the wrists. This activity gave the final thug time to unsheathe his sword and attack, but the swordmaster dropped to one knee and the strike sailed harmlessly over his head.

Alto then sent his blade sideways, chopping off the attacker's legs just below the knees.

Rising back to his feet Alto serenely surveyed his damage. The gang members writhed on the ground amongst severed body parts, losing blood fast. Their screams of agony visibly unnerved Javoko.

Alto flicked the blood off his blade onto the man with no legs and pointed it directly at his leader's face.

"Much like these, your men I defeated before acted like brigands," Alto explained. "I have no quarrel with you sir, but if you persist in accosting me, it shall force me to deal harshly with you."

The gang leader appraised the carnage of his dead and dying men, before looking back up at Alto's sword.

Javoko gave an evil smile. "Have I got a deal for you!"

❁ ❁ ❁

At any hour, the Stormwatch Tavern stayed busy, but the Kan packed the pub to the rafters. Shom walked in and shook off the fog. His fresh bandages attracted a few glances, which soon gave way to indifference when the patrons returned to their libations and conversations. Mal sat at the bar, nursing a tankard. Shom pressed in next to her, leaned over the bar, and immediately hailed the barkeep.

"What happened to your face?" she nonchalantly asked.

"A terminal case of sibling rivalry."

Shom then pointed out a bottle to the barkeep. A drink appeared before him. He downed it quickly, banged the glass on the bar and motioned for another. The bartender shot a thumb at the sign behind the bar—*No tabs. Cash only*—and held out his hand, palm up.

"Oh, for the gods' sake," Shom moaned.

Shaking his head with indignation Shom slapped several silver coins on the bar. Satisfied, the barkeep poured the next drink.

"So now what do we do?" he asked.

Mal calmly pulled back her cloak and revealed the document neatly folded and tucked under her vest. The sight of it made Shom's eyes go wide and he slammed back his second drink.

"I don't know about you," Mal defiantly said. "But I'm gonna go see a man about a ship."

"You sure?"

Mal downed her drink, dropped a couple coins on the bar and swung off her stool.

"Let's go!"

❁ ❁ ❁

Thorn quickly sat up in his bed when he heard the knock at his door.

"Who?" he demanded.

"Soog," came the reply.

He pulled his naked body out from under the covers and, not bothering to get dressed, opened the door.

Soog stood outside, next to Tarrg, holding the visibly mauled canister.

"The raider was gone," Tarrg reported. "We found this in the mangroves along with other jetsam."

Thorn took the tube and examined it, then opening it he peered inside. Holding it upside down and shaking it, a pile of blackened ash fell into his hand, which he rubbed between his fingers. He could tell from the ashes' silky texture that it came from burned vellum.

"Amarenian barbarians," the ironmark spat, shaking his head in disgust, "they destroy what they don't understand!"

The Ironmark wiped his hands and contemplated the ravaged canister for a few moments before sealing it back up.

"Tarrg, Soog, I officially release you from this assignment," Thorn announced formally. "You may return to your Sunals. I will inform the quartermaster and propose commendations for both of you."

Both nodded their thanks before leaving. After he closed the door, a child's voice whimpered from the bed.

"Are the big scary fish gone?"

Thorn lifted the sheets, revealing a naked boy cowering against the pillows.

"Yes, they are, little one," the ironmark cooed. "Now hurry and get dressed, I must get to work. Oh… and tell your poppa his ship is safe from the bad men."

❀ ❀ ❀

Asad leaned over his desk and surveyed the manuscript Mal and Shom had set before him. His face betrayed his confusion and he shook his head.

"Tell me again, what value does this hold for me?" he asked. "Even if I *could* read it, the vellum's been mutilated, and you don't even have the container it originally came in—which might have held some value to collectors."

"The value comes from the information it holds and who you can sell it to," Mal stated matter-of-factly.

"And who exactly might that be?"

"Well, it's damning to both Houses Eldor and Aramos," Shom suggested. "I imagine they would pay handsomely to have it hushed up. Then there's any rival house that might want to use that information for leverage. House Calden immediately comes to mind. I'm sure they wouldn't appreciate an attempt to bypass their commodities exchange. The mayor of Makatooa is a Calden, isn't he?"

The convenience factor perked Asad's interest.

"And what would you ask for such a dangerous piece of information?" he asked.

"I want my ship back," Mal stated plainly, "and a crew."

"I don't have your ship," Asad said.

"I didn't start sailing these waters yesterday Asad," Mal countered. "If My Friend Asad wants something done on this wharf, it happens."

Asad nodded. "Yes, yes, but how do I even know if this document says what you say it does? I'll have to find a translator to verify…"

"You're just gonna have to trust me on this one," Mal said. "Besides, what Spice Rat could operate anywhere in these waters with you as their enemy?"

Asad sat back for a moment staring at the manuscript before offering his hand.

"I believe we have a deal," he conceded.

❈ ❈ ❈

It wasn't uncommon for the Sovereign Patriarch to summon Kerkas de Rophan, the official court scribe for House Eldor, at any hour to record his various thoughts and musings. So, with paper, quill and inkwell in hand, Kerkas hurriedly reported to the family patriarch, Lord Warbel Eldor.

He sensed the oppressive atmosphere upon entering the sovereign's private chambers. Jenki, a tall Picean and Lord Eldor's personal aide, stood at his side, gill flaps fluttering nervously. A crumpled piece of paper and a knocked-over bottle of powerful spirits lay on the desk before him. It was apparent the sovereign had been drinking.

"Sit," Lord Eldor ordered.

Kerkas took a seat, carefully laid out his writing implements before him, and dipped his quill into the ink.

"My son Shann is dead," the king announced.

The scribe's face fell in shock.

"My liege!" he exclaimed. "Please accept my deepest condolences."

Warbel Eldor waved his hand dismissively. He flopped into his chair and picked up the bottle from the desk, examining the remains.

"You will chronicle his death as in the service of the realm," he began, "bravely battling Amarenian pirates. Overwhelming forces overtook his ship. All fought and died to a man. He killed so many of the dirty quims that, after he fell in battle, they cut off his head for display."

Kerkas' eyes teared up, but he kept writing.

"You will arrange a quinte of mourning," Warbel ordered Jenki.

"But your majesty, what of your other son, Shom?"

The sovereign glared at the crumpled piece of paper.

"I have no other son."

❂ ❂ ❂

The Fate of Tomorrow

Mal and Shom stood on the quarterdeck of the newly renovated *Regis,* sailing southbound through the calm waters of the northern Shallow Sea.

"So Shommy, how does it feel to be out from under daddy's yoke?" Mal asked.

"Refreshingly stimulating and absolutely terrifying," Shom replied, smarting from the sting of sea air on his fresh scar. "Of course, we're going to have to do something for money. I doubt your crew will work for goodwill."

"I've got that covered, Shommy," she stated confidently, supervising the activity on the deck of her ship.

"Oh," he said, "I'm intrigued."

"The Amarenians held back a small cask of Noma venom from Asad," Mal explained, "and they hid it well enough from the quartermaster's stooges."

"How did you get it?"

"The shipwright's workers found it," she replied. "It's worth a small fortune as is, but if diluted with the proper cutting agent, it could set us up for life."

"Impressive!"

"Needless to say," she stated, "the shit is really rare. I've only had the chance to move a few small amounts of it, never this much. Luckily, I know an alchemist in Zor who can make the cut."

"I take it that's our destination?"

"Yep."

"Maluria, how could I ever have doubted you?"

"The smart money doesn't."

ACT TWO

The Zorian Quandary

The Amarenian raider *Voola* cut east across the northern Shallow Sea under full sail. Captain Fia's mood drastically improved now that they were making their way from the Spice Islands and, subsequently, Calden waters. There were several times during the past few cycles that she and Mariner Neaux had exchanged knowing glances and the same thought, *we were lucky to have lived.*

Light streamed in from the paned bay window, fully illuminating the rustic quarters. Wooden beams creaked, and the two hammocks gently swayed to the rhythm of the ship slicing through the waves.

The new cabin girl lay naked in one of the hammocks. Now fully 'broken in,' she stared outward to sea with a satisfied smile and absentmindedly played with herself.

Fia moved the compasses across the weathered map open on her desk, sighed, and then paused. A relieved smile crossed her face. In a sudden outburst, rejoicing aloud, she rapped soundly on the table.

"Yes!"

Mariner Neaux was at the helm when the captain bounded up the stairs and onto the quarterdeck. Fia tweaked her nipple playfully before standing at the bow and surveying the sea.

"Well," the captain proclaimed, "we made international waters."

The mariner held one hand on the wheel, while absentmindedly rubbing her favorite spot which was now a smooth indent.

"Yeah, now I guess all we have to worry about are Whitmar slavers," Neaux replied.

The Amarenian captain looked up at the billowing sails.

"We have no currents to help this time," she said, "but at least the winds are with us. We should be out of the Goyan Islands within two cycles."

Neaux furrowed her brow staring off into the distance.

"What the... Captain?!"

Fia turned and concentrated on a dot just above the horizon. She leaned over the quarterdeck rail and addressed her crew.

"Let's slow her down, mariners. Ease the sheets!"

Immediately, the skeleton crew began reefing the sails. Fia reached to her belt and unhooked a collapsed spyglass. Of all the plunder she had ever taken, she considered this her favorite prize. Fia expanded the glass and brought it up to her eye. She stared for a long moment before lowering it with a quizzical expression.

"What is it Captain?"

Fia brought the glass back up.

"Not sure."

The *Voola* continued to approach cautiously, providing the captain a better view, however, Fia still struggled comprehending what she was seeing. An elaborate wooden platform, attached by cables beneath a large, inflated bladder, floated about a hundred feet above the water. There were about a half a dozen people standing on the platform, from what she could make out.

Fia lowered the eyeglass. "What in the name of the Goddess is that?!"

"Captain!" Mariner Betha called down from the poop deck, pointing starboard.

The Amarenian captain turned her glass northeast, toward the shore of House Calden's ancestral home. An armada of fifty ships sailed off the coast of the Island of Tarla. Betha bounded down the stairs from the upper deck.

"Captain, what is going on?"

"Looks like there's a large, multi-house invasion fleet off the shore of Tarla."

Fia lowered the glass.

"It makes little sense," she added. "There are ships in that attacking fleet flying official Calden colors, and even several Caldani Privateers."

Betha stared out at the armada of ships.

"I guess that explains why they weren't fucking with us over in the reef chain."

"Yeah," Neaux added, "because they are alright here."

"This ain't our fight," Fia declared, "and we're not gonna get caught up in it. Fuck these cockloving waters, too crowded and dangerous."

"Mariner Betha, full sails," Fia ordered. "Mariner Neaux hard to starboard, make a course north. We're going to skirt around the top of this chain and slip through the Barketts."

Both mariners exchanged surprised, nervous glances. The Barketts were fifty-nine large, craggy monoliths, perched at the top of the Goyan Islands, connecting the northern tip of Ardon Island to the southern tip of the last area of human habitation, Quell Island Prison. Their north-to-south positioning allowed perfect access to the Shallow Sea from either side, but its treacherous waters and close quarters made it impossible for large ships to navigate and challenging even for small, nimble ships like the *Voola*.

"Uh, captain," Betha stammered. "It's pretty tight quarters in the Barketts, if...."

Fia kept watching through her glass.

"If we're spotted by the wrong side, we don't have the crew to outrun them or the swords to fight them…"

While they continued to watch the armada to the north, the surrounding area went black. All eyes turned skyward, as something massive cast a vast shadow on the water.

The entire crew of the *Voola* stood, mouths agape, as a massive airship passed directly overhead escorted by four sleek, smaller ships with archers suspended from either side. They headed directly toward the embattled island.

"Captain?"

"I don't know what it is, and we aren't stickin' around long enough to find out."

❀ ❀ ❀

The ambassador's ship had docked a short while ago, after following a quick-moving storm front. The trip back to Zor took three cycles, considerably more time than estimated, because they didn't have any of the powerful Goyan currents to carry them.

Adding to their bad luck and delay, the arrival of an Avion delegation completely tied up the dock where they were moored. The three Amarenians watched in exasperation while ten strikingly beautiful, winged men and women gracefully descended on the dock, and then folded their wings.

A winged lizard, baring several containers strapped to its back, landed beside them and its horrific appearance contrasted with the Avions' beauty. It folded its leathery wings and screeched loudly while it careened its long neck around snapping at several nearby fishers. It lowered its head submissively however, when an Avion reached over and smacked it squarely on the snout.

The usual throng of low-level bureaucrats came to greet them. Their leader, a smiling, middle-aged sycophant in bright yellow robes, issued the typical platitudes in a grandiose manner. The Avion leader listened politely and nodded.

Once completing the greetings, the Avion waved his hand, and several overly cautious porters approached the Kell and began removing the various cartons. The beast, now unloaded, shuffled about nervously, screeching and flexing its wings. Two of the Avions grabbed its tether, and all three took to the skies with a rush of wind from extended wings.

"Damn Avions, always acting like they've got a stick up their ass," Sareeta grumbled.

"Never seen one up close," Soshi gasped. "I mean, you see them in the sky all the time with those flying lizard herds... but up close, they are beautiful!"

"Yeah, beauty is only so much," Sareeta sneered. "All of them look down on humans like we're scum. And those Kells are mean as anything you'll ever come across!"

The ambassador remained silent and watched the Avion entourage intently. Sareeta was correct about their naturally snobbish behavior, but this group seemed slightly different. An almost palpable hostility radiated from this Avion delegation.

They reopened the dock for commerce once the procession moved off it. Half a dozen sailors heaved sighs of relief and returned to their duties. These were the pitfalls of doing business in the capital city.

The crowd also dissipated, following the slow parade of delegates making their way up to the main forum complex. The Amarenian ambassador curiously noted that the group of Avions veered to the left and headed not for the forum, but for the diplomatic quarters instead.

Esteemed Sister Alosus, with Sareeta and Soshi in tow, beat a direct path to the forum. Because the incident in

Makatooa had cost valuable time, she kept a brisk pace while addressing Soshi.

"I was hoping you could stay on in Zor to help us out."

"Well, I..." Soshi began.

She glanced over at Alosus' bodyguard and seneschal for a reaction. The last thing she wanted was to become involved in a petty court rivalry. Sareeta nodded discreetly and eased any fears of competitive conflict, which overjoyed Soshi.

"I would be honored, Esteemed!"

"Good, good," Alosus nodded at her, not breaking stride. "Sareeta, please set her up with a room in our suite, and let's get her something to wear."

Sareeta bowed slightly, and broke off with Soshi down a crowded, wide corridor to the market wing of the complex, while the ambassador continued onward into the forum.

"Everything's huge here!" Soshi remarked, looking around in wonder.

"First time in Zor?"

Soshi nodded. Sareeta slowed from her boss's frantic pace and allowed the newcomer to take things in.

"The High Holy City of Zor has provided a neutral meeting place for all sentient races for thousands of grands," Sareeta explained.

She gestured to the multitude of humanoid life forms milling about in the hall.

"Even in the architecture of the humblest sections of the city," she continued, "roads, doorways and rooms are larger to accommodate any of the creatures native to the area."

"Any except us," Soshi qualified.

"That was our people's choice," Sareeta acknowledged with a nod, "and it's what the ambassador is trying to remedy."

She paused briefly and met Soshi's eyes. Reaching up, she gently touched Soshi's chest.

"It's also the cause you just lent yourself to."

❂ ❂ ❂

Mal and Shom supervised the activity on the decks from the bridge of the *Regis*. They were just out from Zor and all hands were on deck preparing to dock.

"I have to admit," Shom approvingly said, "this crew seems quite capable for being suddenly thrown together."

On the quarterdeck just below them, identical twin albino Bailian first and second mates took turns at the wheel. Shom curiously watched them and shook his head. Known for their beautiful pale blue skin, Bailians with alabaster white pigmentation were a genuine rarity.

"Those two together are quite unsettling."

Mal chuckled. "You should have seen it when I first met them. I mean, twin albinos are an odd sight anywhere, but these two share the same name and apparently the same thoughts. Seriously. They just looked at me with their identical deadpan faces and said, 'We are Orich-Taa.'"

"I honestly can't tell the two apart," Shom admitted. "It's fortunate they stand different watches."

"They are definitely ex-Brightstar," Mal noted.

"Oh, I have no doubt as to their abilities," he added, "just their demeanor."

Their focus turned to the main deck, where two human males of medium build with dark hair held a large main rope spanning upward into the rigging. There, a solitary female, lithe and agile adjusted the sails.

"So, what do you think of the new crew Shommy?" Mal asked keeping her focus on the work being performed below.

"That Santo is a weaselly little fuck," Shom said, "and Brados spews more bullshit than even I thought possible."

"Yes," Mal said, "but they might come in handy in Zor."

She drew his attention to the barefoot woman suspended precariously between lines of rigging above them, her blonde hair fluttering wildly.

"Besides," Mal added, "Margo, our little rope queen up there, keeps them in line."

Shom faced his friend with a lecherous smile and quizzical tilt of the head. "She restrains them?"

"No, she fucks them."

"Ahh, ample persuasion if ever I heard it…"

A roar of protest brought their attention back down to the deck. An Outer Clan EEtah carried a large coil of rope up from below. His powerfully built, seven-foot-tall frame bore the burden with ease, but he grumbled in protest with every step.

"Seems that Haak is a constant complainer."

"Yeah," Mal admitted. "Muscle is all he's good for. Besides, Margo's not fucking him."

This caused them both to laugh.

"So, Captain, what's the plan once we hit the docks of Zor?"

"I know a professor at the University of Marassa who teaches poisons," Mal answered. "We'll get his input on how to cut the Noma venom."

"And how is it *you* were hobnobbing around with intellectual types?" Shom asked, chuckling.

"He hired me on as his guide a while back," Mal explained, "when he was working on his Marassa project collecting toxins throughout the Spice Islands. I'll send Mr. Golden Tongue down there to fetch him. The professor should have some answers for us."

"What about your original buyers?"

"They were anonymous, and as far as their concerned, the Amarenian raiders stole the venom."

"Devious as always!" Shom praised.

"A girl's gotta eat."

"This still could be tricky. If an inordinate amount of Noma hits the streets, someone will suspect."

"Tricky is my middle name, Shommy."

❊ ❊ ❊

Ambassador Alosus strode through the crowded hall of the Zorian Forum at a rapid pace, her mind awash with plots, scenarios, and talking points. If possible, she would try to secure a meeting with representatives of House Valdur or Calden before they broke for the Kan.

From behind her, she heard a voice call her name. She slowed a bit and turned back. Adept Conewa, a middle-aged woman in traditional Amarenian court attire—long flowing dress, cinched at the waist with breasts bare—worked her way through the crowd towards her.

"Esteemed," Adept Conewa greeted, almost out of breath, "a word please."

"I'm afraid you'll have to talk as we walk, adept," Alosus said. "Time's not my friend right now."

"As you wish Esteemed," the adept conceded, keeping the ambassador's pace.

As special Amarenian envoy of the Ara-Fel Party, Adept Conewa represented the agricultural sisters wanting to trade with the west. Unfortunately, she also was a bit of a pest.

"Is there any news concerning the support of the western houses?" Conewa inquired, with a dour tone.

The ambassador had been avoiding this conversation.

"Not yet," Alosus answered. "Something called me away for a few cycles on an emergency."

"Sister!" the older woman chastised. "Need I remind you our High Council will vote in three cycles? Without some support from the western houses, we will fail!"

Esteemed Sister Alosus, Ambassador of the Free Amarenian Sisterhood, stopped and spun.

"No Sister," Alosus snapped. "You need *not* remind me! Now if you'll excuse me, I'm attempting that very thing!"

Without waiting for a reply, she turned and hurried off, swept away by the crowd.

By a stroke of luck, she encountered Pierce Calden just outside his chambers, holding an animated conversation with an official she didn't recognize.

Calden gracefully swept away a lock of long brown hair caught in a beard sculptured to accentuate his sharp, angular features. He broke off the conversation when he saw her approach.

"Esteemed," he greeted. "A word in my chambers, perhaps?"

"My thoughts exactly," she replied.

When the door closed, he turned to her solemnly.

"I would just like to state emphatically that my family condemns the treacherous and egregious actions of Houses Eldor and Aramos," he vowed. "You may count on our family, and their charges, for full support of your cause."

Confusion swept across Alosus' face and her throat tightened.

"I'm not sure I know what you're referring to, Ambassador," she confessed.

Now it was the young Calden's turn to appear perplexed.

"Esteemed, I naturally assumed you were aware of the document outlining the invasion of your homeland."

Alosus' stomach became unsettled. Maluria had not destroyed the document!

"I, I..." She stammered. "How?"

"One of the local crime bosses traded it to my brother, the mayor of Makatooa, to curry favor," he explained.

The ambassador's mind raced. She followed multiple scenario threads to their possible conclusions. Would the operation be put into action if the plans somehow made it to the Imperial Bank? No, the plot had already been revealed...

"Esteemed?"

Pierce snapped her out of her trance. She shook her head to clear it.

"Oh, I, uh..."

Alosus quickly composed herself and looked her young ally in the eye.

"Both I, and my people, thank you for your backing and friendship," she said. "I shall convey your pledge of support to our queen."

"Perhaps even the opening of an embassy in your capital?" Calden suggested.

"Perhaps," she admitted with a hint of optimism. "Now, if you will excuse me, I have several errands to run."

"Of course, Esteemed."

Ambassador Alosus bowed and left. She couldn't help but shake her head at the irony of the situation. The revealing of the invasion plans aided them. House Caldens support, with their superior naval and maritime force would be a great asset to their cause. House Valdur's backing, with their airships would seal their victory. She would visit Joc' Valdur at the lifting of the Kan.

❂ ❂ ❂

Hanno's Tavern in Central Makatooa grew crowded and noisy during the Kan. Along with the usual local patrons, the crews of several just docked merchant ships packed the house.

Alto sat in the back of the room and drowned out the din of pub life nursing a tankard of ale. He surveyed the crowd through smoke and the crystal lighting, considering the events of the last few cycles.

Javoko's offer had been generous to a fault. He would set him up with a dojo, a reputation, and a considerable salary. All the crime boss asked in return were his services as a personal bodyguard.

Alto took another sip and stared forward in concentration.

The crime boss even agreed his services would not conflict with Alto's code. Javoko would remain unarmed, giving the swordmaster the right to defend against any attack on him. Javoko also assured he wouldn't involve Alto in any strong-arm robberies or murders.

There were plenty of pros, but only one main con. Javoko. Alto just didn't trust him. Shaking his head with indecision, he took another drink.

"Hey. love," came a sultry voice to his right.

Alto recognized the beautiful brunette in her sheer red dress. He smiled, meeting her gaze.

"Hello Mz. Dasha."

Dasha was his first prostitute hired when he arrived, and by far his favorite.

"You look like you could use some company," she seductively said.

Dasha deftly slipped onto his lap and wrapped her arms around his neck. He leaned forward and put his forehead against hers.

"Too many things on my mind, love."

Dasha's expression of disbelief turned to a sly, determined grin. She put both hands on either side of his face and pulled him in for a quick, hard kiss. While he was recovering, she grabbed his hand and pulled him to his feet.

"We'll just see about that!" she challenged.

He laughed when she yanked him across the floor and out the door, much to the amusement of several regulars who cheered her on. Once outside, she wrapped her arms around his waist and directed him toward his boardinghouse next door.

"Let's fill your head with some different thoughts!"

"Never argue with an insistent woman," Alto declared.

"Smart boy," she said with a nod.

They walked a few more steps, when the cry of a diving seagull snapped him out of his fantasy. The bird circled low and then landed before the two.

"Friend of yours?" she playfully asked.

"One would hope," Alto quizzically replied.

He approached the gull, now walking in a tight circle on the ground and squawking. The swordmaster knelt and the bird came immediately over to him. It didn't protest when he gently picked it up and retrieved the message attached to its leg. He then cast it up into the air. It caught flight, circled once, and then winged away.

Dasha walked up to him and watched his face grow somber reading the message.

"I'm getting the feeling we might have to postpone our session," she uttered warily.

Mora Alto,

I write this letter with a heavy heart. Two cycles ago, someone ambushed and murdered Mora Ferrah. We believe the renegade faction of a rival school to be the culprits. I greatly fear a war between dojos is at hand.

Your assistance is very much needed,

Master Keraso

Alto lowered his hands and stared into space while attempting to assess what he had just read.

"I'm afraid so, my dear," he confirmed. "This is from the Master in Zor. Apparently, we've had some trouble. A good friend of mine was killed and they need my assistance immediately."

Dasha stood silent for a few brief moments, before her mischievous grin returned. She placed her hand on his arm.

"You sure you don't want one for the road?"

Smiling at the thought, he kissed her on the forehead.

"Sorry love, I've got a boat to catch."

❋ ❋ ❋

Captain Rafel de Mirel twirled a lock of his long black hair and looked around the spacious, well-appointed office. A creature of habit, the Zorian spymaster always chose to sit in the same chair, one of two facing his boss' desk, at the beginning and ending of every cycle.

The meetings varied in length but were never omitted. Rafel, a thin, effeminate man with squinting eyes and long thin moustache, took great pride knowing these discussions helped keep any organized gangs out of Zor.

To be sure, crime was abundant in The High Holy City of Zor. However, because of his intelligence network, the draconian methods of the city guards, and the brilliant investigative work of the man behind the desk in front of him, none stayed together long.

Colonel Zekoff de Corab, commander of the Zorian City Guards pulled a good-sized pinch of tobacco from a pouch and filled his pipe, a common sign he was ready to begin the session.

Rafel felt fortunate to work side by side with this man who had come from a small mining town with nothing and worked his way up to his esteemed position by wits alone.

Zekoff was hardly an imposing figure. At the age of sixty, he looked his age, with a long white beard and an ever so slight hunch in his stride. Rafel marveled that he never carried a weapon and, because of his reputation, walked the streets with impunity.

"Anything more on those duels last Kan, Captain?" Zekoff asked, searching the top of his desk for a match.

"Word on the street is it wasn't a duel," Rafel said.

"Oh?" Zekoff remarked, picking up a short orange crystal cylinder and tapping the end of the crystal on the desktop until it began to glow. "A renegade faction of the Zorian Sword Academy ambushed several members of the Rohina Takii Sword School?"

The head of the city guard placed the glowing tip into the pipe and blew out a column of smoke. The white vapors billowed upward and filled the room with the fresh scent of evergreen.

"So," he continued, placing the crystal match within reach. "I guess friendly competition just wasn't enough."

"We talked with the swordmasters of both schools," Rafel said grimly. "The Takii group lost one of their instructors and the Zorian master informed us of the breakaway group."

"And yet another rabble attempts to organize," Zekoff said, shaking his head and expelling another cloud of smoke.

"It seems one of the Zorian senior instructors felt the Wouvian Takii school's opening here was a major affront. He finally snapped and took about a dozen students with him."

Zekoff took a long drag on his pipe and expelled the cloud, contemplating his next action. He opted on the side of tradition. The renegade breakaway sword group would have to be crushed, brutally and publicly, if need be.

"So, Captain, am I correct in assessing that we've got a dozen fanatical expert swordsmen on the street looking to draw blood?"

Captain Rafel began twirling his mustache. "Um, uh, yes sir."

"This can only get worse," Zekoff added. "The Kan is only a few decis away. We need to squelch this *fast*. Get your spies to work, Captain. I'm sure I'll be calling in Red Division at some point in this whole sordid affair and they'll need information."

"Yes Colonel," the spymaster nodded.

❋ ❋ ❋

The *Regis* docked in Slip twenty-three with the Kan's fog rising and the grand turine ringing six times in the harbor of Narian Bay.

The crew secured the ship and Mal dispatched Brados to fetch the Marassa—with the admonishment of not attempting anything clever, just to bring him there.

Before entertaining any guests, Mal then checked in with the harbormaster. They officially logged the *Regis* as empty and ready to receive cargo.

Now, a worrisome amount of time later, the thick, damp vapor consumed all. Activity during the Kan slowed considerably. The rhythmic cadence of the city guard's boots patrolling the streets became the only evidence of constant activity.

Two hooded figures made their way through the murky illumination and up the gangplank of the *Regis*. The lead figure nodded to Haak when stepping onto the deck.

"She waits in her cabin," the EEtah growled.

The hooded man nodded once again, and the two disappeared below deck. Once safely out of sight, Brados, and the Marassa, a very confused older man, pulled back their hoods.

"See?" Brados said, smiling, "Just like I said, safe and sound."

Marassa Yrich took in his surroundings. Several palm-sized crystals illuminated the interior of the ship with a warm orange glow. The foredeck fitted six hammocks lining either side of the moderately sized compartment. Santo slept in one hammock, softly snoring. Margo sat on a container at the far end and was winding thin rope tightly around a much thicker strand. She nodded at the two. Orich-Taa sat back-to-back on the deck, behind the row of hammocks, eyes closed in an apparent trance. Beside him, Brados removed his cloak and offered out his hand.

"May I take your wrap?" Brados asked.

The old man nodded and removed his thick cloak, revealing a long white nightshirt. Brados led the way to the captain's quarters at the stern of the ship.

In the captain's cabin Shom peered over at Mal, who was sitting behind her desk, nervously twirling and balancing her dagger with one hand.

"Perhaps our chatty friend Brados has lost his way?" Shom offered.

Mal merely shook her head and continued manipulating the blade. His next comment was cut short by a soft knock on her cabin door. Mal immediately straightened up and turned towards the alarm.

"Come!"

Brados poked his head through and gave a mischievous grin.

Mal shot him an irritated, questioning glance until he opened the door all the way and she recognized her old friend, Marassa Yrich.

Smiling in relief she rose to greet him and Shom stood as well.

"Maluria!" he bellowed, his face lighting up with joy. "Never in my wildest imaginings…"

"Yrich, you old stick-in-the-mud!"

They embraced warmly. It charmed Shom to see the contented expression on her face.

The Marassa took in the simple furnishings of Mal's private quarters; a hammock, a sea chest next to an enormous desk in front of a six-pane bay window. His focus fell on a half-full bottle on her desk.

"Now then, young lady, am I to believe you would drag an old man out into the damp to catch his death and not offer him a drink?!"

The Spice Rat snickered. She retrieved the bottle, pulled the cork, and handed it to him.

"The last time I drank from a bottle was on this very ship, many grands ago," he reminisced.

Chuckling to himself, he took a swig and then noticed Shom, who remained expressionless. She purposefully hadn't introduced them and, knowing her line of work, he wouldn't inquire. Keeping the bottle, he sat in one of the two chairs facing her desk.

"As good as it is to see you," he started. "I'm sure you didn't bring me out in the middle of the Kan to drink and catch up?"

Mal shook her head and then smiled wistfully.

"Not really," she admitted.

"Well, I am in my nightshirt, and I'm sure my wife is wondering what could possibly be this important."

Mal reached over for the bottle, took a long drink, and set it on the desk.

"I have acquired something that I need your opinion on," she said.

The Marassa furrowed his brow and picked up the bottle.

"An opinion that just won't wait… my dear, you have piqued my interest." With that, he took another drink.

Mal nodded at Shom. The prodigal reached down beside the sea chest he sat on, picked up the small cask and put it on the desk.

"And here," Shom stated, "is what all the fuss is about."

"Go ahead," Mal urged, "open it."

The Marassa slowly and carefully opened the top and peered inside. He quickly slammed the lid closed and looked up stunned.

"Noma!"

Mal nodded. "I know that I just need more details."

Yrik shook his head staring at the barrel. "I know better than to ask how or where you got this much."

"A girl's gotta have some secrets," Mal said with a wink.

"Well, by the smokiness and thickness," the Marassa explained. "I can tell you it is one hundred percent undistilled. In fact, I don't think I've ever seen Noma this pure, or in this volume, ever!"

"So, extremely valuable?" Shom inquired, with a touch of greed in his voice.

"In this amount, yes," he confirmed. "But it is *far* more valuable once refined. The Snake Clan of Virde Island use a special distilling technique called Colaa. It converts the Noma into a powerful hallucinogenic that transports its users into the Middle Realms. Certain alchemists and priests would pay dearly for that concoction."

"Oh, by the gods," Shom moaned. "We're not going back to those forsaken islands, are we?"

"Can you perform that distilling technique?" Mal hopefully asked.

"I can only do a basic distillation," the Marassa said shaking his head. "But you really need the Colaa technique for a proper cut. I must underscore how *dangerous* this liquid is. At this potency, you can't even touch it. If it absorbs into your skin, it's as perilous as ingesting it. You'd be dead in centis. It's dangerous just to be around it uncovered. If the sunlight heats it, the fumes are just as deadly. This cask contains enough venom to kill every living creature on this entire continent five times over."

Mal picked up her dagger and absentmindedly played with it while thinking.

"So, for maximum profit," she concluded. "We have to make another trip back to the islands?"

Shom groaned and slumped back on the sea chest.

"Perhaps not," Yrich countered. "A break-away Snake Clan priest has established his own group on this island, in the foothills to the east of town."

"Oh, thank the gods," Shom said in a relieved tone.

"Snake Clan priests are called Nagas and have a reputation for being temperamental," Yrich cautioned.

Mal gave a determined grin and placed her dagger back on the desk. "Yeah well, temperamental or not, it sounds like this is the person I need to see."

❊ ❊ ❊

The Broken Mast Pub was one of many establishments on Zor's southern waterfront where, a select group of connected individuals known as maparen could be found. Using their services, one could procure anything—from something mundane, like a drink or elaborate, like commissioning a fleet of ships. A barkeep and tavern wenches handled the mundane drinks. Maparen entrepreneurs facilitated the more complex transactions.

Each tavern held a reserved table for one of these entrepreneurs. Such was the case in the rear of the main bar area of the Broken Mast, where the table and base of operations for Waka de Zor resided. It was easy to underestimate the influence Waka held by his appearance.

He looked like an average, clean-shaven human male with a receding hairline and a pot belly hinting at his age. Yet, it seemed everyone owed him a favor. No matter how obscure the want was, Waka could oblige.

The maparen had just completed a small but lucrative transaction with two sailors. When they placed his payment on the table, he saw the tall man enter. Sighing, he gave a conciliatory smile to the sailors who got up and left.

The clean-shaven older human was dressed exactly as he had ben when he first hired him. His black cape had expensive red piping and his clothes implied wealth, as did his demeanor. When he had retained Waka's services, he never gave his name or haggled over the fee. Waka found it unsettling that he'd never seen the man before. Clearly, he must be a broker or agent of some sort, but the maparen knew, and had worked with, all the operatives in Zor.

The man passed the bar and deftly brushed off several solicitations from the Broken Mast's ladies, before pressing through the crowd to the maparen's table. He stood behind the recently vacated chair, staring down expectantly. Waka froze for a moment, then looked up with a forced smile.

"Please sit down, good sir," he offered.

The man's pale, bony features remained expressionless and he took a seat.

"It's so good to see you again!" Waka lied, with an effervescent flair.

The man nodded but his demeanor remained grim.

"Good to see you, Si Waka," he greeted in a deep, somber voice. "My clients have released payment into my care and I now seek to conclude our transaction."

Waka fidgeted nervously.

"Well, I'm glad you brought that up," he uneasily said. "I'm afraid there's been a bit of a setback."

"A setback?" The man remained void of expression.

"Um, uh, yes…" Waka winced slightly. "You see, pirates hijacked the transport ship. They stole the entire cargo."

The Fate of Tomorrow

The maparen waited for a response to no avail. The man sat motionless; his unblinking eyes fixed on the source of the bad news.

"I see," he finally acknowledged in a calm, icy voice, "and the initial fee we paid you?"

"What of it?!"

"Sir, you assured me, and I, in turn, assured my clients, that securing the product and undertaking this endeavor was well within the scope of your abilities. As I recall, I paid a considerable sum to you myself."

Waka was aghast! Did this person not comprehend the way the Goyan maritime world worked?

"Good sir!" he protested. "Surely, you understand that I did not profit from the sum you paid! The amount of venom you requested was difficult to acquire and expensive not to mention dangerous. Avenues needed opening! This too can prove costly. My fee was minimum! There was no guarantee!"

"And yet, those avenues proved inadequate?"

"Yes, well, there is nothing you can do about pirates!"

Once again, the man sat motionless, staring.

"My clients are going to be very disappointed."

Having been in this profession since a young man, Waka had seen his share of unhappy customers, but something about this detached, somber demeanor worried him. Feeling the need to say something to break the palpable tension, he blurted out a halfhearted explanation.

"Piracy affects everyone. We almost lost the *Regis*. Luckily, they could repair her and get her back on the water. She docked just before the Kan."

"It's good to know you have compensated the smuggler, Si Waka, and yet I remain empty-handed."

"I'm truly sorry if those lines are now closed," Waka offered. "Perhaps a substitution?"

For the first time, the man gave a tight, evil grin and the maparen's blood ran cold.

"No," he said, and the grin disappeared when he rose. "I believe we are finished here."

Without another word or glance back, he turned and left.

Once gone, Waka noticed he was visibly trembling. The encounter had totally unnerved him, and he concluded business for this cycle. He had to conceal his shaking hands when he rounded up his few personal items and his knees almost buckled on his way out. Unlike most evenings, he ignored the farewells of the workers and patrons.

Outside, the Kan's coolness surrounded him. He shook his head and chastised himself for being so easily spooked. Taking a deep breath, Waka headed into town.

Fear and the imagination are a powerful force in the human mind. Once infected and the seed planted, simple things can take on monstrous proportions.

With each step, the common street sounds made him more and more apprehensive. In these situations, everyone deals with their dread differently. Waka sang an old campfire song he remembered from his youth to ease his nerves. It was silly, yet meaningful, and calmed him until he wasn't quite so jumpy.

Walking by the next alley, still singing under his breath, a noose lashed out from the foggy depths, wrapping around his ankles. It pulled him off his feet with a violent jerk and when he hit the ground, it knocked the wind out of him. He tried to scream but only gasped when it pulled him off the street and into an alleyway.

In the narrow side street, he made out a dozen Cul-Ta wildly pulling on the rope. Finally catching his breath, he let out a scream until one shoved a dirty rag in his mouth. The bitter taste and smell of feces on it made him gag. He could smell the rat creature's rancid breath when it came within inches of his face.

"Shut up, stupid human!"

Starting off again, they pulled him down the narrow throughway while rocks and debris on the ground tore at his clothing and skin. The mangy creatures halted at an opening with a stairwell leading up.

Eyes wide with terror, he listened to them chatter away, arguing the best way to get him up the steps. After several moments of heated debate, they decided to continue dragging him feet first.

If he weren't the victim, the sight of a group of three-foot-tall humanoid rats, pulling a struggling man up a flight of stairs, might have appeared comical. Occasionally, one of the Cul-Ta would strike him with a small club when his protestations became a burden on the dragging. With each blow, they chattered obscenities at him in their language. Muscling him up the stairwell his back and head collided with each step. This rendered him unconscious by the time they made the first landing.

Waka regained consciousness from the sensation of a warm liquid hitting his face and a dank ammonia smell. When he opened his eyes, he saw one of the rat creatures standing over him, a thick stream of urine arching from a small, pink penis protruding from his furry groin. Thrashing about, Waka screamed obscenities against the rag in his mouth, but his garbled rant only sent the rats into waves of hysteria.

All laughing stopped when the tall man stepped out of the fog. The rats cowered watching him saunter up to Waka with the same unemotional stare. He nodded for one of the Cul-Ta to pull the rag out of his mouth.

Once the filthy gag was removed, the maparen rolled to his side and vomited. The tall man waited patiently, not moving or even blinking. When Waka finished, he rolled onto his back and propped himself up on his elbows.

"I give you one last chance to craft an equitable solution," the tall man offered in his usual monotone.

"Please, please I told you! I don't know where it is. I don't..."

With another nod of the man's head, the Cul-Ta surrounded Waka, lifted him up, and carried him to the ledge.

"No, no, please!!!"

The panicked screams set the rats to giggling and they unceremoniously heaved him over the edge. His thrashing body disappeared downward into the fog. The pleas and crying ended abruptly, replaced by a dull thud when he struck the cobblestone alley below.

In unison, the Cul-Ta cheered, pushing and shoving at each other peering over the side of the building. They squawked in frustration at their failed attempt to get a glimpse through the haze at the body below.

It took a few long moments before the simple-minded creatures realized the show was over. Muttering their disappointment, they turned to face the tall man for their next order. He ignored the rat henchmen and was staring up into the foggy sky. Out of a natural reaction, the Cul-Ta looked upward too.

A short time passed and the wind, normally absent in the Kan, picked up. The rats started mumbling and whispering anxiously while the tall man adjusted his clothing. The wind increased, and the mumbles became nervous squeaks.

"Silence!" he snapped.

The henchmen complied until the two Avion slowly descended into view through the mist, their great wings swirling the fog. The Cul-Ta screeched at once and scattered in all directions. The tall man ignored the skittish rats. He stood motionless, transfixed on the strikingly handsome Avions, dressed in simple white tunics, landing before him.

"My Lords," he greeted, bowing.

Both returned the bow and one stepped forward.

"They call the ship you seek the *Regis*," the man offered, all the while keeping his head bowed. "She's docked in port right now."

"And?" the Avion demanded curtly.

"I'm afraid I have no more information, my Lord."

The Avion sighed and gently put both hands on the tall man's shoulders.

"Loyal Kend," he said, "you are a true friend of the Idonian cause."

Kend met the Avion's eyes with an expression of puppy-like adoration and trust.

"Thank you, Lord!"

"We so appreciate your service," it continued. "More important, your willingness to serve!"

"Yes, yes Lord, anything!"

The Avion raised both hands to either side of Kend's face and leaned in close. The tall man stood enraptured.

"A *true* human friend of the Idonian cause," he whispered, "dies willingly."

A moment passed before the words registered. Adoration turned to shocked confusion. Smiling, the Avion swiftly and violently snapped his subject's head to the right. The neck crunched loudly with the spinal cord shattering. The Avion continued holding Kend's head, smiling and locking eyes, until the last light of life drained out. Then, releasing his hands, the body fell, limp, onto the rooftop.

"A *true* friend of the Idonian cause," he declared.

They unfolded their wings and took off into the fog, their laughter trailing after them.

❀ ❀ ❀

Ambassador Alosus knew the public baths in Zor were perhaps the most important institution in the city, notwithstanding the Goyan Forum. Every neighborhood had one. They served as an informal meeting place for the citizens to mingle, gossip and conduct business.

The Imperial Baths, located just outside and north of the forum, catered to politicians, dignitaries, their families and guests. Larger and more ornate than even the most affluent bathhouses of the Upper North Side, the three mandatory chambers and common area were cavernous by comparison and hosted extra amenities such as massage and steam rooms. They equipped their staff to handle sentients of almost any race.

Now that the Kan was upon them and their work done, Ambassador Alosus, Sareeta, and Soshi exuberantly approached the Imperial Baths' ornate outer doors. The meeting with House Calden unexpectedly produced results beyond expectations and tomorrow's meeting with House Valdur looked promising.

"Oh, I sure need this," the ambassador confessed.

The doors opened for them and they walked into the large entry room. Entering the communal area of any bath took up quite a bit of time, as it was a multi-stage process traditionally conducted naked to symbolize equality.

Three naked, dark-haired, young ladies of demure stature greeted them with accommodating smiles. The young attendants approached when the door closed behind them. Observing proper etiquette, they waited for the signal granting them the permission to continue. Once given, they undressed them with methodical precision. Since Alosus, Sareeta, and Soshi wore traditional Amarenian court dress, the attendants started with the buttons below the bare breasts and worked their way down the abdomen.

The young lady undressing Sareeta grew confused when the fabric caught on something at the bottom of the cinching, just below the waste of the hill sister's long skirt. Soshi spotted the ambassador and Sareeta exchanging amused glances. When Sareeta caught Soshi's bewildered expression, she gestured with her eyes to watch the girl undressing her. Not sure what to make of it, Soshi kept watching.

After a few more tugs, the attendant finally pulled Sareeta's skirt free, and the hill sister's more than ample penis, the cause of the resistance, swung close to the young girl's face. Her look of shock triggered peals of laughter from the Amarenians.

"It never gets old," Sareeta declared in their language.

The poor bath girl's face betrayed a mix of surprise, embarrassment and the vain attempt to keep a professional disposition. The attendants searched the faces of the now-naked Amarenians for their proper reaction.

"She is a Hill Sister," Ambassador Alosus patiently explained in Common. "Blessed with both the male and female organs."

The prep girls nodded their thanks for the explanation and sheepishly led them through another set of doors at the other end of the room. The sound of running water could be heard coming from beyond.

"And the process begins," Sareeta remarked, still in Amarenian.

"Process?" Soshi inquired. "I thought we were going to be taking a bath."

"In this city, the bath is an art form and a social ritual," Alosus explained. "First the pre-rinse. To wash away the everyday city grime. Next comes the bath proper, then the rinse. Only then are you allowed into the large communal baths."

"Seems like an awful lot of work," Soshi remarked.

The prep-girls opened the doors revealing a large room with tiled floors and walls occupied by people of all ages. Wide spouts of water flowed out all along the walls creating a waterfall effect.

"Like I said, an art form," Alosus confirmed, leading the way.

❀ ❀ ❀

"They call themselves Order of the Black Sword," Captain Rafel stated matter-of-factly.

"Rather pretentious, don't you think?" Colonel Zekoff said not bothering to hide his contempt.

"Their leader goes by the name Riess de Nader," Rafel continued, ignoring the colonel's disgust, "and he was one of the Zorian Sword Academy's top instructors."

"Whereabouts?"

"Unknown. I've got people watching the Takii School. Unfortunately for now, the next move is theirs."

"That seems rather dangerous," Zekoff cautioned.

"It's all we have, unless a city guard patrol stumbles onto something."

"Very well," the colonel relented. "So, besides the usual street rabble, the Kan was uneventful?"

The captain grew quiet and lowered his head.

"No sir," he responded. "I found one of my top informants murdered!"

"Murdered?!"

The spymaster bit his lip.

"They bound his feet and threw him off a building between the Southern Docks and the Seven Sisters."

The colonel's eyes narrowed.

"But not before they beat and dragged him through the alleys. My guess is someone wanted information. Most of the wounds suggest Cul-Ta involvement."

Zekoff leaned in to speak.

"There's more…" the captain hesitantly added.

The colonel sighed and reached for his pipe.

"We found the corpse of an unknown human male on the roof of the same building they threw my informant from. Something snapped his neck."

"Related?"

Rafel shrugged. "Probably. We're just not sure how."

Zekoff lit his pipe. "Well, it's a given the Cul-Ta didn't kill the man on the roof."

"But they might have an idea who did," Rafel offered.

"I think it's time we had a conversation with our furry friends in the sewers," the colonel said, exhaling a cloud of smoke. "This one, I'll handle."

※ ※ ※

The heat in the empty, windowless warehouse was stifling. Ten men and two women knelt in two perfectly straight rows, with a black bladed sword placed in the same position before each of them. The students sat motionless, facing forward, with their eyes closed. Sweat dripped off their noses and hair, soaking their tunics.

Riess de Nader, a thin, stern-faced man with a shaved head dressed in a simple white robe, faced them kneeling in the same position. His lecturing voice reverberated off the empty walls. Occasionally, whimpers arose from a group of bound prisoners on the other side of the room. Their cries punctuated his instructions.

"Purge your thoughts!" he charged. "You must be of no mind when you strike. Body, arm and blade must be as one!"

"Hai!" they shouted in unison.

"Ask and give no quarter!"

"Hai!"

"Your blade is your soul. Your soul must be ready at all times!"

"Hai!"

"Your form must be flawless! For that, you must practice proper techniques on authentic targets!"

"Hai!"

"Prepare!"

"Hai!"

The group opened their eyes.

Master de Nader ceremoniously bowed, picked up his sword before him and sheathed it. Gracefully standing, he motioned to two of his students in the front row.

They quickly got up and crossed the room to the captives. Randomly, they pulled an older woman to her feet. Sweat and dirt matted her gray hair. Her ragged dress and grimy skin marked her as one of the nameless street people of the Seven Sisters slums of Zor.

The woman sorrowfully moaned when they brought her before the swordmaster. Her tear-stained eyes widened with fear and she pleaded softly under her breath. When the master drew his sword, the old woman began openly weeping. Ignoring her anguish, he addressed his students.

"Your strikes must be swift and powerful!"

Her eyes followed the blade in horror when he raised it to her stomach level. With a blindingly fast flick, he severed the ropes binding her. She lifted her freed hands, and a brief expression of relief crossed her face. The master continued lecturing, apparently paying no attention to the old woman.

"Unlike your prior instruction, we require absolute reality in training here. We have a serious and solemn duty ahead of us. The honor and purity of our art is at stake. The foreign teachings must be purged along with their accursed school!"

The street lady flinched when he pointed to a spot on the top of her head with the sword.

"The first cut must be the most powerful!"

The woman, still very frightened, watched in confusion. She winced each time he brought the blade up to her body, to explain a technique, but he still had not harmed her. The master went on for another few moments, talking about things she did not understand. Finally, he raised the blade over his head. She tried to read his expression, but his face remained blank with an empty stare.

"Now we begin!"

He brought the blade violently down in a slicing motion on the woman. It split the skull slightly to the right side with a loud crunching sound. The fine Zorian steel severed the spinal cord, heart and, continuing swiftly down at a slight angle, exited out the groin. He arced the sword around quickly and sliced through her with a horizontal cut, severing the lower torso. Sheets of blood trailed the blade when it exited, painting a gruesome red line across the walls, white tunics, and faces of the students.

The victim toppled at his feet in four quarters.

On the far side of the room, the remaining captive street people panicked. Some cried, some prayed, and a few futilely struggled at their bonds.

In one smooth motion, the master flicked the blood from his blade on the quartered corpse and sheathed it.

"Quata Nogu: Quartering Technique!" he instructed, ignoring the cries and protests of those about to die. "There is one for each of you."

"Next!"

❉ ❉ ❉

Ambassador Joc' Valdur was not a man prone to vengeance. Of all the surviving members of his family, he was most known for being clear-headed and a peacemaker. For this reason, an almost decimated House Valdur chose him to represent the family in the Zorian Forum.

It had been a little over a grand cycle since House Eldor's forces swept across the rich agricultural fields of their eastern islands, annexing the Valdurian run islands under the Eldorian standard. Had it not been for their airships, Eldor would have overrun their home Island of Atar.

Naturally, the rest of this once great house cried out for vengeance. Only House Aramos' quick negotiations kept the Goyan Islands from descending into all-out war. Now, in true dark irony their house was smaller but, because of their airships, more powerful than ever before.

Today, Ambassador Valdur entertained Esteemed Sister Alosus of the Free Amarenian Sisterhood in a meeting he considered historic and a high point in his political career. She sat across from him in his forum office and the gravity of the moment gave him pause.

"Esteemed," he began, "I wish to convey my family's outrage at House Eldor's audacity and offer our complete support in defense of your home."

Alosus shifted in her seat. She couldn't help but think, with his youthful features, scraggly mustache and thick black hair swept back off his face, he resembled more of an artist than a politician.

"Thank you, Si Ambassador."

"Please, call me Joc'," he said. "I have a feeling we are going to be working closely."

"Especially if our Ara-Fel Party wins the day back home."

"Especially," he agreed with a chuckle.

"Joc'," Alosus said earnestly, "I can assure you with your family's backing, we will prevail, and our pirating days will become just a distant memory."

"Is your queen fully prepared to renounce the Rayth faction?"

"She is," Alosus assured, "but, as with any significant change, certain groups will be opposed to it."

"Always," Joc' agreed.

"However," she added, "their numbers grow fewer by the cycle."

"You realize this will not be easy?" he asked. "You still have the Ulana faction of the Rayth."

"They have always been a problem," Alosus concurred. "They worship the sea Goddess of chaos and are violent and unpredictable. On top of them, we also have your House Whitmar to contend with."

"I think we can bring House Whitmar around," Joc' offered. "Their queen is about to choose a new husband. The upcoming Consort Ball signifies a different direction for their family."

"Many things to work out," Alosus said.

"All riding on a vote scheduled to take place next cycle," Joc' pensively said, sitting back in his chair. "Thousands of miles away from here."

"A fact not lost on me, Si Ambassador. I will message my queen immediately."

❄ ❄ ❄

The sewer systems of the High Holy City of Zor are some of the most complex in the Annigan. Designed so that waste will not flow into the seas which thousands of sentient life forms called home.

The designers also devised elaborate access tunnels, pipes and filter systems like Sewer Hub Number thirty-two, a fifteen-foot hexagonal recess in the ground. This hub was the intersection point which led to six main tunnels branching outward like the spokes of a wheel. Located just outside the Karobara Plat of the Seven Sisters slums, hub thirty two's elevated, round entrance hatch, rose from the center of the hub and led down to the next level of the sewer complex.

A clean-shaven human in a gray hood stood back from the open sewer hole and reached into a pouch he carried. He pulled out a coin and leisurely flipped it down the hole. It clattered noisily against the sides, plummeting downward, ending in a splash. He let several moments elapse before repeating the action. After the sixth coin, a small, furry head poked up through the hole.

"You have more money?" the Cul-Ta asked with an excited cackle.

"I do."

"What you want?"

"I wish to speak with your leader."

"Leader not here, speak to me!"

"Sorry, but if you want any more of this, I need to go straight to the top."

"No leader here!"

The man sighed. "You force me to take this bag of silver and spend it on drink and whores."

The furry face engaged in a heated conversation in its language with what sounded like several others below.

"You wait!" it ordered the human.

Once satisfied the human stayed, it briefly disappeared back down the hole. Ten armed Cul-Ta emerged from the hatch. The man ignored the implied threat and stood there, smiling. One Cul-Ta stepped forward.

"I Tor-Chu, leader!" it stated, thumping its chest. "What you want?"

"I simply wish a centi of your time," the man stated, tossing the bag of silver at the leader's feet.

All the Cul-Ta stared at the open bag of silver, greed glowing in their eyes. The man slamming the hatch shut with his foot broke their trance. They heard many bows drawn and readied from above. A dozen archers leaned over the top of the hub. Armed city guards stepped out from each of the six tunnels, further panicking the Cul-Ta. The man in the cloak walked away and Colonel Zekoff stepped from the tunnel facing the rats.

Everyone froze while the head of the City Guards approached the Cul-Ta chief. The two leaders stood facing each other, unpleasant recollection etched on both faces, until Zekoff smiled tensely and broke the silence.

"It's been a while, Tor-Chu," he greeted.

"Not long enough!" the Cul-Ta leader sneered.

"Sit with me," Zekoff offered.

He moved towards the raised main sewer hatch, now closed. Once seated, he patted the space beside him for the hesitant rat creature to join him.

"Come on now."

Tor-Chu reluctantly walked over and sat down. Never taking his eyes off the rat, the colonel waved his archers to stand down and then reached for his pipe.

"How long have you run things down here my friend?"

The rat's eyes sparked with anger.

"Zekoff no friend of Cul-Ta!"

"Oh, but I am," the colonel countered. "Did you ever consider why I let you operate in my city with no real challenge? It's with few exceptions that I turn a blind eye to your whole clan."

Tor-Chu eyed him suspiciously.

"I'm serious!" he insisted, lighting his pipe. "Your group is part of the balance that keeps this city in a state of symmetry."

Zekoff brought the pipe down, exhaled, and turned his focus outward towards the slums.

"But something has altered that balance."

"Okay, okay, you nice guy! What you want?!"

The colonel took an extended drag off his bowl and blew a long column of smoke upward. Turning abruptly, he locked eyes on the Cul-Ta with a determined stare.

"I want to know what happened last Kan on that roof."

All the Cul-Ta looked around nervously.

"Don't know!" Tor-Chu cried out.

Zekoff sighed heavily and took another puff off his pipe.

"I can assure you," he began, raising his hand to the archers above, who resumed their aim. "If you do not tell me what I want to know, none of you will leave this room alive. Furthermore, I will place a racial bounty upon your people, both official and civil. One silver piece per pelt, no limit."

"You no do that!" the rat proclaimed rebelliously. "Council no let you!"

"My friend," Zekoff said, laughing, "the Council barely knows you exist. The only information they even receive about you is through me."

Tor-Chu took in his situation. He searched the eyes of his fellow rat people before giving up the truth.

"Tall man hire us," he admitted lowering his head.

"Why?"

"Dead man owed him something."

"What?"

"Don't know."

"So, you threw him off the roof when he couldn't produce it?"

The rat-man nodded.

"Who killed the tall man?"

"Winged men."

"Winged men?"

Again, he nodded.

"What happened?"

"Don't know, we run."

Zekoff took a moment with his pipe to digest the information. If Avions were involved, this whole affair might be taking an unsuspected political turn.

"Very well," he uttered, abruptly standing. "As promised, no bounty on your people. However, you all have just confessed to murder."

The Cul-Ta looked around at each other in confused panic.

"What?!" Tor-Chu bellowed.

"You can't commit murder in my city and get away with it!" Zekoff declared, raising his hand again.

"This no good, you…"

Ten arrows sailed downward and hit their marks with staggered dull thuds. It was over before any of the rat-men could move. Putting his pipe away, the colonel of the city guards peered around at the ten Cul-Ta bodies bleeding on the sewer floor.

"That's it," the colonel calmly said, then turned to leave.

"Sir, what about the bag of silver?" a guard asked.

Zekoff quickly examined it laying in a bloody pool under Tor-Chu's impaled body.

"Leave it."

✸ ✸ ✸

Standing at the crossroads, Mal, Shom and Yrich heard the grand turine in the distant harbor ring four bells, signaling to the several farmers and their carts who shared the main south thoroughfare leading in and out of Zor. The road passed through the Seven Sisters slums and then forked about a mile later. Continuing straight along the coast was some of the richest farmland on the continent. The northern fork, with its overgrown blind turns, led the travelers up into the dense jungle of the Goyan Mountains foothills.

"It's up this way," Yrich said.

The Marassa pointed towards the northern fork, a path leading upward into rough terrain and triple canopy jungle.

"Of course, it is!" Shom sarcastically sniped. "Because meetings in warm, dry pubs with soft women is much too much to ask!"

"Look Shommy!" Mal snapped. "You don't need to be here. Where we're going, there are no pubs or whores!"

"I beg to differ," he countered. "I have a stake in this little endeavor and I'm tagging along to look after my investment."

"Your investment! Why you…"

"No time to argue," Yrich called back, starting up the north road. "The Kan is only a few decis away."

Mal turned to follow. "Well, are you coming or not?"

The road led steadily upward, growing narrower and more overgrown the farther it led into the jungle. The Marassa set a determined clip and Mal caught up with him, leaving Shom trailing, eyeing the forest with suspicion.

"Funny how our roles have directly reversed since when we met," Mal noted.

"Now I am the guide for your project," Yrich said, chuckling. "The circle is, indeed, now complete."

"Do you think she'll help us?" Mal asked. "I mean, the few times I dealt with Banash followers in the past it was in their home islands. You never knew what to expect."

"Who knows?" Yrich warned. "The snake deity she worships is hardly benevolent, but you have something she needs."

"What would you suggest?"

"Caution."

From the rear, Shom cleared his throat loudly.

"You know," he said, "as much as I absolutely adore listening to you two reminisce, and this lovely walk amongst nature, I can't help but wonder about our destination."

Both stopped and turned. Mal appeared irritated. Yrich leaned on his walking stick and smiled.

"Oh," the Marassa said, "you'll know when we're getting close, young man."

With a nod, he turned and set off again. Mal stared at Shom in frustration and shook her head.

"Why the fuck do I put up with you?"

"Because deep down I'm irresistibly lovable."

Shom stepped around her and followed the Marassa.

"Well," he asked, "are you coming or not?"

Mal sighed and caught up. The trio continued for another half mile until the trail forked again. Yrich stopped and stroked his beard thoughtfully.

"Oh, come on," Shom complained, "don't tell me you can't remember the route!"

Yrich smiled knowingly and then started down the right fork path. A large black snake slithered across the ever-narrowing trail. Yrich's smile widened at the sight.

"This way," he confirmed.

They could only travel in single file after another hundred yards. The dense jungle allowed only a few feet of visibility on either side. They proceeded with caution through strange sounds and rustling undergrowth.

Shom's eyes darted nervously from side to side. Something brushed around his ankles and he reflexively jumped out of its grasp.

"Something just tried to grab my feet!" he yelled.

"Probably a snake," Yrich replied calmly.

"Snakes!" he shouted, spinning nervously, "Lovely!"

Yrich pointed to several serpents resting in nearby trees.

"I would get used to them young man."

Shom shuddered and continued following the trail, his eyes never leaving the serpents in the trees. Eventually the trail widened, and the brush thinned, revealing an inordinate number of the reptiles crawling all about the ground and in the branches.

"Do not harm the snakes!" Mal ordered.

"I absolutely cannot guarantee anything," Shom babbled, panic building. "If one of those things lands on me!"

"If you kill one," she warned. "We might not make it out of here alive."

"She's right," Yrich affirmed. "Followers of Banash do not take lightly the killing of…"

A crackle of electricity interrupted the Marassa, followed by a bright, blue flash from just beyond the brush on the trail ahead of them. They froze when a giant green and red snake slowly slithered across the path. Its body, roughly one foot in diameter, dwarfed all the serpents they had seen so far. It disappeared into the bushes on the other side of the trail.

"What in the name of the gods?!" Shom cried out.

Within moments of the serpent moving into the jungle, they heard loud snapping and tearing sounds. The bushes violently shook off a shower of leaves. A tall, lanky man stepped out of the very bushes from which the snake slithered. His entirely naked frame had a pale, greenish, scaly texture to it.

No one moved while he approached the group. Shom noted vertical slits on red irises instead of pupils on his eyes. The green man stopped several feet in front of the group and examined them carefully.

"What is it you seek?" he asked in Common.

"We seek the wisdom of Banash," Mal responded, with a slight bow.

"Do you now?" it questioned, clearly amused. "And what do you offer for such wisdom?"

"That is something best discussed with your priestess," Yrich piped up.

This caused the green man to turn his attentions to the old scholar, carefully sizing him up.

Shom shifted uneasily at the scrutiny. He then noticed the faces of a dozen people peering out of the dense vegetation flanking them along either side of the path. They all appeared human, but with deformities, from large, oozing boils to hideously misshapen, bloated, and scaly bodies. He instinctively placed his hand on the hilt of his blade.

The Fate of Tomorrow

"Don't!" Mal whispered.

Shom reluctantly removed his hand. He noticed a young woman transfixed on him, standing just a few feet to his right. Shom considered she must have once been exquisite, but now her face and neck were bloated. Ruptured boils covered her skin and thick yellow liquid seeped from the openings. She drooled as his hand returned unthreateningly to his side. A long, forked tongue slipped out of her mouth, wiggled about for a moment before returning between her dry, cracked lips.

"The Naga is busy," the green man stated. "We cannot interrupt the Colaa."

"The Colaa is why we seek her," Mal implored. "I have traveled from her homeland with a magnificent prize."

The green man flicked his forked tongue at Mal, weighing her last statement.

"This way," he relented, and walked off down the trail.

Shom gave an uncertain glance at Mal, who scowled disapprovingly back before setting off after the green man. The deformed people disappeared back into the jungle as quickly and silently as they had appeared. They could smell the encampment long before arriving—a nauseating stench with notes of funeral pyre, ammonia, and vinegar accents.

"Once again," Shom noted in disgust. "You have chosen only the foulest of places to visit."

The green man led them to the edge of a large clearing surrounding a cave opening. On either side of the cave stood two crudely sculpted snake statues. Another small trail led deeper into the jungle off to the right of the cave.

Their noses discovered the source of the foul-smelling odor on the other side of the clearing, what appeared to be a giant, elaborate distillation device. A huge pot, containing a thick brownish-yellow liquid, simmered over a low fire. A glass vessel trapped the steam above and redirected it toward a filtration device with many smaller glass chambers. A clear, watery liquid exited a small tube dripping into an open wooden bowl.

Another deformed man tended the fire beneath the still. When the liquid finally stopped flowing, he leaned over the tube, picked up the bowl and ceremoniously raised it above his head. He then walked to the center of the clearing, where one of the most hideous creatures Shom ever laid eyes on reclined on a litter, suspended about three feet off the ground on four thick poles. He could tell at one time this fleshy blob used to be a human female, with a discernible head and short, stubby limbs covered in yellowish-green scales.

The deformed acolyte proceeded reverently to the litter, displaying the bowl above his head, and chanting softly. He stopped before the fleshy blob and slowly placed the bowl before her.

Seeing Shom's pure revulsion, Mal leaned in close.

"She is the Banash Naga," she whispered. "She'll test it for purity before sharing it with her congregation."

With the bowl situated before her, the man backed away and the Naga leaned forward. A long-forked tongue stretched out over two feet and lapped at the liquid from the bloated slit that was her mouth. She leaned back and savored it. Her red eyes turned white, and the Naga emitted a loud squeal.

This started the bushes rustling around the clearing. One by one, the deformed people who surrounded them on the trail shambled into the clearing. Paying close attention to the activity around them, Marassa Yrich grew practically giddy with excitement.

"I've read about the Colaa," he whispered. "But never thought I would ever witness it."

The congregation shuffled towards the litter, tongues flicking in excitement. They gathered around and, each in their turn, bowed to the Naga, dipping their tongues into the bowl. Drawing a small amount into their mouths they sat down at the edge of the clearing. Soon after being seated, all appeared to enter a trance.

"Some elaborate intoxication ritual," Shom scoffed.

"Oh, much more than that," Yrich corrected, never taking his eyes off the ceremony.

When they finished, the green man turned to them.

"Wait here. Do not approach, or make contact with any of the faithful," he warned.

Once assured they understood, he crossed the clearing and worshipfully approached the priestess. He leaned over and whispered. They held a brief conversation before he reverentially backed away and returned to the trio.

"You may approach the Naga," he directed. "Make sure you bow. All communication comes through me."

They nodded and followed the green man when he reapproached the Naga.

The congregation lining the perimeter of the clearing rocked gently back and forth in a deep trance. Shom stared in wonder as a full third of the group, the ones most deformed, appeared translucent. He could see the jungle through them.

Shom must have been lagging while he was transfixed, because Mal grabbed the front of his shirt and dragged him along.

When all three stood before the blob of flesh, the green man bowed and performed a brief introduction.

"You now stand before Mooka, Banash Naga!" he loudly declared.

The group followed his lead and bowed as well.

"Greetings, oh Naga," Mal began. "I am Maluria. It has been my pleasure to have dealt with your great people many times in the past."

The Naga grunted a reply.

"My people cast me out, away from the precious Noma. My people are shit," the green man translated.

Mal stood there stunned, unsure what to say next.

"Nice opening," Shom whispered out of the side of his mouth. "Why don't you insult her mother while you're at it."

Mal shot him a dirty look then returned her attention back to the priestess.

"I have something from your homeland that should greatly interest you," she continued.

"Unless you have Noma, we are not interested," came the translation.

"Great Naga," Mal enthusiastically said. "That is exactly what we brought you!"

The priestess paused and then grunted.

"How much?" the green man asked.

"We have a large supply and would share with you, for your skill at distilling it into a more useful form."

"Our fee is one half," the green man translated.

"Great Naga," Mal countered. "I was thinking perhaps a quarter would be more equitable."

The priestess stared at her through layers of deformed skin and grunt barked at her.

"One-third is the Great Naga's final offer!" the green man returned.

Mal sensed this negotiation would not get any more productive and pushing the issue might have deadly consequences.

"Agreed!"

Negotiations successful, a wave of relief swept across the trio.

"When?" the Naga asked through her translator.

"We should return before the Kan lifts," Mal stated confidently.

The priestess nodded her approval.

"I would ask one favor of the Great Naga."

Her eyes narrowed when the green man translated.

Mal swallowed and continued, "My friend here teaches at the university. I might ask that you would allow him to stay and observe your Colaa?"

This sent the Naga into a long series of grunts. The green man listened intently, before addressing them.

"The Great Naga does not care," he answered. "Watch all you want. Unless you have Banash in your heart, the Colaa means nothing!"

The Marassa bowed. "Many thanks, Great Naga."

"Yes, yes, Banash in our hearts, and gold in our pockets," Shom whispered, smirking. "I just love religion!"

❈ ❈ ❈

Just as he had done every day of their twenty-five-year marriage, Zekoff de Corab picked a flower for his beloved wife when he made his way home. He would then walk the roughly half-mile route past the same shops, down the same streets. Along his trek, the merchants of Shimol Plat would wave, and people would stop him to chat at almost every turn. He never refused a friendly conversation.

By the time he finally made it to his modest home in the neighboring Tuath Plat of northern Zor, the Kan had firmly set in. He would take off his boots by the front door, just as the Kan engulfed the bench he sat on in thick gray mist.

Opening the door, he smiled at his wife, Jaanam, glancing up from setting the table. Her hair was long and gray and the simple blue dress she wore hung loosely on her slender five-foot frame. The fire in the hearth cut the chill and dampness of the outer world, as did the smell of dinner cooking.

"My Zek!" she beamed, crossing the room to him.

Instinctively, he held up the flower. She stopped and blushed a little then took it and sniffed.

"Another for my garden," she cooed.

Zekoff leaned forward and kissed her tenderly on the forehead.

Jaanam spun on the balls of her feet and held the flower in front of her with both hands, as if it were a prize. She moved gracefully back across the room to the table at the far end.

"Dinner is almost ready," she reminded.

She stopped before a vase of flowers in the center of the table and placed the most recent bloom in the vase.

"Did you have a good day protecting the people of Zor?" Jaanam playfully asked.

"There are storm clouds brewing, my love," he replied wearily, while taking off his coat.

"Is it something you should leave out with your boots?"

"Not really," he nonchalantly replied, hanging up his coat.

"Good! Come, let's eat!"

Jaanam opened her arms and they embraced. She held on tighter and snuggled a little closer.

"I missed you today," she confessed, stepping back from the hug.

"Oh?"

"You remember my friend Morga?" She asked, fiddling with the table setting.

"She's one of the people you fish with, right?"

"Yes," she said, pausing. "Her husband just died. He was only thirty-seven!"

The commander of the city guard noted his wife's distress and thoughtfully processed the news.

"The man weighed four hundred pounds as I recall," he flippantly said. "Drank like a fish and whored around any chance he got."

"Zekoff!" she admonished. "It is not good to speak ill of the dead."

"I'll take my chances with the gods," he confessed, walking toward the table.

"Come, sit, eat!"

"Smells like fish," Zekoff teased, sniffing the plate.

"Of course, it is, silly, it's your favorite."

They ate for a few moments in silence before Jaanam spoke while staring at her plate.

"I just wanted you to know how much I love and appreciate you... and well, I just missed you today."

When she looked up, her eyes were moist. He reached across the table, smiled, and took her hands.

"And you," he said, kissing her fingertips, "you are as beautiful and spirited as when I first saw you, so long ago."

They sat, holding hands, gazing at each other.

"I think we should give thanks to the gods for this meal and each other!" she suggested, sitting back.

"Of course."

Jaanam launched into a simple, but heartfelt prayer of thanks, but her husband was not listening. Murderous Avions with possible diplomatic immunity and a renegade sword school dominated his thoughts.

Maybe she was right. Maybe he should have left that piece of trepidation outside with his boots.

❊ ❊ ❊

Mal and Shom watched the filthy streets of Zor's Seven Sisters slums fly past from the seat of their carriage. The Kan's fog and the speed of the vehicle gave pedestrians a ghost-like quality. It surprised Mal these streets always seemed busy, Kan or not.

"I can't believe the coach charged four silver," Mal complained, shaking her head.

"It's not wise to try to find your way around the Seven Sisters on foot during the Kan," Shom defended. "Besides, we'll get there in a fraction of the time."

Mal nodded and watched what she could of the fog-shrouded city go by her window. They moved quickly out of the Seven Sisters and into the Southern Docks area. Mal noticed a flurry of activity ahead on the wharf. Travelers coming and going congested the southern access to Zor, slowing the carriage to a crawl.

Rounding the corner onto the wooden planks, Mal smelled smoke and noticed the fog at the end of the pier glowing red.

"What the..." Mal's voice trailed off when she saw the flames.

The congested throng of people finally halted the carriage. The panicked Spice Rat jumped out of the coach and pushed her way through the crowd.

"No, no, no!" Mal yelled.

She edged her way across the boardwalk to the fire with Shom in tow, elbowing people out of the way, until she stood before the burning *Regis*. By now, flames engulfed the entire ship. She could make out the silhouettes of several bodies suspended from the rigging through the eerily illuminated Kan mist. They dangled and swung while the flames crept up enveloping them.

Then, with a loud crack, the main mast gave way and the entire ship, along with a section of the dock, plunged into the boiling waters. City guards setting up a safety barricade around the inferno stopped her from getting too close.

"That's my ship!" she screamed, pointing.

She stepped back staring helplessly, while her livelihood went up in flames.

"My ship..."

"One cannot help but note the irony," Shom remarked.

Mal had tuned out the world, remaining transfixed on the horror before her. The prodigal noticed city guards milling about the crowd, searching for potential witnesses.

"Mal."

She remained unresponsive.

"Mal!" he shouted.

Slowly, she turned and stared at him blankly.

"I'm going to mill about and see if I can find out what happened," he said.

He motioned over his shoulder at Orich-Taa sitting back-to-back at the edge of the crowd, shivering. They were being watched over by another city guard.

"See what your remaining crew has to say."

Shom disappeared into the inquisitive crowd. Mal stood for a moment and then made her way over to the Bailian twins. The guard stepped between them when she approached.

"That was my ship and these two are what remains of my crew!" she angrily proclaimed.

He paused for a moment, assessing her and then let her pass. Mal knelt before them and their two identical faces turned to her as one.

"They came about a deci ago," Orich stated in his usual deadpan.

"Who came?"

"The winged men," Taa revealed. "The wind picked up, and they landed on the deck."

"Winged men?" Mal asked.

"They killed Haak because he resisted," Orich picked the story back up. "And killed the others because they were human but made a conscious effort to spare us."

"They took your Noma," Taa revealed.

Mal stood and stared at the remains of the *Regis,* now a burnt hulk just above the waterline. She stood, trying to make sense of the calamity and its cause, until Shom walked up behind her.

"Well, I followed the city guards around," he grimly said. "Listening while they interrogated people. All the witnesses, what few there were, corroborated the same story."

"Winged men…" Mal answered numbly.

"Mm-hmm," Shom confirmed. "It seems we now have an Avion issue on our hands."

❈ ❈ ❈

Modaii, by all rights, was an outpost more than a village. Originally composed of only a few interconnected caves in the rocky outcroppings of the central Barketts, Modaii once served as a hideout for pirates during their golden age.

Fia knew this was no place to moor a ship for any length of time—only a quick stopover to take on enough food stores to get them home and a decent place to pick up information. Fia ordered First Mate Betha to procure the food. She chose Mariner Neaux to accompany her gathering intelligence.

They climbed up a damp circular staircase from the small wharf to the Modaii Commons—twin tiers of alcoves lining three of the walls carved out of a cave, seventy feet in diameter with a thirty-foot-high ceiling. The elaborate wooden staircases accessed recesses containing living and working areas. Other stairways led to adjoining tunnels to more caverns.

"Is everything always so wet around here?" Neaux asked, almost slipping.

"Always," Fia confirmed. "They constructed it entirely out of caves."

"It cuts to the bone," Neaux complained, wrapping her cloak tighter across her bare chest.

"Don't worry, we're not staying long," the captain consoled, reaching the top landing.

All the areas were dimly lit by glowing Etheria crystals. Their soft orange light illuminated a few dozen people milling around the stalls of a small, central bazaar. Making sure her crewmember was tightly in tow, Fia led her through the busy marketplace.

"There seem to be an awful lot of weapons for sale here," Neaux noticed.

"Sure," Fia confirmed, "it's their principal export. The iron mines and Lorovan Prison lie just north of here on Quell Island."

They passed one stall comprised mostly of arrows and arrow tips. The captain stopped and eyed a sword displayed amongst a small pile of hand weapons. Neaux watched her captain stare transfixed at the blade.

"Captain?"

Fia ignored Neaux, entered the stall and acknowledged the merchant filing an arrowhead. He nodded and returned to his work. Neaux followed her captain into the shop, even more puzzled. Fia picked up a medium-length blade with a double-hooked tip. Neaux noted the hilt appeared Amarenian in style but didn't recognize the blade design.

"This is interesting," Fia commented nonchalantly to the merchant. "Wherever did you find it?"

The man stopped, pulled back his scraggly, long brown hair, and squinted at Fia, making his rugged face seem even more craggy.

"Ehh," he said, "took that in trade in last quinte."

"Oh?" Fia probed.

She carefully examined the edge feigning interest in making a purchase.

"Yeah," he added, returning to his work. "Taken off one of those crazy Ulana quims, on their way to free Xandar."

"Xandar the Mad?" Neaux blurted. "Isn't that just a myth, captain?"

Fia raised her hand and Neaux stopped. The captain's face grew taut with seriousness.

"Get back to the ship" Fia ordered. "Tell Betha we set sail as soon as I get back. I want to hear what else he's got to say."

❀ ❀ ❀

"Avions…" Mal took another long swig from the bottle on the table in front of her and turned to Shom. "How the fuck do you kill Avions?"

Shom grabbed the bottle from her, took a shot from it quickly, and then set it back on the table.

"Well technically, the same way you'd kill anything else," he answered. "The only practical difference between them and us is the wings. They just think they're superior."

They both leaned forward and reached for the bottle at the same time.

"By all means," Shom relented, moving his hands away. "The real problem is tracking them."

He watched her take another long drink. Mal held the bottle and stared off into space, unresponsive.

"Then there's the larger question," Shom said, continuing his musings. "What would Avions want with Noma? I mean, so much that they'd blatantly murder for it."

Thankfully, because of the late hour, the inn's public room was all but empty, except for three very drunk sailors playing cards at a table across the hall.

"I've lost everything." Mal blurted out.

"I know."

"In a little while, I've got to report this to the harbormaster. Then, they're gonna have to clear what's left of the *Regis* from the harbor. They're gonna charge me for that. Money I don't have…"

Shom put his hand on her shoulder. She stopped rambling and looked him sorrowfully in the eyes.

"Listen, Mal," he reasoned, "the Kan will lift in a few decis. We need to get you up to the room so you can rest. You said it yourself, tomorrow is going to be a big day."

"I'm not tired," she replied distantly.

"Yes, but you should try," Shom advised. "Besides, I've got a few ideas to try out."

Mal's questioning expression made the prodigal wink.

"I'm going to visit a few people," he offered. "And maybe call in a favor or two."

Mal's face turned doubtful.

"Yes, me!" he declared. "Whereas you may be familiar with the more backwater locals, this is *my* city!"

"Really?" she asked skeptically. "Is it?"

Shom shrugged. "I mean, what's the use in having a famous name if you're not prepared to exploit it?"

❂ ❂ ❂

The High Holy City of Zor's Forum is a four-thousand-grand-cycles-old structure dominating the face of Harmony Mountain. Its main entrance looks down upon the Goyan Coast and Zor, the largest city in the Annigan. A wing just off the massive main forum floor houses several sub-chambers, each capable of hosting a large meeting.

In sub-chamber three, Colonel Zekoff self-consciously glanced down at the mysterious stain on the front of his disheveled tunic. Just a little while ago, Jaanam had sent him out the door neat and clean. Now, standing before the four Avion ambassadors, all he could practically think about was that little stain.

"My lords," he began, clearing his throat. "I would like to thank you for meeting with me on such brief notice."

Ambassador Donis of House Eacher ran her fingers through her hair brushing blonde curls off her face and disdainfully eyed Zekoff's stain.

"You said it was urgent, Colonel," she reminded.

Ambassador Straza of House Solas, a tall male Avion with short dark hair and an apparently permanent intense glare, sat beside her.

"Yes, yes," Straza demanded. "What could be so urgent the colonel of the City Guard summons *us*?"

Zekoff scanned the four sets of eyes studying him and swallowed nervously.

"Your kind have been accused of several incidents involving murder and property destruction," he stated cautiously, "and I am diplomatically obligated to inform you that a full investigation is underway."

"Our *kind*?!" Ambassador Vatra of House Pyre asked indignantly.

"Vatra," House Azar's Ambassador Sifo interceded with a soft, lyrical voice, "he meant no disrespect."

She smiled diplomatically at Zekoff. "Please, continue."

"Over the last two cycles," Zekoff started, placing his hands behind his back and pacing. "There's been multiple murders where reliable witnesses described the killers as winged men."

The colonel stopped when the four broke into their Avion tongue, chattering amongst themselves.

"Is there anything else?" Donis asked over the prattle, attempting to get the meeting back on track.

"Yes, milady," Zekoff said. "This last Kan, they burnt a ship moored in the Southern Docks and killed almost the entire crew. The two surviving Bailian crewmembers testified the winged men killed the rest of their crew simply for being humans and deliberately left them alive."

When he concluded, Zekoff noticed Ambassadors Straza and Vatra exchange quick looks of recognition.

"Would any of you have any information to offer which might aid this investigation?" Zekoff asked after a few moments of awkward silence.

This brought the Pyre ambassador to his feet. "Exactly what are you insinuating?!"

The Fate of Tomorrow

"Vatra!" Sifo gently admonished. "The man is merely doing his job."

This didn't calm the Pyre ambassador.

"I, for one," he snapped, "will not sit here and let a mere municipal servant insult me, a *human* one at that!"

He regarded the colonel disdainfully before storming out. All eyes followed him while he made his way to the door and a stunned quiet permeated the room.

"Colonel, I'm afraid I have no information on this matter," Ambassador Donis offered, breaking the tense silence.

"Nor I," said Sifo.

Straza sat, staring out into space, saying nothing.

"Any idea of what house they may belong to?" Donis asked.

"No, milady," Zekoff responded, thankful for a relevant question. "I hoped you all could shed some light on this."

Both female Avions shook their heads, but the Solas ambassador remained silent, lost in contemplation.

"We shall contact our respective houses and inquire if they know anything," Donis offered.

"I thank you My Lady." Zekoff said and bowed.

Taking his cue, the colonel exited into the main forum. Straza stood and began to leave as the Azar and Eacher emissaries chattered about what had transpired.

"You've been awfully quiet, Straza," Donis probed. "Any ideas, what say you?"

"Perhaps," he replied, moving for the door. "Perhaps."

It took a few moments of searching, but Straza caught up with Vatra across the forum on his way to the Otick Temple of the Golden Avatar, remembering him mentioning a meeting with the High Priest.

"Vatra!" he called out. "A centi of your time?"

"What is it, Straza?" the Pyre ambassador demanded.

"Oh, I think you have some idea," the Solas ambassador retorted.

"I really don't have time for this!"

"Save your indignation for the humans, my friend. You and I know who's behind this."

Vatra said nothing and turned to leave. Straza caught him by his arm.

"If the Idonians are being this brazen," he said, "something big is going on."

"The Idonian Cabal is none of my concern," Vatra said with a vile grin.

"This could be catastrophic," Straza implored. "Your house knows more about the Idonians than any other, seeing it was House Pyre that spawned them."

Vatra looked down contemptuously at Straza's hand.

"And House Solas only too readily embraced it," he reminded, yanking his arm away. "As I said, the Idonians are none of my concern."

❀ ❀ ❀

Alto noted there was nothing on the front of the Rohina Takii Dojo which gave its location away from the street. One had to know what they were looking for. A simple circular symbol, carved above a plain wooden door, beckoned to all who desired to study the Wouvian Sword Schools' discipline.

Alto slipped off his sandals, placed them to the right of the door, and stepped through. He bowed before entering the training hall, a large single-room structure empty of furnishings or people. He walked barefoot across polished pale blue tile floors which seemed to magnify the room's actual dimensions. Painted inspirational symbols and phrases covered the walls, so the students could always see them.

Off in a far corner, the master gave a private lesson to someone Alto assessed as a less-than-average student. The raw-boned man, with short hair and a clean-shaven face, attempted technique after technique, not really getting the hang of it. The master, a petite elderly man with delicate features, patiently demonstrated the maneuver again after each bungled attempt. Another failure and demonstration followed, with the master guiding the limbs of the much larger man.

Alto lowered himself into the formal kneeling position and waited. He found this pairing strange. With so many instructors below the master, they rarely allowed basic trainees access to him. The lesson stretched on, and Alto slipped into a meditative trance.

His eyes opened when he sensed the master silently approaching across the tile floor. Alto instantly assumed a kneeling attack position and drew his blade. The master stopped just in front of him. Alto lowered his head and presented his sword with both hands.

Takii Master Keraso slowly examined the perfectly maintained, razor-sharp blade with silent approval. Reaching out, he placed his hand on Alto's head.

"Your master's confidence was not misplaced," he softly encouraged. "Rise."

Alto ceremoniously sheathed his blade, and stood, head still bowed.

"Thank you for coming so quickly, Mora Alto," Master Keraso said grimly.

"Of course, Master Keraso," Alto said, lifting his eyes.

"I know Mora Ferrah was your friend. You trained and tested together for many grands," the old master kindly said.

"We didn't just train together," Alto mournfully replied. "I was his second at his wedding and in several duels he fought. I introduced him to his wife."

"We all miss him, none more than me, but you must not think of revenge. Already there has been talk amongst some students of retaliation but I stopped it. The Zorian guards are the best at these sorts of matters. We must allow them to do their jobs."

"Master, I only pray I am balanced enough to draw upon this wise counsel when needed."

Keraso turned his attention back to his private student in the corner, still energetically but erratically swinging his wooden sword. He put his hand on Alto's shoulder and walked toward the young man practicing the sloppy kata.

"Mora Alto, you have a new student," the master announced. "I want you to meet Tate Whitmar."

Alto stared over at the old master in disbelief while approaching the flailing pupil.

"That's *Ambassador* Whitmar," Keraso clarified.

❈ ❈ ❈

"Shom Eldor!" the young man cried out, rising from behind his desk. "I heard you were dead."

Joc' Valdur, House Valdur's ambassador to Zor, slipped around his workstation and gave the prodigal a brief but sincere hug. Joc's tall, lanky frame towered over the smaller, thinner Shom.

"Wishful thinking," Shom responded with a wink.

"It's great to see you!" Joc' exclaimed.

"And you!"

"Nice scar," the ambassador noted, rubbing the stubble on his square jaw and eyeing the battle mark marring Shom's once babyface.

"A little memento from Makatooa," the prodigal acknowledged, "and how's your... lovely bride?"

Shom was never sure how to refer to Joc's wife, Tracee, since she was also Joc's twin sister. The Royal Valdurians' believed their incestuous heritage kept their lineage pure. Shom really didn't care about who Joc' slept with. He just didn't want to insult his friend.

"Pregnant again," Joc' replied. "Sit!"

"How many does that make now?" Shom asked taking a seat in front of the ambassador's desk.

"This latest will make six," Joc' replied brimming with pride.

"Gotta keep the lineage strong," Shom jokingly remarked.

"The wife's obsessed with it," the ambassador reported.

"And I suppose you just go along for the ride?" Shom teased

Joc' leaned over, grinning and shaking his head in disbelief.

"So, when did you get in?"

"Just before the Kan."

"So how long are you here and where are you staying?" Joc' inquired warmly.

"We're at an inn by the docks."

"We?"

"Yeah," Shom responded. "I'm afraid I've partnered with Maluria again, and what's left of her crew. Her ship was the one that burnt in the Southern Harbor last Kan."

The Valdurian emissary's expression grew concerned.

"Yes, I heard something about that."

"And that, in part, is the reason for my visit," Shom confessed. "I need a favor, Joc'."

"Name it!"

"It's a big one," Shom conceded.

"I owe you big," Joc' declared.

The prodigal knew this to be true. During the brief but deadly Unification War, last grand cycle, Shom singlehandedly thwarted the Eldorian assassination plot on Joc' and Tracee.

"I need the use of..." Shom began with a wince, "perhaps even *extended* use of... one of your smaller airships."

The ambassador sat back and exhaled. This was a tall order. However, they could spare the Resistance Class Cruiser he'd just authorized for minor repairs.

"I imagine you'll need a pilot?"

"Initially," Shom optimistically conceded. "Just for training."

"I don't understand."

Shom shook his head in wonder.

"Mal latched onto a fascinating set of Bailian twin helmsmen, ex-Brightstar."

"Really?" Joc' asked, unconvinced.

Shom leaned forward and folded his hands on the ambassador's desk.

"They have an affinity for navigation, possessing some weird telepathic abilities. Natural born pilots."

"Shom, I hate to pour cold water on this, but there is a big difference between helming a ship, even an Ukko one, and piloting an airship."

"Give them a chance is all I ask."

Joc' pondered for a moment before nodding.

"I'll have my pilot show them the ropes. If she says they're fine, then it shouldn't be a problem."

Shom slumped down in relief. "Thank you!"

A mischievous grin crossed Joc's face.

"Oh," he added, "you need to hear the best part before you thank me."

The royal prodigal looked up, cautiously. The ambassador leaned forward.

"Almost every part of that ship is proprietary," he explained, his tone serious. "Especially the engine. Every sentient that crews or commands one takes an oath to destroy the ship before it falls into the wrong hands."

"I think I can sell that," Shom confidently assured.

"Otherwise, it's a deal breaker, my friend."

"Well, we'll just test how stubborn Maluria can be."

Joc' sat back and chuckled knowingly—Mal always was a handful.

"So," he slowly drawled, changing the topic, "what happened in Makatooa?"

Shom paused to collect his thoughts.

"Quite simply, my father used me as an unwitting pawn to deliver House Eldor's Amarenian invasion proposal to House Aramos. Rayth raiders unwittingly intervened by stealing Mal's ship. Once we hooked up with the Amarenian ambassador, she interpreted the war plans, and it became a group effort."

"Alosus?" Joc' confirmed cautiously.

"The same!"

"You worked with her?"

"Why yes, it got quite hairy there for a bit."

Joc' stroked his chin again, staring directly at his friend deep in thought and shaking his head.

"I have a meeting with her," he admitted, after an uncomfortably long silence, "early Kan."

"Oh?"

"Yes, Pierce Calden will be there too. Were you aware that the Amarenian Council is voting this cycle to give up piracy and open negotiations with the west?"

"I knew it!" Shom shouted, gloating over his correct assessment. "I mean *no*, technically I didn't, but it was a logical guess."

"We're going to discuss our options based on the way the vote falls. I'd like you to be there."

Shom nodded. "Mal should be there too."

Joc' raised an eyebrow.

Shom stayed firm. "She was right there in the thick of it."

Joc' processed the request for a moment and then slowly nodded his head.

"Sure," he stood and offered his hand. "Meet me in front of the Demon's Gate at seven bells."

"I will be there my friend!" Shom said, shaking hands.

"So, you and Mal... back together again?"

"Romantically?" Shom reeled in surprise and grinned. "Gods no, most times I irritate her by merely breathing!"

❀ ❀ ❀

Jaanam let out a long, contented sigh and leaned on her broom. The house was finally clean, and she could relax for a while before she started dinner.

Walking past the table, she stopped and admired the vase of flowers she referred to as her love garden. She reached over and plucked one that had wilted. Zek would bring a replacement when he came home. Ever since they courted—he, the youngest captain ever promoted and she, the colonel's daughter—he always brought her flowers. She smiled at the thought of seeing him when he came home every Kan.

Crossing the room to the door, she tried to open it to throw out the wilted flower. To her surprise, it would only move a little, and there was a single, annoying squeak. Not understanding how it could have gotten stuck, she pulled a little harder. The effect was the same. The door inched inward and squeaked. Huffing in frustration, she placed both hands on the door handle and pulled hard.

The squeaking intensified when the door finally gave way. It flew open, knocking Jaanam backward. She fell and gasped in horror when the colonel's wife discovered the source of the squeaking. Eight Cul-Ta rushed through the door and were on her before she hit the ground, biting and clawing.

In between their frenzied squeals, she heard them repeating, "Zekoff's mate! Zekoff's mate! Zekoff's mate!"

She flailed her arms striking out, but their numbers and the element of surprise overwhelmed her. They shredded her clothing. Their claws raked her wrinkled skin. Serrated teeth ripped away chunks of flesh.

Jaanam attempted to scream but one bit through her neck and she could only gurgle. Shock finally set in while the rat creatures continued their deadly assault and she slowly lost consciousness. Fading away, she looked around her home for the last time, her gaze settling on the beautiful flowers of her love garden.

❁ ❁ ❁

The grand turine rang three bells.

The lone gull circled twice in the cloudy sky, then landed on the balcony of Ambassador Alosus' quarters. It squawked loudly, pacing back and forth on the ledge.

Alosus heaved a sigh of relief and held the bird tight to her chest upon reading the simple message.

"Ara-Fel victorious."

❁ ❁ ❁

Colonel Zekoff shook his head in revulsion. The killing made no sense. Something cleanly snapped the unarmed apothecary's neck, and yet there wasn't even a sign of a struggle. Three city guards searched through the shop's displays of bottles filled with expensive liquids and powders, none of which had been stolen.

"I want to see any records you find," he ordered.

They nodded, and Zekoff stepped out into the street. A light rain fell from a slate-gray sky. He assessed the weather and slipped the hood over his head. It was a short walk from there to the Northern Docks.

Captain Rafel fell in beside him.

"I have some *positive* news," the spymaster proclaimed.

"I could use some positive news," Zekoff replied.

"Witnesses saw two Avions fly east from this location."

Zekoff stopped and faced Rafel. Rainwater running off his hood created an opaque mask effect.

"The mountains, of course!" he blurted. "And by the quickness of the attacks, I'll bet they're close, too!"

Rafel looked over at the mountain peaks.

"Shall I put together a search party?"

The colonel followed Rafel's gaze.

"Only ten huntsmen," he answered, "mostly archers, but don't deploy yet. I'm going to see if my Avion contacts will help with a little scouting."

"Who would know better how to hunt them than their own kind?" Rafel concurred.

"See to it, Captain," Zekoff ordered. "Excellent work. You've earned your quinte's worth of wages on this one."

Rafel smiled. "Thank you, sir."

"Now, apparently, I'm needed on the Northern Docks," the colonel stated wearily, turning to go.

Heading west, down to the wharf, he felt the rain turn into a fine mist. Passing a small row of buildings, a young boy, soaked from the rain, ran over to him. The lad smiled up at him with large brown eyes and an angelic face, framed by wet black hair. Zekoff couldn't help but think about Jaanam's three stillbirths and what their children might have been like.

"Yes?" he probed in a friendly voice.

The boy motioned to the nearby buildings.

"I'm afraid I'm too busy to go with you, young man."

The boy gave a wide, toothy grin and motioned again. This time he reached out and took the colonel's hand. Curiosity piqued, Zekoff let the boy lead him behind three merchant shop buildings to a small access road.

Nothing in the back alley appeared out of place and Zekoff saw no one else.

"What do you have to show me?"

Instead of answering, the youngster let go of his hand and motioned him to follow.

"What is it?" he inquired.

Zekoff took a few more steps, and still seeing nothing, turned back to the boy, but the child had disappeared.

"You're a hard man to get ahold of," Avion Ambassador Straza's voice echoed over the rooftops.

"It's been a busy day," the colonel responded watching the Avion descend through low heavy clouds.

"I have something you are going to want to hear, Colonel," Straza said ominously while silently landing in front of him.

"Coincidentally," Zekoff said, "I also wanted to speak with you."

"I know of the ones you seek," the ambassador stated, matter-of-factly.

The colonel pulled back his hood.

"As does Vatra," Zekoff declared.

This gave the ambassador pause.

"You can expect no help from House Pyre."

"I concluded that with our first meeting," the colonel conceded. "The question is why are *you* willing to help?"

"Allow me to explain *who* you are dealing with," Straza answered quietly. "That should answer your question."

Zekoff gestured for him to continue.

"There is a secret, *very* radical faction of my people called the Idonian Cabal," the ambassador explained. "To them, humans are a blight upon the Annigan. They breed too quickly. They ruin lands. They subjugate other life forms. All of Avion society tends to hold prejudices against humans, but the Idonian Cabal seeks to eradicate your *entire* species."

"So, you know the members of this cabal?"

"Not specifically," Straza answered. "Their society is most secretive. They rigorously screen and only invite zealots who they feel share their hate filled ideology. We *do* know these terrorists originated in House Pyre and have spread through the Avion Great Houses, even mine."

"I'm not sure I'm following you," the colonel said. "If they're so secretive, why aren't they covering their tracks?"

"My point exactly!" the ambassador answered. "If they are being *this* bold, something terrible is about to happen."

Zekoff nodded grimly and instinctively reached for his pipe. Noting the weather, he abandoned the idea.

"Thank you, Si Ambassador," he said. "This all leads to the reason I wanted to talk with you."

❈ ❈ ❈

The hunting cabin sat on the edge of a forested outcropping in the western Goyan foothills just east of Zor. The location was ideal, close enough to be a short flight to the city but far enough away from civilization for privacy.

They killed the original inhabitants—a human family of four—as a matter of course and dropped their bodies in a deep ravine nearby. Animals would take care of the remains. The new occupants, ten members of the Idonian Cabal, stood in morbid reverence.

"I cannot believe our good fortune!" Vezeto of House Pyre, the cell leader rejoiced. "I had feared our cause lost."

Nine Avions murmured in agreement standing around the small cask of Noma on a table in the center of the cabin.

"Do we have what we need to divide it up?" Vezeto asked.

An elderly Avion nodded, retrieving a container borne by the Kell. He opened it, revealing a series of glass bottles stolen from the dead apothecary.

Vezeto nodded in approval. "I leave you to your duties."

"You two assist him," he ordered. "Follow his instructions to the letter."

Two Avions stepped forward and moved to the side of the alchemist, awaiting orders.

"The rest of you, slaughter and prepare the Kell. Tonight, we feast. Tomorrow will be a glorious day for the Idonian Cause!"

※ ※ ※

The river of blood ran from under the door and formed a pool in the street. A young sergeant guarded the entrance, face pale, with a puddle of his vomit cooling on the ground beside him. The colonel approached with six additional city guards and placed his hand on the sergeant's shoulder.

"You alright?" he asked.

The young man weakly nodded and the colonel moved by him, stepping over the blood and filth. The old colonel nearly gagged from the stench of death when he opened the door.

The sight combined with the malodor caused the two guards following behind him to throw up.

Random body parts littered the large, bare room, strewn about in a sea of crimson. The guards' boots left grisly footprints in the blood covering almost the entire floor surrounding the corpses. Upon closer examination, Zekoff grimly deduced each of the victims had been neatly quartered. He noted severed ropes and bruising around the appendages' wrists and ankles.

"It appears there were twelve bound victims," Zekoff observed.

"Colonel?" one guard called out.

The commander crossed the room. Six silver pieces lay glistening on the gore-stained floor. They fell out of the split pocket hanging from the bottom quarter of a man.

"They didn't take their money," the guard said.

"Robbery wasn't the motive," Zekoff declared. "This was sword practice."

He turned and slowly surveyed the scene, before moving for the door.

"Let's get this place cleaned up," he ordered.

"But sir, don't you want us to run your usual discovery process?" the sergeant questioned.

"Not necessary," the colonel replied, "I know who is responsible, Sergeant—that renegade faction of the Zorian Sword Academy. The question *is*, where are they right now?"

As Zekoff exited the building, Captain Rafel approached with two guards. They hurriedly splashed through the puddle-dotted street.

"Colonel, there's been an incident," Rafel said grimly.

Zekoff exhaled noisily and ran his hand through his drying hair. This was shaping up to be a deadly day.

"Oh?"

"It's your wife…"

"What about my wife, Captain?"

"Sir, I'm afraid she's dead."

❈ ❈ ❈

Shom returned to the room a little before the Kan, carrying a small bag. Mal was just waking up, Taa was standing by the door and Orich stood motionless staring out the window.

"Well, isn't this a cozy bunch," he chirped.

Mal pulled her legs over the side of the bed and scowled at her friend through bloodshot eyes.

"What the fuck are you so cheerful about?" she sneered.

He held up the bag for her inspection, before casually tossing it onto the bed beside her. She watched it land and then looked back up at Shom. He held her gaze and then nodded toward the bag. She sighed, reluctantly picked it up, and opened it. Peering inside, her eyes widened.

"There must be at least *twenty secors* in here! Where did you get this?"

"Twenty-five," Shom said, grinning. "I told you I was going to call in a few favors. One of them just happened to owe money."

"This helps," she said, optimism creeping back into her voice.

Mal reached in and pulled out two secors. She tossed one to Taa, by the door, who caught it without looking. She pitched the other at Orich, still facing out the window, who snatched the ingot from the air without turning around.

"Two other things," Shom added.

Mal turned back to her friend.

"I have a meeting at seven," he said, "and I think you are going to want to attend."

"Meeting?"

"With the Amarenian ambassador no less."

This caused Mal to sit up attentively.

"Alosus?!"

"Unless you know another," he said with a sly wink "but first, I've got something to show you."

"You *have* been busy," she observed, slipping on her boots and rising with a wobble. "Orich-Taa."

"Yes Captain?" they replied in unison.

"You can go and…"

Shom interrupted by clearing his throat.

"We need them to come with us too."

Mal raised her eyebrow questioningly.

"Trust me on this one," Shom assured.

❈ ❈ ❈

Patrol Captain Gasata, a stout, barrel-chested man sporting a thick, perfectly groomed mustache and a scowling face, stood at the front door of Zekoff's cottage barking commands. His orders set the city guards under his command abuzz with activity.

"Question anyone in the area!" he yelled.

Gasata noticed Colonel Zekoff and Captain Rafel rapidly approaching the scene of the crime. He took a deep breath before addressing his superior.

"We arrived within the deci, sir," Gasata reported trying to keep a professional demeanor. "The door was open. A neighbor discovered the body. We're still questioning her."

Zekoff, still in shock, stared at him blankly before reaching for the door handle.

"You don't have to do this sir," the captain warned. "The Cul-Ta viciously attacked her. She's chewed up pretty bad."

Zekoff gently placed his hand on the captain's shoulder.

"Thank you," he said in a hoarse whisper, "but yes, I do."

He opened the door, slowly entered, and closed it behind him. This time, he kept his boots on.

Colonel Zekoff didn't come back out until after the grand turine rang six and the Kan mist had rolled in. He walked past Gasata and Rafel, his face pale and eyes swollen, seemingly oblivious to their presence. He then stopped, lowered his head and turned to them.

"I'm going to check in at the Demon's Gate Inn," he said, voice barely audible. "Send Trenton there immediately."

With those orders, the colonel ambled off into the fog. Rafel quickly set off for the forum to collect Captain Trenton. The Patrol Captain watched them leave and slowly shook his head. Trenton was the head of Red Division. Death was coming to the streets of Zor.

❈ ❈ ❈

Built deep into the slope of Harmony Mountain, Valdurian Air Station Three was the largest structure in Zor. It's landing bay protruded outward fifty-feet into space, casting constant shade on the upper-scale businesses and residents below. Black silhouettes of airships sailed across the city, merging and emerging from its giant shadow.

Mal, Shom and Orich-Taa stood before a sleek airship in a corner of the main hangar. It stood twenty-five-feet-long and twelve-feet-high, tapering at each end. Glass covered the front taper, where the pilot and navigator sat. A large, empty hull took up the middle with a drop door on either side. The rear end tapered down to an opening one foot in diameter, surrounded by four aerodynamic fins.

Mal fought back a sense of astonishment at the operation's sheer size and scope. She had greatly underestimated Shom's influence. All around them, air crews loaded and unloaded a variety of airships of many sizes. Ground crews manned the massive landing bay, receiving and dispersing flights. After the initial shock to their senses, the quartet's found their attention focused on the lone figure who stood between them and the craft.

The Valdurian flight instructor stood just five feet tall, but her intensity made both Mal and Shom fidget. She wore her shoulder-length black hair pulled into a ponytail. Porcelain pale skin set off wide, hazel eyes, which matched the color of her olive-green jump suit. One shoulder displayed the circular patch of the Valdurian Scouts—ace pilots with a reputation as daredevils—and the other, the double-sideways chevron revealing her captain's rank. She scowled with her hands on her hips and assessed her new students.

"My name is Captain Edzo!" she stated authoritatively. "I am the ambassador's personal pilot! He has ordered me to train you in the piloting and navigation of this craft!"

"A bit intense, don't you think?" Shom whispered to Mal out of the side of his mouth.

The captain stopped and stared impatiently at the prodigal.

"I have stated my disapproval of this plan to the ambassador," she continued, "in the strongest of terms! Nonetheless, I have my orders. But rest assured, the only way into *there*…"

She turned on her heel and pointed at the airship.

"…is through me!" she concluded threateningly. "Now, if there are no further comments!"

Orich-Taa stared past her and scanned the craft, taking in every detail while Mal's attention remained riveted on

Captain Edzo. Shom however fought back the unproductive compulsion to laugh.

"This is the *Haraka*," the flight instructor announced, patting the side of its polished Ukko wood hull. "She is a Resistance Class Cruiser! They mostly use this class of ships for extended scouting operations, archer assault support and rapid insertion of marines!"

The captain abruptly finished her exuberant monologue. Her intense gaze focused like a laser on Shom, who absentmindedly peered around the room. Edzo stepped up into his face.

"Am I boring you?!" she barked.

Shom leaned away fighting back a smile.

"Gods yes!" he admitted.

She pushed aggressively forward. Shom held his ground and unsuccessfully fought back his amusement.

"Umm, Captain?" the royal asked in a commandingly flippant tone. "It *is* captain, is it not? I am *not* some raw recruit for you to berate. I *am*, however, a close childhood friend of Ambassador Valdur. Contrary to whatever you assume, I assure you, my needs are more than a mere joyride around the capital. And another thing, I am *not* your student. I will *not* be piloting this vehicle. That task falls to my two very strange friends here."

He pointed to Orich and Taa who slowly walked in sync along either side of the craft, running their hands across the buffed Ukko panels. Edzo hastily did a double take at the twin albinos.

"Hey, you two," she ordered, "get back over here!"

Orich-Taa ignored her and continued examining every facet of the airship's exterior.

"They don't hear you," Mal calmly explained. "They're actually melding with the ship."

"So, Captain Edzo," Shom continued, "as much as I would love to stay and witness your irrelevant melodrama, the lady and I have a previous engagement to keep."

Captain Edzo stared fuming with silent disdain.

"Rest assured," he added, "we will subscribe to any oath concerning the secrecy of this craft."

Shom pointed to Orich-Taa, who converged on and now explored the fins near the opening in the stern.

"I believe you will find our friends more than exemplary students," he assured, "and best of all, no berating needed… So, dear captain, we bid you good Kan."

With that, Shom took Mal by the arm and led her away.

❀ ❀ ❀

The Demon's Gate rose like giant antlers from the dense fog of the Kan. Its wide expanse and gently sloping arches welcomed all to the thriving mercantile area in the Shimol Plat neighborhood of northern Zor. When constructed more than a thousand-grand-cycles-ago, it represented the last vestiges of civilization, before one ventured out into the wilderness beyond.

The initial courtyard just beyond the gate contained six medium-sized merchants: a lapidary, a tailor, a rug merchant, a cobbler and the Rohina Takii Sword School. All were flanking the Demon's Gate Inn, one of the largest structures in the Shimol Plat. The same family which originally built it still maintained and ran the facilities. Their ancestors constructed the three-story building over five hundred grand cycles ago to represent a true marvel of the carpenters' craft.

At a table by the window, Colonel Zekoff stared out at the street traffic abating. Reaching over, he poured amber liquid from a plain brown bottle into a glass. In a single motion, he downed it and stared at the man seated across the table.

The Fate of Tomorrow

Captain Trenton de Uutu stared intensely back at his commander. "Please accept my heartfelt condolences. How may I serve you, my colonel?"

Zekoff carefully considered his next order. Captain Trenton was the commander of the feared Red Division. Much like the ironmark, if they deployed the Red Division then sentients were going to die. The question was, how horrifically—and to what extent—would they unleash their fury.

Trenton was a hard looking man, with sharp features and a scar that ran the entire length of the right side of his face. He was born, as his name suggested, in the Uutu Plat of the deadly Seven Sisters slums. Unlike the people he grew up with, many now dead, he would eventually learn to channel and regulate his aggression. This brutal upbringing made him one of the most savage men the colonel had ever worked with.

"I want that furry scourge eradicated from my city!" Zekoff growled filling his glass once more.

Trenton's eyes flashed at the prospect of a mass slaughter. "You honor me, by allowing Red Division to be the instrument of your vengeance, my colonel!"

"One silver piece per pelt, no limit. Kill on sight, no quarter," Zekoff's eyes were cold and vacant while he gave the fateful order.

The captain gave a nod of approval with an evil grin.

"Restrictions?"

Zekoff snapped out of his trance and focused on his angel of death.

"No collateral damage, *period*," he ordered, his tone serious. "No innocent sentients are to be harmed."

The colonel paused to take a sip.

"I waive this, of course, if you see anyone committing a crime with any Cul-Ta."

The captain nodded knowingly.

"I'm *serious,* Trenton, if an innocent merchant or citizen is harmed just because they're in the vicinity…" he said, tapping nervously on the table, "I will personally hang that guard!"

"I will see to it my men understand," Trenton assured.

Zekoff's broke his intense stare when glancing up. Leaning back, Trenton saw his superior's eyes widened in recognition. Turning, he saw a large female step through the door. She wore a simple cloak and on her hip was a medium-length short sword. Long, light brown hair hung in a ponytail over her bare chest. Her eyes swept suspiciously across the room. Seeing no threat, she stepped back outside. Moments later, two pale skinned, dark-haired women in simple tunics, one older than the other, entered.

Trenton snapped a quick questioning glance back at Zekoff.

"The Amarenian ambassador and entourage have just entered, and it appears they are attempting anonymity," the colonel stated calmly, not taking his eyes off the women.

They crossed the room and settled at a large round table in the hall's rear. The old colonel tugged at his beard, contemplating the situation.

"Excuse me, I'll be right back." Rising, he straightened his tunic and made his way through the crowd.

Seeing him approaching the table, Sareeta stood protectively. A gentle touch from the ambassador and she slid back into her seat. Alosus' eyes twinkled in recognition at the bearded man before her table. Rising, Soshi and Sareeta clumsily followed.

"Colonel Zekoff, it is good to see you!" Alosus beamed.

Zekoff nodded through the introductions, then finally turned his attention to the ambassador. "Esteemed, I am pleasantly surprised at your presence in this rather humble setting."

Alosus smiled warmly. "Sometimes, the greatest things can only get accomplished away from the view of the gods."

The colonel glanced around at her party. "Well, I just wanted to say hello. I'll leave you to your business."

Turning to leave, he stopped and peered back.

"Esteemed, please remember, you have friends in this room."

The ambassador nodded and Zekoff returned to his table where Trenton was more than a little inquisitive. Not wanting to answer questions, he played to the captain's bloodlust as a distraction.

"You may begin immediately, captain!"

❀ ❀ ❀

Riess stood in the center. Twelve disciples in matching white tunics resembling ghosts stood forming a silent circle in the fog. Twelve swords were drawn, all pointed at him.

"Black Sword triumphant!" they chanted in a low voice.

Riess stared at the woman facing him. She lowered her blade and bowed. The man next to her followed her actions lowering his blade. Then the swordsman to his right, and so it went around the circle. By prior orders, no one sheathed their blade. Their leader knew well they could never outdraw the Takii sword style.

"No quarter!" he ordered.

"Hai!" they snarled.

Silently, they broke their circle and Riess led them out of the alley and into the fog-shrouded street of the Shimol Plat.

❀ ❀ ❀

Seven bells rang out across the city. As promised, Joc' Valdur stood at the base of the Demon's Gate and searched the foggy streets for Shom and Mal. The intersecting boulevards and Demon's Square were still fairly busy, but the crowds were thinning considerably.

Catching movement off to his left, the ambassador turned, fully expecting to see his childhood friend. Instead, the sight of a dozen sword wielders, weapons drawn, caused his eyes to widen in surprise, and he slipped back into the foggy shadow of the gate.

They moved silently, six on either side of the street. When they passed through the gate and into the square, he heard them softly chanting in unison.

The young ambassador wasn't sure what was going on; he just knew it would not end well.

❈ ❈ ❈

Mal and Shom approached Demon's Square via one of the several side streets. Joc' would wait for them at the gate, but Shom preferred not to enter in front.

"So, does anyone know what this meeting is about?" Mal inquired when she saw the square just ahead.

She had been so caught up with the sudden influx of money and a new airship, she hadn't had time to consider the nature of the appointment.

"But of course," Shom admitted.

"Care to let me in on it?"

"The Amarenian High Council voted last cycle to give up piracy and open trade with the west," Shom explained.

"So, you were right all along!"

The prodigal sighed contentedly and stole a quick glance over at his friend walking beside him. "I never tire of hearing you say that."

"Yeah, well don't get used to it," she retorted. "It doesn't happen that often."

"All the more reason for my joy."

"So why am I invited? I don't give a shit about politics. Besides, Alosus may have a bone to pick with me about not getting rid of those invasion plans."

"I insisted," Shom emphatically stated. "I told the Valdurian ambassador you had been in this whole sordid mess from the beginning and deserved a place at the table."

Mal stared down at the street, considering this latest revaluation while they entered the plaza.

Shom's arm suddenly reached over in front of her, disrupting her thoughts. He barred her upper chest and brought her to an unexpected halt. Abruptly, he was pushing her back with him around the corner.

Looking up in surprise, she saw why.

There, crossing the square, were a dozen figures in white tunics, with black bladed swords drawn.

❀ ❀ ❀

Every Rohina Takii sword class officially ends with the students facing the master and giving a bow of thanks. Tonight, there were two instructors addressing the aspiring sword wielders.

Master Keraso had Alto run the class this evening, which allowed him to sit back and observe the young mora's teaching style. The master was well pleased with students' reaction to Alto's instructions.

Once the class of twenty disbanded, most broke off into smaller groups of friends who chatted excitedly about the evening's training. Unlike his fellow pupils, Tate Whitmar made a direct line to the head of the class. Alto was speaking with Keraso and Tate stopped at a discreet distance and waited. Once the two instructors bowed toward each other and parted, he stepped forward and bowed.

"Mora Alto, I was hoping we could talk about my private training schedule?"

It had been a long, full day, and the swordmaster had not been expecting to teach. Tate was enthusiastic but not very coordinated and could be trying.

"I'm sure we can set up a regimen that will be suitable for both of us," Alto assured, putting his arm around the new student's shoulders to guide him towards the door.

"Thank you, Mora, my schedule is flexible and…"

A woman screaming from just outside cut off his statement. Throwing the door open, Alto witnessed several beginner students being cut down by assailants in blood-stained white tunics. Through the mist, he could make out two others futilely attempting to defend themselves.

"Get the master!" Alto ordered.

Vaulting out the door, he drew his weapon in mid-leap.

❋ ❋ ❋

Zekoff was finishing his drink and saying his goodbyes to Captain Trenton, when he glimpsed a young man, he recognized entering the room via the kitchen door.

"This gets more and more interesting by the deci," the colonel thought aloud.

The captain watched the young man greet the Amarenians and sit down at their table. "Isn't that the Calden ambassador?"

"It certainly is," Zekoff cautiously validated.

A woman's scream and the clash of blades just outside caused the Zorian Guards to whirl about in their seats. Both peered out the window in time to see a dozen figures in white attacking the sword school just letting out.

Trenton flew up out of his chair and rushed out the door, simultaneously drawing his sword and blowing his emergency whistle. The shrill notes cut through the clash of arms and reverberated down the streets.

Out in the square, several beginner students were doing their best to hold off the attackers by fighting back-to-back. The Black Blades however, proved much more advanced, by using better footwork and more powerful well-timed strikes.

Moving into the fray, Trenton raised his blade to attack the nearest assailant only to trip on a body hidden by the fog. He landed next to a teenage girl whose torso had been almost severed in two. She stared outward, with dead eyes. Enraged, Trenton stood up to see Alto leaping through the air, sending his blade into the skull of a Black Blade who had just cut down a young man.

❀   ❀   ❀

Mal and Shom watched in disbelief at the seemingly vicious, unprovoked attack. When Shom reached for his sword, Mal saw Alto leap from the dojo door and strike.

Crying out in surprise, she drew her blade and charged into the square with Shom trailing just behind.

"Yet another fracas!" Shom lamented, unsheathing his weapon and running after his friend.

❁ ❁ ❁

Trenton's eyes blazed with fury. Blowing his whistle again, he resumed his attack, cutting down one of the female attackers.

For several long moments, the square rang with the clash of swords. Alto was exchanging blows with what was proving to be an exceptional student when he felt something heavy brush against his back.

He quickly jumped to the side, fully expecting to engage several combatants. To his relief and surprise, he saw Mal, who had just run through a Black Blade sneaking up from behind. The attacker's lifeless body fell and disappeared into the fog.

The sound of many boots quickly approaching caught the attention of the remaining white-clad attackers. With a shout from Riess, they disengaged and ran south, followed closely by ten city guards now led by an irate Trenton waving his sword above his head and howling.

❁ ❁ ❁

The entire incident was quickly over and an eerie calm descended on the square. Curious citizens meekly stared from their windows and doorways. Joc' Valdur stepped out of the gate's shadow. Tate Whitmar, along with Master

Keraso, exited the dojo. All stared about tensely, adrenaline still pumping through their bodies. Realizing the danger had passed, weapons were slowly lowered.

Alto sheathed his blade, and his gaze finally fell on Mal, who stood five feet away, staring at him. A sly smirk crossed her face. She glanced down at his fallen would-be ambusher and then back up at Alto.

"Hey, how ya been?" she quipped with a wink stepping up to him.

Their eyes locked before she reached out and grabbed him, pulling him close. The kiss was quick and passionate. When she stepped back, Mal playfully punched him in the chest.

"It's about fucking time you showed up!"

A mock-incredulous look swept across Alto's face. "May I bring up that you were the one to sail off without so much as a goodbye?"

Mal placed her hands on her hips and was about to respond when Shom interrupted, "Well I see you've been practicing that move I showed you!"

Alto chuckled and nodded his head.

"It's good to see you too, my friend," the swordmaster said, extending his hand.

"All very touching," came a voice from behind.

Everyone turned to see Colonel Zekoff approaching at a leisurely pace, hands clasped behind his back. "Now, is someone going to tell me exactly what happened here?"

❂ ❂ ❂

When the warning signal of a bird call arose from the point man farther up the trail, six men crouched down disappearing into the ground fog. They were a mile north of Zor heading upward into the foothills. High above, Sargent Barton saw the reason for the alarm. Flying several hundred feet above, an Avion circled slowly, then landed on a rocky outcropping another mile away up the steep, rugged hillside.

"Just where they said they'd be," he said, nodding with satisfaction.

Captain Gasata's intelligence from the Avion's House Solas apparently had proved correct. Glancing back at his men, he raised his fist in the air, flexed his hand open, then back into a fist. All six rose and gathered around their commander.

Barton de Goya was thin and wiry, with long, greasy brown hair which always seemed to have leaves and twigs in it. His face's bony features contained a permanent unshaven stubble. The sleeve of his tattered green jacket displayed the patch of the Zorian City Guard, Patrol Division, but it was the patch on the other arm that truly defined his duties.

The double-crossed arrows showed he was leader of the Volunteer Huntsmen, an informal group of hunters normally providing the undomesticated meat to the butcher shops of Zor. Some traded their tracking skills to patrol the wilderness areas around the city instead of paying a hunting tax. The group of equally scruffy archers focused attentively as the ex-Zerian Ranger instructed them.

"They appear to be up there," Barton said. "Who's the fastest runner?"

All pointed to a small, thin young man with blonde hair and a baby face.

"Get back to Zor as quickly as possible," he ordered the young hunter. "Find Colonel Zekoff. Tell him we have located the targets and we're going to need a squad of city guards for backup."

The young hunter nodded, slung his bow and then took off running back down the path.

Barton turned to the five remaining. "Let's get up there and see what we can see."

"Do we take 'em out, Sergeant?" one archer asked with sadistic anticipation.

"On my command or if they try to make a break for it," Barton instructed.

❀ ❀ ❀

City guards filled Demon's Square, marking bodies and talking to potential witnesses. The colonel milled about the scene, confident in his team's abilities. His attention turned to Alto and the surviving victims. Deftly, he retrieved and filled his pipe.

"Well," Zekoff said, "everyone's version is basically the same…"

From down the street, a commotion caused all heads to turn. Out of the fog, Trenton marched victorious. Behind him was the detachment of guards he had led in pursuit. They muscled three bound, very resistant Black Blades back into the square and before Zekoff.

"We caught up to 'em right before Tuath Plat," Trenton excitedly reported, his face streaked with blood. "They put up a bit of a fight—nothing we couldn't handle. There's three of 'em in the streets back there."

Zekoff examined the three, their white tunics heavily stained with red, faces contorted in rage.

"Were these the people who attacked you?" the colonel inquired of the group standing around Alto.

All nodded yes.

The colonel sighed and turned to Trenton. "Hang them at the lifting of the Kan."

The sentence calmly pronounced; Alto stepped forward in front of Riess.

"As a matter of honor, I should beseech this man to let me kill you in combat!" His voice was low, his tone ominous.

This level of controlled malevolence caused Mal and the entire group to shift uncomfortably.

"But you, you are a man without honor!" he paused, staring intently into Riess' eyes. "I will rejoice in seeing you hang like a common thief!"

In a final defiant act, Riess spat at Alto's face. A simple turn of the swordmaster's head caused the ball of spittle to fly harmlessly by.

Alto scoffed, looking him up and down. "You are as predictable as you are devoid of honor. It would have been too easy to kill you."

"Then fight me!" Riess screamed, struggling fruitlessly against his bonds and guards. "Fight Me!"

Zekoff nodded, and they led them away. Riess continued bellowing as they disappeared around the corner. Alto stepped back and stood beside Mal. Her arm reached out and slipped around his waist. Smiling broadly, the swordmaster put an arm around her shoulder.

Gripping his pipe in one hand, Zekoff tapped on the tip of a crystal match with the other, causing it to glow. "Well, that's that. Now, I guess I can give murderous Avions my full attention."

Bringing the match up, he puffed until the pipe lit.

"Avions?!" Mal perked up, breaking her embrace with Alto and stepping forward.

Zekoff blew out a thick cloud of smoke that obscured his face. Waving the match out, he blew a hole in the smoke cloud. Their two bewildered faces stared at each other.

"Avions," he casually confirmed.

"Those fuckers burned my ship last Kan and killed most of my crew!"

Zekoff pulled the pipe slowly from his mouth and studied Mal. "Why do you think they would do that?"

"How the fuck do I know?!" Mal incredulously said. "They're not even my species!"

"True," the colonel expounded, pointing the tip of his pipe for emphasis, "but I've found motivation crosses the species line."

He pulled a drag from his pipe. "Except for the Otick, yeah, talk about discipline! Those crabs have got the lock on... oh, sorry, I've been distracted lately... you know the crazy part about the..."

His voice trailed off, and he stared blankly, puffing his pipe. Mal, Shom and Alto exchanged baffled glances.

Zekoff continued his incoherent ramble until Shom spoke up, "Umm, I'm confused as to the point of this conversation."

Mal impatiently surveyed her surroundings. "Are we done here?!"

This seemed to break Zekoff out of his babbling trance. "Um, uh... just be available later."

"Yeah, well my airship is being checked out over in Air-Station Three." Mal jerked a thumb northward in the building's general direction. "You can probably find me there."

Reaching down, she grabbed Alto's hand. "But that'll be later."

Pulling the swordmaster along, she started across the square toward the inn. "In the meantime, the gentleman and I have some serious undisturbed catching up to do."

Shom grinned watching Mal drag Alto behind her with the same determined lustful look he had seen many times before. A good fight always made her horny.

"Best of luck old boy!" the prodigal offered when they passed him.

Following helplessly, all Alto could manage was a shrug and a slightly embarrassed smile.

❂ ❂ ❂

The flames of several small braziers, along with the fumes from the cooking Noma, made the air inside the cabin heavy and pungent. Scattered across the top of the single table was a maze of glass tubes and containers filtering the deadly poison into a single, small container.

The renowned court alchemist, Karaca of House Solas inspected the process. He nodded in satisfaction, ignoring the heat and smell.

"We are just about ready," he calmly declared.

Raising his hand, Vezeto signaled all to gather around.

"Brothers and sisters, long have we waited for the day when we could make a significant impact in ridding the Annigan of the human scourge. Today is that day! We kept details of this operation secret for security reasons, but the time for secrecy is over. We will strike the water supplies of all ten human cities on this continent!"

The Idonian Avions shouted their approval.

"The dose is ready," Veeto continued, holding out a handful of small sticks clenched in his fist. "We shall draw lots to see who shall begin this Goyan purge. The first target will be the slaver city of Nier, to the north."

❂ ❂ ❂

They both rolled back from an embrace and lay on their sides, facing each other. Mal swallowed hard and tried to catch her breath. Long moments passed just staring into each other's eyes. Reaching over, Alto stroked Mal's hair and moved a sweaty ringlet off her forehead.

"Tell me, how is it a beautiful woman, such as yourself, becomes a smuggler?"

"Revenge," Mal responded simply.

"How so?"

"My parents fished," she began. "We were part of a small hamlet on the reef side of Scoth Island."

"You said Scoth?" Alto's tone changed, from tenderness to concern.

Mal nodded slowly.

Being a native of the Spice Islands, he understood Scoth Island rested between the two island chains making up the Spice Islands, the Zerian Reef Chain, controlled by House Calden; and the Outer Zerians, controlled by House Aramos. Both laid claim to the island. They each hired privateers to keep the other off it. Scoth became a no-man's-land, accessed only by Spice Rat smugglers and foolhardy profiteers.

"One day, while I was out gathering firewood," Mal explained, with a distant gaze, "the Aramosi came. They killed everyone and burned our homes to the ground. I took on with the next passing Spice Rat and the rest is history."

"Something tells me there is more to your history," he said, tracing the long scar branded across her back.

"Yeah, a little bit."

"So, I would imagine there's no love lost between you and House Aramos?"

"Or Calden, and you can thank the Whitmar slavers for my back," she said, pausing thoughtfully. "It's been my life's mission to fuck with their entire operation in the Spice Islands."

"Perhaps it is time to think about a new life's mission."

Mal rolled over and snuggled into his chest.

"I know you're quick to spout that philosophical bullshit," she chuckled, tracing circles on his chest with her forefinger, "but in this case, you just may be right."

"You may think of my words as folly but, I too, have a similar story."

"Really?"

She stopped playing with his chest hairs and they met each other's eyes.

"It's true," he explained. "My father and uncle trawled the Zerian Reef. When I was ten, Reef Piceans killed them over territorial fishing rights."

Mal nodded sympathetically.

"My mother found herself with no means of support," Alto continued. "It forced her to sell me into servitude."

"They made you a slave, like me?!"

"I was proud to serve my village and feed my family."

"But still a slave."

"My contract was for two grand cycles."

"What did they have you do?" she asked.

"Like you, they turned me over to the slavers of House Whitmar. From there, they assigned me to the rice fields of Northern Wou."

"You picked rice?"

"That and more. I became a part of the Teekia Rice Collective. They treated me well."

Mal tilted her head and raised a skeptical eyebrow.

"I was not a prisoner like you, I was under contract. You were under sentence." Alto explained. "Mine was not punishment slavery. I was indentured. The local boss, a man named Seefa, and his family, were kind to me. I was like family."

"I can understand why they took a liking to you," Mal said, leaning forward and kissing him lightly. "So why didn't you stay?"

Alto sighed and lay silent for a moment.

"One day," he said, "I was part of a group tasked with taking a load of rice to the port city of Quana. Thieves ambushed us. They waited for us to sell our load and knew we had money. I was eleven at the time. I remember being so frightened."

Mal tenderly brushed his cheek.

"Then, this stranger passed by as they held a knife to my friend Aboki's throat." Alto continued. "He wore a long black robe and a wide-brimmed black hat. The stranger stopped and demanded they set my friend free. The thieves just laughed at him. So, he demanded a second time and they threatened him. He did not demand a third time. At first, I didn't know what I was watching, as he effortlessly killed all three of the bandits. I just knew it was the most graceful thing I had ever witnessed.

"When my two grand cycles of service ended, I did not return home, where they would have welcomed me as a hero, instead I sought that man out."

He kissed her forehead.

"And the rest, as you say, is history."

❈ ❈ ❈

Zor was deep in the Kan. The grand turine in the harbor rang twelve times, echoing through the near-deserted streets.

Otof de Kaya glanced out the front entrance of the Pijon Inn and spat onto the fog filled street. Grunting in disgust, he slammed the door closed. He had only taken in three coppers this evening and was in a foul mood. At this rate, he wouldn't be able to pay his business tariff. Perhaps he would beat his wife, he evilly mused, running his hand through his greasy brown hair. The soreness in his fingers reminded him how he had just beaten her yesterday for spilling a beer.

He turned when he heard the door open. Alosus, Soshi and Sareeta entered. He noted two of them were of average height, attractive, with brown hair and nicely dressed. The other, however, towered over them. She wore pants and carried a short sword.

"We're closed!" he snapped, turning back, and walking to the bar.

The two nicely dressed women followed him.

"Good sir, I would ask your indulgence," Alosus beseeched.

Otof prepared to spit out a nasty comment when he heard the distinctively recognizable sound of metal clinking on the bar. Soshi placed five gold pieces down. He stared at the money, licking his cracked lips, then back up at the ambassador.

I'd rather do a threesome with you twats. Otof thought, undressing them in his mind. *I'd bend the two lookers over the six-foot-tall quim and fuck the gold pieces out of them like broken piggy banks. I know whores when I sees 'em. I wonder who she fucked for that gold?*

"We would like to rent your hall for a few decis," she asked softly.

"Sure," he grunted, reaching for the gold. *And I'd like to rent you hussies for a few decis.*

Soshi's hand quickly covered the coins.

"Alone," Alosus added.

Otof stopped and looked back at her.

"Sure," he mumbled. "I got stocking to do in the back." *And a little sticking to do in your back ends.*

Alosus gave a nod and Soshi stepped back from the bar. The grizzled innkeeper reached out, snatched up the gold and exited out a door behind the bar.

Otof stood in a short hallway, thinking about how odd the situation was while wiping his hands on his pants. This had to be worth checking out. He slipped into the stockroom and sat on a keg of beer near the wall. He gently pulled a loose knot of wood from its boarding. From this position, he could see and hear everything that went on in the main room.

Alosus and Soshi sat at the largest table, while Sareeta guarded the entrance. Within a few moments, Shom Eldor led Tate Whitmar, Pierce Calden, and Joc' Valdur through the door and they took a seat at the table with the ladies.

Otof didn't recognize anyone, but he was certain of this meeting's importance. Perhaps even important enough that Captain Rafel might pay handsomely for what's learned from it. He pressed his ear against the hole in the wall and listened carefully.

"You know," Tate Whitmar declared obstinately, staring down the Amarenian ambassador, "I don't give a dick for a dandy about any mutual defense pact if it means my family loses the slave trade!"

Alosus took a deep breath and steeled herself.

"Ambassador Whitmar, no one is asking your family to give up anything," she explained calmly. "May I remind you, our culture too, relies on conscripted labor? All we ask is that your house itself cease taking slaves."

"Now, I'm aware you claim that your kind just outlawed piracy," he said, "but you know some of your hardcore will just keep at it!"

"Yes," Alosus conceded, "but they would then be criminals, and therefore subject to Punishment Slavery. Seeing how we no longer take slaves; my people would commission your people for the labor we need."

The young Whitmar paused and nodded. "Huh, well, now that's a scrap I can take back to the dogs!"

"What about embassies?" Pierce Calden inquired.

"With open trade they will be a necessity," she offered. "I believe my queen will act quickly and favorably."

"Well, I certainly hope so," Shom interjected. "Time is something we don't have a lot of. They must reach a formal agreement quickly and confidentially. These kinds of secrets tend not to stay secret for long."

Joc' Valdur scanned the group. "I agree, it must remain a secret until we've all signed."

"If my father gets wind of this pact, he will do everything in his power to see this endeavor fail," Shom grimly advised.

"He's right," Joc' concurred. "House Valdur knows full well what treachery Eldor and Aramos are capable of."

From behind the peephole, Otof's eyes were wide in astonishment. He swallowed hard. This *was* important and, potentially, *very* profitable.

"I'm heading home at the lifting of the Kan," Tate chimed in. "Just received word grandma returned. They instructed me to let you all know a Consort Ball is officially being arranged."

A collective groan went up around the table.

"Ah, yes, so the White Queen returns," Shom remarked with a slight sarcastic tone in his voice.

Tate shrugged. "Yeah, and I get some rich, snot-nosed noble who's even younger than me as my new grandpa."

All the men laughed. This outburst caused the Amarenians to exchange perplexed glances.

"Forgive us, Esteemed," Shom explained, noting their uncertainty. "The White Queen of Whitmar is… well… old."

The women still appeared confused.

"*Very* old," Shom continued.

"I've not heard of this Consort Ball," Alosus admitted, her face a mask of confusion.

"That's because they held the last ball quite a while before your appointment here," Tate explained. "We all dread it but it's how House Whitmar survives."

Pierce Calden spoke up, returning to the matter at hand. "So, we're all in agreement?"

All shook their heads.

"Alright," he continued. "I suggest we all contact our various superiors and let's get this done quickly."

Otof saw the meeting ending. He quietly replaced the knot in the board and stood up. It was going to be difficult to contain his excitement at the thought of how much this information would fetch.

"One last thing," Shom said, while everyone was standing.

All eyes turned to the Eldorian prodigal.

"It would be helpful," he asked, "if someone could monitor my dear uncle, the Eldorian ambassador, to see if he's planning anything."

Soshi winked. "I can do one better than that."

This offer obviously surprised Shom. The former Secret Sister had remained quiet the entire meeting.

"I would ask," he started, "but I'm not sure I *want* to know. So, I say thank you and please do!"

"You been here *too* long!" Otof bellowed, entering the room. "You go now!"

Alosus turned to the innkeeper and bowed slightly.

"We were just leaving, good sir," she said. "Thank you for your hospitality."

Alosus nodded at Soshi, who handed Otof another gold piece. He grinned widely, while he quickly snatched and pocketed the coin. This night might have completely turned his fortunes around. With the money Spymaster Rafel would surely pay, he might finally get ahead of the game.

When Otof locked the front door behind them he heard the turine rang fourteen bells. The Kan would lift in just a few decis, but he was too excited to sleep. Leaving by the back door, he made his way to the forum while the conversation stayed fresh in his mind.

❀ ❀ ❀

The *Voola* rocked violently in her slip, while the last remnants of a passing squall battered all six boats in Modaii's tiny marina. They scrounged meager provisions, just enough to get them home, and she was ready to sail. When Captain Fia climbed aboard, all hands were eager to hear what she had discovered.

"Looks like we're heading back to a different world than the one we left," she stated, with a touch of melancholy.

The crew exchanged confused glances.

"Neaux said something about Xandar the Mad?" one young mariner spoke up. "I thought he was just a legend."

"If the ones I spoke to are to be believed," Fia said. "A large band of our Ulana sisters came through here, about a quinte ago. Said they were going to release him from his imprisonment in the Middle Realms."

This perplexed Neaux. "Even if it is true, why would they do that?"

"Chaos," Fia responded. "Remember, they worship Ulana, Goddess of the chaotic sea."

"But Xandar is a man!" another piped up, still confused.

"Like I said, a different world," Fia solemnly repeated. "The Ulana sisters apparently took over the ruins of Darkspur Castle. We avoided all the Human Houses banding together to crush them. That's what we encountered that forced us to change course and how we ended up here in the Barketts"

"What were those flying things?" another asked.

"Those belong to House Valdur," Fia explained. "They've harnessed some form of sorcery from Nocturn to make their ships fly."

The crew started nervously chattering and Fia needed them to focus.

"Let's set sail," she ordered. "The storm has passed, and it's time to find out what's going on at home."

The Fate of Tomorrow

❦ ❦ ❦

Judgement Square was in the upper end of the Northern Docks. The jail, courts, City Guard Station, barristers and scribes, all surrounded a large common area where they permanently displayed their gallows, stocks, chopping block and a torture cross. Someone always occupied at least one of these ominous instruments of the city's wrath there.

Alto stood in the pre-morning chill and dampness of the Kan, reflecting how he had left a bed warmed by a beautiful, naked woman to be here. His face betrayed no emotion when they placed the nooses around three necks. He looked Riess squarely in the eye when the platform unceremoniously dropped, launching the trio's spirits into the Middle Realms.

The swordmaster watched the bodies sway in the morning breeze while the fog receded from around his feet. Riess was twitching violently his tongue bulging from his mouth. Catching the strong scent of feces Alto knew that they had released their bowls.

Sentients of all types milled about the square in their morning rituals. Most only glanced at the bodies when they passed by, but a few stood and gawked. Some even threw things at the lifeless pendulums.

Alto felt no vindication or joy in death, now that he'd avenged his childhood friend. He only regretted not killing Riess himself, but the Takii way viewed vengeance as a sin. It had no place in his school's philosophy.

Chastising himself, he remembered an old Takii axiom. *One can master physical technique in but a few grands. Mastering one's temperament will take a lifetime.*

Alto reflected on that wisdom while he turned to go.

❂ ❂ ❂

Mal and Shom were already there, standing beside the *Haraka*, by the time Alto made it up the steps to the main hangar of Air Station Three. The flight deck was coming to life and pilots prepared their crafts. The first landings of the morning arrived and traffic moving in and out of the air station started to pick up.

Orich-Taa stood beside the craft's open side doors speaking with Captain Edzo. Unlike their previous encounter, the captain was all smiles and shook Orich-Taa's hands before walking off. She glanced disdainfully at Shom when she quickly passed by him pausing in front of Mal.

"Well, I gotta say captain," Edzo remarked in a chipper tone. "These two are amazing. What they mastered in a cycle would normally take grands of constant practice."

"Yeah, they're *something* alright," Mal admitted.

"I wish you luck in whatever your endeavor is." Edzo said before shooting another dirty look at Shom and moving off.

"Greetings, captain," Orich-Taa chanted, nodding at Mal.

"Well boys," she said, eyeing the *Haraka*, "you've been at this all Kan. So, what have we here?"

Orich-Taa's faces lit up.

"A truly beautiful machine!" Taa asserted, patting its side. "The propulsion system is like nothing I've seen."

"The steering system felt sluggish, however," Orich added. "So, you might put it in for a tune-up."

"Do you foresee *any* problems?" Mal asked.

"Not at all," Orich concluded confidently. "We can more than compensate. However, I recommend a trip soon to the Air Yards on Zer for a refitting."

Mal exuberantly spun around and faced her friends. It relieved both Shom and Alto to see her ecstatic expression.

"What say we take this baby for a shakedown flight and see what she's got?"

"A wonderful way to start the day!" Alto agreed.

"I'm in!" Shom responded.

Mal spun back to her Bailian crew.

"Well in that case…"

She cut her order short when six city guards approached at a double-time march. Four women and two men formed two disciplined rows of three. All wore blue blouses, with a single red circle on the left sleeve, and a short compound bow slung over their shoulders. Arrows filled lined special quivers attached to their ankles and left forearms.

They halted before the group, separated, and turned facing each other. Colonel Zekoff walked leisurely between the two rows and approached Mal.

"It's a fine morning for a flight," he amicably stated, while surveying the craft.

The Spice Rat's face turned serious and she stepped forward to greet the head of the City Guard. Alto and Shom flanked her one step behind.

"What can I do for you, Colonel?"

"Something's been bothering me," he announced, clasping his hands behind his back. "Why would Avions attack *your* ship?"

He slowly paced in a tight circle. The city guards of the Red Division remained at rigid attention behind him.

"I've already told you," Mal answered defensively, "I don't *know* why!".

Zekoff stopped and pivoted to face her.

"Young lady, you need to understand that I've got a fanatical, murderous Avion cult operating in my city. They have a specific hatred for humans and something big is about to happen. Any information you may have could save many lives."

"Look, Colonel…" Mal began.

"Of course," Zekoff coyly continued, "anything you may wish to share won't be held against you,"

Mal stopped and studied the colonel's grim expression. Her resolve for secrecy faded when she remembered the old Marassa's words, *"Enough to kill every living thing on this continent, five times over."*

"Noma," she admitted weakly. "We had a small cask of pure, undistilled venom."

"I... I know where they are!" Zekoff sputtered with horrific recognition. "We've no time to lose and it appears your ship is prepped to fly."

Mal glanced nervously back at Alto and Shom.

"I'm commandeering this craft, with or without you!" Zekoff warned.

"He appears to have the upper hand," Alto whispered in Mal's ear.

"And a certain indebtedness by local authorities," Shom whispered in the other ear, "might come in handy one day."

"Agreed," Alto continued, "besides, this could fit in perfectly with your new direction."

Mal whirled, facing her two advisers.

"Shut up, shut up, shut up!"

Resignation overcame her defiance and she turned back to Zekoff.

"Oh, for fuck's sake, get in," she conceded.

Orich stepped to the side of the open hatch and the colonel pointed to the ship's interior. Six archers quickly climbed inside. Shom and Alto followed and sat along the bare hull, directly behind the navigation station and pilot's wheel. Mal and Zekoff, along with Orich-Taa, were last. Taa closed the hatch while Orich took his place at the wheel. Zekoff frowned at the empty interior.

"Sorry for the sparse surroundings," Mal sarcastically apologized. "We haven't had time to fix her up."

Zekoff ignored the jab and eyed her cautiously.

"So, Colonel," she continued, "where are we going?"

"Up in the foothills just north of…"

Mal held up her hand cutting the colonel short and waved Taa over. Zekoff held his thought, curiosity overcoming his irritation. The Bailian focused on his captain as he approached, avoiding meeting Zekoff's eyes.

"I need to know where we're going," she demanded.

The pale white humanoid's face remained expressionless. He nodded and reached for the colonel's head. Instinctively, the City Guard commander recoiled.

"Relax," Mal assured, "they're navigation savants. He doesn't care who you're fucking."

Zekoff reluctantly lowered his guard. Taa placed both hands on the sides of his head and closed his eyes in concentration.

Within the briefest of moments, Orich—still manning the ship's wheel—connected with Taa and they silently passed the location between them. The craft shuddered slightly when the Etheria engines whirred to life.

Mal addressed the guards in the rear, "I'd have a seat and hold on if I were you."

The *Haraka* ascended and whirled towards the hangar entrance, knocking Zekoff and his squad off their feet.

"She did warn them," Shom snickered to Alto, while the ship slipped rapidly into the post-Kan sky.

❊ ❊ ❊

"Sergeant, there's movement," one of the volunteer huntsmen whispered.

Barton peered through the bushes at the cabin. He was right. Something was going on.

"Ready, lads," he said, rallying two archers next to him.

He cupped his hands around his mouth and trilled out a bird call. An answer came from a hundred yards away on the other side of the outcropping. A human target couldn't escape, because the huntsmen's arrows covered the only exit and any who fled on foot would meet a deadly crossfire. Avions could fly, however, giving them a whole different avenue of escape. That was fine with the sergeant. The crafty ranger had a plan.

"Alright, let's light 'em up," the sergeant ordered.

One archer, who had amassed a small pile of kindling. produced a thin piece of flint from his pouch and struck it against a rock, showering the pile with sparks. The kindling quickly caught fire. He then reached into his quiver and extracted an arrow. After wrapping the shaft in an oil-soaked cloth just beneath its tip. He nocked and drew, dipping the arrowhead in the flame. The cloth immediately caught fire. Aiming at the cabin, he let loose the arrow. The others crouched, arrows at the ready.

※ ※ ※

Everyone looked up when they heard the arrow hit the roof. Panic set in when they saw the smoke.

"Protect the Noma!" the alchemist shrieked, wings fluttering nervously.

The leader turned to the young Avion who had drawn the short straw. He took a small waterproof pouch from the alchemist and quickly handed it to him.

"You know your mission!" he grimly reminded.

The young Idonian locked eyes on his leader, then turned and headed for the window.

"Cover his escape!" he ordered the two flanking him.

The three exited by the window facing outward to the cliff. One by one, they unfurled their wide wings sending them into the air.

Two Avions unsheathed their short swords and flew upward assessing the danger. They were little more than a blur to the archers on the ground and the first volley of arrows sailed harmlessly past them. With the huntsmen distracted, the Avion with the pouch, leapt from the window and glided north.

The other two pulled their wings back and dove into the volunteer huntsmen. Their short swords decapitated one archer and split another's skull from crown to neck. Eventually it became impossible for them to evade the torrent of arrows.

Multiple projectiles struck them and they plummeted to the ground. One crashed through the now-enflamed roof, showering the interior with fiery debris. The other writhed about on the ground, his wings flapping futilely.

❀ ❀ ❀

"Captain, I believe we have located our destination," Taa announced.

Through the windshield they saw a large plume of rising smoke. The *Haraka* sped closer and began its descent, rapidly approaching the burning cabin.

"Damn!" Mal blurted out viewing the spectacle below.

Zekoff stood behind the navigator's chair and watched volunteer huntsmen and Idonians trade arrows around the burning hovel. Avion and human corpses littered the grounds surrounding the building.

"Put us down there!" Zekoff requested, pointing to a small clearing next to the building. "Red Division, prepare to deploy!"

The Red Division archers immediately unslung their crossbows and began loading their bolts.

Mal noticed how the craft's descent affected Orich-Taa. Taa sat sweating in the navigator's seat, silently transfixed on the burning structure, while Orich calmly manned the helm. When they were a hundred yards from the ledge, Taa broke his stare and turned to his twin. Their eyes locked and the ship's interior pulsed with a strange energy.

"Hold on!" Orich warned.

He jerked the wheel hard to starboard. The *Haraka* banked steeply, accelerating suddenly from the cliffside. The airship's passengers screamed obscenities while the turbulence threw them around like toy soldiers. Zekoff was about to protest, when the entire outcropping on the mountainside disappeared in a massive, silent explosion of blue light.

Waves of energy pelted the craft and the ship rocked violently from side to side. Mal held on to her seat while she watched Orich struggle to regain control of the helm. Once the ship stabilized, she could see the blast completely wiped away the entire ridge, and part of the mountain above it, leaving a smooth rock bald spot surrounded by trees and vegetation.

"What the…" Mal gasped in disbelief.

"Well," Shom said, shaking his head, "I guess now we know what happens when you ignite an enormous amount of raw Noma."

"What in the name of the gods just happened?" Alto wondered aloud examining the barren area.

"We felt it building," Orich-Taa revealed in unison. "If we had stayed there, the portal they unwittingly opened would have sucked us in with them."

"Where did they go?" Mal wondered, staring in disbelief at the blighted expanse.

"Unknown," Taa replied. "They could be anywhere in the Annigan…"

"…or trapped on any of the planes of the Middle Realms," Orich continued.

"We've got other things to worry about," Zekoff announced ominously. "One got away."

He pointed to a dot racing toward the horizon.

"Do you think they have any of the Noma?" Mal wondered.

"Can we take that chance?" Zekoff answered, meeting her eyes.

She locked on his gaze for a moment, before spinning to face Orich-Taa.

"Go!" she ordered.

❂ ❂ ❂

It took practically no time at all catching up to the fleeing Avion. Keeping up with his erratic flight path across the rugged hills proved problematic.

Taa scanned the precarious terrain.

"He appears to be heading northeast," he announced.

Suddenly, the Avion's wings folded slightly, and he quickly descended into a wide ravine. Without hesitation, the *Haraka* dove after him.

"We would suggest holding on to something," Orich-Taa warned in their emotionless monotone over the din of bodies being thrown about the cabin.

Shom and Alto barely kept their footing, gripping the sides of the ship.

"I really hate flying!" Shom announced.

"Have you flown before?" Alto curiously inquired, with a tilt of his head.

Shom swallowed back his nausea and glanced at the guards piled in a heap about the stern.

"First time."

The Avion deftly maneuvered along the snaking canyon at an astounding speed. The *Haraka* kept pace, mirroring his actions, directly above the precipice.

"Magnificent creatures," Taa stated. "Perfectly suited for flight."

Zekoff stood braced against the captain's chair and hull. He witnessed firsthand the connection between the twin Bailians. The one in the navigator's seat acted as another set of eyes for the one behind him at the helm.

Zekoff caught motion out of the corner of his eye and turned to the windshield. The winged humanoid shot upward, out of the canyon, right in front of the *Haraka's* bow. Orich banked hard to avoid collision. The Avion passed within twenty feet of the craft, performed a flawless right arc, and dove for a nearby stand of ancient trees.

"What the fuck…" Mal gasped.

"Impressive!" Orich-Taa complimented.

The Avion sped toward the woods low to the ground and the *Haraka* held a tight pursuit.

"Captain," Taa announced, "I believe the Avion will attempt navigating that forest."

"Looks like it," Mal admitted, eyes narrowing. "Stay tight on his ass. Force him to enter the forest full bore. Don't pull up until he clears the tree line."

"Yes, Captain," Orich answered from the helm.

"Our speed and elevation make our odds of succeeding *very* slim," Taa warned, his normally dispassionate face now masked in concern.

"Yep," Mal calmly answered.

"Captain?"

Mal stared down the rapidly approaching forest. The Avion disappeared into the trees.

"NOW!" she ordered.

Orich pulled the craft into a steep ascent. Blue sky filled the windshield while branches broke and scraped along the hull. The speeding craft clipped the outer limbs of the forest canopy, limbs and leaves showered the *Haraka*. Forest debris streamed past the windshield leaving a trail of green confetti, while the airship cleared the trees and leveled off. Taa scouted the canopy below while his twin maneuvered in a gentle circle just above the treetops.

Shom heaved a loud sigh of relief, then slumped back against the hull. "Excuse me while I remove my balls from my throat."

Zekoff's eyes bored a hole in the back of Mal's head.

"Your decision almost got us killed back there, young lady!" he scolded. "Are you sure this is what…"

"The captain's strategy worked perfectly," Orich said, interrupting the indignant colonel.

Mal and Taa silently stared out the windshield, searching the forest below. Zekoff glared at Orich in disbelief.

"She forced the Avion to navigate the forest at the highest speed possible to increase his chance of a mishap," Taa added in his typical monotone, his eyes never leaving the ocean of green beneath them.

"There!"

He pointed to a flock of birds, streaming up through swaying branches.

"Find a spot to set us down," Mal ordered, ignoring the surrounding conversation.

While Orich adjusted their course, Mal turned in her chair to address Zekoff.

"The trees probably did the work for you," she said, "but you'll need to be sure."

"Captain, I located a small clearing," Taa announced.

Mal gave Orich a thumbs-up while he gently steered the wheel and stared back at the bearded colonel with a satisfied smirk. Zekoff lowered his gaze.

"You have my sincere apology, young lady," he offered. "I haven't been myself of late. Perhaps there is something I could do to make this right?"

Mal rolled her eyes. "Well, you could stop calling me 'young lady' for starters."

"I'll try," Zekoff said with a sad smile. "However, you very much remind me of how I envisioned my daughter might have been."

They stared silently at each other for a moment, and Mal unsuccessfully fought back a blush. The colonel broke the trance and turned to his guards.

"Red Division, prepare to deploy!"

❀ ❀ ❀

Rafel used the ropes still attached to the headboard and rolled over onto his back in bed, savoring the way his naked body glided across the luxurious sheets. The welts on his buttocks warmly ached and feeling semen leaking from him onto such expensive bedding made him giggle with sheer decadence.

He propped himself up on his elbows and watched his lover dress. Rafel's eyes drifted downward, as the muscular man, with long salt-and-pepper hair and beard, buttoned the shirt covering his thick, hairy chest. Rafel licked his lips, gazing at the now flaccid member swinging between Hoyt Eldor's legs while he pulled on his pants.

"This was a surprise sir," he said. "Thank you for a wonderful evening."

Hoyt buttoned his trousers and fastened his buckle then glanced over at the naked spymaster. A superior, dominant smile crossed the ambassador's face staring down at the man's small but insistent erection. Rafel continued with his nervous post-coital small talk.

"I mean, it's not every day you're admitted to the Eldorian ambassador's private chambers."

Now fully dressed, Hoyt walked over to the bed. Rafel couldn't take his eyes off him, and his heart pounded at his approach. His erection quivered and balls ached from an evening of repeatedly being taken to the edge and then denied an orgasm. Hoyt stood over him and examined the effeminate man who looked back with adoring eyes.

The ambassador reached down, grabbed Rafel by his long black hair, and pulled him close. Rafel gasped in excitement when Hoyt kissed him hard, biting his bottom lip. The ravaged spymaster tasted blood and his cock jumped. For a moment, he feared he might release without permission.

Letting go of his hair, Rafel fell back onto the bed and stared up at his lover's confident face.

"I feel like I can tell you anything, sir," he cooed through bloodied lips.

Hoyt leaned down and playfully slapped his face.

"Because you can," he assured in a deep gravelly voice.

The Eldorian ambassador then turned to leave. Opening the door, he looked back at Rafel, aroused, and writhing in bed.

"You may release when I'm gone," he permitted, before stepping into the hall and closing the door behind him.

Hoyt Eldor's gait was almost effervescent walking toward the main forum. He'd satisfied both his intellect and his loins in one session. The information the enamored spymaster gave up should prove extremely interesting to his Aramos allies. They will probably call for a mutual defense pact between the Amarenians and the other houses, possibly calling for even more drastic measures.

❋ ❋ ❋

When they opened the side doors of the *Haraka* the pungent smell of the woodland filled the cabin. Zekoff winced at the cacophony of bird, insect, and wildlife noises.

Archers of Red Division piled out the open hatches, three to each side, crossbows at the ready. Colonel Zekoff calmly climbed out onto the forest floor and took it all in.

Three-foot high ferns covered the clearing and extended twenty feet out from the ship. The colonel's boots crunched down the undergrowth when he waded through the waving sea of green. Sticky seedpods attached themselves to his pants with every step. He tried brushing them off, only to find the resilient spores sticking to his hands. Waving his arms comically, the pods finally dislodged and flew off.

Shom chuckled from the doorway. "Not exactly what you find on the docks of Zor, eh Colonel?"

Zekoff shot him an unamused look and continued to assess his surroundings. Ancient trees reached up hundreds of feet into the sky. Their massive trunks resembled pillars to a forest temple. Smaller trees and thick vegetation composed the second and third tier of the canopy, making visibility difficult. The upper branches were alive with birds flying and monkeys playing. The archers warily circled the perimeter and awaited orders.

"I should accompany them, Captain," Taa stated, joining Mal in the doorway.

"Not a chance!" Mal snarled at the Bailian.

"Captain, I believe I am the only one that can guide them through."

"That's probably right," Zekoff agreed. "He could save us valuable time slogging through the bush."

"The longer we spend on the ground, the greater the peril to the craft," Orich reasoned.

The Fate of Tomorrow

Mal looked around, addressing her detractors.

"Fine, fine, just bring my navigator back in one piece!" she conceded.

Taa stepped out of the craft and joined Zekoff in the tall ferns. Hearing rustling behind her, Mal turned to see Alto leaving the ship adjusting his sword belt.

"Where the fuck do you think you're going?" she incredulously demanded.

"Your navigator and the Colonel are unarmed," Alto said with a smile and shrugged.

"You're hardly ranger material." Mal said, pointing out the door into the dense woods.

He continued smiling, while his eyes tracked Taa and the Colonel moving toward the edge of the clearing.

"Then it is a good thing that I will not attempt any ranger-like activities."

"Yes, and, well, he needs the practice," Shom jabbed.

The swordmaster turned toward the prodigal. "And it is…"

"Yeah, yeah," Mal interposed, "it's all about your damn code!"

"Alas, I cannot help it," he lamented with a resigned expression.

"Yeah, well, one of these days, you're gonna have to fill me in on all the details of this code of yours. Personally, I think you're making half this shit up as you go along!"

Reaching out, he touched her cheek and met her eyes.

"I will return in no time," he assured.

She stared up at him, softened, and pulled him in for a lingering kiss. When they finally separated, she paused with eyes closed, lips still pursed, and head tilted upward.

"You fucking better," she whispered, opening her eyes.

Hopping out the doorway, Alto addressed Shom.

"Will you also be accompanying us?"

The prodigal looked at the swordmaster as if he had lost his mind.

"It's a good chance to hone your skills," Alto suggested. "You said it yourself."

"Gods no," Shom answered. "I detest rustic locals! Besides, someone's got to stay with the ship."

"I bid you good day then," Alto said, giving a casual two finger salute. "I shall expect to see you upon my return."

He waded off through the ferns to where Zekoff and Taa conferred with the archers.

"Does he always speak that way?"

Mal and Shom turned to the source of the monotone query. Orich sat cross-legged in his brother's chair, eyes closed. They grinned at each other.

"Pretty much," Mal acknowledged.

❈ ❈ ❈

Taa could feel his brother's presence back on the *Haraka*, leading the column of the dreaded Red Division archers through the brush. The feeling of the ship, its Ukko wood and structure, calmed him. A sailor by nature, he felt completely out of his element in the forest. Orich was always with him, however, and together they were strong. Now, as he pushed past bush and briar, he realized how much he missed being on the water. Sea or not, he still knew instantly which way to go. He had seen it. He could find it.

Four archers crouched and silently followed him with crossbows at the ready. Twenty feet to his right, he could hear Zekoff and Alto leading their team of archers. Both squads followed parallel paths tracking northwest with an occasional course correction necessitated by trees and undergrowth.

Suddenly, Taa stopped his group with a raise of his hand. The unmistakable odor of blood wafted in from the jungle ahead. Turning to face the archers, he waved his hand questioningly under his nose.

Did they smell it?

All nodded.

The archers resumed their cautious posture and Taa led on. He took two steps before disappearing, followed by a crashing of brush and the splash of water.

They rushed forward and peered into a six-foot deep ravine camouflaged by fallen branches and leaves. The albino appeared unharmed, lying on his back in a small field of gelatinous egg sacs deposited along the shore of a small freshwater pool. Taa's impact burst almost all of them, covering him in gray slime and embryo parts.

A swarm of giant mosquitoes raced out of the hole enraged over their destroyed brood. Taa focused on the snout of the first mosquito speeding toward him. Raising his arm and lowering his head, he sought to make a small target of his vital areas.

He could smell the rancid, dried blood on its proboscis when it pierced his upper arm and a searing pain coursed through his body. He braced for a second attack but felt nothing, and instead, he heard the buzzing of their wings flying away.

❋ ❋ ❋

"I don't give a fuck Shommy!" Mal snapped. "As soon as this little adventure is over, I'm out of here!"

They sat cross-legged before the open side doors of the airship, facing each other.

"What about Alto?" Shom asked. "I mean, granted, he's irritating, but you stood him up back in Makatooa."

Mal took the flask from Shom's hands and downed a large gulp. She nodded and stared through him.

"Yeah, he'll understand."

Shom reached over and retrieved his flask.

"And then what?" he asked incredulously. "You're just going to steal this airship? I can assure you, your success—if you succeed—will be *very* short-lived."

"The way my luck has been lately..."

Shom groaned loudly and raised his eyes skyward. "Oh, for the love of the gods, stop it! You know what your problem is, just as well as I do."

Mal fixed her gaze on the rarely serious Shom.

"And just what might that be, Shommy?" she impatiently inquired.

He drew nearer, meeting her eyes.

"You're afraid."

"Afraid of what?"

"I think," he said, "for the first time since your parents, you love someone, and that scares the shit out of you."

Orich screamed suddenly and bolted up in the pilot's seat, wrenching Mal and Shom from their conversation. The pilot sat rigidly and stared into space. They looked over at the Bailian and then back at each other.

This didn't feel good.

❈ ❈ ❈

Zekoff's team scrambled through the thick brush towards the sound of buzzing and screaming. Alto led the way, drawing his short sword and dagger while leaping branches and bushes. Two female Red Division archers flanked him, meeting his pace, and keeping their crossbows in firing position.

They arrived in time to see a swarm of foot-long mosquitoes attacking the other team. The large insects covered two archers on the ground, their proboscises buried deep within their chests. The archer's faces, paled by massive blood loss, stared up lifelessly. Three monstrous insects harassed one of the two standing archers, while the other fired bolts at any bug he could get a bead on.

The female archers flanking Alto broke the clearing and let loose their projectiles, solidly striking two of the assaulting bloodsuckers. The bugs flapped wildly falling and erupting in a shower of blood covering the immediate area.

With a defiant cry, Alto vaulted off a bowed limb and launched himself into the fray. He slashed at the bugs draining the life from the prone archers.

"Aim for the flying ones!" he screamed.

Alto spun and sliced two more flying at him. The velocity of the attack caused the engorged insects to explode in crimson geysers. The remaining archers calmly picked off the flying attackers from the clearing's edge while Alto deftly removed any lingering parasites.

An arrow silenced the final buzzing of a wounded mosquito spinning on the ground and a hush descended over them. Alto offered a hand to Taa as he struggled to climb free and noticed the Bailian's left forearm swollen with purple bruises from the bite.

"I have you, my friend," he consoled and pulled him up.

❈ ❈ ❈

"Orich! Talk to me!" Mal ordered.

The albino didn't acknowledge her but continued to sit and stare blindly into space.

"Look!" Shom said.

Orich's eyes fluttered back and forth as if watching some event. This caused Shom to shoot Mal a concerned glance.

"Has he ever done this before?"

"Not that I know of," Mal answered, "but I've never seen them apart this long before either."

※ ※ ※

Clearing the final outcropping of brush, Zekoff heard the distinctive sounds of a battle's aftermath. When he finally broke through the last bit of undergrowth, he was unprepared for what he encountered.

Blood covered the thick vegetation surrounding the shallow ravine and pool. Three archers lay dead, their pallid corpses drained and staring into the trees above. The remaining members of Red Division tended to their wounded.

Alto knelt by Taa and examined his wound. Creeping veins of blue-black poison spread just beneath his pale skin.

"You clearly were bitten…"

"Yes," Taa answered, wincing at his touch.

"And yet they did not try to drain you."

"Apparently," Taa answered with a touch of curiosity, "my blood is unappealing."

※ ※ ※

Orich snapped out of his vision with a jolt causing Shom to jump back in surprise. He looked back and forth wildly from Shom to Mal.

"Poison!" he breathlessly gasped.

❋ ❋ ❋

Alto watched the wound on the Bailian's arm continued to swell and fester. He turned to Zekoff.

"I need a fire, quickly," the swordmaster demanded.

Zekoff motioned to an archer who gathered a small pile of dry brush. She produced a steel shiv, struck it against a rock, which showered the kindling with sparks, and it ignited immediately.

Alto wiped the gore from his dagger and held it over the small flame until the tip glowed. He turned back to Taa who eyed the blade indifferently.

"I apologize my friend," Alto warned, "but this will be painful."

❋ ❋ ❋

Orich fell back into a catatonic state immediately after his outburst. Mal and Shom stood on either side of him, sharing bewildered looks. The Bailian suddenly convulsed and cried out in pain. Mal watched as a red welt in the shape of a dagger tip appeared briefly on the Bailian's upper arm before fading.

His pain threshold exceeded, Orich's eyes rolled back, and he passed out, tumbling over into Shom's arms. Shom studied Mal's apprehensive face and nodded at the unconscious albino resting against his chest.

"I'm open to any suggestions."

❋ ❋ ❋

Zekoff assessed his depleted force. Other than Alto, there were three survivors of Red Division, one man and two women. This left only four able-bodied fighters should any mishap occur. They retrieved as many of their own bolts as they could find and confiscated the quivers of the dead.

"It should be just beyond that grouping of boulders," Taa said, pointing with his good arm.

"Stay hidden and flank the area," Zekoff ordered an archer. "Only fire or reveal your position if we get into trouble."

The young woman nodded and slipped away into the thick vegetation.

"Alright, let's go have a peek."

When they rounded the boulders, they caught the distinct stench of ammonia mixed with feces and charred earth. They pushed back their revulsion and cautiously entered a strangely blighted area.

The point of the Avion's impact atrophied the jungle in a thirty-foot-long, ten-foot-wide cone of destruction. It grew narrower leading away from them, finally settling on a once-majestic giant tree trunk, now bark less and quickly decaying. Exposure to Noma left all florae brown and withered, void even of insects and animals.

They searched the area for the Avion's corpse, spreading out through parched bushes and undergrowth. The brittle vegetation crunching under foot made stealth impossible.

"This is where his flight ended," the male archer stated, cautiously circling the dead tree trunk, "but where's the body?"

"Something's not right," Taa said, perplexed by the desolation. "It feels like a portal but it's hard to pinpoint."

A sudden loud, inhuman shriek reverberated around them, followed by a very human cry of anguish.

The creature which was once an Avion stood now beside the dead tree, shifting between a translucent and a solid state. Hideous deformities riddled its formerly beautiful, humanoid body. Leathery bat-like flesh replaced the soft white feathers that covered its wings. Oozing boils corrupted its flesh with a sickly grayish hue. The previously angelic face now had no discernible nose, just two large bulbous eyes. Seven-inch, dagger-like claws extended from freakishly long arms impaling the male archer, who gurgled incomprehensibly before going limp.

Without hesitation, the female archer whipped around and fired two bolts in rapid succession, but by the time the projectiles found their mark the creature had returned to its ethereal state. The short arrows passed harmlessly through and buried themselves in the dead tree. The deceased male archer, no longer held aloft by a physical presence, fell to the ground.

It screeched again, unfolded its wings, and took after the female. Its disembodied form covered ground quickly and the lone arrow she rapidly fired passed through it, sailing into the jungle canopy. When the monster descended upon her, it retook its solid form and raked its claws across her. They split open her skull, ripping off the crown of her head. The force of the blow sent her body tumbling into Zekoff and knocked him into a large batch of dead briars.

The creature went incorporeal again and wheeled around for Alto. The swordmaster drew his blade and guardedly watched it approach. The monstrosity solidified when within five feet. Its blow made contact, but Alto deflected the wraith's attack. Its sheer power surprised him, and the collision knocked him to the ground.

It returned to an intangible apparition and advanced on him again. Alto shook his head attempting to clear it, while it closed the distance in a single hop. It landed squarely over him with a leg on either side of the swordmaster. The beast reared back, bellowed, and sent its gnarled claws plunging downward while switching to physical form.

Alto felt the creature's legs go solid. He raised his short sword and rolled against its now tangible leg. His weight threw it off balance and deflected the plummeting talons into barren ground beside him.

The beast went spectral again immediately following the attack. Alto tumbled back through its leg and up on one knee, just before the monster's next screaming lunge.

He moved his blade up to shield himself and watched the creature grow solid, bracing himself for impact. The mutant Avion's face suddenly contorted in pain. He heard the distinct thumps of three crossbow bolts piercing its back. It screamed in agony and slowly faded away.

Alto eventually composed himself and sat up. Zekoff and the last remaining member of the Red Division team slowly climbed out of the brush across the desolate clearing, picking thorns from their clothes. Taa approached as Alto rose to his feet.

"It would appear that the archer banished the creature," the Bailian said. "I no longer feel any open portals."

The surviving archer scanned the area, her crossbow still at the ready. This was the first time Alto had taken any notice of her. She was only five feet tall with short brown hair and a slightly turned-up nose. From her delicate appearance, he marveled at her ability to load and fire her weapon with such speed and accuracy. Lowering her crossbow, she warily approached the group.

"My lady, I am in your debt," Alto said, bowing.

The Red Division archer grinned shyly but remained silent.

"We got lucky on this one," Colonel Zekoff said, stroking his beard. "It could have been catastrophic."

The others sighed in agreement.

"Alright then," Zekoff ordered, "let's take care of the bodies and get back to the ship."

❊ ❊ ❊

Ambassador Bartol Aramos wrung his pudgy hands nervously and peered over his desk at the two men facing him.

"You're absolutely sure?" he anxiously probed.

Ambassador Hoyt Eldor carefully shifted his six-foot-three frame in the relatively small chair. His chiseled good looks and naturally jovial demeanor was now drawn and serious.

"My source is very reliable," Hoyt answered.

The Aramos Ambassador to Zor anxiously shifted his corpulent frame, making the chair he occupied creak in protest. "The very gods we worship fuck us at every turn!" Bartol whined.

The outburst caused Hoyt to shoot a worried glance at Stryder Aramos seated beside him. Stryder broke into a cruel smile. His thick, black hair, stylishly shaved above the ears, was accentuated by thin dark eyebrows over light blue eyes. A thin mustache complimented his regal aquiline nose and

Hoyt thought the youngest Aramos brother and head of the Quartermasters Guild, seemed bored.

"The Amarenians conspire against us and there is *nothing* we can do about it!" Bartol fumed.

"I wouldn't say, 'nothing,'" Hoyt calmly remarked to Stryder, ignoring Bartol's tantrum.

Stryder's eyes twinkled at the prospect. "Oh?"

"I don't see how you two can just sit there so calmly," Bartol added, nervously playing with one of his thick caterpillar-like eyebrows. "A mutual defense pact could prove disastrous to both our families!"

"We've got to slow down this pact," Stryder addressed Hoyt, absentmindedly stroking his mustache.

"Agreed," Hoyt answered, "and I may just know how to buy us some time."

"Excuse me!" Bartol exploded. "I'm sitting right here! I believe *I'm* still the ambassador!"

"You are, dear brother," Stryder cajoled, "however, I think we've moved beyond diplomacy."

The two brothers stared at each other for a few tense moments.

"What exactly are you saying?" Bartol asked suspiciously.

Stryder leaned forward in his chair. "I'm saying, that in our current situation my people are going to be more effective than any diplomatic efforts on your part."

Hoyt reclined, observing the edgy exchange between siblings and covered his mouth to hide his sadistic amusement. Bartol twitched and fidgeted under his younger brother's intense gaze.

"Father will hear of this!" he angrily blurted out.

Stryder kept his evil grin, nestling back in his chair. "Father already knows."

Bartol felt panic rise and shifted his gaze nervously between the two men. "I… I don't believe you."

"I really don't care," Stryder said shifting in the chair. "There are some situations, such as this one, where, given your official position, you must maintain credible deniability."

"So, you're saying I'm purposely being kept in the dark!" Bartol protested. "This... this is outrageous!"

"Be that as it may, brother," Stryder replied, "but this is the reality of the situation."

"We'll just see what Father has to say about this!"

"Indeed, we will."

The younger Aramos cleared his throat and stood to leave. Hoyt followed his lead.

"Rest assured, dear brother," Stryder calmly said, "we will keep you informed of all relevant activities. Now, if you will excuse me."

Bartol was speechless watching the two leave his chambers. A small part of him realized Stryder was right. Outraged at his exclusion, he drummed his fingers on the desk's surface and clenched his jaw tightly.

Outside in the hall, Stryder and Hoyt made their way to the main forum.

"I trust you enjoyed that?" Stryder quipped.

"Immensely!" Hoyt confessed, no longer able to contain his amusement. "May I be blunt?"

"Always."

"Between my father's recklessness and your brother's ineptness, our goals are doomed to fail."

"Oh, we have goals, have we?" Stryder asked, navigating the busy corridor.

Hoyt smiled slyly, "Indeed we do. I need to contact some people first, but a mutually beneficial plan could happen."

"I'm all ears." Stryder finally looked over at him.

"In order for any plan to move forward, I'm afraid we might have to remove certain family obstacles," Hoyt whispered.

"I admit to considering the same thing," Stryder confessed. "There's only one problem."

"And what would that be?" Hoyt cautiously queried.

"Eliminating family members from the picture will only raise attention to any endeavor we might put in motion."

"What would you suggest then?"

Stryder grinned malevolently. "Make them irrelevant."

❂ ❂ ❂

Mal turned around in her chair for the hundredth time since they had taken off from the clearing. She looked past Taa beside her, nursing his wounded arm; past Orich at the wheel, deftly maneuvering the *Haraka* over the rooftops of Zor; and her leering gaze settled on the surviving member of Red Division. The bitch was sitting entirely too close to Alto!

The way her lingering gaze was so attentive, along with her constant flirtatious smile was really pissing Mal off. The swordmaster remaining oblivious to the blatantly obvious attention to him somehow angered Mal even more. However, the fact it bothered her, proved the most infuriating.

Shom sat against the hull opposite Alto and watched Mal's predicament with amusement. When Orich banked the craft for final approach to Air Station Three, it sent the Red Division archer sliding into Alto and he caught her with his arm. They immediately separated, but the incident proved enough to send Mal into a brief fist-clenching moment.

Shom looked over at Zekoff, seated beside him, wondering if he had noticed the drama as well. The colonel apparently saw nothing and just sat cross-legged staring into space, but the gentle thump of the airship touching down broke him from his trance.

Everyone got to their feet when the craft settled, and the engine whirring died. Mal's eyes bore holes into Alto. Alto caught her death stare, and quizzically shrugged.

The group disembarked and stood beside the ship in the hangar. Zekoff turned to the young archer and put his hand on her shoulder.

"You did well today," he said in a low, tired voice. "I'm putting you in for a commendation. You are dismissed."

She nodded her thanks to her superior then glanced over at Alto. Her lips seemed to purse when the corners of her mouth rose slightly. The swordmaster returned the smile and bowed slightly. Mal smacked him on the arm when the archer walked off.

Alto was genuinely confused. "May I ask what that was for?"

Mal put her hands on her hips, giving him the *"you know"* expression.

When Shom snickered at the interaction, Mal reached around and smacked him too.

"Hey!" he protested, rubbing his arm.

The colonel ignored the antics and looked over the group with a somber expression.

"This city," he began. "And probably the whole continent, owe you a great debt of gratitude. I'm sure once they read my report, we can find a more practical way to express our thanks."

Zekoff gazed off into space. For a moment, his exhaustion became evident to the others.

"Now, if you will excuse me," he said, "the Kan will be upon us shortly and I have something important to tend to."

With that statement, Zekoff turned and trudged off. His sense of melancholy lingered in the air around them.

"Well, I don't know about the rest of you, but saving the Annigan is thirsty work!" Shom offered, breaking the mood. "I say a bit of refreshment is in order here."

The others nodded in agreement.

"Splendid!" he proclaimed. "I know an inn that makes a goose pie *so good* you'll be willing to turn to a life of crime to get more."

"You *can* eat goose?" Shom asked, addressing Orich-Taa.

"Yes," they replied in unison.

"Then we're off."

Shom noted Mal still giving Alto the silent treatment while they left the hangar.

"Good thing you're not the jealous type," Shom whispered in her ear.

❉   ❉   ❉

Colonel Zekoff stood for what seemed like an eternity staring at his cottage. The red security rope laced across the front door dramatically contrasted with the white walls and green trim.

After a long sigh, he walked up to the porch, removed the rope, and entered. The room was exactly how he had left it two cycles ago. He looked around at the broken furniture and blood-stained floor.

Jaanam was there too, just as he had left her. He walked over to the table where she lay. The same table she had served countless meals on. The same table they had made love on when they first got it.

He approached her linen-covered body and touched the "love garden" bouquet lying on her chest. Leaning down, he kissed her forehead.

"It's time, my love," he whispered.

He retrieved two silver coins from his pocket and slowly placed one over each eye before gently picking her body up. He carried her outside and stepped into the street, turning toward the docks.

The walk was thankfully short and he stared straight ahead the entire time, tears streaming down his face. He ignored those all along his path who stopped and bowed their heads in respect. He ignored the flies buzzing around the enormous pile of Cul-Tal pelts stacked in the center of Judgement Square.

Zekoff stopped just beyond the Northern Docks at the Temple of EEtah House Nur. He had passed by that building countless times over the years. Now, walking up the three steps to its landing, it all seemed so different.

When he passed through the gigantic, inverted shark-fin architecture looming over its massive double doors, a seven-foot-tall female EEtah in orange robes stepped out to greet him. She stood before the grieving human and her black, unblinking eyes betrayed no emotion.

Zekoff nodded to her. She reached up and removed the two silver pieces from Jaanam's eyes, before tenderly taking the body from the colonel. She walked ceremoniously through the cavernous main temple with Zekoff trailing behind, head bowed. They exited out the rear of the temple, onto a short, wide dock, with a lone platform sticking out over the water. The Nur Priestess placed Jaanam on the platform and turned to Zekoff, who stood on the other side.

"Do you have anything to say?" she asked in a guttural tone.

Zekoff stared down at the lifeless body of his enduring companion and brushed away the tears.

"Goodbye my love," he choked, touching Jaanam's forehead. "Soon, we will always be together."

He collected himself, and then nodded at the priestess. She turned to face the sea, raised her hands, and uttered a quick prayer in her own staccato language. Then, reaching down, she tipped the end of the platform and the body slipped into the water.

Zekoff stared at the area in the water where she went under. The flowers of her "love garden" bouquet surfaced when the ripples faded away. Zekoff watched them float out into the Shallow Sea and his tears finally stopped when he lost sight of them. The commander of the City Guards then teetered and toppled over unconscious onto the deck, finally succumbing to grief and exhaustion.

❈ ❈ ❈

Stryder Aramos sat one of the four round tables containing the high stakes card games in the Shimol Plat Casino. A noisy, upper-class human crowd, sprinkled with the occasional Bailian and Outer Clan EEtah packed the gaming club. faces.

He tuned out his surroundings and focused on his fellow players' somber expressions, while fighting back the urge to rejoice over the cards he just drew. Perhaps his luck *was* turning around. Nearly out of gold, he decided to cash out if he lost this hand. He tossed two gold coins from the dwindling stack before him into the pile in the table's center.

"I'm in for two," he proclaimed.

He watched the reactions of the other three players. They all matched his bet. A man across the table, whom he had never played with or even seen before, looked back with a stone face.

"And I will raise your bet five gold," the man confidently proclaimed, moving his money into the pot.

Stryder saw, from the corner of his eye, the players on either side folding their hands. They grumbled about it being too rich for their blood. The young Aramos studied his opponent warily. They appeared roughly the same age. His opponent's clean-shaven face, short blonde hair and blue silk shirt radiated wealth.

"You're bluffing!" Stryder announced.

"Maybe, but it's going to cost you five gold to find out."

Stryder smiled deviously. "Very well then, five it is... and another five, just to make it interesting."

The royal moved his remaining coins into the pile. Their eyes locked. Stryder detected a hint of doubt, as perfectly manicured hands called the raise and placed the additional five.

A moment passed with the two gamblers assessing the situation and each other.

"So, I guess this is it..." Stryder laid his cards out before him.

The man's face fell when he saw the three Tower Cards.

"Well, I guess it was just a matter of time before your luck changed," he conceded, watching Stryder rake in the gold pieces.

The young royal felt a wave of exhilaration at the win, and relief as he stacked the coins. A losing streak always put him in a sour mood which would last long into the next cycle. Pocketing the coins, he felt a distinctive change in the room's atmosphere. His loins tingled slightly when a small but palpable sexual energy swept around him.

That's when he noticed Soshi adorned in her royal-blue court dress. Stryder found himself transfixed by the way her long brown hair swept down around her face and rested just above the gentle curves of her bare breasts. He knew he wasn't alone in his feelings. The entire inn, both male and female, watched her gracefully cross the room and stand at the bar.

"My luck has *definitely* changed," he stated as he rose, all the while keeping Soshi within his bedazzled gaze. "Deal me out,"

He approached her confidently, despite the lustful tingling that increased with each step. He had to keep reminding himself that this was business. Even though she was the newest member of the Amarenian Ambassador's Court, she still more than likely had valuable information. His wit and charm had always served him before, he reasoned, so why not see how it works on an Amarenian?

By the time Stryder made it to Soshi's spot at the bar, she had already attracted a small group. The two men and one floor prostitute placed themselves strategically around her, all attempting to strike up a conversation. She smiled politely at each but remained silent. A stern expression and nod of the head from the royal scattered the three away. She finally looked up at him when he leaned against the bar facing her.

"You should buy me a drink." Stryder assertively began.

"Why would I buy you a drink," she asked with a sly smile, "when at least a dozen people in here are trying to buy *me* one?"

"None of them are me," Stryder confidently said.

"Tavernkeep?" Soshi called out to the bar. "A bottle of your best and two glasses." Turning her attention back to Stryder she gazed seductively. "I try not to miss an opportunity to enjoy the company of a creature as handsome as you."

"I completely understand," Stryder said pulling out the stool and sat next to her. He indicated the seat next to her and she demurely sat down.

"Your dress is striking," he said, his eyes lingering on her exposed breasts. "Amarenian, is it not?"

"Yes," Soshi said with a nod, "I just arrived four cycles ago."

The bar tender set the bottle and two glasses before them. He turned to the noble for payment, but Soshi smiled and slid the man a gold coin. He looked confused for a moment and then smiled back, lingering in the presence of two aesthetically captivating humans.

"That will be all, thank you," Stryder said curtly.

"Yes… Of course, my lord," the tavernkeep sputtered before quickly turning his attention to other patrons.

"I'm Stryder," he proudly proclaimed, "Stryder Aramos."

"Soshanna," she said melodically, offering her hand.

He immediately took it and raised it tenderly to his lips.

"So, what brings a lovely woman out into the dampness of the Kan?" he asked, his breath warming the back of her hand.

Soshi gently removed her hand from his and picked up her drink from the bar.

"Quite simply, you."

With that simple, yet sultry declaration, she took a sip. For some unexplained reason, the statement unnerved him a bit, but he felt the distinct beginnings of an erection.

"Flattering," Stryder admitted, sipping his drink. "Why would that be?"

She stared into the glass for a moment before answering.

"My sisters and I differ in opinion as to who our new friends should be."

"Interesting."

Soshi pouted her lips. "I just think if you're going to choose friends, then they should be powerful ones."

Sipping her drink again, she gazed into his eyes.

"Don't you agree, Lord Aramos?"

"I do," Stryder concurred.

"And you being so handsome is a rather fortunate bonus to diplomacy."

The royal returned his gaze to her breasts and her nipples hardened under his scrutiny.

"A toast then!" he suggested enthusiastically.

Soshi nodded, raised her glass, and touched his.

"To a profitable business union!" Stryder toasted.

Soshi took the last sip from her glass and hungrily eyed Stryder. "Well, hopefully not *all* business?"

Stryder placed his empty glass on the bar. He stared briefly at it, then back up at the doe eyed beauty looking longingly at him.

"The baths are just next door," he offered, in a low, suggestive voice.

"That sounds wonderful."

❄ ❄ ❄

Sareeta exercised caution, as usual, in answering the door during the Kan. She let Soshi in and led her back to Alosus' private chambers, which reeked with the musky odor of recent sex. They sat on the side of the ambassador's bed while the Hill Sister stood watch.

"I'm sorry to disturb you, Esteemed," Soshi began.

Alosus waved her hand dismissively. "Nonsense, you have something?"

Soshi nodded, a concerned look etched upon her face.

"I just left a session with Stryder Aramos," she said, shaking her head in disgust. "That is one evil man!"

"He's the head of the Quartermasters Guild," the Amarenian ambassador replied, "that goes without saying. So, what did you discover?"

"He and the ambassadors of Eldor and Aramos plot to disrupt and even stop our talks with the other houses."

Alosus silently pondered how Stryder could have discovered their plans. After a moment, she gave a heavy sigh shaking her head.

"The tavernkeep was spying on us," she concluded.

"Esteemed," Soshi began, leaning forward and placing her hand over the ambassador's, "they'll stop at nothing to make sure our mutual defense pact, and any diplomatic trade, fails."

"Why?"

"Eldor still has designs on commandeering our fields at home. The only bright spot is, House Aramos secretly doesn't want Eldor gaining a stranglehold on all food production, since they already hold the eastern agricultural islands."

Alosus contemplated Soshi's last statement. "This could be helpful in the future. Right now, we've got to get these negotiations beyond prying eyes and ears."

Soshi glanced over quizzically. "Esteemed?"

"Sareeta," Alosus ordered, "go to Ambassador Valdur's chambers. Soshi, you go get Ambassador Whitmar. I'll find Pierce Calden. Meet back at The Demon's Gate as quickly as possible. The Kan will lift soon."

The bewildered expression still framed Soshi's face. Alosus stood, looking determined.

"They wanted embassies in Amarenia," she explained. "This will be the perfect excuse. We're going to take this little party home with us."

❋ ❋ ❋

Patrol Captain Gasata de Munn was always an early riser, a habit he developed in his youth while working on the family farm in the Munn region north of Zor. Now, as the grand turine rang fifteen bells, he stepped into the foyer of the Main City Guard Station in Judgement Square. He opened the door, nodded to three guards on their way out, and quickly shut the door behind him.

He closed his eyes and took a deep breath, glad to be away from the stench of the ever-growing pile of Cul-Ta pelts rotting in the plaza. When he opened them again, he discovered both Stryder and Bartol Aramos standing beside the Command Sergeant's desk.

"Well," Gasata commented, not hiding his surprise, "you're both up early."

"Captain," Bartol asked, stepping forward, "if we could have a word?"

Gasata nodded to the sergeant on duty and walked past the desk. "In my office."

The Aramos brothers followed down a short hall into a spartan room with only a sizable desk and two chairs for furniture. On one wall, a giant map of the city displayed the boundaries of the various patrol divisions. The adjacent wall held a large roster of names, times and dates.

The captain stood at his desk and briefly scanned the copious reports which had arrived during the last Kan. Bartol Aramos fidgeted nervously, occasionally stroking an eyebrow.

"Captain," he said, "we apologize for ambushing you just as you arrived."

"No need to apologize," Gasata said glancing up. "I've just come from visiting Colonel Zekoff."

"Oh, yes, we heard, how is the colonel?"

Gasata turned his attention back to sifting through the paperwork before him.

"Still unconscious," he said after a moment. "He's over at the Clerria House. They say he'll be fine."

"Excellent, excellent," Bartol exclaimed, with a hint of sarcasm. "We would hate to lose such a fine civil servant!"

The Fate of Tomorrow

The captain stopped and slowly peered up at the ambassador.

"Colonel Zekoff is the finest commander I have ever served under," he said defiantly. "The man is sixty-one. He just lost his wife two cycles ago and still managed to personally close two major cases before the Kan set in!"

"Captain," Bartol said, opening his arms in a gesture of sincerity. "Please, I meant no disrespect..."

Unconvinced, Gasata returned to sorting papers. "What can I do for House Aramos today?"

Stryder cleared his throat.

"Well, Captain," he began. "To be brief..."

"I would appreciate it."

"We need you to detain the Amarenian ambassador's party!" the head Quartermaster said, bristling at the captain's arrogance.

The Patrol Division captain stopped sorting papers and faced the two.

"You want me to arrest the Amarenian ambassador and her entourage?" he incredulously asked.

"No," Bartol said, again raising his hands in a placating gesture. "No, not arrest, merely detain."

"On what grounds?!"

"We suspect one of the ambassador's party of espionage," Stryder said, leaning in close.

"Shouldn't you be taking this up with our Spymaster then?" Gasata asked.

"No," Stryder countered, "it concerns smuggling, which is why it's quartermaster's business. Naturally, it's classified."

"Naturally."

"With Colonel Zekoff being, well, um, indisposed," Bartol added, "we naturally came to you."

The representatives of House Aramos now held Gasata's full attention. He finally sat down behind his desk and offered them a seat.

"How in the name of the gods do you propose we do this without starting a diplomatic shitstorm?" he asked.

"This calls for delicate handling," Bartol softly suggested. "We only have suspicions and need to ask some questions. It cannot appear like an arrest. Simply bring them to the Aramos Embassy in the forum."

"And should they refuse your invitation to chat?"

"Well," Bartol said, laughing nervously, "I hardly think an ironmark or the Red Division would be necessary."

Gasata stared at them, unamused.

"What I mean to say is," Bartol continued, "we must place a gentle emphasis on the *importance* of the meeting, for sake of diplomacy between East and West."

The captain sat back and eyed the two suspiciously.

"No matter what, Captain," Stryder added confidently, "we shouldn't allow them to leave the city until they are cleared of these suspicions."

Captain Gasata held his wary stare while he gathered up the papers and stacked them noisily.

"I'll assign my top lieutenant and have him take a six-guard contingency," the captain offered. "I imagine they're in the Amarenian Suite?"

"Very well," Stryder said, standing, "we know you are busy. Thank you for your cooperation, Captain."

Bartol rose and bowed slightly. "Yes, yes, thank you."

Gasata remained silent but his expression clearly said, "fuck you," and they turned and left immediately.

❀ ❀ ❀

The Fate of Tomorrow

Tate Whitmar threw a piece of clothing into an open traveling case, his shirtless muscular chest heaved, and his face furrowed in uncertainty when he turned to face Soshi.

"I'm sorry but I've got a ship to catch in less than a deci, ma'am," he protested. "We can't keep Grandmama waiting, you know."

"Ambassador," Soshi insisted. "I can assure you it is of critical importance!"

"You said that already," he flatly stated.

Tate reached down and tossed a shirt in the over-packed case and struggled to close it.

"Aramos and Eldor has somehow discovered our intended mutual defense pact," Soshi pleaded. "They will do everything they can to stop it!"

"They can't do shit," he proclaimed, forcing the case shut. "Now if you'll excuse me, I've got family duties at home."

Soshi stared in appreciation at his back muscles flexing when Tate reached across the bed to grab the last remaining shirt. She reached inside her skirt's side pocket and withdrew her little finger, its nail coated with white powder While he pulled the tunic over his head, she snorted the powder up her nose.

"Please express my sincere apologies to Esteemed," Tate said adjusting the fit.

After strapping on his short sword, he slowly faced her. The eroticism of Soshi's features, not present before, suddenly made the Whitmar ambassador catch his breath. For what seemed like an embarrassingly long moment, his gaze followed every twisting lock of shoulder-length brown hair framing her dark round eyes and pouty, sensual lips. Eventually, he fixated on one ringlet falling across on her bare breasts. How had he not noticed this beautiful woman before?

His heart raced when she stepped closer. She sensuously pouted and placed a gentle hand on his chest. A jolt of electricity pulsed through him with her touch and settled in his groin.

"It's very important," she purred, looking up at him.

His resolve melted and he leaned into her soft and warm kiss. When Soshi's tongue slipped through Tate's lips, he felt light-headed. Breaking, Soshi stroked his cheek.

"We really must go."

Tate shook his head to clear his mind. He reached over, grabbed his travel case, and pulled it over his left shoulder.

"Fine," he said, meeting her eyes. "Let's go see what's so important."

❂ ❂ ❂

Lieutenant Vanir de Tuath looked down both sides of the T-shaped corridor and then back to his squad. He ran his hand through his thick red hair and nodded grimly. Six veteran sergeants, three women and three men, stared attentively. He pointed out a door.

"The Amarenians are there," Vanir said to the three female guards.

Turning his attention to the remaining men, he pointed down the opposite end of the hall and raised his other hand.

"Calden," he said, raising one finger.

"Whitmar." He raised a second.

"Valdur." A third went up.

"Make sure there are no Amarenians in their chambers," he said, handing out keys. "Knock first. If there is no answer, enter and look around. Send for me immediately should there be an encounter."

Nodding again, the guards took the keys and headed off in opposite directions. The female guards arrived at the Amarenians door first, but no one answered their knock.

The male guards were almost upon Ambassador Calden's room when Tate and Soshi stepped out from the room next door. Both sides froze, clearly surprised at the sudden encounter.

Lieutenant Vanir's throat tightened. He nervously gripped the hilt of his sword, composed himself and stepped forward.

"Ambassador Whitmar!" he condescendingly greeted. "An early start for *you*, isn't it?"

Tate eyed the guards warily.

"An early ship to catch."

Vanir smirked and nodded knowingly at Soshi. "And your friend?"

"She's coming with me," Tate stated firmly.

"I'm afraid not, Ambassador," Vanir countered. "My superiors request her presence for an urgent meeting."

Tate clenched his jaw and puffed out his chest. He deliberately met each man's eye until his gaze finally rested on the lieutenant.

"A meeting she's going to miss."

Vanir clasped his hands behind his back and shook his head. "Ambassador, I..."

"There really isn't any discussion here," Tate interrupted, "Lieutenant Vanir, isn't it?"

Upon hearing his name, Vanir felt his palms perspire.

"Y... Yes."

"Let me spell this out for you," Tate continued. "This woman is in *my* custody. I have to be on a ship in less than a deci or there *will* be an international incident."

The lieutenant cleared his throat, nervously nodding. "I understand, sir, b-but you must understand I have my orders."

The Whitmar ambassador's brow furrowed. He casually jerked a thumb down the hall.

"Do your orders also include violating diplomatic immunity by breaking into the Amarenian ambassador's chambers?"

Vanir's heart pounded when he turned in time to see the three female guards unlock the door and enter. He tried speaking but couldn't form words fast enough. Sensing fear and confusion, Tate pounced.

"Look Vanir, you're Zekoff's prodigy, so I know you're not *stupid*. Are you really going to detain the Sovereign Hand of Whitmar? That would be a career-ending decision. You *do* want to make captain, don't you?"

Tate motioned to Vanir's three guards frozen in place.

"Are your fine sergeants here interested in advancement?"

He took Soshi by the arm and insolently walked past them.

"We never met."

Vanir's fists clenched watching them leave. His freckled and normally youthful face contorted with rage and he reluctantly turned away.

The three female sergeants returned from investigating the Amarenian quarters. Wordlessly, they shook their heads. Vanir slowly felt the anger recede, replaced by the driving desire to uncover what was *really* going on, and perhaps find a way to avenge his humiliation.

"Follow them," he ordered two of the female guards.

They immediately trotted off after Tate and Soshi. He addressed the remaining four.

"We're going to Demon's Gate."

"Sir?"

"Patterns, sergeant, patterns."

❂ ❂ ❂

The Fate of Tomorrow

Tate and Soshi made their way out of the sprawling complex just as the forum came to life. Soshi's heart still raced while the Whitmar ambassador guided her by the arm out into the major boulevard.

Soshi attempted to turn toward the Shimol Plat and Demon's Gate when they approached the first intersection, but Tate continued his gentle but firm grip heading the other direction. Soshi resisted and it surprised her when he just pulled her along.

"You can't go to meet your friends, Soshi," Tate said. "You're going to have to come with me."

Surprise turned to indignation, and she snatched her arm free.

"Horse shit!" She spat. "This is important!"

Tate spun furiously, feeling his frustration rise at yet another delay.

"Don't you think we're being followed?" he asked. "If you leave my side, they have you!"

Soshi's eyes widened with a building panic. Tate leaned forward and, with a simple smile, broke the tension.

"Look, I'll get us there, I promise," he assured. "We'll just be a few cycles late, but we need to leave now!"

❀ ❀ ❀

Heavy morning traffic rolled through the Demon's Gate. Empty wagons pulled into the Shimol Plat to be filled with goods and handiwork from the many high-end merchants and crafters calling the neighborhood home. Once loaded, they made their way down to the docks for shipping. Streams of people navigated the congested streets seeking the various wares.

Sareeta stood before the ambassadors, keeping a watchful eye on the crowd. Pierce Calden and Joc' Valdur listened intently to Alosus making her argument for moving negotiations to her homeland.

"You really think House Aramos and Eldor would try something?" Joc' asked, his face betraying his skepticism.

"I'm certain!" Alosus demanded. "Soshi got it out of Stryder Aramos last Kan."

"What do they have in mind?"

"I don't know exactly," Alosus responded. "However, they used the term, *'drastic measures.'*"

Pierce and Joc' traded anxious looks.

"Esteemed!" Sareeta called out.

They turned to see Lieutenant Vanir across the courtyard pointing them out to a squad of city guards.

"I don't know what he wants," Pierce said, sighing, "but it doesn't look good.

"I'm not so sure I want to stick around and find out," Joc' added.

"Where's Tate Whitmar and your assistant?" Pierce asked Alosus.

She nervously glanced around. The teeming masses slowed the guards crossing the courtyard towards them.

"I don't know," she said, "but we've got to get out of here now!"

When they turned to make their way down the street, the guards picked up their pace. Alosus nervously turned and watched the pursuing guards close the distance.

"Sareeta, we need a distraction!"

The Hill Sister scanned the crowds and noticed the owner of a wagon laden with linens, standing on the buckboard in a heated argument with another wagon driver blocking his path. Sareeta quickly drew her short sword and poked the horse in the hind quarter. The beast whinnied loudly and reared up on its back legs, sending driver and bolts of brightly colored fabric into the busy street.

This mishap instigated a domino effect, causing the other horse to panic and buck furiously, throwing the second driver into a cluster of citizens fleeing the mayhem. Several small casks of oil lurched out of the wagon's bed and cracked open on the street. People and animals began slipping on the slick cobblestones.

"This way!" Pierce directed, motioning to a small side street.

They slipped from the square and rushed toward an adjoining avenue with Sareeta holding rear guard. Exiting onto another busy road Alosus looked over questioningly at Sareeta.

"They didn't follow," the Hill Sister noted.

Nodding, the Amarenian ambassador swallowed hard and turned to her western counterparts.

"What now? They're probably watching the docks too. Securing passage will be all but impossible."

"I've got an idea," Joc' said, stroking his chin slyly.

He suddenly headed north up the street.

"This way!"

❈ ❈ ❈

The Valdurian ambassador and party's arrival on the main deck of Air Station Three transformed the normal bustle of activity into a frenzy. The Air Boss, a short, thin man with gray hair, just finished signaling a large transport to take off when he noticed Joc'. He placed his hand over his heart and briefly bowed his head.

"Good morning, sir. What brings you around our humble operation?"

Joc' casually scanned around the hangar and put his hands on his hips.

"We're looking for the *Haraka*."

The air boss pointed. "She's over there. The captain hasn't arrived yet."

Joc' nodded his thanks and motioned for the others to follow. He took a few steps and turned back.

"How many marines are on duty?" he asked the air boss.

"Standard security detachment of six, sir."

"Send their commander over."

He bobbed his head and disappeared in the assortment of workers and airships. Joc' turned and saw both Amarenians staring about in wonder.

"It can be a little overwhelming at first," he reassured. "Now, let's go have a look."

They found the *Haraka* with both side doors open. Orich knelt in the back, adjusting one of the tail fins bent skirting the forest canopy. He stopped and turned to face them when they approached. Taa stepped out from the ship and onto the ramp, wiping his hands on a cloth. The ambassadorial party failed to hide their surprise at the sight of the twin Bailian albinos.

"Good morning!" Joc' called out.

Orich-Taa gazed at the group blankly and chanted their reply together in their usual deadpan, "Good morning."

"We haven't met," Joc' said, approaching the two. "I'm Joc' Valdur and these are my friends."

The albinos continued their slightly unnerving stare.

"We are Orich-Taa," they intoned in unison.

"I understand your captain has not arrived," Joc' continued. "It is critical that we get in touch immediately."

The twins turned to face each other, their expressions blank, but their eyes seemed to speak to each other.

"Meaning time is a bit of a factor," he added.

"Very well," they droned.

The Fate of Tomorrow

Orich-Taa closed their eyes and began a low, identical incantation under their breath.

❊ ❊ ❊

Mal slept in Alto's arms with her head resting on his chest. The rise and fall of his breath acted like a metronome, lulling her into deep slumber. Then, a rhythmic pulsing rose from the depths of the darkness. It started slowly and then built to a rousing shout, pushing past her curtains of unconsciousness.

The Spice Rat cried out, shoved herself away from Alto and sprung up to a sitting position in the bed. Alto bolted up beside her, simultaneously reaching up to the headboard and unsheathing his short sword. Mal heard the steel being drawn and placed a reassuring hand on his chest.

"No," she panted.

Alto lowered the weapon and sheathed it.

"A bad dream?"

Mal tried to compose herself. She shook her head no.

"We need to get to the ship, *now!*" she emphatically stated when she could finally speak.

❊ ❊ ❊

Shom stumbled out into the daylight. His head pounded, but he figured he had stopped drinking just short of begging the gods for the sweet release of death. He needed a remedy and, on the south docks of Zor, that only meant one thing. It had to be hot, meaty, and greasy. In short, a steaming bowl of Yugo.

Standing before the stall, Shom basked in the odoriferous steam that poured out into the street. The smell of meat, vegetables and noodles made him feel better just standing there.

The middle-aged food vender, with her hair pulled up, tersely snapped Shom out of his hunger trance.

"Hey! What you want?!"

The badly hung-over prodigal pointed to the large pot simmering behind her and gestured for a single serving. When she turned, he placed a single copper coin on the narrow counter. While the merchant filled his bowl, Shom surveyed the hectic streets around him.

He could hear the rhythmic sounds of street musicians just within earshot to his right. Normally, in his current state, he considered this form of entertainment a cacophony to avoid, but this was different.

The food vendor thrust the bowl upon the counter and moved on to the next customer. Shom picked it up, sipped the broth and his eyes rolled back in his head with pleasure.

"Ambrosia, my dear lady!" he trumpeted his approval.

The lady looked over and grunted. He took another sip and turned back to the street. While Shom walked, he continued to drink and munch on the sublime concoction, gravitating toward the music. With each step it called to him. The rhythm resonated in his mind, and he found himself chewing to the beat.

Shom stood before three percussionists, each oblivious to their surroundings, totally immersed in the moment. The prodigal stared at them, his foot tapping to the cadence, and finished the last bit of the grease-soaked bowl of grain.

He could hear it plainly now. It was right there in the rhythm. Their music was speaking to him.

"Get to the ship."

"Get to the ship."

"Get to the ship."

❋ ❋ ❋

Mal's heart raced from practically dragging Alto across the flight deck of Air Station Three, heading for her airship. Flight crews stopped and stared at the five-foot-six woman, pulling the much larger man by the hand.

"Perhaps you could give me a clue to the reason for this expediency?" Alto inquired.

"I'll let ya know when we get there," she replied.

To her relief, she found the *Haraka* just where she left it. While Orich-Taa attended to the ship, Ambassador Alosus stood on deck before the open door to the bridge, talking with two men she didn't recognize.

Mal nodded at Sareeta when she yanked Alto past her advance guard. The Hill Sister snickered at the helpless expression on his face. Orich stepped before her at the top of the gangway.

"Good morning captain," he greeted, "Sorry to disturb your rest, but these sentients insisted on your presence."

"It's okay, Orich," she said with a forced smile. "I had to get up anyway."

Mal let go of Alto's hand and approached the group. Alosus' face erupted in delight seeing her, and she broke from the two strangers and advanced with open arms.

"Maluria!"

The Spice Rat met Alosus' warm embrace with a reserved clasp. The Amarenian ambassador's lips moved to Mal's ear.

"I *am* glad to see you," she whispered. "But we need to talk about that document you were *supposed* to destroy."

Breaking, the two stared at each other, before Alosus returned to her two companions.

"Sovereign Hand Joc' Valdur and Pierce Calden, may I present Maluria de Scoth, the commander of this vessel."

"Yeah," Mal said, meeting their formal bows with a nervous nod, "good to meet you."

Introductions complete, all eyes turned to Alto standing behind her silently. Observing their scrutiny, he stood at attention and slightly bowed.

"Alto de Gom, at your service!"

Alto's formal greeting pleasantly surprised Joc' and Pierce. Mal just shook her head and took a step closer to the trio.

"He may talk funny," she said scoffing and grinning at the same time. "But he's a genuine badass. So, what the fuck's going on?"

"Well, isn't this a pleasant surprise!" Shom announced loudly from across the hangar. "I recognize everyone here!"

"You look like death on a cracker!" Mal yelled back, annoyed at the interruption. "Where have you been?"

"I've been consorting with the common folk of the Southern Docks," Shom said, crossing over to them. "Lovely people, don't you know… naturally a certain amount of inebriation is always required for any long-term exposure… be that as it may…"

Shom noticed all eyes fixed on him.

"A qualifying question before I proceed any further," he added, raising a finger. "Is my presence necessary to this conversation?"

"No!" Mal and Joc' answered in unison.

"Is there anything I need to know?" he asked, chuckling.

"We're leaving soon," Mal tonelessly replied.

"Splendid!"

Shom teetered a bit, spun facing the *Haraka,* and gestured drunkenly toward the open hatch.

"I do believe I'll go and secure my spot."

Shom then staggered up the ramp and disappeared into the craft.

The air boss approached Joc' with the marine commander. His massive frame filled his green jumpsuit. A full-sized crossbow hung from his shoulders, with bolts holstered along each thigh, and he kept a short sword sheathed horizontally along the small of his back. Joc' nodded at him.

"If you will excuse me," he said to his companions.

When Joc' stepped aside with his two subordinates, Mal turned to the other two ambassadors. "Is there anyone missing?"

"Soshi," offered Alosus.

"Tate Whitmar," replied Pierce.

Mal tensed her lips watching the marine and air boss scurry in different directions while Joc' hurried back.

"Decision time!" she stated ominously.

"I guess we're on our way to Amarenia!" Joc' announced.

"Should we leave Soshi and Tate?" Alosus asked the Valdurian ambassador.

Joc' shrugged helplessly.

"I don't see that we have any choice."

"Yeah, well, we really don't have any choice now!" Mal proclaimed, noticing Vanir's squad entering from across the flight deck.

"Let's go!" she ordered.

Everyone hurriedly boarded the *Haraka* and took their stations. Alto glanced over at Shom passed out in his seat and reflected how obliviousness was a gift.

Vanir's eyes busily searched the crowded hangar. He was sure they were here somewhere. He was just about to order his crew to spread out, when five Valdurian marines confronted them with crossbows lowered, but at the ready. The two sides nervously faced off until the marine sergeant broke the tense silence.

"Good day, lieutenant," he said, "I am Sergeant Ajax of the Valdurian Marine Security Detachment. What is your business here?"

"Good day, sergeant," Vanir answered, slightly amused. "I wish to speak with your commanding officer."

"Sir, I am in command."

"Oh, I see," Vanir said, his tone shifting from amused to condescending. "Sergeant, here's what I need. We believe there are individuals…"

"Sir, with all due respect," Sergeant Ajax snapped. "Providing for your needs is not my duty. The security of this station *is*, however."

The two stared at each other. Vanir felt his anger rise but forced himself to keep a civil demeanor.

"Sergeant, technically I outrank you and…"

"Sir, I would remind you we are not under the same command," the sergeant countered. "Also, you and your guards are, by law, now standing on Valdurian soil!"

Mal and Joc' stared out the windshield of the *Haraka* at the confrontation and traded worried glances.

"The air boss cleared us for priority departure status," Joc' stated.

"Well, why didn't ya say so!" Mal said, swinging forward in her chair. "Orich-Taa, get us the fuck out of here!"

Taa closed the hatch and jumped into the seat next to her while Orich fired up the engine. Joc' watched Lieutenant Vanir tremble with frustration before spinning abruptly and leading his men out of the hangar. The *Haraka* slipped out of the massive opening and into the blue skies of Lumina.

"We're still gonna have to put down somewhere and take on provisions," Mal warned. "We got nothing."

"Yes, our departure was rather abrupt," Alto agreed.

Mal turned back to the ambassadors. "And I'd still like to know how we're getting paid for this little trip?"

The Fate of Tomorrow

"House Valdur will compensate you well," Joc' assured. "If you play your cards right, you might just get an airship out of the deal."

Mal shot him a skeptical eyebrow raise. Joc' pointed over to Shom, who was reclining against the hull of the craft, sleeping soundly.

"Who do you think arranged the use of the *Haraka* with me?" he asked.

Mal looked at Shom, who was drooling a bit, and then back at the ambassador.

"You must have lost some kind of big-time bet to owe him like that," she said, laughing.

"He saved my family," Joc' replied, without smiling.

"The Unification War?" Mal asked, clearly astonished.

"Agents of House Eldor came for us," Joc' said, nodding solemnly. "Shom tipped us off and got us to safety. That act cost him dearly in his family's eyes and left him a prodigal. I imagine his father gave him the responsibility of couriering the secret invasion plans back in Makatooa as one last chance to prove himself."

Mal considered her snoring ex with a newfound respect.

"Yeah, and we all know how well *that* went."

❄ ❄ ❄

Three frustrated men clustered around the corner of a conference table and stared each other down. The tension in the room grew palpable. Bartol Aramos fidgeted and drummed his fingers on the table.

"I knew it!" he yelled. "I just knew it wouldn't work!"

"For the love of the gods," Hoyt roared, bolting from his seat, and leaning over the table into Bartol's face, "you whine more than a puff boy with a cock up his ass!"

The Aramos ambassador reeled back in his chair, his eyes locked on the enraged man before him. Bartol opened his mouth but could only sputter. His eyes bulged, a vein on the side of his neck protruded and throbbed.

Stryder reached over and gently touched Hoyt's arm.

"This accomplishes nothing."

The Eldorian ambassador yanked his arm away and plopped back down with a huff. Stryder took a few moments to make sure the scene calmed enough before proceeding.

"Alright, our last plan did not meet with success."

"You mean it failed miserably!" Bartol said, finally finding his voice. "I told you this was a ridiculous plan from the start!"

Stryder eyes narrowed, and nostrils flared, but he remained silent. With a final, discouraged growl, Hoyt abruptly stood and pointed at the two brothers.

"I've had it with the sibling drama!" he said, glaring at Stryder. "We tried it your way. Now, we try it mine!"

❈ ❈ ❈

Zekoff's eyes popped open, and he saw yellow fans.
Clerria House. Good!
The grand turine rang fourteen bells in the distance.
The Kan will be on us soon. How long have I been here?
His eyes darted back and forth, taking in the few details found in the mostly bare room. They settled on a tall, thin red-headed young man, seated by the bed. He stared at the

now conscious colonel, face lit up with surprise and pleasure.

Vanir.

"Sir, I'm so happy you're back!" the red head gushed.

Vanir rose and stepped over to the open door. In a low but adamant voice he called down the hall. Two women dressed in purple robes quickly entered the room. Vanir addressed them enthusiastically.

"He's awake!"

Their wide eyes sparkled—the only thing visible through their purple headdress. They moved around the colonel, running their hands over him and nodding satisfactorily to themselves.

"He appears to be fine," one told Vanir. "He just needs a little more rest."

The lieutenant nodded his thanks and the two women in purple left. He looked down at his mentor and heaved a sigh of relief.

"I must return to duty, sir," Vanir said, "but I'm glad you're back with us, as I'm sure the entire guard is."

Vanir stood at attention, saluted, and left. Zekoff lay there, drifting in and out of consciousness. Each time he woke, he felt himself returning closer to normal.

The new normal. Alone.

Seventeen bells, the Kan...

"Colonel Zekoff?" A Clerria's gentle voice called from the door bringing him back to the surface. "Colonel?"

"Yes?"

"There's someone here to see you."

He nodded weakly and motioned for them to enter, but he caught the smell of fish long before he saw who it was. A short round woman with long gray hair and a kind face stepped into the room. She held in her outstretched hands a steaming plate of food. She smiled sweetly and approached the bed. Zekoff slowly sat up and gestured his approval.

"Hello, I'm..."

"I know," Zekoff said, smiling. "You're Jaanam's fishing friend Morga."

"We all decided…" she said, blushing at the fact he remembered her. "Well, we know you're a busy man and, well, we just want you to know, we'll take care of feeding you. Now that our beloved Jaanam is, well…"

She looked down and cleared her throat.

"So, we cooked you today's catch."

"Thank you, Morga," Zekoff said, holding his sad smile. "This is most kind, but truth be told… I never cared much for fish."

Morga visibly recoiled in shock.

"But all the years she fished with us and cooked for you? She said it was your favorite!"

"Yes, I know," Zekoff answered quietly, turning away to hide his sorrow. "Even though I never liked fish, she did, and I *loved* her."

❈ ❈ ❈

Soshi's hands trembled, and her eyes fluttered.
White powder coated the tip of her little finger.
Only a little, just before bed.
We land tomorrow.
Big day.

Sleep.
Dreaming.
She's on an island.
A city she knew intimately, but never visited.
A beautiful, erotic, and immortal White Queen.

The Fate of Tomorrow

❋ ❋ ❋

Captain Fia experienced a rush of emotions when the gentle spires of Mostas appeared on the horizon. She felt relieved to be back home at the Amarenian capital at last. Extended raids took a toll on the ship and the crew, this one especially. Yet, she felt trepidation because, for all intents and purposes this raid failed, costing over half her crew. She knew there would be some sort of reckoning for that.

Which led to a bigger concern. What kind of homeland would she be returning to?

Fia stared up into the rigging and the wind swirled the hair about her head. The *Voola* moved full sail flying Rayth colors proudly. She turned to the woman at the helm and sighed dolefully.

"Let's take her in, Mariner Neaux."

R.W. Marcus

ACT THREE

The Amarenian Legacy

The old farmer watched the approaching banners waving above the sea of wheat which stretched to the horizon. As one of the largest land masses in the eastern agricultural islands, harvest time kept the wheat fields of Otomoria especially busy. Their yield helped feed thousands across the entire Goyan Islands. He smiled and tapped the shoulder of his raw-boned son busy examining the blade on his scythe.

"Lancers passing through," he announced.

The large young man turned to catch the lancer tips just above the banners, glinting in the late-day sun.

"Good," the son said, "I came across a nest of Makas this morning. I got two of them but the rest scattered."

"They damn near destroyed the far west field last few cycles," the father replied, adjusting his wide-brimmed hat. "Ate damn near everything."

The farmer reached over and broke off a thin stem of wheat and began chewing on the end.

"Let's offer them a place to break for the Kan," he suggested. "That'll take care of our Maka problem."

They both chuckled and were thankful their number one pest was a highly sought-after delicacy for passing patrols. The farmer and his son watched the patrol of the Sixth Eldorian Lancers slowly turn toward them down the ten-foot-wide row between fields. Calmly chewing on his wheat, the father couldn't help but notice that something seemed odd when the column leisurely approached.

❈ ❈ ❈

They advanced in columns of two. Most focused their attention straight ahead, watching with distrust the female lieutenant riding next to the sergeant leading the group.

"I tell ya Reed, it ain't right!" snarled Ollie, a youthful lancer scratching his three-day-old stubble. "It's bad luck I tell ya!"

Reed, a lanky young man with long brown hair, wasn't listening. His eyes carefully scoured the wheat field to his right while he rode.

"And what with her wearing the uniform and all…" Ollie continued.

Reed suddenly spun on his horse, deftly slid the lance from its side holster on the saddle and thrust it into the thick of wheat near the ground. A high-pitched shriek pierced the monotone of horses' hooves. Reed's face lit up pulling his lance back and saw a two-foot-long animal with protruding buck teeth, mammoth rear legs and a long rat tail writhing on the tip.

"Hey look!" he cheerfully announced to the horsemen before him. "Dinner!"

Several lancers glanced back and smiled. Reed pulled the creature up to him and snapped its neck.

"You say something Ollie?" he asked, turning to his friend.

Ollie de Toriss glared at Reed.

"Her!" he barked, motioning to the front of the column. "Lieutenant Treena!"

Reed peered forward while casually tying a cord around the Maka's legs to secure it to the saddle horn.

"Yeah, she's a bit of a looker," he agreed. "Not big on talking though."

"It's bad luck!" Ollie whined, sounding nearly panicked.

Reed sighed but kept his eyes on the female rider.

"Ollie, what the fuck are you yammering about?"

"Thirteen!" Ollie protested, leaning over in his saddle. "Lancer patrols should number *thirteen*—that's twelve lancers and a sergeant! Fourteen is bad luck—and with a woman to boot!"

"You actually believe that horseshit they've been feeding you?"

"She's not one of us I tell you! Ask anyone, nobody's seen her before!

"So?"

"So!"

"Yeah, so what?"

"W... Well..." Ollie sputtered in frustration. "Do you really think they would promote someone no one's seen before, especially a quim..."

"I really wish you wouldn't use that word."

"... *especially a quim,* to the fucking rank of lieutenant? Even Sergeant Jork kisses her ass!"

"Look brother," Reed said, turning to face him, "we're the new grunts in the unit. The rest of the guys will naturally have a go at us. You know, feed us some legendary horseshit. We'll be doing it to the next new guys, and you know it."

The conversation ended when the leader's hand went up and the column halted.

❈ ❈ ❈

The old farmer and his son peered up at the balding, bearded sergeant in weathered leather armor. Lieutenant Treena, an attractive blonde woman, with short, cropped hair and delicate features turned downward in a dour expression, sat beside him. Behind them were the usual twelve lancers in brown and tan striped tunics.

"Gabe," the sergeant nonchalantly greeted, leaning forward in the saddle.

"Jork," Gabe responded in kind, removing the wheat stem from his mouth.

The old farmer's gaze settled on the woman whose uniform carried a lieutenant's rank. Their eyes locked for a moment before he quickly turned away, unsettled by her intense stare. There was something about her entire demeanor. She radiated waves of malevolence and sadistic brutality.

"Kan's coming soon," he remarked, scanning the sky. "We've got a spot for ya, if ya want."

"Having Maka troubles, are ya?" Jork asked, grinning down at his friend.

Gabe chuckled and returned the stem to his mouth.

"The boy here will show you where to set up camp."

Lieutenant Treena shifted impatiently in her saddle and loudly cleared her throat. Jork's face went serious. He sat up straight and turned in his saddle.

"Reed! Ollie!" he bellowed.

Reed's face lit up hearing his name. Ollie groaned. Both immediately broke rank and rode from the rear of the column to their commander.

"You will accompany Lieutenant Treena," Jork ordered. "Follow her orders to the letter. Do you understand?"

Both nodded but refused to meet the woman's eyes.

"This will be your first side patrol men," the sergeant said, timbre softening. "And it ain't what any of us would call a normal one. Make me proud."

He then addressed the lieutenant. "Your objective is about five miles to the northwest."

Treena solemnly nodded thanks to the sergeant and then, motioning with her head, wordlessly instructed Reed and

Ollie to follow. Jork and Gabe watched the trio ride off with a sense of relief.

"Alright men, let's make camp!" Jork commanded.

❂ ❂ ❂

Taa slowly lifted his hand from the top of Alosus' head. He stared off into the distance while he processed the Amarenian's life and knowledge. His normally blank expression betrayed a sadness and understanding.

"Your people have suffered much," he said in fluent Amarenian.

Alosus' eyes opened wide in surprise, "How?!"

"We were born this way," he stated flatly.

Orich peered over from the wheel.

"It almost cost us our lives," he affirmed, also in flawless Amarenian.

Alosus studied the twins inquisitively. Taa sat back in the navigator's chair, his face evocative with memory.

"Before the revolt in our home city of Immor-Onn," he recalled, "a racial purity movement had taken hold. It swept across the western Twilight Lands, fueled by a bewitched queen and corrupt general. We felt the tide of resentment building and fled before bloodshed began."

Not understanding Amarenian, Shom's attention returned to Sareeta. She stood in the stern of the *Haraka* attempting to teach beginners' Amarenian. The crew sat cross-legged around her, repeating basic words and phrases.

"What do you suppose those three are discussing?" Alto asked Shom in a whisper.

The question broke the royal's fixation on the Hill Sister's breasts. He turned and squinted at his friend. "Hopefully, a way to make these little adventures we seem to keep falling into pay off."

Alto chuckled. "We're richer than we know, my friend, and you might actually learn some of the words if you paid attention to our teacher."

"I really don't think so." Shom's said with a casual confidence. "Although I *have* been paying attention, in my own special way. I find, I learn new languages best in bed with partners who speak the tongue."

Alto tilted his head and gave an unconvinced look.

"It's true!" Shom defended. "I guess the act of love breaks the language barrier and plants it permanently in my mind… a gift, really."

The craft suddenly rocked, nearly knocking Sareeta off her feet.

"Sorry," Orich apologized, breaking off the conversation in Amarenian and returning to Common. "The portal from the Banok Atoll to the south appears to be more powerful than expected."

Mal swiveled back from her lesson.

"What have we got?"

"Nothing we can't handle captain." Orich replied course correcting again.

"Be glad we're hundreds of miles from it," Taa offered, gazing southward over an ocean stretching to the horizon.

Mal eyed them both. "Let's keep it that way."

❈ ❈ ❈

Fia saw the *Mahilia* waiting on the Mostas docks. They stood at relaxed attention, clothed only in blood-red crop pants. A matching weaponized sash they called lurohs, diagonally crossed between their breasts. The sash featured two functioning metal bolo balls at the ends which rested on their thigh. She immediately spotted the leader by the ranking bars she wore on her luroh.

The skeleton crew struggled against the deeper, more aggressive seas of the eastern ocean and the *Voola* clumsily entered Mostas' harbor. Once they finally secured the ship, Fia assembled her crew on deck.

"The Mahilia are here," Fia warned ominously. "They're probably going to want to talk to me."

"Captain…"

"So, I'm gonna talk to them," the Rayth captain continued. "You all need to keep a low profile while I'm gone. I doubt they'll let anyone else leave the ship."

"What if they want to search the ship?"

"Is the ship empty?"

"Yes Captain!"

"Then let them search," Fia ordered. "Keep your eyes and ears open to the way the political winds are blowing. I told you this was going to be a different world we were returning to."

She held up her finger.

"Remember, mouth closed, eyes and ears open."

The mariners nodded in agreement. Sighing, Captain Fia turned and disappeared down the gangplank.

✺ ✺ ✺

Ollie and Reed's wet clothes clung to them like an irritating second skin, restricting their movements. The rough material chaffed their flesh and every shift in the saddle grated their tender parts, intensifying their already miserable mood.

The two of them glared at Lieutenant Treena leading them who appeared unfazed by the weather. She brought her horse to a trot when the shower finally passed and the sun burned away the clouds.

"Nothin' like a steam bath," Ollie grumbled, watching vapor rise from the rows surrounding them.

A half a mile ahead, the wheat fields gave way to a large clearing. The wide furrow between fields turned into a crude, muddy road leading between two ancient, solitary oak trees into a hamlet beyond. The trees seemed out of place in the vast expanse of open fields. Their stoic trunks and massive green canopies took on the appearance of arboreal sentries for the human outpost.

Reed spotted two forms lying at the bottom of one of the trees. He knew immediately what was happening even before he heard their cries of anguish. Riding up, he stopped to stare at the naked male and female humans bound spread-eagle on the fallow ground beneath the branches. They had staked the man face up and the woman face down. Ollie came to a halt beside his partner just outside the drip line.

"Poor bastards," Reed sympathized.

"My ass!" Ollie spit on the ground. "There's a reason it's called the Tree of Vengeance."

Reed remembered they reserved the face up position for capital offenses. The man had obviously been laying there for quite a few cycles and the acid given off by the tree's leaves had already taken their toll. His eyes were sunken into hollow black sockets and small circular burn marks covered his entire body. Writhing in wordless agony against his bounds, he would probably die before the next cycle.

The female staked out face down indicated she had committed a lesser crime. They probably caught the woman stealing and would soon release her. The same round burn marks peppered her entire backside. She sobbed continuously knowing she would carry those scars for the rest of her life.

"I never much liked this punishment," Reed admitted. "Too cruel."

Ollie snorted contemptuously. "Eh, that soft heart of yours is going to get you killed one day!"

A gust of wind whistled across the fields and shook the tree limbs. Collected raindrops fell from the leaves. The staked victims thrashed wildly when the acid-laced drops struck their skin forming nasty red welts. The woman screamed, and the man, unable to speak, groaned loudly. They could see a wet leaf had fallen inside his blackened mouth and completely disintegrated his tongue.

Ollie chuckled. "Bet that hurts!"

Reed shot his partner a disdainful sideways glance and turned back to see the victim lifting his head in his general direction. The man kept mouthing a single word through cracked, burnt lips. The lancer didn't need to hear it to know he begged for mercy. Reed reached back and unholstered his lance.

"You've suffered enough," he declared.

Reed plunged the lance through his chest. The condemned man gasped when the tip pierced his heart. Relief flooded his face, as the pain, along with his life, rapidly faded.

"You'll have to answer for that!" Ollie sneered.

"He was going to die anyway."

"Yeah, but they wanted it to be slow."

"Hey!" the lieutenant yelled from just up the road. "If you two are done fucking around you can return to duty!"

Her horse fidgeted nervously from the intensity in her voice, and she struggled to keep it in check. Irritation riddled her normally serious face. The two lancers felt an indefinable menace emanating from her tone, and they spurred their steeds, trotting her way.

"Wouldn't ya know it," Ollie grumbled, "the first words the quim speaks to us, and it turns out she's a ballbuster!"

❈ ❈ ❈

Tate Whitmar leaned against the railing of the ship and watched the Port of Brinstan grow larger on the horizon. He ignored the bustle of sailors on the deck and allowed himself to take in the moment. The sea air stung his face while the wind in the sails whistled a melancholy song announcing the approaching harbor.

"A bittersweet homecoming?" Came a female voice from behind.

He turned and realized Soshi had been standing there watching him. Gathering her windblown hair, she pulled it to one side and joined him at the rail.

"Nah, more of a pain in the ass, really," he answered. "We should be on our way to Amarenia right now."

"So, why aren't we?"

"Grandmama has returned. We all gotta pay our respects, in person."

"Yeah," she agreed. "I've heard that before, and you've been kinda tight-lipped this entire voyage. I'd really like to know what to expect. Unless you just want my first diplomatic efforts to fail."

Soshi smiled, tilted her head and pouted sensually. The residual effects of the Oldust she ingested upon awakening began influencing the conversation. Tate gave her a forlorn smile and then focused on the port.

"Grandmama isn't just really old," he confessed, "She's literally one of the first humans."

"How?"

"The truth?"

Soshi nodded.

"She's cursed," he whispered.

Recoiling, she stepped back, mouth agape.

"Relax, it doesn't rub off," he said. "It affects only Grandmama. However, she must return after every husband dies and choose a new one. Hence, the Consort Ball."

"So, really old?"

"I mean like, five thousand grands," he answered. "She's got the wing scars on her back to prove it."

"*Wing scars?*"

"Yeah," he added, "and I'll tell ya, she's got no love for the Avion House Pyre."

"Why?"

"They're the ones who cursed her."

Tate could see the confusion in the Amarenian's eyes while trying to process what she was hearing.

"Are you telling me, you really don't know that all of us, *every damn human in the Annigan*, is descended from Avions?" he asked.

Soshi stood there, dumbfounded. She didn't know what to say. She'd only been taught the Amarenian creation stories of the moon-centric Legend of Mia-Ta.

"How?" was all she could manage.

"The short version?"

"Please."

Tate sighed. "There was once a great house of the Avions known as House Solas. They made an alliance with the forces of Nocturn and started a war against Lumina. All the other sentient races of Lumina united to defeat them. As punishment for their treachery, they cut the wings from the rebellious Avions and scattered them throughout the northern Goyan Islands. These wingless survivors gave birth to what we now know as humans."

Soshi struggled to find her voice. "You said, 'she must return after every husband dies.' Return from where?"

"She got bored with the Annigan shortly after her first thousand grands," he answered. "The Middle Realms are her playground. She can choose to be just about anywhere, places we can't even imagine, but we all like to believe she thinks of this one as home."

"She was in my dream last night," Soshi blurted out.

Tate turned to her. "If she visited you in your dreams, she already knows all about you."

A few awkward moments passed in silence.

"'Was it a pleasant dream?"

Soshi blushed a bit. "Yes, it was very erotic."

"Well," he said, chuckling, "you might just have quite a powerful ally there."

"So, I get to meet the family?"

"You bet!"

❀ ❀ ❀

The cross breeze felt good on Fia's face while she stood at ridged attention. She could hear the bustle of the Mostas docks below from the open second-story windows, but the woman seated at the desk before her held her attention.

"Captain Fia, thank you for coming so promptly," she stated flatly, continuing to focus on paperwork.

"I really had little choice, Astute," Fia replied, eyes fixed forward.

Astute Sister Mernasi, the Amarenian Maritime commander, peered up from her reading.

"No, I don't suppose you did," she coldly admitted.

The commander dropped the papers on her desk and sat back in her chair. She kept her thigh-length gray hair gathered into an elegant mane over her left arm, which hung limp at her side. The trusses ran gracefully down and around her left breast, resting on her bright blue crop pants. She peered up at Fia with a stern yet sympathetic gaze.

"Captain," she said, "I'm going to give it to you straight. Three lunas ago the High Council voted to disband the Rayth Faction."

The Maritime commander paused for a moment to let her latest revelation sink in. Fia remained silent and at attention. Her face tightened, and her mouth clenched, drawing her lips into a taut, horizontal line.

"I understand your anger, Captain."

"Do you, Astute?!"

Mernasi remained calm. "Yes, I too was once Rayth."

"With all due respect Astute Sister, you gloriously gained your retirement in battle. Mine will be because my sisters have said my kind have no place among them."

"You have a place here, Captain. Just in a slightly different role."

"Astute, leading a ship in combat is all I know!"

"And I would be a poor commander, and a fool, to use you for anything else."

Fia studied her superior's face. It took all her resolve to fight back her rage.

"If you officially renounce the Rayth Faction," Commander Mernasi continued. "I can guarantee you a commission in the newly forming Amarenian Navy. We would refit your ship and you would still hold command."

Fia stared at the floor and weighed the options.

"Tell me, Captain," Mernasi asked, "how long were you on mission?"

Fia's response was automatic, her mind still wrestling with choices. "Twenty lunas, extended raid."

"And how many mariners did you lose?"

"Ten."

"And what spoils did you return with?"

"None."

"Captain," the commander reasoned, voice softening, "it is simply a matter of economics. We as a people will gain so much more by trading with the West instead of stealing from them."

Fia still stood at attention but trembled in frustration. A single tear crept down her right cheek. Mernasi sat up and resumed sorting through her paperwork.

"Take this offer back to your crew. We will provide them positions in the navy. We will make every effort to keep them together as a crew. You have one luna to decide."

Fia hated ultimatums. The structured life of a naval officer was a far cry from the freedom of the hunt unfettered by strict supervision and specific missions.

"I demand an audience with the queen!" Fia insisted through clenched jaw.

Mernasi glared solemnly. "As is your right."

※ ※ ※

Ollie and Reed followed the mysterious lieutenant into a small farming hamlet which resembled every other farming village dotting the northern half of the Continent of Otomoria. The narrow dirt road passed by a handful of small dwellings, including a common longhouse, livestock pens, a granary, barn, and silo storage area.

She stopped them outside the barn. Two older farmers busied themselves threshing a large pile of wheat in front. They peeked up at the trio when their horses restlessly snorted. The lieutenant sat up straight and perfectly still in her saddle.

"Kalaka?" she asked.

Both men exchanged uncertain glances.

"Kalaka?" she asked, in a much sterner tone.

Ollie and Reed watched the farmers chatter their regional dialect at each other in response to the strange question. Not understanding the language or the situation, the lancers shifted nervously in the saddle when the lieutenant raised her voice.

"Kalaka!" the lieutenant shouted over the farmers babbling.

Both stopped talking and quaked under her daunting presence. One silently pointed north with a trembling hand. She assessed the farmers for a moment and, apparently satisfied with their honesty, snapped the reins on her horse and led the two lancers north, out of town.

They rode about half a mile when Reed could not contain his curiosity.

"Uh, Lieutenant, ma'am," he called out.

"What is it lancer?"

"If you could tell us what we're searching for, perhaps we could be of more help."

"Not what," she replied. "Who. Any further details remain classified. So, the best way you can help is to watch my back."

The next mile passed slowly due to the oppressive rising heat and humidity. From the corner of his eye, Reed could swear Ollie was sleeping in the saddle. Suddenly the lieutenant spurred her horse into a cantor, shocking them both out of their dazed boredom.

Just before they caught up with her, they spotted a man walking calmly on the side of the muddy road. He appeared to be in his late thirties with dark brown skin. Filth covered his thin, nude body, with matted hair and dirt caking his five-foot-four frame. An enormous cloud of flies extended a half dozen feet around his entire body. It moved with him as he shambled along with the aid of a long, gnarled walking stick.

The lieutenant caught up to him first, slowing her mount to a walk, and keeping pace with the man who completely ignored her presence. Ollie and Reed trailed behind with lances ready in case of trouble.

"Kalaka?" she asked commandingly.

The man peered at her through the cloud of flies, before returning his attention to the road ahead.

"Kalaka?!" she repeated.

The naked man slowed his pace, eventually stopping to face her again. Several flies buzzed around Reed's head, and he swatted at them absentmindedly. Flies now circled the lieutenant too, which she ignored, concentrating on the man.

He silently reached down and plucked a locust crawling up his leg. The rookie lancers could not contain their disgust when the naked man slowly put it up to his mouth and bit it in half. Reed fought the urge to vomit from the crunching sounds when the man chewed the insect with his mouth open.

Both lancers stared in repulsed amazement when he offered the uneaten half to the lieutenant. She reached down without hesitation, took the grasshopper's bottom half, and popped it into her mouth. When she chewed and swallowed, the naked man's attitude completely changed. He relaxed and leaned on his staff.

"Why you want Kalaka?" he asked in Common.

"I need his help."

"Kalaka no can help you!" the man said, erupting in laughter. "Kalaka old. His time over. He ready to pass on to Middle Realms."

"I can change his mind."

"Kalaka no can help you," he said, cackling.

"Let me try!" she pleaded. "Where is he?"

The man grew quiet for a moment and turned to face towards the east.

"You will find him where he began."

The naked man said nothing more. He nonchalantly pivoted and continued his slow progression down the road.

❈ ❈ ❈

Tate and Soshi walked down the gangplank toward the bustling docks of the Whitmar ancestral home city. A single person greeted them. She was tall and lanky with no discernible figure beneath loose silk clothing subtly conveying wealth. A thin-bladed short sword bounced against her thigh and she fidgeted with excitement.

Even with her head shaved, Soshi couldn't help but notice the strong Whitmar family resemblance. She looked like a female Tate.

Spotting them, she rushed forward with arms open wide when they descended onto the dock. Tate set his travel bag down and braced himself. She almost knocked him over with her enthusiastic embrace.

"Tay-Tay!" she cried joyously. "Oh, it's been too long."

She rocked him back and forth until Tate broke the hug. He stepped back and seemed genuinely surprised she stood almost as tall as him.

"How's my favorite sister?" he asked playfully.

She scrunched up her face and swatted at him. "Your only sister, silly!"

Tate grinned and motioned toward Soshi.

"Kacha Whitmar this is…"

"Lady Soshanna," Kacha interrupted, offering her hand.

Soshi gave a bewildered smile and took it.

"Kacha is the family information oracle," he said.

Kacha rolled her eyes and leaned into Soshi.

"It does sound better than spymaster," she whispered.

Tate shook his head and picked up his travel bag. Kacha placed herself in the middle of the two, locked arms with them, and led them to a waiting carriage.

"Mother and Father got your room ready, Tay-Tay" she said. "We've got a guest room for you, Soshanna."

"Please call me Soshi."

"Soshi it is," she said tilting her head and grinning widely. "Grandmama has been asking about you, Soshi."

The Amarenian's surprise left her speechless.

"You said she was in your dream last Kan," Tate reminded her.

"Yes, but I didn't think…"

"I told you she would know all about you," he knowingly said.

"Father arranged for a banquet tonight," Kacha excitedly added. "Having the family all together will be such a treat!"

Tate faced her and put his hands on her shoulders.

"I'll be here for the banquet, Kacha, and to pay respects to Grandmama, but we've got a meeting in Amarenia to attend. I wish we could stay longer but we set sail at the lifting of the Kan."

"You won't even stay for the Consort Ball?" Kacha asked pouting.

"You, more than anyone," Tate said, resting his forehead against hers, "know how important it is that these talks go well. I've got to get her home, Sis."

They stopped before a small, private carriage. Kacha nodded her head in acknowledgment.

"I know," she said, "and so do Mother and Father. Now let's get the festivities started!"

Kacha jumped in the driver's seat and motioned for them to climb into an empty bench in the back. She then reached forward and snapped the reins, starting off across the teeming city. Soshi leaned into Tate smirking.

"Tay-Tay?"

"When we were very young, she couldn't pronounce Tate," he said, blushing. "Somehow the nick-name stuck with her. I can't tell you how many fights it got me into when I was growing up,"

Soshi sympathetically patted his arm. She could see the towers of Castle Whitmar extending above the rooftops of the city while Kacha deftly maneuvered the carriage through the crowded streets. Soshi could feel the presence of the White Queen increasing with each city block.

The Amarenian peered upward in wonder at the massive castle rising above the five bridges crossing the Brinstan River. She couldn't resist the lure. The distinct sadness of the energy attracted her, along with a sense of wonder.

✸ ✸ ✸

The massive termite mounds rose in stark contrast to the lush fields surrounding them. The horses whinnied uneasily and the sound of their hooves echoed off the imposing, desolate structures. Both lancers eyed the brown, earthen columns surrounding them suspiciously, slowly following the shadowy lieutenant. Ollie nervously searched the long shadows they cast and spat on the ground.

"These things give me the fucking creeps," he said.

"This must have been a stand of trees once," Reed offered, glancing up at some of the taller ones.

The lieutenant slowly surveyed each vertical mass and the surrounding area. She occasionally would stop and inspect one closer. Unsatisfied, she continued scanning the surrounding mounds.

They had almost crossed to the other side of the termite field when she jerked on the reins and halted her mount before a mound on the border. To the bewildered lancers, the towering column seemed identical to the others. She leaned forward in the saddle and carefully examined the ground around it.

Without a word, the lieutenant gracefully slipped from the saddle and knelt before the earthen tower. Her hands ran over the earth and took a pinch of ground. She brought it up to her nose to smell the soil and stood thoughtfully. Stepping closer, she examined the side of the pillar, then gently touched its surface.

"What in the name of the gods is she doing?" Ollie whispered.

Reed shrugged, watching the lieutenant continue to run her hands with reverence over the surface. Suddenly, she walked to her mount, led it over to Reed, and handed him the reins. She motioned towards a small clearing about thirty feet away.

"Make camp over there," she ordered. "This may take a little while."

✦ ✦ ✦

Everyone slept quietly inside of the *Haraka* except Taa, who relieved his brother at the helm, and Mal, who stared fascinated out the windshield. For Mal's entire life in the Goyan Islands, the sun had always maintained its constant station directly overhead. Now, flying eastward toward Amarenia, it sank into the western sky behind them, growing noticeably dimmer. The clouds parted in the distance ahead of them revealing a small yellow globe sitting low in and illuminating the eastern sky, glittering off the ocean's surface.

"What the?!" Mal cried out.

"That is the Moon," Taa explained.

The Bailian gave her an understanding smile, for she had only known the sun-drenched skies of Lumina.

"It will pass soon," the albino helmsman added. "We should be near our destination when it appears next. In the

Goyan Islands you use the Kan and Turine Tidal Clocks to mark time, everywhere else in the Annigan uses the moon."

The commotion roused Alto from his slumber. He quickly rose to his feet and walked up behind her in awe of the sight. Placing his arms gently around her waist and looking over her shoulder, they stared transfixed at the spectacle before them.

"That is *amazing*," he softly said unable to mask his astonishment.

The moon mesmerized them while they cruised across the sky. It calmed Mal, leaving her smiling at the passing clouds set against the darkening heavens and the shimmering orb adorning them. Alto yawned and bent over, kissing her on the top of her shoulder.

"I'm going back to sleep," he whispered.

Not a bad idea, she thought, feeling her eyelids grow heavy. Mal followed him to a vacant area beside the hull, slipped into his arms, and a deep slumber.

❈   ❈   ❈

Fia slammed the doors to the queen's outer chambers so hard it startled both Mahilia standing guard.

"Show respect in the Queen's Palace!" one admonished, stepping forward.

"Fuck off!!" Fia spat, not bothering to slow down.

The antagonistic guard, used to sisters respecting her authority stood speechless. Noticing the Rayth markings on Fia's face and chest she decided not to test their reputation of savagery.

Tension coiled in the pirate captain's body like a spring. She had never felt so betrayed, so isolated, *and by her own people!* She wouldn't become a shipbound clerk serving at the beck and call of farmers. Storming out of the palace and into the busy square, she turned toward the docks.

❂ ❂ ❂

Ollie shivered in the fog and moved closer to the fire warming his hands. Reed rotated a spit roasting the carcass of an anteater just above the flames. A short distance away lieutenant Treena sat cross-legged before the termite mound. She rocked back and forth, all the while speaking softly in a strange tongue to the monolith's side.

"She's just been sitting there for almost a whole cycle," Reed remarked, giving the spit another turn.

"Crazy quim hasn't shut up the entire time," Ollie said in frustration, glancing over his shoulder. "And what language is that? It *ain't* any language I've ever heard. Just who in the name of the gods does she think she's talkin' to?"

Reed swatted several flies away and returned his attention to cooking.

"Don't know," he whispered, "but just the sound of her voice makes me jumpy. *It doesn't sound human.* You just may be right this time Ollie, she's *not* one of us."

❂ ❂ ❂

When the moon returned the weather grew progressively worse. The *Haraka* descended through a light gray sky providing moderately choppy winds and a steady drizzle.

"Captain, we approach our destination," Orich announced from the helm.

"But we have no official location to land," Taa added from the navigator's chair. "Our arrival will be quite unexpected."

"Find an open spot to put us down and try not to hit anything or anyone," Mal ordered, pivoting to address both. "Take us in fast and steep—the less hang time the better. Word of us will spread fast enough once were on the ground."

Alto and Sareeta sparred in the aft-most part of the ship beneath the sternpost. They glared intently at each other smiling confidently, stripped to the waist, and brandishing short swords. The sudden rocking of the ship challenged their balance and both glistened in sweat struggling to keep their guard up. The rest of the crew had gathered, seated along the side of the hull to watch the contest.

"Time to end the fun and games you two!" Mal ordered over her shoulder.

"Bravo!" Shom marveled, applauding from where he was sitting. "Such amazing skill and stamina!"

Both challengers cast an irritated glance at the smirking royal. The rest of the group missed his sarcasm and murmured their agreements watching the competition unfold.

"However, I needn't remind you," Shom added, with an obnoxious grin. "The nature of the wager does not depend on the conditions. The first one to fall, whether struck down or losing their balance, for whatever reason, loses."

Both Alto and Sareeta held position with eyes locked. Each waiting for the other to make the first move.

"Why does it always come down to dick measuring?" Mal rhetorically asked, turning calmly back to Orich and raising a finger. "Do it."

With a single pull of a lever, the Bailian sent the *Haraka* into a steep dive. Mal felt her stomach lurch and the *Haraka* tilted nose forward. The angle of descent proved too much for the sparring partners and both tumbled forward to the bow of the craft. Mal glared at the two piled up in front of her and chuckled watching them untangle.

"You're both losers," Shom laughingly announced.

"Captain, I have located an area sufficient to land on," Taa stated, keeping his attention focused on the rapidly approaching ground.

"Put her down," she ordered. "Alright, Ambassador Alosus, here's your chance to shine."

※ ※ ※

Captain Tara Ungar stared at the plain beige envelope delivered just moments ago. The courier exited through the light rain down the gangplank of her ship, the *Raptor*. The Maritime commander's seal on the envelope revealed what it contained.

Two lunas ago, she signed the vow to give up her Rayth charter and this marked her first commission in the new Amarenian Navy. They scheduled her ship to be fitted for naval use in two lunas, but she had lost half of her mariners when they abandoned their posts rather than renounce their raider lifestyles. They disappeared, along with deserters from the rest of the fleet, into the depths of the city to form the Rayth Underground.

The wind blowing into Mostas' inlet drove the light rain at a steady angle across the harbor. Captain Ungar pushed locks of damp blonde curls out of her eyes. She just knew the weather would be miserable this entire luna cycle.

Turning to head inside out of the oncoming storm, she noticed movement above her out of the corner of her eye. A mysterious object fell almost straight out of the sky and headed for the docks close to where she had moored the *Raptor*.

Workers gawked upward in shock and disbelief all along the main harborside as the cylindrical object drew rapidly closer. They shouted and pointed upward while male slaves panicked and ran. Captain Ungar's remaining crew joined her on the deck watching the object drop rapidly at a forty-five-degree angle. It suddenly pulled out of the steep dive fifty feet above them and leveled off. Ungar made out tapered ends with fins in the stern and realized it was a type of ship.

The *Haraka* came in dangerously low, running along the length of the main dock. A wave of startled cries preceded her and people dropped to the soggy deck. Still maintaining a perilous velocity, it passed twenty feet over the *Raptor*, whose crew also dove for cover. Ungar remained standing and followed the flying vessel when it passed.

"By the Goddess!" she stammered, her eyes wide with wonder.

While people returned to their feet, everyone watched the *Haraka* glide to an empty slip at the end of the wharf. It came to an abrupt halt from full speed and spun to face inward towards the waterfront. The strange flying ship hovered serenely above the vacant jetty, then gently set down. The crew of the *Raptor* crowded around their captain approaching the now motionless airship.

"Captain, what is that?" a mariner asked in amazement.

"The future Mariner," Ungar replied unable to take her eyes off the flying marvel. "The future."

❂ ❂ ❂

The Fate of Tomorrow

The pre-dinner meet-and-greet was already in full swing when Tate and Soshi descended the stairs through the grand foyer of the Whitmar Palace. Activity filled the opulent room. Tray-bearing servants bustled to and fro serving drinks to Whitmars of all ages mingling about the hall talking and laughing.

A female bard sat on a small corner stage of the antechamber playing a fourteen-string lute. Her fingers blurred performing a complex melody which sounded like two distinct pieces of music weaving through and complementing each other.

All activity centered around the lady standing in front of the huge dining room doors. She looked to be in her late twenties to early thirties, tall and slender with waist-length snow-white hair. She wore a clinging blue gown with a plunging neckline dramatically highlighting her porcelain-white skin.

Soshi recognized her from her dreams and her vulva tingled at the remembrance. The moment seemed totally surreal, and she felt lightheaded. Taking Tate's arm to steady herself, she navigated the last few steps.

The White Queen chatted with Kacha, and two people Soshi didn't recognize. A large city guard and two obvious attendants stood at attention behind her. The two ladies-in-waiting wore lavish matching green court dresses. They surveyed everything around the queen with stern expressions of entitled judgement.

When Soshi stepped off the final landing onto the floor, the queen made direct eye contact from across the crowd. The Amarenian felt a jolt of energy surge through her snatching her breath away for a moment and Tate heard her gasp.

"Are you alright?" he quietly asked.

"So… music and everything," she said, quickly composing herself. "I'm impressed,"

"Yeah," he said, chuckling, "it only happens once a generation, so we go all out. This is only the official *beginning* of the activities leading up to the Consort Ball. And she isn't *just* a musician."

"Oh?"

"The music the bard plays casts a protective dome over the room in case of a psychic or magical attack."

"Really?"

"It also extends an aura of general wellbeing to those within earshot."

"Come to think about it, I do feel pretty good," Soshi admitted, letting him assist her across the ballroom.

"Well, I'm glad to see the money wasn't wasted," Tate quipped.

Crossing the antechamber took quite a while, because family members stopped Tate and her at every turn, greeting them warmly. They seemed to wholeheartedly accept Soshi even if she wasn't part of the Whitmar clan.

Soshi felt the pull of the White Queen, however, with every step, to the point where simple conversation grew challenging. The Oldust coursed through her system like she had just snorted a hit. When she locked eyes with the queen again the rest of the room became a blur and her heart raced. The monarch then pursed her lips and smiled enticingly. An ethereally erotic wave suddenly passed through her and she found herself mindlessly approaching the queen.

Tate broke from a conversation when he saw Soshi walking away. He rushed to catch up through the crowd, reaching her just as she stood basking before the queen's receptive gaze.

"Grandmama!" Tate exuberantly greeted.

The queen's demeanor remained subdued, but her eyes conveyed genuine affection. Tate kissed her on each cheek with diplomatic grace and she gently touched his arm.

"You've been so busy of late," she said, in little more than a husky whisper. "I feared you wouldn't make it,"

"Grandmama," he asked, turning to Soshi and extended a hand outward, "may I present Mz. Soshanna Kael, Ambassador's Council to the Free Amarenian Sisterhood."

Soshi bowed, and Tate continued.

"And you stand before Dariel Whitmar, sovereign and sole matriarch of the Whitmar name."

She took the queen's hand when offered. It was ice cold and another wave of arousal pulsed through her.

"It is an honor to make your acquaintance," Soshi said, blushing under the queen's scrutiny.

"It is always good to meet a fellow traveler," the White Queen confided, grinning knowingly. "We should talk later this evening, after all the fuss has died down."

"At your pleasure," Soshi offered.

The queen patted her hand. Soshi felt honored, intrigued, and, most of all, aroused, but also strangely apprehensive.

"I'll send for you," the queen added, "but now, I imagine all of you must be famished."

Two attendants pressed through the crowd and swung open the giant twin doors to the dining hall.

"Dinner is served!" One loudly announced.

❀ ❀ ❀

Alto untangled himself from Sareeta on the floor of the bridge. Mal scowled at them while they stood around the command seats peering curiously out the windshield.

Joc' Valdur stood and stared at the Bailian twin pilots, marveling how they integrated with the *Haraka*.

"*That* was some damn fine flying! He said with an appreciative nod.

"Thank you, Ambassador," they answered in unison.

"To be honest, Orich-Taa," he continued, "even with Captain Edzo's vote of confidence, I had my reservations about handing this craft over to you, but I just gotta say, you are top shelf pilots! If you ever tire of hanging around with the likes of these miscreants, we've a spot for you in the Air Scouts."

The Bailians stared quizzically at each other, completely missing the intended humor.

Alosus smoothed down her court dress trying to make herself presentable, she'd wore the same one for three cycles now.

"It would be best if I went out first," she advised. "The Mahilia should arrive soon."

"Would those Mahilia happen to wear red pants?" Mal asked, gazing out the windshield.

"As a matter of fact, yes."

"Already here," Mal announced.

Alosus peered out the windshield. A dozen of the Mostas' city guards straddled the dock, preventing any exit. They stood in two rows at relaxed attention. All the Mahilia kept their lurohs by their sides at the ready. Alosus recognized Astute Sister Mernasi as the official in command. Although she previously only had brief encounters with the maritime commander, she remembered her to be cold and efficient.

"This is where I earn my keep," Alosus said.

"Alright then, open the hatch," Mal ordered Taa.

The moment the Mahilia heard the latch opening, they clacked together the two metal balls on the end of their lurohs in perfect unison. The resulting percussive rhythm escalated the tension on the dock, increasing in speed with the hatch slowly opening. The cacophony rang across the wharf drawing attention to the potentially serious scene.

Sareeta appeared in the open hatchway first, immediately followed by Alosus. Mernasi's expression relaxed with visible relief and she exhaled loudly. The Maritime commander raised her hand and the clacking ceased.

"Esteemed." Mernasi coolly greeted.
"Astute." Alosus responded in kind.
"Highly irregular," Mernasi remarked in a deadpan tone.
"Irregular circumstances call for irregular actions," Alosus countered.

The maritime commander's appraising gaze slowly swept over the airship while Alosus continued to stare at her.

"One more thing," Alosus added.

Mernasi froze and gave Alosus a suspiciously quizzical gaze.

"There's also a diplomatic delegation from the western houses on board."

"Well," the Maritime commander said, raising an eyebrow, "I guess we better get you to the queen."

❂ ❂ ❂

When the Kan set in again, Ollie and Reed decided to keep moving to stay warm. They tethered the horses and brushed them down. Then, after sharpening their lances and blades, they stacked the weapons neatly beside the steeds, and finally ran out of tasks. Even by the campfire, the damp chill of the fog cut to the bone.

Lieutenant Treena didn't seem to notice the cold, still sitting and swaying before the termite mound. She hadn't eaten or drank anything in two cycles and didn't even take a break to piss or shit.

The two lancers shared a single rabbit for dinner. Reed wiped his mouth on his sleeve and swatted the flies away with his greasy hands. Ollie scowled gnawing a leg bone in search of more meat.

"I bet you didn't even have to hunt this skinny hare," Ollie grumbled. "It probably gave up due to malnourishment."

"Right?" Reed agreed, smirking. "And you'd think the Otomoria bunnies would be fat from plundering crops."

"Maybe it was on a diet," Ollie offered, "watching its wee figure."

This cracked them up until a fly bit Ollie on the back of the neck. His laughter ended with an abrupt snort. He swatted at it and another bit his cheek, which he slapped hard enough to cause Reed to start cackling again.

"These fucking flies!" he cried out, exasperated. "The food must be attracting them."

The air slowly began thickening with annoying insects. Soon they both waved their arms about, but it proved an ineffective defense against the building swarms. Neither lancer noticed the large stream of ants carrying their weapons away into the mist.

"There's gotta be something you can do?!" Ollie snapped.

"Why ya askin' me?!" Reed responded in surprise.

"You're a country boy, Reed! I figure you'd know some kind of... um... *natural* way to get rid of them. I'm from *the city*, for fuck's sake!"

"What? They don't have flies in the city?"

Both turned when a loud cracking sound from the termite mound cut their squabble short. The lieutenant still sat calmly, but the side of the monolith developed several large cracks. With an even louder snap, the entire front of the mound broke loose, hanging by a sliver of surface veneer. The separated wedge teetered briefly and exploded, sending hardened chunks and dust outward.

Treena appeared unharmed and sat motionless, her face and hair covered in dust. Reed and Ollie stood transfixed, frozen in horror, when a lone figure ascended from the depths of the broken mound.

In a panicked scramble, they searched the area where they had stacked their weapons, but only the tack remained.

"What the fuck!" Ollie screamed.

"There!"

Reed pointed out a trail left behind from the dragged equipment. His eyes followed it, and, when a gust parted the fog, he saw the weapons slowly moving away.

They ran after them but suddenly stopped. Spiders, scorpions, and centipedes covered their belongings. The ground seemed to move beneath the fog. The entire earth undulated as millions of creeping insects scuttled over and around each other surrounding them.

A little old man with pale white skin stepped from out of the ruins of the mound. He held a long staff over his head and stood angrily over the lieutenant. They couldn't understand his words, but the emphasis seemed obvious. He gesticulated wildly at the calmly seated woman and crawling insects covered her.

Ollie and Reed recoiled watching the creepy crawlers cover her body and, worse yet, her face. Insects slithered in and out of her mouth when she suddenly called out to them.

"Do not move!" Treena ordered. "Do not interrupt for any reason!"

Both froze in shock when they realized the frail old man—who hadn't even acknowledged their existence—held an ocean of pestilence in check.

❋ ❋ ❋

Alto cast a concerned glance out the *Haraka's* open hatch. He adjusted his sash and slipped his swords into place.

"I have heard the vast majority of the population does not like men," he said, shaking his head.

Mal grinned mischievously and playfully smacked his cheek. "Don't worry sweet cheeks, I'll show you around and take care of you."

"I was not aware you had visited here before," Alto said with a touch of optimism.

"Oh, I haven't."

"Somehow your assurance is not very reassuring," Alto said, rubbing his jaw.

"Taa, come with us," Mal ordered. "Orich, stay with the ship. Allow no one on unless you're certain of them. Ambassadors, it's showtime!"

Her gaze finally fell on Shom, who smiled lecherously.

"And *you*," she said. "You better fucking behave yourself! The last thing we need is some fucking incident!"

Mock concern crossed Shom's face.

"Has anyone spoken to you lately about your excessive use of the word fuck?" he asked.

"Yeah, they have," she replied. "Fuck you!"

She raised up on her tiptoes and gave Alto a quick peck on the lips. "Let's do this!"

All eyes were on them when they moved down the ramp in the drizzling rain. Alosus and Sareeta gave reassuring nods, but Astute Sister Mernasi remained expressionless. Mal's party nervously eyed the dozen Mahilia and the curious crowd gathering behind them.

While Alosus skillfully introduced everyone and Mernasi extended the reception, Mal's eyes scanned the docks. They came to rest on a ship four slips down which seemed quite familiar. Seeing it turned her positive disposition into a vengeful cold scowl. She kept reading the ship's name across the stern, *Voola*, and fought to curb her rage to kill.

Mal surreptitiously reached behind and poked Shom without turning away, for fear it might just disappear like an illusion. He initially assumed he'd committed yet another infraction and gave her a defensive shrug, but she stared beyond him. He followed her gaze to the *Voola*. It took a moment, but his face lit up in recognition. He glanced apprehensively back at Mal, unsure of what to expect next.

"...and I'm sure you all must be weary after such a long journey," Astute Sister Mernasi said, finishing her welcome. "You are our honored guests and if you'd follow me, we'll get you to your quarters to freshen up. I'm certain the queen is eager to grant you an audience."

When the maritime commander turned, the Mahilia formed a corridor through the crowd. While Mal's party followed, the mob scrutinized the outsiders every aspect. Increasing her pace slightly, Mal made her way to the front of the procession, close behind Alosus.

"I need to know about a ship in your harbor called the *Voola*," she said, quietly.

The Amarenian ambassador discreetly noted the vessel's name and nodded. Mal's mind raced with dozens of vengeful scenarios, she leaned in close to Taa.

"Tell Orich to stay on board and monitor the ship moored four slips down from ours," she whispered.

The Bailian quickly glanced in the ship's direction. "Yes captain."

❇ ❇ ❇

The *Voola* rocked gently in her moorings while rain pelted the multi-pane window behind Captain Fia's desk. She stood aggressively, arms crossed, and leered angrily at her remaining six crew.

"*What* did the queen say?" one asked, apprehensively.

"That cock lover betrayed us and our heritage!" Fia spat.

The mariners erupted in a barrage of nervous chatter.

"Mariners!" Fia shouted, "like I said before, our home is a different place than what we left. I hereby release you from any contracts. You are free to go. The newly formed Amarenian Navy will offer you all positions."

This set off another round of chaotic banter until Fia's commanding voice quieted the rabble.

"I, however, will not be joining any navy! Rayth is all I have ever known and it's the root of our very culture! Any are welcome to sail with me. As for the rest, you may go with no hard feelings."

A solemn hush descended over the room. Mariners nervously searched each other's eyes for a hint of the other's intentions.

"But know this," Fia continued, "if you join the navy, we will officially become adversaries. *I am now an enemy of the state!*"

"Captain," Mariner Betha spoke up, "I've served under you for many a luna. You've treated me fair. I tried to be a good first mate to you. I gotta say though, sailing the Shallow Sea and *not* having to run or look over my shoulder sounds really good!"

Fia watched grimly as one by one they left her cabin, heads bowed. Only Neaux, her pilot, remained.

"This is the first time in my life I've been able to live as *I* want," she declared, "and not just fulfilling someone else's expectations. Rayth judges me by my abilities, not my bloodline or wealth. I would rather set my own course and die free as a raider."

Fia gazed fondly at Neaux. She found it ironic the newest member, and the one who least resembled a Rayth, would be the one to stick by her.

"Thank you," she murmured, taking her in her arms.

"What are we going to do now, Captain?"

Fia pulled her in for a kiss. This surprised Neaux, but she warmed quickly and returned it with passion. The mariner felt herself become wet as their tongues danced. Fia broke the embrace and pushed Neaux down on her desk. The mariner's eyes widened and gasped with passion and her chest heaved.

Fia reached down and grabbed the stout mariner's large breasts and felt the nipples harden in her palms.

"First, I'm going to spend some time bonding with my new first mate," Fia said, spreading Neaux's legs, "and then we'll go look for a crew."

❂ ❂ ❂

When the Kan broke, and the direct rays of the sun pushed the receding fog from the wheat fields. Ollie and Reed gasped at a sea of insects surrounding them. Worms crawled in solidarity with roaches, scorpions, ants, and spiders. They slithered just inches outside Ollie and Reed's protective circles. Flying bugs of all kinds darkened the air.

The old man and the lieutenant still sat facing each other by the broken termite mound. Neither had moved, but they traded staccato sentences in their cryptic language.

"They didn't shut up all damn Kan!" Ollie bitterly noted through chattering teeth.

Reed rubbed his shoulders in the sunlight trying to warm himself.

"What could they talk about for so long?" he asked.

"Fuck if I know," Ollie answered. "Ain't never seen anything like this before."

Just as suddenly as it began, the conversation stopped. The old man raised his staff above his head with a shout, following several long moments of silence. The swarms dissipated, and then disappeared.

The old man and lieutenant stood. She bowed to him, turned, walked past the lancers, and picked up her saddle on her way to the horses.

"Return to your patrol," Treena coolly ordered.

The two lancers stared in stunned silence when she unceremoniously saddled her mount and rode off.

"Like I said," Ollie said under his breath, "she's not one of us."

A sudden buzzing sound bought their attention back to the termite mound. An immense swarm of wasps hovered above the old man. He moved his hand in the air and their large black cloud followed him. He then brought both hands upward and swept them down to his sides. The swarm swayed and oscillated around him. When he crossed his arms over his chest, the wasps formed a flowing cloak around the old man's nakedness.

The old man spun three times in his living cloak and stamped the ground with his staff. A humming sound rose in the distance. The southern skies blackened, and the darkness moved over them when a storm cloud of locusts blocked out the sun.

Both horses whinnied and kicked in a panic when the swarm descended on them. The lancers ineffectively swatted at the teeming grasshoppers inundating the area, before diving to the ground and covering themselves with saddle blankets.

The old man spun his staff in the air and the massive host of destructive insects rallied around him forming an insect tornado. He spun the staff faster with each rotation and the swirling vortex of locusts obscured the man. The swarm cyclone slowly lifted off the ground and carried the old man with it.

The two lancers peered from beneath their blankets and watched it fly east over the horizon.

"No one's gonna believe this!" Ollie said, rushing to attend to the agitated horses.

Reed continued to gawk, not daring to blink.

"I'm not sure *I* believe it."

❃ ❃ ❃

"May I present your liaison, Attina," announced Astute Sister Mernasi.

The young Hill Sister bowed. "Pleasure to meet you."

She met everyone's eyes, but her gaze amorously fixed on Shom. For a moment, his mouth hung agape and he returned the enamored stare.

"This is gonna be good," Mal softly said, elbowing Alto.

They watched their friend puff out his chest and try to switch on his normal roguish charm. Alto couldn't help but smile at the obvious chemistry.

Even though she stood a full head taller than the royal, there was no doubting her beauty. She kept her chestnut brown hair pulled back into a tight ponytail, framing delicate, cherubic features. In Amarenian tradition, she only wore a pair of brown crop pants. Their color perfectly matched the areola of her nipples. Her firm, high breasts obviously captivated Shom's attention.

"Thank you for your hospitality," Mal said, "but I wouldn't want to take Attina away from anything important just to babysit *us*."

"Speak for yourself," Shom flirtatiously interjected.

"She is to act primarily as your translator," Mernasi replied.

"No need," Mal countered. "My man Taa speaks your language fluently."

"Of course," Mernasi said diplomatically, "but our customs may seem foreign to you and…"

"My man Taa is familiar with your customs," the Spice Rat interrupted.

Mernasi's expression tensed slightly, taking on an air of superiority Mal wanted to smack off her face.

"Be that as it may, she's been assigned by the…"

"Where are the ambassadors?" Mal cut in again.

"We escorted them to their accommodations in the royal complex," Mernasi answered, taking on a business-like tone. "Your quarters are here and…"

"Yeah, yeah, I got it," Mal said, turning away.

Astute Sister Mernasi's nose flared, and her lips grew noticeably taut, as if she smelled something foul.

"If there's nothing else," she said, glaring. "I bid you good day and leave you in Attina's capable hands."

Mal threw a condescending smirk at the maritime commander marching off while Shom and Attina struggled to keep their eyes off each other. The Hill Sister liaison finally broke her attention from the royal and addressed everyone.

"If you'll step this way…"

She pulled a lever beside the tautly hung door beads and parted them. Their suite comprised four private rooms just off a round common area.

"I'm sure you'll be comfortable here," Attina assured, escorting them in. "I'll return shortly, and we can refresh ourselves. It's best if you don't wander the city unescorted."

With that, she paused for a lingering glance at Shom, and then left.

"A most comfortable prison," Alto said, taking in his surroundings.

✺ ✺ ✺

The Fate of Tomorrow

Soshi changed into the silk robe she found draped across her bed and inspected the small gift basket of toiletries which had arrived with it. A gentle knock rattled door and startled her. She closed the robe and walked over to the ornately carved barrier.

"Who?" she asked through the door.

"An invitation," a voice creaked from the other side.

"Invitation?"

"The queen requests your presence."

Soshi spun and turned her back to the door. She closed her eyes, and her breathing grew heavy. She quickly composed herself and hurried to the side of the bed to retrieve a small leather pouch. Examining it, she weighed it in her hand and then put it in the robe's pocket.

"Come," she invited.

She twisted the latch and the door silently swung open. An elderly, hunched man stood naked but for a simple loincloth in the darkened hallway. He held a glowing crystal in his frail left hand.

"Come with me please," he croaked, turning to lead the way.

Soshi quietly fell in behind while he lit the hallway before them. His solitary light cast moving shadows against the walls adorned with paintings ang hanging tapestries. She couldn't help but notice the Whitmar sideways letter W branded in the center of his back amidst a mass of crisscrossing whip scars. She felt a wave of sympathy contemplating what horrors he must have faced as House Whitmar's prisoner.

They passed briskly through a series of empty corridors, before stopping in front of a wall displaying a large tapestry with a simple yet striking geometric pattern. He reached over to pull a gold tassel and the floor shook from the sound of shifting stone walls. He then peeled back a corner of the tapestry revealing a short corridor.

"The queen awaits," he announced, gesturing her onward.

The wall slid back into place when Soshi entered, but, oddly, she felt no apprehension. She wrapped the robe tighter around her naked body and moved toward the light at the end of the hall. The sweet, musky smell of burning incense drifted from behind an ornate beaded curtain and She heard the unmistakable sound of music. Soshi recognized it as the same style and type of lute she'd heard at the dinner party. The bard's complex tune spread the general feeling of well-being over her like a warm blanket.

She paused before the hanging beads. A soft orange light came from beyond the doorway. She reached into her pocket, pulled out the small pouch with the remaining three doses of Oldust. With careful rationing she could have made that amount last six cycles. She put the pouch up to her nose and inhaled it all.

A blinding rush shocked her body like icy water. Her mouth watered panting until it passed. Her nipples ached against her robe's delicate fabric, and she felt wet. Taking a deep breath, she parted the curtain and entered.

A single orange crystal cast a seductive glow while Incense and music drifted in the air. Mirrors of every shape and size covered the room's round walls, interspersed with small pornographic frescoes depicting every sexual act, combination, and kink. A large round bed covered in black satin sheets and pillows took up the center of the room.

The White Queen stood beside the bed wearing a sheer floor-length, red nightgown prominently contrasting her alabaster skin and silvery hair. A white gold collar around her neck clasped the two swaths of the translucent silk holding the garment together.

Soshi gasped slightly upon seeing her which delighted the queen. The monarch opened her arms and glided across the room.

"My little traveler," she beamed.

Soshi melted into the queen's embrace, shivering and sighing when only silk separated their two bodies. The White

Queen's cold skin heightened the erotic experience and Soshi found herself craving more of what would normally be an uncomfortable body temperature.

The cold both comforted and aroused her at the same time and she found herself falling under the spell of this ancient seductress.

Sensual jolts coursed through Soshi's body when the queen ran her icy fingers up and down her back. They both lingered in the moment and nuzzled each other's necks.

When they finally separated, they intimately gazed upon each other's faces. Soshi could make out dozens of shades of white in the queen's eyes. They seemed to peer beyond her face and scrutinize her very soul.

The White Queen sat back on her bed without breaking eye contact.

"Sit," she said, smiling.

Soshi demurely complied and snuggled up against her.

"Sovereign," she asked, "why do you call me traveler?"

The queen seemed genuinely surprised by the question. When she leaned in close to her, Soshi gasped again, the music and Oldust amplifying her arousal.

"We both know the Middle Realms," she whispered seductively.

This, in turn, surprised Soshi.

"Sovereign, I don't travel, I merely poke at its veil."

The queen ran her hand lightly across Soshi's hair.

"You still bear the marks," the White Queen said.

Instinctively, Soshi ran her eyes across her body.

"What marks?"

This caused the queen to laugh. "Not all marks are visible to the human eye. You are special. The dust you inhale has made you so."

Soshi lowered her head in shame. "So, you know about my affliction?"

"Yes, and it matters not."

"Why?"

"Because all visit the Middle Realms sooner or later," the queen said, gently cupping both sides of Soshi's face, "but we travel there by choice. It can be ours to command together. I can show you."

Soshi grinned in recognition and shifted even closer, putting her face within inches of the queen. She pursed her lips and gently brushed them across the monarch's mouth.

"I'm so honored to have you as my guide," she said in a low sensual voice.

The queen wrapped her arms around her and whispered into her ear, "Even though you were previously unaware of your power, I have been waiting for thousands of grands for someone with your aptitude."

Soshi could barely consider anything except the monarch's warm breath on her neck. The queen lounged back, letting her hands run across Soshi's thighs.

"Why do you want me, Sovereign? I'm not that old or wise."

"I may be old, but I'm not that wise," the White Queen admitted. "Cirok, the one who cursed me so long ago, and I clash constantly across the Middle Realms."

"Constantly?"

She gently placed her forehead against Soshi's.

"Yes." the queen whispered, "even now he stalks me."

"What happens?"

"Endless pain," she said, "for both of us. Resolution for neither."

"How can I *help you*," Soshi implored.

"Together we both can make the difference," the White Queen said, with a sad, sweet smile. "But there is something that you must do to crossover. Something that I cannot ask. Something you must offer."

Soshi stroked the queen's long white hair. The queen peered up, took Soshi's hands, and kissed them. Soshi ran her nose and lips up the queen's white forehead, planting soft kisses at her hairline.

"I know what is needed," Soshi said her voice carrying a touch of melancholy. "And I'm willing to sever my ties with this plain of existence if it means being with you and breaking the curse."

"Consider well your offer, my little traveler," the queen softly warned.

Soshi retained her poignant smile. "I'm certain with your guidance, I could become a *true* traveler."

Soshi paused and peered down at her lap.

"You said you knew of my longings?" Soshi asked with a twinge of guilt. "I've spent enough time in the underbelly of society to see my future. I cannot satisfy these cravings, and there is no cure. I would rather give myself to something noble than confront my inevitable deterioration out on the streets. Together we can lift both our curses."

You are the catalyst," the Whitmar sovereign proclaimed. "That is why I reached out to you in your dreams."

The queen captured her hands again and rose before her. Gently embracing, their noses touched.

"Let me try," Soshi plead, her voice husky and seductive.

She reached up, without waiting, and released the clasp on the collar around the queen's neck. The pretense of a garment slipped to the floor.

"Sovereign, please let me help," she cooed, drawing close for a kiss.

"Dariel," the ancient ruler intimately purred. "My name is Dariel."

Soshi opened her robe and let it drop. She delicately touched Dariel's face guiding her in.

"Together, we can help each other... love each other." Soshi cooed, just before their lips finally locked in a passionate kiss.

❈ ❈ ❈

The streets of Mostas had mostly cleared when the moon slipped below the horizon, beckoning the moonless phase of the luna. Now the sun which hung low in the western sky was the only illumination, bathing the Amarenian capital city in a faint orange glow. Attina led the procession down one of the main boulevards with Shom by her side. Mal, Alto, and Taa trailed behind. They drew stares everywhere they went. Many of the female citizens still out and about displayed open suspicion. Shom however, didn't notice. He was too busy clinging on Attina's every word, pointing out passing architecture and culture.

By the time they arrived at their destination, Shom and Attina were walking very close to one another, brushing up against and indiscriminately touching with intimate familiarity.

Like all buildings in Mostas, the structure was round with semi-circular attachments. Smoke escaped from the building's side appendages and Alto caught the distinct odor of meat being roasted. An arched header covered the wide entrance and a thick curtain of opaque beads hung across it.

"Tonight, as honored guests of the queen," Attina announced, turning to the group, "you are invited to experience one of the central aspects of our society, the Gustare'. It's kind of a bathhouse and tavern all in one. They're everywhere in Mostas, but this one is my favorite."

Shom immediately perked up. "Bathhouse, hmm, does this mean we'll be getting naked?"

"That's usually how we take baths around here." Attina said, winking slyly.

"Singularly or collectively?" Shom suggestively asked.

"That depends," the Hill Sister smirked.

The three-feet thick bead curtain enveloped each person passing through them. When they emerged from it, they found themselves in a large, circular room. An old woman sat behind a small podium to their left.

"Please wait here," Attina beseeched. "I have to secure a private bath."

She stepped over to the old woman and began negotiating. Beyond her in the main room, a large oval pool dominated the center and many alcoves on either side provided refreshment and private baths. Naked women lounged throughout the Gustare', while male waiters dressed in collars and loincloths served each group.

When Shom peered into the expanse of naked people his face lit up with lurid delight. Alto stepped up beside him and joined his voyeuristic pleasure.

"I think I'm going to like this place," Shom confessed.

"I understand," Alto agreed.

"You know Shommy," Mal slyly said, stepping up to him. "Odds are your new girlfriend is a spy."

"Oh, I'm counting on it," Shom gleefully assured, never taking his eyes off the naked spectacle. "It's the guarantee I'll get laid!"

Alto snickered and Mal punched him in the arm.

"Don't fucking encourage him!"

Attina returned, smiling at her accomplishment. "Please follow me."

The Hill Sister led them through the crowded Gustare'. Much like on the streets, their presence drew everyone's full attention. The chatter echoing off the walls trailed to an abrupt silence while they walked through the crowd.

Their private bath comprised a large pool accompanied by two smaller ones. Low tables lined the walls surrounded by scattered pillows. Two male slaves stood just inside the beaded curtain awaiting instruction. Attina gave them a few clipped orders in Amarenian. They bowed and quickly left.

"You may disrobe there," she said, pointing to an alcove.

Shom's attention moved down to one of the smaller side pools, then back to their hostess.

"Shall I claim this one for us?" he asked with a salacious grin.

Mal, Alto and Taa exchanged amused looks at Shom's obvious infatuation.

"I think that would create a very favorable diplomatic position," Attina said, eyeing the royal hungrily.

Alto was on the verge of laughter when Mal reached over and smacked him. The swordmaster recoiled.

"Oww!"

"I told you *not* to encourage him!" she playfully scolded.

Shom and Attina didn't have the presence of mind to notice. The two enamored humans focused their attentions solely on undressing each other.

"It would appear we've discarded all subtlety," Taa said, pulling off his clothes.

Mal and Alto quickly stripped as well and eased into the warm water across from Taa. Shom took the longest to undress. Attina struggled with all the buttons and hooks on his ruffled shirt, multi-buttoned pants, and knee-high boots.

Shom simply pulled down her crop pants with one swipe of his hands. His eyes widened at the sight of Attina's ample semi-erect penis springing up.

"Why, my dear," he said, "you are just *full* of surprises!"

Mal and Alto could no longer contain themselves and began snickering loudly. Shom eyed his amused friends.

"I take it you were aware of the situation all along?"

Both nodded and pointed at Taa. The naked albino peered at Shom with his usual deadpan expression.

"And they say I don't have a sense of humor," Taa calmly declared.

Shom raised an eyebrow with a bemused expression. Attina ran her arm around his waist and whispered in his ear. Shom whispered in agreement and the two climbed into the smaller pool and sat close to each other.

Within a few moments, the slaves returned with a large platter of food and two oversized pitchers. Attina waved her approval and motioned where to set them down.

"I've taken the liberty of ordering some refreshments," she said.

"Wonderful!" Alto piped up. "I'm famished."

As the luna wore on and alcohol flowed, Shom and Attina went beyond touchy-feely to downright frisky. They vigorously masturbated each other underwater, oblivious to how uncomfortable it made the others.

"It's like watching an execution," Mal whispered. "You know you shouldn't, but you just can't look away."

Taa suddenly snapped his head in the door's direction. He remained motionless for a few brief moments then turned toward Mal.

"Captain," the Bailian quietly said. "My brother reports that most of the Amarenian crew have departed and gone their separate ways. There appears to be only two still on board."

"I think it's time I paid them a little visit." Mal announced, her mind racing with vengeance scenarios.

"Aren't you forgetting something?" Alto asked. "I believe they instructed us not to travel unaccompanied."

Mal jerked a thumb toward Shom and Attina, who were practically on top of each other.

"I think that obstacle will take care of itself," she assessed, standing up.

Mal cleared her throat and interrupted the amorous duo mid stroke.

"Well, this has been a wonderful experience," she said. "I think it's time we should return to our rooms. It's been a pretty busy day."

"I think that's a capital idea!" Shom cheerfully concurred, without breaking contact.

Attina, in a complete state of obvious arousal, leered back at Shom. "As do I!"

❇ ❇ ❇

Attina immediately grabbed Shom's hand and practically dragged him through the common area of their suites into his room. The beads slammed rigidly closed behind them.

"Yeah," Mal said, giggling, "she's gonna hurt him."

"I would never have guessed his preference," Alto commented, shaking his head.

"*Preference*?!" Mal blurted in amused astonishment. "Shom's *preference, hmm*?! Well, let's see… they must *still* be breathing… and *not* repulse him, but enough intoxicants could probably overcome that!"

Her giggling turned into outright guffaws and Alto found himself chuckling along with her. Even Taa smiled.

"Fuck," she continued, "I almost had to physically restrain him back in Makatooa from joining a threesome with a random Bailian couple."

A soft knock rattling the door beads interrupted their laughter. Alto stood beside the thickly closed beads. His right hand hovered just over the handle of his short sword and his fingers lightly danced across its pummel.

"Who?"

"Sareeta."

Alto relaxed and pulled the latch parting the beads. The Hill Sister stuck her head in and addressed Mal directly.

"The captain of the *Voola* is a Rayth Faction loyalist who goes by the name of Fia," Sareeta recounted. "Word on the docks has it, the Maritime Council disbanded Captain Fia's crew today and she's trying to recruit a new one before they seize her ship."

The Spice Rat's face grew taut. Sareeta showed no emotion and, not allowing any time for thanks, quickly withdrew her head.

"I've got to move fast!" Mal declared, stepping toward the center of the room, and stripping off her shirt. "I've finally got a name!"

"Your last act of vengeance?" Alto asked, closing the door and turning to find a topless Maluria. His eyes roamed across Mal's bare chest lingering on her small, perfectly formed breasts.

"I approve of the look," he added.

"You just like it because my tits are hanging out."

The swordmaster shrugged and grinned in appreciation.

"Like I said..."

"Yeah, well," she said, shrugging, "this way I won't stand out as much."

When Mal pivoted to leave, Taa noticed the sideways W branded across her back. He approached her with a curious look on his face.

"Excuse me Captain," her navigator asked, "is that the Whitmar prisoner brand on your back?"

"Yep."

"I've never seen one before, may I examine it?"

"Sure, but I got places to go…"

"I'll be brief."

The albino Bailian brought his face within a foot of his captain's back, taking in every detail.

"So, captain," he deduced, "by the size of the brand I can only assume…"

Mal turned and faced him. "That's right, I'm a runner. There's a sizeable bounty on my head."

Taa and Alto both were taken completely aback at her revelation. Their reaction caused the Spice Rat to glare defiantly back at them.

"Why do you think I've agreed to all this low-paying, dangerous shit?" she asked. "I'm sticking around because these negotiations could mean a reworking of the slave trade and the lifting of my death sentence."

"Captain, I believe I should accompany you on this expedition," Taa offered.

"As should I," Alto added.

"Yeah, Taa I get—translation and all that kind of shit—but you?" She turned to Alto and shook her head. "Your standards are *way* too fucking high for this shit."

"You obviously will be engaged in the business of vengeance," Alto said, with a bob of his head. "I'll come to look after our unarmed navigator."

"Alright then," Mal agreed. "let's go kill us some fucking pirates!"

"I would just like to reiterate," Alto said, slipping his blades onto his sash, "my participation in this little endeavor of yours does not necessarily include killing anyone."

"Yeah, whatever," Mal said slipping out the door.

❈ ❈ ❈

The White Queen's handmaidens rose long before the lifting of the Kan. Sweeping through the halls of the Whitmar palace, they heard the passing whispers of how the queen privately entertained a guest during the Kan. Concerned about encountering a sensitive situation, they agreed diplomacy and discretion would be the order of the morning.

Diplomacy first, they gently knocked upon the White Queen's bed-chamber door. Then discretion, they quietly entered and discovered what lay beyond. Five green dresses surrounded the queen's bed, staring at each other in confusion and near panic.

Soshi lay naked on her back, staring lifelessly at the ceiling. Her eyes were open in wonder and a satisfied smile rested upon her lips, which had turned blue.

Between her legs in an obvious scissoring position lay a pile of ash in the shape of a human. One of the ladies in waiting saw something glittering in the dust of what once was her hand. She reached down and retrieved a small ring.

Holding it up, they all gasped.

"The queen's favorite ring!"

"The quake that rattled the palace during the Kan…" One surmised, peering down at the intimate positioning. "You don't think…"

"The White Queen is dead!" another proclaimed.

"But how?"

No one answered.

No one could.

"The curse is lifted!" another declared.

❈ ❈ ❈

The rain had finally stopped and a damp, chilly wind was all that remained. It blew across the docks from the deep northern ocean, signaling the beginning of colder weather. Mal stood, shivering, three slips down from the *Voola,* regretting her wardrobe choice. She crossed her arms over her chest and rubbed warmth into her shoulders.

When the various Amarenians passed, they would take the time to welcome them with a nod and smile. Taa stood beside Mal silently greeting them.

"Is it just me," she asked, "or is everyone being really friendly?"

"It would appear so," Taa answered.

"It's a shame Alto can't see this," she said.

"Captain, he's right behind us," the Bailian replied, "in the building's shadow. He sees."

"Right."

A tall, slender middle-aged noblewoman, with an entourage of three attendants, stopped and stared at Mal's bare back before addressing her in rapid-fire Amarenian. Mal's expression betrayed her ignorance to the language.

"This is Lady Coben," Taa interpreted. "She sees that you are an outsider but noticed the brand on your back. She wishes to convey her heartfelt regrets at your past suffering. Lady Coben also pledges to extend the welcoming hand of amnesty and, perhaps, one day, even citizenship, if you so wish."

The stranger's kindness completely took Mal aback. She stood dumbstruck for a moment. Lady Coben just smiled.

"Please convey to the Lady I am truly touched," Mal replied, "and would consider it an honor to walk amongst them as an equal."

Taa translated the message and the Lady's face lit up with delight. A short-haired, brunette attendant, in a traditional court dress, stood next to her clutching a small leather bag. The Lady Coben held out her hand and the attendant swiftly slipped her fingers into the bag, retrieving a small green coin. She then handed it to Lady Coben, who in turn offered it to Mal.

The Spice Rat hesitantly reached out, unaccustomed to such generosity. The elderly noble clasped Mal's hands when she passed on the coin, speaking rapidly and fervently in her native language.

"This is her personal Simikort," Taa translated.

"Simikort?" Mal asked, perplexed.

"An Amarenian calling card," Taa clarified.

"How do you say thank you in Amarenian?" she asked, still holding hands.

"Rahmat," Taa answered.

"Rahmat!" Mal enthusiastically repeated.

The Spice Rat smiled gratefully and squeezed the Lady's hands. The Amarenian noblewoman bowed her head, before turning and leaving with her entourage down the docks toward the city center. Mal ran her fingers across both sides of the intricately carved green coin.

"Captain," Taa said, when the Amarenians were out of earshot, "upon further observation, I believe the crowds are being exceedingly friendly because the Whitmar brand enamors them to you."

"Good," she said shivering. "At least I got something out of this besides standing here freezing my tits off!"

"Captain..." Taa interrupted, peering over her shoulder.

Mal turned in time to see Fia and Neaux walk down the gangplank of the *Voola* and onto the docks. A sinister smile crept across the Spice Rat's face and suddenly her burning hatred seemed to make her oblivious to the cold. Her mouth twisted into a sneer watching them walk away.

"Let's take a walk."

❀ ❀ ❀

The bead curtain to Shom's bedroom clacked open and the prodigal stumbled into the suite's common area rubbing his glazed eyes. He walked somewhat awkwardly and kept readjusting the towel wrapped around him.

Attina swaggered out behind him also clad only in a towel around her waist. Her pale skin glistened with sweat and she carried a satisfied smirk.

"You're fun!" she declared, slapping him on the ass. "You took it like a champ, *and* you're a good sport."

Shom turned and stared at her, trying to focus.

"I can't feel anything below my waist," he confessed.

Attina grinned and strode over to a table to poured two cups from a pitcher.

Shom faltered trying to cross the room after her and his towel dropped to the floor. He knelt to pick it up and lost his balance, stumbling backward onto the low couch behind him. The prodigal just sighed, sitting there naked, holding his towel and staring off into space.

Attina casually crossed the room and offered him a cup. He blinked weakly at her and took it.

"We'll get you in shape," she assured, taking a sip.

"Huh?"

"You know," Attina said, winking, "you've got a lot of creativity. We just need to work on your stamina."

The Hill Sister suspiciously looked around, noticing they were the only ones in the common area. The other bedroom curtains were pulled back and she saw the rooms were empty.

"Um, serious question," Attina asked, "where are your friends?"

"My who?"

"Your friends, Shom, the people you arrived with!"

"Just because I arrived with them, does not necessarily mean they are my friends."

"Shom, I'm not kidding!" The Hill Sister forcefully said.

The prodigal recoiled and covered his ears. He raised a finger and shook his head.

"There is absolutely no reason to raise your voice."

"Where are they?!"

Shom straightened up and gazed around the room. He obstinately turned back to the distraught Amarenian.

Well, they're definitely *not* here," he snapped. "How would I know where they went? Perhaps they went out for a drink because they didn't want to listen to us."

"Exactly what do you mean by that?!"

"*You must be joking*! *We were howling like monkeys!*"

"That doesn't matter!" she yelled. "I asked them not to go anywhere without me!"

Shom finally took a sip from the cup. He sputtered twice and examined the contents.

"I'm truly sorry," he said, "but we were occupied for quite a while…"

"Not as long as you think."

"Be that as it may. I wasn't here to witness or try and prevent their departure. I imagine my absences will only become prolonged after my, *endurance training*."

"This is serious, Shom!"

"I have no doubt!" he snapped. "However, I would remind you, again, we were just in there fucking. I don't *know* where they are!"

Attina's body trembled in frustration. With an irritated huff she pointed at Shom.

"If you had anything to do with this!"

"Are you fucking kidding me?!" he asked, exasperated. "We haven't been able to keep our hands off each other since we met. I haven't left your side! Hardly the acts of a conspirator."

"I've got to report this," she conceded.

Shom took another swig, then slumped back down.

"I would imagine so."

"I've got to go."

Shom glanced back up and nodded weakly. Reaching down, she put a hand on top of his head.

"I want to believe you," she said.

Shom shrugged without returning her stare. She moved quickly back into Shom's room, dressed, and left.

While the door beads still rattled from her exit, Shom sighed heavily and took a long swig.

"Well, piss."

❂ ❂ ❂

Blenda didn't feel good about having to kill her captain. She'd grown fond of Captain Lage after serving nearly eight grands as her first mate on the Rayth raider *Craven*. Lage took her on as the first Hill Sister in the entire Rayth.

However, the captain accepted a charter in the Amarenian Navy against the wishes of her twelve-member crew. Now the die was cast. Now Blenda was in command. They would preserve the Rayth heritage on her ship. The political winds were quickly shifting, and she realized time was of the essence.

She now moved through the long, shadowed streets of Mostas, absentmindedly twirling the three-foot war hammer which pulped the captain's head only a little while ago. Her destination was a specific Gustare' in the northeastern side of Mostas, catering to Rayth mariners.

"Captain, shouldn't we be setting sail?" her new first mate inquired, attempting to keep up with the Hill Sister's much longer legs.

"We need to know who and how many are with us," Blenda replied. "I got word of this meeting last luna from our Rayth sisters. Once we dispose of Lage's body, we'll be out of here before moonrise."

"They're placing her in an alley," the first mate said. "It will look like a robbery."

This satisfied the new captain, and she kept her determined stride down the dimly lit boulevards. The circular avenues became much less congested with the passing of the moon.

She slowed her gait when she spotted two figures across the street from her destination. One was obviously a male Bailian from the shape of his elongated, bald head. The other, was a human woman in a terrible imitation of

Amarenian garb, sporting the distinctive brand of the Whitmar slavers across her bare back. Blenda tapped her first mate on the shoulder and motioned to the duo.

"Now, this is interesting."

❂ ❂ ❂

Alto paralleled Mal and Taa across town, never losing sight and keeping to the shadows. The two Rayth raiders they were following had entered a Gustare'. He watched the Spice Rat and navigator confer, probably strategizing on how best to enter the establishment.

The sound of others approaching drew his attention down the street. The commotion was caused by two women; one was obviously a Hill Sister, and the alpha of the duo. The other appeared a typical Rayth mariner, bare chested with crop pants and short sword. Both walked up to Mal and Taa with an unaggressive stride. He couldn't hear the dialogue when they struck up a conversation, but the subject of the interaction was obviously Mal's Whitmar slavers brand.

The alpha did all the talking and Taa translated. She seemed gracious to the point of being awestruck. When the conversation became animated and receptive, he could hear their laughter. Mal and the Hill Sister hugged, before walking together into the Gustare'.

Alto pulled his head back into the shadows. He leaned against the wall and felt his heart rate rise and mouth go dry. He resisted the urge to follow and protect, silently running through his Rohina breathing exercises.

Mal clearly used the Hill Sister and her first mate as cover. Mal knew what she was doing. His anxiety eased and the swordmaster resigned himself to the fact that waiting was his only option.

❋ ❋ ❋

Six small boats fished without the moon just offshore of the Mavara inlet. Although hardly profitable, it was a time-honored way to feed one's family, if not much more. The fishers had to leave before the light of moonrise, when the larger trawling vessels set sail for deeper waters.

The older Amarenians groaned at their bad luck when they saw the immense black cloud rising on the horizon. It appeared to quickly head their way. They immediately began pulling fishing lines and anchors. Storms off the deep ocean were common this time of the season. They often passed quickly but could easily sink small boats on the water.

The older fishers gawked at the billowing blackness and then back at each other in bewilderment. It didn't move like a normal stormfront. It undulated, shifting back and forth around a central hub in a tornado-like fashion.

Pointing upward and calling out, anxious chatter erupted between the boats. They quickly grabbed oars and desperately paddled for the shore. A thunderous buzzing filled the air when the cloud overtook them. The swirling blackness passed low over their heads. The sound grew deafening, causing the older women to cringe and place hands over their ears. It roared passed, shooting over the horizon, and leaving an eerie quiet across the waters. They sat in their boats in stunned bewilderment.

The cloud passed mostly unseen by the sleeping inhabitants of the Amoso-Dor territory. It swirled and churned above the fields of grain, rapidly making its way to the outskirts of a small farming hamlet at the base of the Breust Mountains, immediately east of the province's capital of Amoso.

The swirling cloud of vermin settled to the ground beside a large barn, kicking up its own dust storm. Within moments, the tight cyclonic vortex shifted and broke up, unleashing millions of locusts.

Kalaka, the Itori insect mage, emerged from the cloud supported by his walking stick. He adjusted his cloak of hornets, closed his eyes for a moment, and listened to the humming of a million wings, before pointing his staff at a nearby cornfield. He shuddered, recoiling at having brought with him the same destructive insects he spent his life trying to control.

"Well done, my friends," he heard himself saying. "A feast awaits you for your service."

The cloud immediately moved off, covering the tall stalks of corn with countless ravenous insects.

Kalaka raised his staff and stamped it three times on the ground. The soil erupted with thousands of long white larvae digging out of small holes. They formed a massive wave inching across the ground toward the barn. The horde covered the entire surface seeking entrance, invading every crack and crevasse in the walls and roof.

The old shaman hobbled over to the barred doors. He placed the head of his staff against the large plank securing the door and blew a warm breath over the surface. The wood rotted and crumbled to the ground.

The doors swung open to reveal thousands more larvae already at work, devouring the grain inside. He listened to the tiny creatures within, chastising himself for his helplessness. The blonde woman's seductive voice drifted hauntingly through his head. It commanded him to do abhorrent things. Acts which tore at the very fabric of who he was.

The old shaman woefully paused at the destructive sight. His stomach knotted and he felt sick. This went against everything he had dedicated his life to. The destruction of crops tore away at his conscious, but the female lieutenant's beguiling voice and demeanor overshadowed his guilt.

He grinned sorrowfully and hobbled through the open doors.

"Yes, yes, I'm coming."

❀ ❀ ❀

"You have joined us at a pivotal point in history," Blenda proudly announced to her guests.

Mal and Taa stood in a room full of thirty hardened female Rayth raiders in a heated debate. Captain Fia sat at a table with two other captains and the rest of the mariners sat scattered about the main pool.

There were no men present, not even male slaves. The Spice Rat felt thankful she had Taa beside her to translate, but his gender drew attention. Mal hoped they wouldn't care about him since he wasn't a human male.

Fia climbed atop of a table in front of the main bathing pool. She stomped her boot several times. The room quieted and gave her their attention in between gulps of ale.

"You all know me!" she announced, straightening her shoulders. "I will not bow down!"

This sent the room into a rousing clatter of approval.

"How many ships do we have?"

"Three, including yours," came a voice from the crowd.

"Four!" Blenda announced proudly. "The *Craven* sides with the Rayth!"

All heads immediately turned to Blenda.

"You speak for the crew?" Captain Fia demanded.
"I do!" the Hill Sister confirmed.
"But Lage is captain of the *Craven*," Fia said.
"Was!" Blenda said with a sneer.
This set off a murmur through the crowd.
"*I* am captain of the *Craven* now, and the entire crew stands with our Rayth sisters!"
The room erupted in applause and accolades. Fia joined in with the enthusiastic group.
"Four ships," Fia confirmed. "How many mariners?"
A moment of silence greeted her question during the headcount.
"Twenty-seven in all," a voice piped up.
"This will work!" Fia said. "We can take back our ships, but we must act before moonrise!"
"Where will we go?" another skeptically wondered.
"Durik will welcome us," Fia stated confidently.
This set off another round of murmurs. The captain of the *Zurina* stood up insolently.
"Durik?!" she asked incredulously. "As in Durik-Dor and the crazy Ulana sisters?!"
"Yes," Fia confirmed.
"You're joking, right?" the captain asked. "I mean they just tried starting a war with the Western Houses and had their asses handed to them!"
"This will make it easier for us to deal with them," Fia responded with a wicked smile. "The new cock loving Amarenian government has opened trade routes between the Twilight Lands and the Western Houses. This means new hunting grounds for us. We'll be the queens of a new Rayth dynasty."
The room exploded in a wave of excited voices. Mal watched Captain Blenda move in front of them and stand beside Fia.

"I believe Captain Fia's vision is our future!" Blenda declared. "If we truly value the Rayth lifestyle, we have no other choice. There is nothing left for us in Amarenia!"

The room once again flared into verbal chaos.

"Our ships are on the northern docks! Fia yelled. "The moon rises soon! The time is now!"

"Yes!" screamed Blenda, sending the room into hysteria.

Mal and Taa stood in the rear of the room near the backdoor. Her face revealed a mixture of concern, curiosity and hatred. Taa caught the expressions and returned a skeptical glance. Mal met his eyes before returning her attention to Captain Fia.

"As a Spice Rat I can sympathize with their cause," she whispered, "but they don't stand a fucking chance. I just want a chance to kill the quim leading them with my own hands before anyone else does."

Taa nodded solemnly. "I respect your honesty, Captain."

❀ ❀ ❀

From the shadows, Alto watched while the meeting disbanded and the Rayth crowd spilled noisily into the street led by Captain Fia. He heaved a sigh of relief when he saw Mal and Taa come into view, but they moved with the mob en masse toward the northern docks.

The swordmaster shook his head in resignation. *This will not end well.*

❀ ❀ ❀

Mal kept Fia locked in her sights. Their attempted escape from the city should create enough chaos to provide the perfect cover for calling in her long overdue blood debt.

Taa stopped walking. His face took on a blank expression and he stared off into space. He snapped back and quickly turned to Mal.

"Captain," he said, "Shom's returned to the *Haraka* and Orich reports a rapidly growing presence of city guards arriving as we speak."

A jolt of adrenaline coursed up Mal's spine. "Tell Orich to get the fuck out of there. Take her out to a safe distance but be available. We may need to leave quickly."

Suddenly Blenda rushed up, face flushed and panting in excitement.

"I told you we're gonna make history!" she exclaimed.

She tweaked Mal's nipple before disappearing back into the crowd. Mal recoiled at the Amarenian's touch and glanced down at her bare chest.

"It's a Rayth custom," Taa mentioned, slightly amused. "Equivalent to a pat on the back."

"Yeah, fine…" Mal said, still taken aback.

The Spice Rat positioned herself only ten feet away from Fia's while they marched down the street. Taa kept to the shadows of the passing buildings. They followed the Rayth throng moving through the streets running in concentric circles and ringing the city of Mostas.

When they arrived at the wharf walkway, leading out to the spherical docks, a dozen Mahilia stood at attention and drew their lurohs. The city guards set their bolos clacking and sounded the alarm.

❁ ❁ ❁

Orich kept the *Haraka* hovering just offshore above the Mostas docks. Shom glared out the windshield, helplessly watching the unfolding conflict below.

"I'm pretty sure we should be ready to retrieve our friends," Shom advised.

"I have my orders from the captain, Shommy," Orich said calmly. "However, any other observations you may offer are welcome."

"I'm sorry," Shom replied, *"what did you just call me?!"*

"I'm sorry," Orich answered, perplexed, "but Shommy is the term the captain most often uses to address you. I thought it appropriate to…"

"No," Shom interrupted, "it is *not* appropriate!"

Orich adjusted the wheel slightly to face the docks. The prodigal's turned his attention back to the situation on the wharf below.

"As I said before," Shom reminded, "be ready to yank them out of there."

✸ ✸ ✸

Clack. Clack. Clack.

Blenda belligerently charged to the front of the mob and stood before the row of guards.

"Get the fuck out of our way!" she ordered.

Clack. Clack. Clack.

The Hill Sister captain sneered at the city guards, raised her war hammer assertively over her head and gave out a blood curdling scream.

❈ ❈ ❈

"Perhaps a slow circle over the area at a safe distance?" Shom asked Orich.
"An excellent strategy, Shommy."
Shom angrily whirled and pointed a trembling finger at the Bailian.
"Do not fucking call me that!"

❈ ❈ ❈

The dock erupted in pandemonium the moment Captain Blenda's scream reverberated down the waterfront. The Rayth raiders rushed the Mahilia. The clacking of the luroh balls went silent, replaced by battle cries. The guards feinted backward and synchronized the twirling of their lurohs in a deadly figure eight before them. Each Mahilia coordinated perfectly with the guard next to them and formed a deadly wall of rapidly spinning metal balls.

The charging Rayth raised their swords to block or entangle the bolos. The lurohs smashed down several raiders, but the sacrifice left the guards' line breached. Fighting progressed across the dock with the Rayth attempting to get to their ships.

Mal pushed Taa into the shadows of an alley and drew her blade. She surged forward towards Fia, who was busy attacking a surprised young Mahilia guard.

The Rayth captain sliced a horizontal wound across the guard's abdomen. Intestines spilled out on the decking and the guard fell at Fia's feet when Mal ran, unobserved, up behind them.

I'm going to enjoy this, Mal thought, raising her blade.

She swung downward at Fia's head with a savage cry. Mariner Neaux bounded from the crowd, slipping between Mal and Fia. Raising her short sword, she deflected the blow with a jarring clash of metal. The unexpected block jammed Mal's arm, and a searing jolt of pain ran from wrist to shoulder. The Spice Rat cried out in anguish and staggered back, struggling to hold onto her blade.

Hearing the conflict behind her, Fia turned, her face warped with rage, and joined in on the attack. She assaulted Mal from above while her first mate struck from below.

❈ ❈ ❈

Alto reached Taa's position in the alley when a rain of arrows fell onto the docks from archers on the deck of the *Craven*. The projectiles struck many of the Mahilia and they dropped screaming to the docks.

The Rayth now outnumbered the remaining city guards. Alto heard clacking coming from down the main road behind the walkway, signaling reinforcements on the way.

"To the ships!" Captain Blenda screamed when another volley of arrows peppered the docks.

❈ ❈ ❈

Mal's arm burned with pain and she vainly strove to defend herself. She feinted to her right, attempting to keep one attacker in front of the other and minimizing the number of strikes.

The second volley of arrows fell dangerously close to them. A Mahilia guard's body dropped between Mal and her attackers, giving the Spice Rat a moment to regroup.

"Leave her!" Fia ordered Neaux. "Get to the ships!"

Fia broke off and ran but Neaux's blood lust overwhelmed her, and she resumed her onslaught alone.

Sweat stung Mal's eyes, her chest heaved with exhaustion and she knew her arm couldn't deliver many more blows. She managed to block the next attack, but it knocked the sword out of her numb hands.

Neaux, seeing Mal disarmed, lunged forward using her body's momentum to sweep the Spice Rat's legs.

Mal tumbled onto her back, staring at her sword, now completely out of reach. She glared up helplessly at Neaux advancing, her short sword raised above her head, poised to strike.

"Your friends are leaving," Alto said from behind her. "I would join them if I were you."

Neaux turned to see a smiling Alto standing mere feet away. She sneered at this male's audacity when he hadn't even drawn his weapon.

"Stupid fucking dag!" she spat.

Mal watched in horror as the pirate swung her blade at her lover's head. Dread became amazement when Alto clapped his hands together and caught the blade between his outstretched palms. He swung his arms in a large circular motion and pulled the mariner off-balance while guiding the blade downward.

Neaux reeled when her weight shifted uncontrollably forward in the direction of her blade. The tip of the sword embedded in the deck. In a smooth, single motion, he drew his short sword and sliced open her now exposed throat.

Streams of blood erupted, painting the dock and her bare chest in gore.

Fia was already halfway up the gangplank of the *Voola* when she turned just in time to see Neaux topple over beside Mal.
"No!" she screamed and started back down.
Two mariners, heading up the gangplank at the same time paused and held her back.
"Captain, we must leave now!" One shouted hoping to convince their leader.
Hearing the approaching clacking of the Mahilia reinforcements, Fia relented, and the two mariners quickly escorted her on board.
Fia watched the docks fill up with city guards just as her ship pulled away. She eyed Alto sheathing his sword and committed his face to memory
"This ain't over, dag," she swore. "I'll find you."
On the dock, Alto knelt and helped Mal to her feet. She hugged him and watched the *Voola* sail away. Resting her head against Alto's shoulder she gave a frustrated sigh.
"One day," she said in a frustrated growl, "I'm gonna kill that fucking bitch,"
"It's good to see you too," he replied, kissing the top of her head.

❈ ❈ ❈

Nell Warburr rose with the moon, just as she had done every day of her sixty grands. The low sunlight and full moonlight crested the Breust Mountains and flooded her bedroom's simple, dignified furnishings with a warm glow.

The Fate of Tomorrow

The Crone of Warburr Banja, one of the richest farmlands in Amarenia, stretched her thin, muscular frame. She nodded in satisfaction, when seeing her clothing for the day meticulously folded in a nearby chair.

"Toho!" she bellowed.

Her male house slave rushed into the room. Toho bowed and smiled apprehensively. Nell took a moment appreciate the whipping welts streaking his radiant copper skin.

"Yes, Masha?"

"I'm feeling a little stiff this morning. Assist me in dressing."

"Yes, Masha!" he said.

Toho eagerly removed his only garment, a utility apron, and set it down. The crone watched the naked slave approach and smiled at his lack of genitalia. She studied the castration scars between his legs and reflected on the wisdom of emasculating at birth. A slave without distractions is far more productive.

Toho held out a pair of neatly folded leather pants and knelt before her. She nodded her approval and gazed absentmindedly out the window while he guided her legs into the garment. Her long, amber toenails caught on the fabric, and she lost her balance, tumbling backward onto the bed. She sat up astonished and slapped him hard across the face. He cowered from her blow.

"What are you trying to do, kill me?!" she screamed.

"No, Masha!" Toho cried, bowing deeply. "I'm sorry Masha! I'm so sorry!"

She grunted and half-heartedly smacked the back of her house slave's lowered head.

"Be more careful!" she scolded.

"Yes Masha."

Toho tentatively grabbed the waistline of the pants and finished pulling them up. Once fully dressed, Nell let the incident pass and returned her attention to the window. He gently washed her face and began applying makeup.

"Sing for me, Toho," she ordered, eyes glazing over. "You know, the song I love."

The young man swallowed hard and, despite mouth breathing to avoid her repellent odor, recounted a slow, sad ballad in a high tenor voice. The crone continued her vigil while Toho painted her face. The ballad ended when he finished penciling in her arched eyebrows.

The crone finally turned her attention from the window and studied the face of the man she bore over thirty grands ago. His birth was the cause of her family's precipitous drop in social ranking, and she never let him forget it.

"Ah, Toho," she said, chuckling, "how many times have I tried to kill you?"

The house slave kept his eyes on her cheekbones while he powdered the hanging skin to soften her sunken features.

"Too many times, Masha." He said, nodding sadly.

Now ready for the cycle, Nell stood regally before the kneeling naked man. She nodded at a three-foot wooden cane with a worn, wrapped leather handle leaning against her chair. He glowered mournfully at the instrument responsible for all his scars, before handing it reverently to her. She attached it to her belt and signaled for him to rise.

"Breakfast," she demanded.

Toho rose to his feet and put his utility apron back on.

"I've prepared your favorite," he said, "and Bea is already at the table."

"And just how is my youngest daughter this moonrise?"

"Still sad," he answered, fastening his apron.

The crone sighed and rolled her eyes. She took Toho's arm and they walked through the estate to the common area. He escorted her to a large table where a voluptuous young Amarenian with short black hair sat staring mournfully into her breakfast brew. He helped the crone into her seat before excusing himself and headed for the kitchen.

"There's absolutely no point in sulking, Bea!" Nell scolded, face hardened. "It's done!"

"I don't see why I couldn't go," she moaned, keeping her eyes turned downward.

"We've been through this!" Nell snapped. "Your sister is more than capable of trading a wagon of potatoes for a new field slave all by herself. She doesn't need your help."

The young woman finally glanced up. She appeared on the verge of tears, but the crone remained unfazed.

"You're attending the Kaefom Ritual in the next few lunas," Nell reminded. "Getting pregnant should be your sole focus!"

"It *is*," Bea said, weakly returning her focus to her drink.

"Then act like it!" Nell admonished.

"But I've never even *seen* the capital."

"If you think I'm going to risk your well-being by letting you traipse off with your sister into the city unchaperoned, you are very much mistaken!"

Bea was about to offer another sorrowful protest, but Nell wasn't hearing it.

"Just think, Bea," Nell wondered aloud. "A female born into this Banja could elevate us two full social ranks."

"Status is all you think about, isn't it?!" Bea spat.

The crone leaned over the table. Her mother's intense stare forced the youngest maiden to flinch when they locked eyes.

"*Yes*," Nell hissed, "*it is!*"

Toho emerged from the kitchen carrying a platter of steaming food and drink. He rounded the table to place the service down when the front door flew open. A robust male field slave burst into the room and collided with Toho sending the entire platter clattering down on the tabletop.

Hot food and scalding liquid splattered across the surface. Bea jumped from her chair just as a stream of scalding liquid poured into the seat she had occupied.

"Why you!" The crone erupted in a rage.

Nell grabbed Toho by his throat and slammed him down on the table. She leaned over him within inches of his face. Toho's eyes widened with horror, too shocked to react.

"If you endanger my daughter again," she warned, "especially if she is with child, I'll cut your worthless throat and piss in the wound!"

The field slave began cleaning the mess up nervously, unsure what else to do. Nell stood up and released her grip on Toho's throat. He gasped for air while she detached the whipping cane from her belt.

"Assume the position!"

Toho slowly stood up from the table with a resigned expression on his face. This would hardly be the first time he received a beating for something not his fault. He turned around, bent over the table's edge, and presented his bare backside already crisscrossed with scars.

The field slave bent on one knee in a frantic gesture and bowed his head. "It was my fault, Masha!"

"Not now!" the sadistic crone snarled.

Her cane landed its first blow and Toho winced in silence. Bea rushed around the table and placed her hand on Nell's striking arm, tears streaming down her face.

"It wasn't his fault," she insisted, "it was an accident!"

Nell yanked her arm away from her distraught daughter, ignoring her. Two more blows landed in rapid succession.

"Masha!" the field slave cried out.

She spun and pointed the cane at him, "I told you, not now!"

"Masha, please!" the field slave begged, panickily pointing out of the open door.

"What is it!?" the crone huffed in frustration.

Her curiosity getting the better of her, she scowled down at Toho. "Resume your duties!"

He quickly recovered and scampered off. Nell turned back to the field slave.

"Well," she demanded, "show me what's so important!"

The Fate of Tomorrow

When the slave led her out the door, Bea heard her matriarch gasp in shock. The maiden subconsciously wrapped her short cape over her bare chest, focusing on the open doorway. Nell poked her head through the door. Her face was grim.

"No matter what," she said, "keep this door secured!"

Bea nervously wrapped her cape tighter and sobbed.

"*No matter what!*" Nell reinforced, slamming the door behind her.

Nell's throat tightened in horror surveying her property. She trembled and nervously tapped the tip of her cane against the side of her boot. Locusts had devoured every plant and blade of grass as far as she could see.

The cornfield to her right still swayed under the weight of the swarm of locusts hungrily clinging to each stalk. She could see that the cone of devastation emanated from the barn. Pursing her lips in anger she swatted her boot with a defiant crack of the cane.

"With me!" she ordered a field slave cowering behind a large barrel.

The field slave walked at her side and she set out across the barren compound for the barn. The ground crunched beneath her feet with each resolute step. She passed two more field slaves, still reeling from shock in the ravaged farmyard.

"You two!" she commanded, gesturing with her cane for them to follow.

The family matriarch led them over to the barn. She stopped before its large wooden doors and tapped the cane against them.

"Open them!"

They moved quickly and together tugged at the sizable iron rings. The hinges creaked, but the door moved only a little. Something was obviously jamming it.

"Come on," she barked, swatting the slaves with her cane, "put your backs into it!"

Painful motivation forced them to double their efforts. The doors slowly pulled back, before suddenly giving way and throwing her bondsmen to the ground.

When Nell peered within, she cried out in indignation at the sight of millions of insects devouring her entire wheat harvest. The insect shaman leaned on his long walking staff in the center of the large, open storehouse. She lifted her cane and pointed it at the old man with sunbaked skin and a shimmering brown cloak.

"What is the meaning of this?!" she screamed, shaking violently.

Her antics confused the insect shaman. He casually picked up a nearby caterpillar and popped it into his mouth. He chewed openmouthed and tilted his head side to side curiously watching her.

"By the Goddess, I'll beat the truth out of you!" she roared, raising the cane over her head.

The old man's face went serious, and he lifted both arms over his head. When he lowered them, the cloak dissolved and broke into thousands of angry wasps. Nell screamed and the swarm surrounded her and attacked.

The hornets were quickly joined by other flying, stinging insects biting her. They started on her exposed skin but quickly began burrowing into her clothes. With seemingly malicious precision they targeted her most sensitive body parts: breasts, nipples, inner thighs and vulva.

Nell tried to scream but they were swarming into her mouth, up her nose and down her throat.

The bites and stings burned like itchy fire when they invaded her vaginal and anal cavities. She felt her eyes and throat swelling shut and threw herself to the ground in a last-ditch attempt to roll them off her. The besieged crone's efforts proved futile when the larvae and worms covering the ground joined the winged attackers and began burrowing into her flesh.

Inside the house, Bea gasped in terror peering out at her mother thrashing her cane futilely against the swirling cloud. Toho joined her at the window and together they watched the matriarch disappear beneath the swarms.

The stinging insects already covered two of the field slaves, writhing and howling on the ground. The third ran across the compound with a swarm in close pursuit.

Bea stood transfixed by the horrific spectacle. Toho placed his hand on her shoulder.

"Don't look, Masha," he sorrowfully advised.

She continued staring out, tears streaming down her face, oblivious to the slave's voice. She winced with their screams and attempted to look away but found it impossible. Eventually the cries slowed, and then subsided, replaced by only the buzzing of a million wings.

From Bea's vantage point, she could just make out her mother lying on the ground inside the barn, her skin red and bloated from the stings. She watched the barndoors close, seemingly by themselves, and the remains of the Crone of Warburr Banja disappear behind them.

Inside the barn, the insect shaman stamped his staff and the host of wasps reformed into his cloak. He then pounded it again and armies of spiders, caterpillars, and silkworms spun webs sealing the barndoors and windows.

❈ ❈ ❈

Her name was unimportant, forgotten long ago when she joined the Darek Sisterhood, the ancient shamanic midwives of Amarenia. Over the grands, her alignment with earth magic, in service to fertility and nativity, overshadowed her personal identity.

A cool wind swept down from the peaks of the Breust Mountains wildly blowing through her long gray hair. Pods of Brom riders soared above the steep, rolling southern foothills, racing the gale force winds, and bounding the thermals. She swept the hair from her eyes and marveled at the sisters who caught and trained the giant dragonflies.

In the valley below, she spotted the wild Brom hovering a foot above the surface of the lake. Something didn't feel right about how they moved but she couldn't put her finger on it. Back onshore, the smoke rose from campfires nestled in the small hamlet of elaborate tents called pabells.

A cry of anguish brought her out of the trance-like musings. She ducked into the dim interior of the open pabell behind her. Inside, a small fire cast wavering shadows on the ceiling and filled the air with a light yet aromatic smoke.

Three middle-aged nurses surrounded a naked, very pregnant young woman suspended in a sling. The young woman's dilated cervix told her all she needed to know—birth was imminent. The head nurse approached reverently.

"Venerable Darek," the pod leader said, "it is an honor that you attend this birth."

"Of course," she answered, "I seeded her in the last Kaefom. You didn't think I would miss harvesting the fruits of my labor, did you?"

The young woman grimaced in agony.

"Soon, my child," the Darek said,

She pushed the sweat drenched hair from the woman's brow. The mother-to-be smiled in recognition at her through the pain. The Darek addressed the three nurses.

"Why have you not applied the Prowda Balm?"

"She refused the balm, Venerable Darek," the pod leader explained."

This initially surprised the Darek, and she glanced back at the patient for confirmation. The mother-to-be just sneered while another wave of contractions racked her body. The Darek huffed in resignation.

"Oh, very well, no balm it is!" she conceded, "I get it, Brom rider, you're tough! Get me the bit."

"Venerable Darek, she has also refused the bit."

This caused the Darek to point a bony finger at the obstinate woman.

"You can't command Broms if you bite your tongue off giving birth," she said. "You'd regret this moment of bravado for the rest of your life!"

The Darek turned to the nearest nurse without waiting for permission.

"Bit!"

❋ ❋ ❋

The constant clatter of bugs colliding against the windows tightened the knots in Bea's throat and stomach. Toho assisted the distraught maiden to a seat at the kitchen table. She sat shuddering, staring panic-stricken about the room, unconsciously clutching the tablecloth with her fists.

Bea screamed and started whimpering when the outside door began rattling on the other side of the chamber. The handle jangled and Toho noticed it remained unlocked. He stood up and warily approached the thin, vibrating barrier. The rustling and scratching intensified when he drew nearer.

Bea's anxious gaze followed his every step. He caught her eye and nodded with a forced smile to try and calm her.

Reaching for the lock, his fingers contacted the metal latch, which vibrated rapidly under his touch. He hurriedly threw it to lock the door, but in his haste, it bounced off the mount. His fingers felt thick with panic. Fumbling nervously with the latch it finally fastened with a loud click.

Toho let out a sigh of relief and turned back to face Bea. She looked past him and screamed in horror when clouds of sawdust and termites exploded from the doorline. A vanguard of cockroaches followed them and tore through the deteriorated wood. They scurried across the walls before disappearing in cracks and crevices.

"They're everywhere," Toho gasped.

He dashed across the room, turned the kitchen table on its side, and pulled Bea to the floor. He covered their bodies with the tablecloth and held Bea tightly in his arms, praying their death would be quick.

A long, tension-filled moment passed and nothing happened.

"Can you hear it?" Toho asked, cocking his head.

"What?"

"It's stopped."

The maiden listened. An eerie quiet had replaced the sound of marauding insects and they pulled the tablecloth from over their heads. When the kitchen began growing darker, he stared in horror at the windows.

"By the Goddess," he whispered, mouth hanging open.

Bea screamed at the sight of waves of silkworms crisscrossing the glass, spinning out reams of white silk, obscuring the view outside.

"They're sealing us in!"

❀ ❀ ❀

The first-time parent lay back in the birthing sling recovering with her newborn twins. The female child suckled on her doting mother's breast, while the male clung to a scowling wet nurse who seemingly would rather strangle the male infant than feed it. The Darek stood outside the pabell consulting with the nurses and pod leader.

"I will perform the Najuka in two lunas," she informed. "We must let the boy gain strength before I separate him from his manhood."

"Thank the Goddess, she delivered a new sister to us this day," the pod leader joyfully hailed.

"Praise the Goddess!" they chanted in unison.

More Broms joined those just hovering on the lake over the water. Occasionally they fluttered their wings erratically and made loud clacking sounds clashing their mandibles together, almost as if frustrated or restrained.

"The Broms have been acting strangely since last luna," the pod leader noted, shaking her head.

"Something is definitely amiss," the Darek added. "I felt it the instant I arrived."

She watched three returning Brom and their riders land next to the lake. They hastily dismounted and headed for the group with grim expressions and a determined pace.

"You've returned early," the pod leader asked a scout. "Is something wrong?"

"Sister," the Brom rider said, "there is a massive horde of insects devouring the crops ten miles west of here."

"Locusts?"

"Not just locusts," she answered, "Every kind of destructive insect swarming together."

The Darek eyed the scout warily. "Together?!"

"Yes, Venerable Darek."

"I've never heard of such a thing…"

From out on the lake, the Brom started clacking their mandibles more rapidly. All the Broms in the area soon joined in and the volume rose to a deafening level.

A scream rose above the cacophony. The Derek looked on in stunned horror watching the Broms attack the riders unsaddling them. One of the scouts fell to the ground, her severed head caught between the giant dragonfly's powerful mandibles.

The lead scout ran off to assist but stopped in mid-stride when all the dragonflies took off in unison. The pod leader appeared absolutely devastated watching their prize herd of mounts fly westward and out of sight. The camp descended into pandemonium with confused pod members running about with panicked looks chattering nervously with each other.

"They're flying toward the horde!" a scout yelled.

"They go to join it," the Darek said grimly.

"What can we do?" the pod leader asked.

"I must see what I can do," the Darek said, facing westward. "Stand ready to move the pod. The horde could eat everything in its path, not just vegetation."

The women stared at her aimlessly, still in shock.

"Do you understand?" the Darek asked.

They slightly nodded their assurance but were only half listening.

The Derek then hurried to the nearest large tree, its six-foot trunk and massive root system standing directly on the bank. She sat between two large roots and laid back onto the thick green moss, mouthing a low chant. Within moments, the moss enveloped her and crept around her body. It pulled her down into the soft, moist earth until she disappeared.

"Praise the Goddess," the pod leader uttered frailly.

❈ ❈ ❈

Mal stared at the walls of the common area of her suite like a caged animal. She restlessly flipped her dagger into the air, caught the solid-black handle with the other hand, and then flipped it back, before repeating the process. Alto knelt on the floor across from her sharpening the blade of his short sword with a whetstone.

"It's been *two fucking lunas*," Mal grumbled. "How much longer are they going to hold us prisoner?"

"Well, to be fair," he said with a shrug, "you instigated a rather deadly altercation."

Mal snorted.

"And technically," he continued, "we're not prisoners."

Mal caught the dagger with her right hand, reached back and threw it into the wall next to the beaded curtain. It embedded next to dozens of other knife marks.

"Yeah," she said, smirking, "and the guard outside our door is just for our own protection."

Alto held his short sword up and, closing one eye, surveyed his work against his other two blades. He held the steel out at arm's length checking the edge.

"They let us keep our weapons," he countered. "Hardly the act of a captor."

"Still…"

A single knock at the door interrupted her. Without waiting for a reply, the beads parted. Sareeta, now wearing the red crop pants of the Mahilia, stepped through the threshold.

She noted the embedded dagger with wry amusement, pulled it out as she passed, and tossed it back to Mal, handle first. The Spice Rat snatched it out of the air, mid arc, and sheathed it in one fluid movement.

Alosus and Joc' Valdur followed the Hill Sister into the suite, closing the curtain behind them.

"It's about fucking time!" Mal declared, standing up.

"They have sorted things out," Alosus explained. "We determined, that even though you went out without a guide, the people you fought were insurrectionists stealing ships. I spoke on your behalf, and they will press no charges."

"This is good news," Alto said. "Thank you, Esteemed, we are in your debt."

"How fortuitous that you should say so, sir," the Amarenian ambassador said, grinning.

"Wait a fucking centi here Alto," Mal growled, pointing a finger at him. "You can't just go *indebting* us!"

"Uh," Joc' said, clearing his throat, "to clear things up a bit, the *Haraka* is on loan from the Valdurian government."

Mal scowled at the Valdurian ambassador.

"My queen requests you perform just one small task," Alosus offered, "the simple transport of two passengers. This will erase the dock incident from official memory and serve to elevate all of your standings in our community!"

"It's never that simple!" Mal retorted.

"The trip is little more than a hundred miles that direction," Joc' Valdur said, pointing eastward. "It'll take you less than a luna and you're done."

"Why us?" Mal suspiciously asked.

"They need to get there quickly," Joc' answered.

"I don't know," the Spice Rat reflected, shaking her head indecisively. "I've already put this crew through enough crap for little reward."

"Do this," Joc' added, "and the *Haraka* is yours."

"Deal!" Mal quickly agreed, offering her hand enthusiastically.

She then gave Alto a quick kiss on the cheek.

"Apology accepted."

"Wait, what?" Alto asked, bewildered.

"So, are *you two* coming with us?" Mal asked the Amarenians.

"No," Alosus answered, "we're not the passengers. Sareeta and I must return to Zor. I *am* the ambassador they tell me."

"Hey, if you ever find out what happened to Soshi," Mal asked, "send a gull my way, will ya?"

"I will," Alosus assured.

"Speaking of the *Haraka*," Joc' interjected. "Where is the ship?"

"Safe," Mal assured. "I sent her off when the shit went down on the docks."

"I, and my people, appreciate that," Joc' said. "But time really is of the essence here."

Mal peered back over her shoulder through the open door at the albino meditating in his bedchamber.

"Orich-Taa, recall the ship."

"Yes Captain," the Bailian said, breaking his trance.

Alosus and Sareeta hugged Mal, and everyone said their goodbyes while Alto sheathed his blades.

"This begins another tale to build my reputation," he stated enthusiastically "*and* I get to do it with you."

This caused Mal to snort again.

"Yeah," she said, "Shommy's just gonna *love* this."

❈ ❈ ❈

There is always a way.
The paths are there if you know them,
and the Darek did.
The living roots guided the way.
Faster through the trees,
Slower through the grass,
Until...
Near the surface,
So many grubs, worms, caterpillars.
Death beyond.

The path is gone with the crops.
This was the place.

❀ ❀ ❀

Shom noticed the special two passengers waiting on the docks beside his friends when the *Haraka* broke through the clouds and descended onto the Mostas wharf. One, was a tall, long-limbed woman with a shaved head and solemn features, dressed in flowing black robes, sporting an enormous bow across her back. The other, a mousy-looking brunette with thick features and a nervous twitch, wearing the bright blue crops of a government worker of some sort.

Shom met them at the hatch. "Hello ladies, I'm…"

They moved past the royal, ignoring him. The bald one paused and serenely scanned the interior of the craft.

The prodigal's exasperated glance fell upon Mal, who entered the craft immediately after them.

Hmmm, taut mouth, beady eyes, yeah, he's pissed. She defensively held up her hands. "Shommy…"

"I've just spent the last two lunas orbiting this city with nothing to do or *drink*," he ranted. "And, my only companion, let's just say, wasn't a *sterling* conversationalist!"

"No offense, Orich!" He yelled back to the albino at the wheel.

"None taken," he responded peering through the wheel's spokes.

"Then, the first new people I meet in days, act like I don't exist," Shom whined. "I need a bath, a meal and something a little more fun than water to drink!"

Overhearing his friend's lament, Alto snickered when he entered the craft with Taa by his side.

Mal patted Shom on the shoulder.

"Soon," she said in a placating voice.

"Soon!" Shom erupted. "What the fuck does that mean?!"

The indignant royal shook his finger at the new passengers. "*And who the fuck are they?*"

Mal calmly took her seat.

"It means we'll talk about it once we're in the air," she answered, shutting him down. "Let's go, Orich-Taa."

Shom reluctantly took a seat, grumbling the whole time, just before the *Haraka* lifted off the Mostas docks. While everyone settled into their respective places, Alto watched the lanky archer woman retire to the rear of the ship.

She removed the bow from her shoulder and ceremoniously placed it on the deck in front of her. Holding out her right hand before her, a shower of blue sparkles erupted from her extended palm and a long arrow, with bright-red fletching and no arrowhead, appeared in her hand. She reverently placed it next to the bow. The archer knelt before them, closed her eyes, and slipped into a trance.

The mousy brunette settled down across from Alto and Shom.

Mal swung her captain's chair to face her. "You *do* know where we're going, right?"

"Amiea," the Amarenian said with a touch of irritation in her voice.

"Where?" Mal asked scrunching up her face.

"No," she replied, "my name, it's Amiea, Amiea Roko."

"So, Amiea," Mal asked, feeling her impatience rise. "Do you know where we're going?"

Amiea nodded enthusiastically, "Yes, it's…"

Mal waved her hand dismissively and shook her head. Confused, the woman abruptly halted. The captain nodded to Taa who stood up from the navigator's chair and joined them. Amiea eyed the approaching albino with suspicion.

"He's gonna need to touch your head," the Spice Rat said in a calm, matter-of-fact voice.

The young woman's uneasy frown fluctuated, back and forth, between Taa and the captain. Panic grew in her eyes when he placed his hand on the top of her head.

"Relax, it's painless," Mal added with a smirk.

With the destination secured, the ship turned southeast and picked up speed.

Alto leaned over to a sulking Shom and motioned toward the meditating woman in the stern of the *Haraka*.

"An archer with only one arrow is either a grand master or a fool," he whispered.

※ ※ ※

The moss bubbled between two huge, gnarled roots at the base of the ancient elm tree on the Warburr estate. The green carpet slowly took on a humanoid shape. When the moss pulled away the Darek sat up and took in her surroundings.

The blight spared the elm and a small strip of vegetation around it, but ravenous insects decimated the bordering fields. The farm complex was a hundred yards away, in the center of the devastation.

She counted three Broms, roosting on the roof of a barn keeping a lookout and another three on the silo connected to it. It was unnatural behavior for them to remain motionless for this long without a rider. She surmised they must be drawn to the originating source of the psychic field. Someone—or something in the barn was controlling them as well as the other pestilence surrounding them.

The three Broms on the silo caught sight of the Darek when she rose to her feet and took off directly for her. She knew their superior vision registered even the slightest movements and chided herself for standing so quickly.

She calmly bent over, scooped up an enormous pile of dirt in both hands, and flung it up into the air directly over her head. The dirt fell over her and she disappeared.

The giant dragonflies covered the distance quickly. They circled the area, saw nothing, and flew back to the silo.

The Darek took refuge beneath the moss several feet away. She watched the giant dragonflies return to their unnatural roosts and contemplated her next move.

Her clairvoyant senses registered a distant connection with another empath or empaths. She felt this unfamiliar energy drawing closer from the west. Turning her head, she saw a cylindrical object approaching in the clear western skies. Within it contained the presence she felt approaching.

❈ ❈ ❈

Mal's mouth hung open in amazement at the extent of blighted ground they passed over. Taa also stood transfixed at his commander's side. Amiea joined them at the windshield and looked on with a troubled scowl.

"Fascinating," Taa said, betraying no emotion.

"It's *far* worse than reported," Amiea gasped, unable to take her eyes off the destruction.

Mal angrily faced the woman. She could feel her body tighten and face flush. *So much for a simple transport!*

"Okay, I've just about had it with the mystery! This is my ship and we're risking our asses! Who the fuck *are* you, Amiea Roko?!" she tersely demanded. "And *what the fuck* did you get us involved with?!"

Amiea shifted nervously. "I'm afraid that's classif…"

Taa turned in his seat. "Amiea Roko is an appointee to the queen's new Pasturage Group."

"*Pasturage Group?*" Mal asked, confused.

"Part of a secret new plan to standardize farming, animal husbandry and the like," the navigator explained.

The Spice Rat chuckled at Amiea's shocked expression.

"Sorry about that, secret agent," Mal said sarcastically, "you probably shouldn't have let him touch your head."

"They assigned her to study this extremely fast-moving swarm of destructive insects," Taa added, turning his attention back out the windshield.

Mal nodded towards the person in the stern of the ship.

"What about the strong, silent type back there?"

"Wostera's here to protect me!" Amiea spoke up.

"She doesn't look like much of a bodyguard to me," Mal said, unconvinced.

The Amarenian official glared insolently.

"Just get us there!"

"Captain!" Taa interrupted, unusually alarmed.

Mal twirled and glared out the windshield. Three rapidly approaching Broms filled the sky before them.

"What the fuck are they?" she asked.

"Brace yourselves!" Orich yelled.

He pulled hard on the rudder, sending the ship into an almost vertical dive. The Bailian helmsman twisted the ship from side to side in a seemingly chaotic pattern during the plummeting descent. The whiplash turns buffeted bodies about violently, crashing them into one another.

They could hear the scraping sounds against the hull when the Broms landed on the surface of the craft. The giant dragonflies tapped the ship a few times, probing with their mandibles before flying back and joining the others at the barn.

Orich landed the craft west of the compound, facing the buildings. The swarm had already completely encased the barn and the main house in giant silk cocoons.

"What just happened?" Mal asked. "Why did they leave us alone?"

"I mimicked a falling pod or insect that was too tough to eat," Orich responded calmly. "It has bought us some time."

"As the gods are my witness, the next piece of civilization we arrive at, we are having seats with belts installed!" Shom yelled, getting to his feet and rubbing his back.

The royal then gripped an interior beam and helped pull people out of the pile of bodies around the piloting station.

"Alright, sister!" Mal sneered at Amiea. "This is where you and your friend get out!"

"You are not worthy to be called my sister!" Amiea said with a sneer.

"Get the fuck off my ship!" Mal exploded.

Shom watched the interaction with amused interest. There was something he found undeniably sexy about a cat fight. Alto tapped him on the shoulder and nodded to the aft. The kneeling archer remained deep in meditation during the whole erratic descent. Her equipment still placed exactly before her.

"I'm going to go with grand master," Alto said.

❈ ❈ ❈

What was this strange object that fell from the sky? A giant cocoon? No, the insect shaman detected no gestating insect life within. *An oversized nut or berry, perhaps?*

Placing a discarded Brom skull on his head he raised his staff to the barn's rafters.

"Investigate," he impatiently ordered. "I wish a closer look."

Two Broms took flight from the roof crest.

Allow no distractions, the voice of the beguiling blonde lieutenant commanded in Kalaka's head.

❊ ❊ ❊

"Captain," Taa said, "I am definitely picking up two separate psychic energy sources. One emanating from the barn and the other about fifty yards behind us."

"It truly *is* fascinating," Orich continued. "For all the destruction and chaos, I detect no real malevolence."

"Yeah, well the big bugs out there seem pretty fucking malevolent," Mal said, kneeling against the back of her chair to face the group. "As far as I'm concerned, we've done our job. We got our passengers to their destination."

"The lady makes a point," Shom concurred.

"We can't just leave them here," Alto protested. "Those things will most certainly kill them."

"Not my problem," Mal countered with an evil grin at Amiea.

"Well, you are the captain," Alto said, shrugging. "However, if you force them to get out here, I must disembark with them."

Mal froze and briefly paused. Her expression tightened.

"Fine, they can stay. Wouldn't want to break your code."

Shom placed a hand on the swordmaster's shoulder.

"When she says it that way," he whispered, "I'm pretty sure she doesn't really mean it."

The contentious scene was interrupted with Amiea's scream.

Two giant, round, iridescent dragonfly eyes peered in at them through the windshield.

❊ ❊ ❊

The shaman's mouth dropped open, shocked at the images of the flying wagon revealed from the Brom's eyes.

He could feel the destructive suggestions of the female lieutenant overpowering his natural curiosity, but he had to know if it was a threat.

"I'd like a better look at that flying covered wagon!" he ordered the large ant mound around him. "Fetch it for me."

The mound briefly trembled before hundreds of thousands of large ants poured out under the door and into the courtyard.

❊ ❊ ❊

Everyone stared in horrific fascination at the Brom hovering directly in front of the *Haraka*. They all felt a sudden jolt and the craft began slowly inching along the ground toward the barn.

"We're moving—why the fuck are we moving?!" Mal asked.

Taa pointed past the Brom. A massive, rolling, black carpet of ants drew them toward the compound and barn. Mal marveled at the stream of insects carrying her ship but didn't relish the thought of being drug into the structure.

"What the fuck?!" she frustratingly said. "Take her up about a foot and remain stationary."

"Yes Captain," Orich-Taa answered.

※ ※ ※

"I must do something to reveal the hidden!" the Darek vowed, "Make things clear! Bring all into the light!"

She picked up a long, thin twig from the ground, held each end, and raised it above her head while softly chanting. She slowly lowered her arms bending the wood. As the twig bent, all the wooden planks of the front of the barn mimicked the angle of the twig's stress. Nails popped loose from their architectural moorings. Boards creaked under the strain until they exploded outward, littering the courtyard, and exposing the interior.

Thousands of cocoons of various sizes filled the barn. The pillow-like nests hung from the rafters and clung to the walls and fixtures. The insect shaman stood tangled in the silk webbings, knee-deep in a massive ant mound. A Brom's skull covered his head and he held his long staff aloft while streams of bugs flowed in and out.

※ ※ ※

Watching from the ship, Mal gasped in disbelief.

"Are you fucking believing this?!"

"Captain," Taa answered, "I believe this is the source of the blight."

"Do ya think?" Mal sarcastically asked.

Orich gently tapped the rudder and the *Haraka* lifted away from the moving wave of ants carrying them. A loud screech came from inside the barn causing the remaining Broms to take off, heading directly toward them.

The one hovering just outside the cockpit assaulted the windshield and the craft rocked slightly when the mandibles struck.

"That's it," Mal ordered, "Orich-Taa get us the fuck out of here!"

The helmsman manipulated both rudder and throttle, but the craft only shuddered and remained in place.

"Captain, their hindering our ascent," Orich calmly said.

"You two *truly are* masters of the obvious," Mal said in exasperation.

"Captain," Taa added, "if they breach the windshield…"

Mal ignored her navigator, nervously glancing about the ship's interior until her attention fell on the archer kneeling in the back.

Wostera, Grand Bowmistress of Taia-Dor's eyes suddenly opened.

❈ ❈ ❈

The Darek watched giant dragonflies land atop the object and hold it down, while two others assaulted the bow of the ship., The ants on the ground climbed on top of one another, forming a living ladder until their numbers could reach the craft. In a torrent of flowing blackness hey began quickly spreading out over the hull.

The Darek scooped up a handful of blighted earth and, crying out, she forcefully cast it away from her into the wind.

Simultaneously dried earth and sand blew all around the craft, building into an intense storm. The swirling winds blew the ants off the craft and unsettled the Broms.

The Darek's closed her eyes focusing the last of her strength, while she swirled her hands maintaining the intensity of the sandstorm. She chanted furiously and didn't see or hear the Brom approach. Feeling a rush of wind, she opened her eyes in time to see the mandibles of the large insect sever her head.

The beast swooped past, not breaking stride. It carried its prize several feet before dropping it. Still conscious after decapitation, the Darek saw her headless body teeter for a moment, spewing pulsing geysers of blood. It eventually collapsed to the ground and the dying Derek faded into oblivion, eyes fixed on her motionless corpse.

※ ※ ※

The interior of the *Haraka* descended into near chaos. The roaring buzz of the wings above and the pounding of mandibles on the windshield returned, panicking the crew.

Mal watched Wostera calmly collect her implements from the floor and stand up. The bowmistress walked up to the bridge, nodded her head at Taa, and indicated he should open the side hatch. The Bailian looked to his captain.

The Spice Rat shrugged. "Sure, what the fuck."

Taa turned the latch and the door quickly lowered. Wostera stared straight ahead, silently pressed the bow across her chest, and calmly stepped into the buzzing maelstrom surrounding the *Haraka*.

One of the Broms took off after the bowmistress when she gently floated to the ground. She landed, readied her bow, and immediately adopted a wide sideways stance facing the oncoming dragonfly.

At an unhurried pace, she nocked her only arrow, drew her arms in a large arc, aimed, and released in a single fluid motion.

The charging Brom was a mere thirty feet away when the tip-less Ukko arrow penetrated its skull and the dragonfly's head exploded. The arrow continued through the body, cracking the exoskeleton when it passed, blasting out the thorax in a shower of insect gore, before disappearing in a tiny blue spark. The eviscerated Brom crashed to earth, creating a large furrow in the dry ground stopping mere feet away from the archer.

The bowmistress gracefully extended her right hand and the arrow reappeared in it with another blue spark. She nocked the arrow again searching for her next target.

"That's some trick!" Shom marveled.

"And now we know why she only requires one arrow," Alto added.

Wostera deftly dodged an attacking Brom, it sailed past her, missing by inches. She repeated the elaborate aiming ritual before letting the arrow fly.

Mal stared with worry when hairline cracks formed on the windshield from the attacking dragonfly's mandibles. An arrow, accompanied by a distinct whooshing sound, punched a large, neat hole in the attacking Brom's head. It hung briefly, before toppling to the ground. Another took its place and smashed into the glass, spreading the cracks.

"This isn't good!" Mal yelled.

On the ground, the arrow reappeared in Wostera's hand just as another Brom dived at her. She side stepped it, and the creature sailed past, ripping part of her sleeve. It was then she noticed a large stream of ants had broken off from carrying the ship and were headed her way.

Alto had seen enough. He picked up his swords and slid them into his sash. Mal turned towards him in disbelief.

"And just where the fuck do you think you're going?"

"She needs my help," he answered.

"You're out of your damned mind!" Mal insisted. "You can't go out there!"

"She will die if I don't," he replied. "Taa, open the hatch please."

Mal put her hand on Taa's shoulder.

"Stop," she ordered. "Please don't go out there."

He stepped over to her and touched her cheek.

"Just be ready to lift off at a moment's notice," he solemnly said.

❈ ❈ ❈

Alto opened the hatch and vaulted to the ground, drawing both swords in mid bound. He cleared the distance in two leaps and stood behind Wostera just as the Brom soared in for another pass.

He swung his short sword upward, aiming for the pinching mandibles. His blow deflected the attack, but the blade lodged in the hard skin and the creature's velocity wrested the sword from Alto's grip. It twisted him around, and at the end of the spin, he used the momentum to strike with his long sword, chopping one wing in half. The Brom broke into an erratic flight pattern and disappeared over the barn with his short sword still lodged in its head.

Alto whistled a warning and directed the bowmistress' attention to the ant horde almost upon them. She scanned around quickly and spotted a large rain reservoir parallel to the courtyard.

Firing her arrow towards it at an upward angle its impact created a large hole before it flashed back to her hand. A sheet of water cascaded out and across the courtyard, washing away the advancing frontline of insects.

❋ ❋ ❋

The Broms abandoned their attack on the *Haraka* to focus on the sword and bow masters on the ground. Mal stared down at the battle through the cracked windshield and the ship finally began an ascent. The Broms now circled, rising and diving for Alto and Wostera.

"Push through them the next time they ascend to attack," Mal ordered Orich-Taa.

"Yes Captain," they responded.

The Broms rose upward for their next attack and Orich accelerated through the giant insects. The maneuver broke their attack pattern and caused them to fall back to regain order.

"Put her down there," Mal ordered, pointing to a location just north of the combatants. "Be ready to secure them on board."

"Captain, if I may," Taa offered, "my brother and I believe we may have a resolution to our dilemma."

"All ears. I got nothing."

"The enemy is not the insects," Orich explained. "The enemy is within the walls of that barn."

Mal nodded glancing back out at the barn.

"That should be the bow master's target," she agreed, "but how do we get word to her?"

"You will need to take the helm," Taa answered, "and be ready to lift off, if need be. My brother and I must work together, uninterrupted."

"This means you're working the door," Mal said to Shom.

"Wostera's arrow works off the principle of a Flavian microloop," Taa explained.

Both traded blank stares with the albino. "A what?"

"Once the arrow reaches a certain velocity, distance, or whatever trigger the archer has set for it, it slips into the Middle Realms for a brief ellipse and slingshots from that dimension returning to the archer's hand."

Mal and Shom's eyes seemed to glaze over as they attempted to process the information.

Taa let the concept take root, then continued, "Once the arrow enters the Middle Realms, my brother will hold the portal open for a few ellipses longer, and I should be able to attach a psychic message to it."

Shom's face contorted in skepticism. "Will that work?!"

"Theoretically," Taa answered, "It may be our only chance. You can't really hear much in that chaos *and* she doesn't speak our language."

"Alright then," Mal said, "let's do it!"

She traded places with Orich behind the wheel. Shom positioned himself by the side hatch. They watched the mirror-like effect of the identical twin albinos leaning forward and touching foreheads.

❄ ❄ ❄

Flying vermin filled the air, biting, stinging, and obscuring Alto's vision. He deliberately drew the attention of the remaining Broms, distracting them from Wostera. The giant insects were now coordinating their diving attacks on the swordmaster and he patiently awaited an opening. When the next attack came, Alto parried one set of lunging mandibles and dodged the next by dropping to the ground. He rolled back to his feet, watching the skies for the next arial assault. The Broms soared into striking position, but before they could dive, the *Haraka* plowed through them and disrupted their attack.

Wostera released her arrow while the dragonflies struggled to regroup. It pierced the wing joint of a Brom trying to right itself, before disappearing in a blue flash. The entire left wing exploded and the Brom spun out of control and crashed.

The bowmistress reached out to catch the returning arrow but felt nothing in her hand except swarming insects. She gazed down at her outstretched palm shaking her head in astonishment. Just as she grew concerned, the arrow appeared.

This has never happened before, she inwardly lamented. *It's never returned late.*

She grasped it and stared at the projectile intensely while the whirlwind of flying insects coursed around her. She could hear Alto through the deafening buzz, urging her back to the *Haraka,* which had landed just ten feet away.

Ignoring him, she continued staring at the tardy arrow while the insect flurry stung her and clung to clothes and skin. Alto persisted with his alarm, shouting and waving his hands, pointing at the airship's opening ramp.

Suddenly she understood. *The barn! Of course, it was so simple*!

In a supremely surreal moment, Alto witnessed a look of comprehension cross Wostera's face. He screamed for her again just before dodging the remaining dragonflies' attempted attack. An expression of serene resolve crossed Wostera's face, nocking the arrow and beginning her ritual arc, this time aiming at the barn instead.

Alto's chest heaved and sweat stung his eyes. His limbs were growing heavy and he could feel fatigue setting in.

In a moment between Brom attacks he saw that the four-foot-wide column of marauding ants were only inches away from the bowmistress. Dropping to one knee in front of the archer he swept the flat of his blade across the advancing bugs. More ants quickly replaced the ones he brushed aside, but she was able to fire the arrow.

Alto desperately kept sweeping the ants while he watched the arrow fly. The magical projectile traveled straight, blasting through the wooden paneling along the lower right quarter of the barn.

The insect swarms immediately began dissipating and the remaining Brom flew away. The column of ants diverted course to a more natural meal—the fallen Brom's remains.

Once again, Wostera held out her hand again, but the arrow did not return. Her face tensed and brow furrowed. She eyed the barn suspiciously and lowered her bow.

Quiet had now settled in and the crew cautiously emerged after the *Haraka's* side ramp lowered to the ground. Mal ran over to Alto and threw her arms around him. After a prolonged hug, she stepped back and grabbed each side of his face.

"Why the fuck do you keep doing crazy shit?!"

Shom and Orich-Taa walked the grounds, taking in the devastation. They carefully scanned the exposed barn and main house.

"Captain, I am no longer detecting any major psychic fields," Orich reported. "There are, however, two human life essences originating from within the farmhouse."

"Dig them out," Mal ordered.

Wostera stepped before Alto and spoke a single sentence in a gravelly language he didn't understand.

"The Grand Bow Mistress of Taia-Dor requests your assistance," Amiea translated. "For her to ask for your help is a *great* honor and shows much respect."

Alto straightened and bowed. "I would be honored."

Wostera turned and walked into the embattled barn. Alto quickly followed. Mal's face fell when she lost sight of them.

"What the fuck…" she said, shaking her head. "Taa!"

Upon hearing his name, the albino's attention returned to his captain. Mal motioned towards the barn. He nodded and trotted after them.

❋ ❋ ❋

Hatched cocoons and broken silk nests littered the floor within the outbuilding. Wostera traced the arrow's path to the insect shaman's body lying face down in a pool of blood. The entire center of his torso was missing. Only a bloody cavity remained where the arrow penetrated and a spattering of gore on the wall opposite the entry hole.

"Where did the arrow go?" Alto asked.

Wostera uttered a growling phrase.

"She says *he* stole it," Taa translated, entering the barn behind them, "and she claims she's going to get it back."

"How could he steal *anything*?" Alto asked. "He's dead."

"In theory his essence left his body for the Middle Realms in the same instant the arrow also passed through them on its way back to the bowmistress," Taa speculated. "Perhaps he simply grabbed it on the other side and prevented its return."

The Bailian knelt over the body and gently rolled it over. Removing the Brom Skull he tossed it aside.

"This was how he was able to see through the Brom's eyes, he reported.

The old man's face, now finally revealed, seemed peaceful in death. Taa placed his right hand on the dead man's forehead.

"His prime essence has passed,' Taa said with closed eyes, "but there still are residual memories…

"His name was Kalaka, an insect shaman from the Island of Otomoria. He wasn't evil. In fact, I'm sensing a long life of service to his community. These actions were not in his nature. A very powerful entity beguiled him into destroying these crops. It took the face of a blonde woman wearing a lieutenant's uniform. Things are fading, but I sense House Eldor was behind all of it."

Alto sighed and closed his eyes at the news.

"Shom isn't going to like that."

❀ ❀ ❀

"You wanna explain to me how it's my ship, but I've still got to run errands for House Valdur?" Mal asked.

Alto squeezed her thigh under the table. With his other hand he gestured to Mal.

"What I *believe* the captain is trying to express," the swordmaster interjected, "is her heartfelt thanks for House Valdur's generous gift. She's simply inquiring as to the nature of our future relationship."

Joc' Valdur smiled at the attempted diplomacy.

"It's called a Loose Charter."

Mal shook her head skeptically. "What the fuck does *that* mean?"

Alto squeezed again. This time she swatted his hand away. Joc' and Shom couldn't contain their amusement. Broad grins stretched across both their faces. It took a moment for the Valdurian ambassador to compose himself and adopt his business demeanor.

"It means you can operate the craft for your own private gain," Joc' offered, "so long as you break no Valdurian laws or treaties. And, if it's not out of your way, we may ask you to run an errand or two … for full compensation of course."

Mal sat, silently contemplating the offer. She checked Shom, and then Alto, eager to get their reaction. Both nodded their approval. Her attention returned to Joc' with a satisfied smile.

"Fine, deal!"

"I think you made the right decision," Joc' said.

The Valdurian ambassador picked up a medium-sized flat leather pouch at his feet and placed the satchel on the table before him. He withdrew two large sheets of paper folded in quarters. He placed one on the table.

"This is your official charter from House Valdur."

Mal grinned exuberantly at the piece of paper. Joc' placed the other piece on top.

"And this is your official commission as a captain in the Valdurian Air Service."

Mal shook her head in surprise. She picked up the paper and excitedly examined its contents. Her exuberant mood quickly turned confused.

"I can't read this!"

Joc' grinned knowingly. "Both are official documents from House Valdur. They're written in Valdur-Ya."

"Yeah, but…"

"Maluria, don't be boorish," Shom said, annoyed at his friend's unsophistication.

Mal refolded the paper and sat back.

"Thank you, Ambassador," she said sincerely.

Joc' placed two more folded sheets in front of Mal.

"These are for Orich-Taa," he said. "They both now hold the rank of pilot in the Valdurian Air Scouts."

The albino twins exchanged surprised expressions.

"Thank you, Ambassador," they uttered in unison.

Shom fidgeted in his chair and drummed his fingers on the table.

"This is all well and good for those folks who fly about like vagabond birds. I, on the other hand, was hoping for something a bit more grounded."

"Never change my friend," Joc' said, grinning.

He retrieved five wafer-thin Ukko wood one thousand secor commodity notes from his pouch and stacked them on the table.

"One for each of you."

"Please forgive me for doubting," Shom apologized with a greedy smile.

One by one, each crew member picked up their piece. Alto and Orich-Taa curiously examined theirs, having never seen a commodity note before. The three inch long and two-inch-wide rectangles bore the outline of an airship burned into its surface on both sides. The Imperial number one thousand was positioned in the middle, marking the value at ten thousand struck gold coins.

"I've also arranged for repairs to your craft," Joc' said.

"Seats with belts!" Shom abruptly suggested.

"Don't worry Shommy," Mal said, chuckling, "we'll get you *something* to sit on. Maybe Attina's available."

"The closest air station is in Immor-Onn," Joc' continued. "It's newly built and fully operational. They're expecting you."

The name of their birth city caught Orich-Taa's attention. Mal noted her crew's excitement and cautiously grinned

"Why so generous?" she asked. "What's the catch?"

"You think *this* is generous?" Joc' asked. "We haven't even gotten to the Amarenian queen's appreciation yet. Let's not forget you successfully enabled the historic first diplomatic mission to Amarenia. And you helped to save the agricultural economy of the entire continent. I'd say that warrants compensation, wouldn't you?"

"Sure," Mal agreed, "but up till now I didn't think anyone else fucking would!"

Mal fiddled with the commodity note before sticking it inside her vest.

"Besides," she continued, "I've always wanted to visit the Twilight Lands."

Joc' grinned broadly and reached into the pouch again.

"I'm so glad you said that."

Mal's eyes narrowed. "Here it comes."

He pulled another one thousand secor note from the bag and set it before her.

"Seeing how you're going that way, anyhow…" he began. "We *do* need a small errand performed."

Mal glanced from Joc', down to the note, and then back.

"Talk to me."

GLOSSARY

Spoiler warning: *The following is a master glossary for all the books in this series. Reading beyond specific word or phrase searches could result in spoilers.*

Term	Explanation
Adad Sunal	EEtah war collage belonging to House Bran. Its specialty is conducting internal security for House Bran.
Agress	Etheria Crystal, Green w/ red striations, which opens and closes doors, windows and hatches, negating any locks but not traps or wards.
Aiken	Semi-sentient clouds sent out across the Annigan by the Ghas-Tor. When placed against the backdrop of a blue sky they appear to be glowing blue clouds, all but indistinguishable from other clouds. They are remote viewing devices and record everything they experience, both on the ground and in the air across the Annigan. Aiken immediately send the visuals back to the mountain, which is the epicenter of air magic, however recent images remain in its limited memory. Avions and anyone possessing psychic abilities can access their recent

	memory by flying through them and communing.
Akina	Humanoid fox creatures native to the Barrens in the Twilight Lands. They're sly and excellent thieves.
Amarenian	Female human race formerly noted for their hatred and slavery of men and piracy.
Angona	Roasted eel on a stick. Sold from vendors' carts all over the City of Immor-Onn.
Annigan	The name of the world which is the setting for the various stories in the Tales of the Annigan Cycle.
Anointed Sister	The title for the Amarenian Queen.
Aquamarine	Pale blue Etheria crystal which reveals things true nature.
Ara-Fel Party	Political party of Amarenian farmers.
Arapa Fish	This large fish native to the back waters & tributaries of the Otoman River is torpedo shaped with large blackish-green scales and red markings. Streamlined and sleek, its dorsal and anal fin are set near its tail. Unlike other fish it has a fundamental dependence on surface air to breathe. In addition to gills, it has a modified and enlarged swim bladder composed of lung-like tissue, which enables it to extract oxygen from the air.

	The Dreeat especially covet its tough scaly skin to use as armor. The scales are so abrasive they sell them for nails.
Ash-Ta	Avion derogatory term (winged monster) for the humanoid bats which inhabit the rocky crags in widespread colonies stretching across of The Spine of the World. There have been six distinctive tribes noted by Avion scholars in the Ash' Ta Garia: the Molossi, Acero, Chiro, Ptero, Diaemus and Desmodus. Ash-Ta are allies with the Tiikeri and share an enemy in the Do-Tarr.
Astute	Amarenian title for high level politicians. Usually paired with the term "sister."
Aur-Quaz	Iridescent Etheria crystal stimulating energy.
Available Regions	Uninhabited areas of Immor-Onn waiting for the residence displaced by the recent Black Pearl Revolution to return and inhabit.
Avion	These proud sentients are the rulers of Lumina's sky. Incredibly beautiful and graceful to behold and unabashedly elitist, especially towards their distant cousins the humans. Avions refuse to wear any sort of armor and yet these fierce fighters have led the way in almost every major

	war fought. They are skilled Kel handlers, tending to huge herds of the flying lizards used as beasts of burden or harvested for food. Their scholars have contributed a great deal to the knowledge of everyone on Lumina. The four Great Houses occupy the air space and mountain tops of the Goyan Islands.
Avion Great Houses:	
House Azar	Avion House inhabiting the City of Mitar, on the Island of Dal, in the Tellasian chain, ruled by Queen Averin. Their territories include the skies over the Tellasian Chain, Otomoria, Zer-Tal Twins, and the Zerk Atoll. They are known for their healing Clerics of Neami and their beautiful music.
House Eacher	Avion House inhabiting the Island of Wou, City of Picon & surrounding airspace. Ruled by King Sindil.
House Pyre	Eldest, largest, and most powerful of all the Avion Houses. They inhabit the skies above the Island of Goya. Their magnificent city stronghold of Darmont Keep sits on the north face of Mt. Goya. Unlike the other Avion Houses who utilize air magic, they are the masters of Fire Magic drawing their power

	from the constantly erupting volcano.
House Solas	Smallest and weakest of all the Avion houses. They inhabit the city of Adean on the island of Temil in the Outer Zerians and control the surrounding airspace.
Awal	First of the ten Quinte Grand Cycle, spring.
Azurite	Purple Etheria crystal which connects to the Middle realms.
Bailian	Predominate race of the western Twilight Lands. Descended from the Piceans they are a beautiful humanoid race with pale blue skin and large eyes.
Banja	Amarenian noble families. There are seventy-seven of them, eleven for each of the various seven provinces called Dors. There is a strict pecking order within each Dor and each Banja is always trying to elevate its status.
Banok Atoll	Island ring in the Southeastern Ocean of Lumina. It is the location of one of the largest permanent Flavian Portal. Its ripples extend out hundreds of miles and affects the entire southeastern Deep Ocean of Lumina.
Banok Run	Final test for admittance to the elite Brightstar Sailors of the Calden Navy. It comprises sailing a tight circle through the turbulent seas around the Banok

	Atoll, without the giant Flavian Portal located in those waters pulling you into it.
Bespoke Lords	Members of prominent families who have Bespoke Names and are advisors to the sovereign in a respective noble human house in the Goyan Islands.
Bespoke Names	In the Goyan Islands, these are personalized family names indicating wealth and status which can only be bestowed by a governor or higher, usually in reward for exemplary service to the crown.
Black Mural	Magical record of the Annigan in the Rod-Ema Trench in the Deep Oceans of Nocturn. It records each act of imbalance on the planet from great to small. When one side grows too powerful, it grows so large, it plunges into the planet's core killing all life, allowing it to start anew.
Black Talon	Special forces of the Aramos Army, the Fosvara Guard.
Boustian Mage	Bards who perform magic by singing, playing music and storytelling, located in the larger cities of the Goyodan Chain.
Brightstar	Elite sailors of House Calden qualified to sail the deep oceans and the storm-tossed waters of the twilight areas of the world. All captains in the Calden Navy are required to be Brightstar

	qualified. Brightstar only allows acceptance to their ranks upon completion of a sailing around one of the two massive Flavian portals, the Innaca Deep or the Banok Atoll. Once inducted they are qualified to wear the coveted star over swan pin.
Brom	Horse-size dragonflies which inhabit the steep southern foothills of the Amaren Mountains.
Brom Riders	Amarenians who catch, train, breed, and ride Broms.
Calcite	Clear Etheria crystal with aids in navigation.
Caldani	Privateers hired by human House Calden to patrol their waters.
Calden Intelligencer Service	Elite spy, protection, and secret police for House Calden. They draw almost all from the Calden Maritime Legion.
Calden Maritime Legion	House Calden's marines
Calisma	The main library in the University of Marassa, Zor.
Cali	Branch libraries and scriptoriums in the five human capital cities in the Goyodan Island Chain.
Carbana	Chewing tobacco rolled into a tight tube.
Cavernite	Etheria Crystal, pale green with pink striations. When placed on the interior side of all the structure's exterior walls it increases physical dimensions of

	the interiors size. The size of the increase will depend on the amount of Cavernite used and the amount of PSI it's powered with.
	This crystal must receive a constant supply of PSI power or the dimensions will revert back to their original size. For this reason, they are almost always attached to an Obsidian PSI battery.
Centi Elipse	Called a Centi for short. Unit of time in the Goyan Islands equaling a minute.
Celot	Amarenian term for a priestess.
Cevot	Large sentient spider creatures that inhabit the Os-Oni Mountains of the Twilight Lands, known for their silk.
Ched	Seventh of the ten Quinte Grand Cycle, autumn.
Cluster	Name for the grouping of ten cycles. The Annigan's version of a week. There are five clusters to a Quinte.
Cobalcite	Deep pink Etheria crystal used for healing.
Common	Short for the Common Tongue, a spoken only language used mostly by humans and those that do business with them.
Cocoonessa	Cocoon city of the Tinian Moth creatures on Mt. Natal in the Land of Mists, Nocturn. Also called the Silk City.

Corporal Reach, The	Otherwise known as the prime material plain of the middle realms. It is the Annigan resides.
Coxeter	Both the language and magic system of the Tinian race is a complex form of three-dimensional geometry. It is revealed in two different ways. The actual written language which is a cryptic mathematical notation using lines dots. The other more complex variation is in the three-dimensional mapping which is the way their mind perceives all math. It is displayed best in their silk weaving. Intricate geometric patterns are used to create everything from the simple walls created by the larva to the delicate patterns woven by the adult Tinians. Much like the rings of a tree a dissected pod wall revels when it was made and age of the maker. These patterns when combined with Etheria Crystals can be used to perform spells.
Croquis	Magitech mapping devise which projects a scalable three-dimensional holographic image of a desired location, including other planes and the multiverse.

Cub Prince	Heir to the throne of the Tiikeri Empire. All Tiikeri kings are a rare black tiger. Once a generation the king must breed an heir. All the prominent Tiikeri families offer their most eligible daughters to breed with the king. Only one will conceive a black tiger. All other cubs produced from this union are killed. The complete family that bore the Cub Prince are then moved into the palace and are also considered nobility. The Cub Prince is immediately groomed for the throne. When he comes of age, he must kill his father then take the throne.
Cul-Ta	Humanoid rat creatures found in almost every City in Lumina.
Cycle	Time period equivalent to a day.
Dag	Amarenian term for a common slave. A derogatory slang word for a male.
Darek Witch	Amarenian earth shamans acting as midwives and perform other shamanistic duties.
Darian Silk	High quality silk spun by the Cevot Spiders. They trade it to the On'Dara.
Darwan	This race is a cross between the Balians and the Fudomi. They are the most prolific humanoid native to the Barrens. Their villages are situated around Ghorn temples

	and must pay a tribute to the Onay horde of its region. Villages close to the borders of the hordes are always under threat. These creatures raise a herd animal called the Ng'Ombe which is the major food staple in the Barrens.
Dasam	Tenth of the ten Quinte Grand Cycle, winter.
Deci	Time unit in the Goyan Islands equivalent to one hour.
Derde	Third of the ten Quinte Grand Cycle, spring.
Diamond	Clear Etheria crystal which transfers power.
Diplomat Stone	Slang name for the Etheria Crystal, Larimar. It allows translation of all languages and to communicate from a distance. They are issued to diplomats serving in foreign lands.
Doggin	Derogatory term used for slave dock workers in the city of Aris.
Dolin	Etheria gem hunters mostly of the Gila race. They travel the Barrens in small caravans harvesting raw Etheria Crystals. They then take them back and sell them to the Zadim lapidaries of the Oasis in the Dark Waste Desert.
Dor	Title of the seven various provinces in Amarenia. Taia-Dor, Denat-Dor, Mivira-Dor, Amoso-Dor, Kinning-Dor, Rackam-Dor, Durik-Dor.

Do-Tarr	Sentient mantis hive mind creatures from the Land of Mists in Nocturn. They comprise two large hives in the north and south with precise tunnel networks beneath the ground. They are expert builders and are neutral in all forms of politics.
Dreamer in the Lake	Demi-God of the Os'Tor Forest and a Harbinger of Balance. She rests at the bottom of a large lake encased in mud and manifests herself on the lake's surface as a multicolored lotus. Her accolades are sentients from every race who sleep around the lake's shore. They send their ethereal bodies out into people's dreams and guide them.
Dreeat	Humanoid crocodile people who inhabit the area at the end of the western fork of the Otoman River in Otomoria. They grow sugar cane and make healing candies from it. They also harvest a meaty river fish as a major part of their diet. For thousands of grands, ever since their arrival humans have been attempting to eradicate them.
Dronning Mare	Female horse chosen to breed with the On'Dara chief.
EEtah	Large, powerful and aggressive humanoid sharks, professional warriors of Lumina trained in martial schools known as Sunals.

	After their egg birth in the hatcheries and their first year in the nursery they are sorted to one of the various Sunals of their House.
	Females enter House Nur and the males go through a highly competitive Sunal scouting, recruiting process with the nursery's called The Garess. Sunals then hire out bodyguards, sentries, mercenaries and virtually anything martial. This, and weapon manufacturing and sales, are the main revenue streams for the great houses.
EEtah Great Houses:	
House Nur	This Noble house is female only. Co-ruled secular Queen Mother and spiritual High Priestess.
	Temple of Drulain headquartered in the High Holy City of Zor. Specalties: Scribes, Clerics, Healers, Politics, Domestics.
House Crom	Three Sunals in the Tellasian Chain:
	Sedar Sunal on Roe Island. Specialty: Bodyguard.
	Boril Sunal on Uma Island. Specialty: Crom Internal Security.
	Zorod Sunal on Tel Island. Specialty: Castle and Town Defense.

	House Bran	Four Sunals in the Goyodian Chain:
		Garf Sunal on Quell Island. Specialty: Long term inland duty.
		Tukk Sunal on Mobis Island. Specialty: Shipboard Security.
		Adad Sunal on Creos Island. Specialty: Bran Internal Security.
		Farak Sunal on Roust Island. Specialty: Bounty Hunter, Vengeance.
	House Zed	Three Sunals in the Wouvian Islands:
		Dakor Sunal on Owling Island. Specialty: Shock Troops.
		Jut Sunal on Tor Island. Specialty: Zed Internal Security.
		Morrak Sunal on Billow Island. Specialty: Police, Executioners.
Elipse		A Unit of time in the Goyan Islands equaling a second.
Esteemed		Amarenian title for an ambassador, usually paired with the term 'sister'.
Etheria Crystal		Crystals that contain magical properties. Mostly found in the form of trees in the Barrens of the Twilight Lands. They harvest and process the crystals in the oases of the Dark Waste Desert. They are the primary form of magic in Nocturn.

Flavian Portals	Portals through space crossing to different points in the Annigan and seemingly instantaneously accessible. Each Flavian Portal is different. There are several large, fixed portals on both Lumina and Nocturn and hundreds of smaller dedicated Flavians. Certain animals, intoxicants and magical items can open smaller portals. Every Flavian Portal connects to its destination by passing through the inter-dimensional Middle Realms.
Frozen Sea	This vast expanse of open ice flows covers the vast majority of Nocturn and is the largest centrally occupied area in all of Annigan. The ice ranges from a slushy mixture with icebergs near the land masses to several hundred feet thick in the eastern areas.
Forsvara Guards	This is the rank-and-file foot soldier army of House Aramos.
Fudomi	Sentient humanoid ram creatures that inhabit the western Os-Oni Mountains of the Twilight Lands. They are constantly at odds with the Cevot Spider broods. They steal and sell the spiders silk and their eggs, which are considered a delicacy.
Galeb	Sea Gulls bred with a psychic connection to a handler. They are

	used to transporting messages across Lumina.
Garf Sunal	EEtah War college belonging to House Bran. Their specialty is long term inland duty.
Gar-Kal	Fish head humanoids living on the ocean floor of Nocturn. They are of low intelligence and aggressive.
Geta	Amarenian title for a master at a skill or craft, especially if they teach it.
Ghas-Tor	This is the tallest peak on the Annigan. It reaches upward 32,000 feet in the Os'Ani Mountain range, Twilight Lands. It is more than a mountain; it is a sentient being and the epicenter for Air Magic in the world.
Ghorn	Necromancers of the Barrens in Twilight Lands.
Ghost Suit	A grey, skintight jump suit used mostly by Valdurian forces to blend into the Kan fog.
Ghosts of the Kan	Mariners term for Rayth raiders. This is because of the ghost white chalk which covers their bodies and acts as camouflage when they attack during the Kan fog.
Gila	These are the main sentient race populating the Dark Waste. Their original stock comprised Bailian pilgrims and a now long-gone sentient lizard native to the region. They are an advanced

	race which occupies the three large oasis of the desert.
Golden One, The	Otick term for the Golden Avatar.
Goy-Ardia	Goyan fire mages trained at the University of Marassa.
Goyan Calander	Method of time keeping found only in the Goyan Islands.
	It consists of a Grand Cycle (year) which is comprised of 10 Quinte (months) named; Awal, Teine, Derde, Kvara, Peto, Sesto, Ched, Merve, Tisa and Dasam. Each Quinte is divided into 50 Cycles (days) with each cycle being divided into 50 Deci (hours) 25 being in sun and 25 in Kan. 10 cycles equal a Cluster (week) with 5 Clusters per Quinte.
Grand	Short for Grand Cycle. Time period equivalent to a year.
Grass Eater	Singa insult
Gustare'	Amarenian bath house and tavern.
Gyronite	Etheria Crystal which maintains balance.
Hackney	Etheria driven taxis of various sizes found in the major cities of Lumina.
Hand of the Wind	Assassin's guild of Annigan. All members worship Orad, goddess of death. Upper levels are clerics of Orad.
Hakim	A judge in the High Holy City of Zor.

The Fate of Tomorrow

Harbingers of Balance	Sentient creatures of all types who have given themselves to monitoring the balance of the Annigan and giving warning when something is about to upset the balance.
Hasteen	City of the Dreeat crocodile people.
Hill Sister	Hermaphroditic Amarenian warriors who inhabit the northern foothills of the Amaren Mountains. Even though they possess both male and female sex organs, they cannot procreate. Amarenian nobility use them as seneschal/bodyguards partly because they can have sex with them and not violate their 'no man' pledge.
Hoon	Word used in Zor to denote a pimp or the manager of a brothel.
Howlite	Grey Etheria Crystal used for glamour, disguise and polymorphing.
Humans	The human race is descended from the Avion race. In 5070 PA rebellious Avions which had joined Xandar the Mad doomed Great Kraken Incursion had their wings severed as punishment before they were banished and scattered to the Goyodan Chain. One hundred seventy-one years later the 7th Avatar Sang "The Song of Rebirth" and they evolved into a separate race.

	They formed their Great Houses and spread out across the Goyan Island Chain and eventually beyond The Shallow Sea.
Human Great Houses:	
House Aramos	This is the largest and wealthiest of the great human families directly descended from the First Men. The Capital city of Aris is on the Island of Vakai in The Goyodan Chain of Islands in the Northern Shallow Sea. They control the banking and finance in Lumina and are constantly hatching Machiavellian plots to expand their power over the other houses.
House Calden	This great house controls the seas with the largest military and commercial fleets. Their Capital City of Nader is on the Island of Tarla in the Goyodan Chain, but they command the island chain of the Zerk Atoll where their sailors are trained.
House Eldor	This great house control virtually all the agricultural islands of the eastern Goyan Islands. Their Capital City of Rophan is on the Island of Tolle in the Goyodan Chain of Islands in the Northern Shallow Sea.
House Valdur	This house is known for their incestuous practices to keep the family bloodline pure. Their capital city of Dryden is on the

	Island of Atar in The Goyodan Chain of Islands in the Northern Shallow Sea. They were all but destroyed in a surprise invasion by House Eldor called the Unification War. It was only through the discovery of lighter than air travel that their home island was spared by a fleet of war balloons. The rest of their agricultural lands were lost to Eldor. Their entire culture revolves around them now being a powerful Air guild, The Valdurian Air Service.
House Whitmar	This family runs the organized and sanctioned slave trade on Lumina from the city of Nier on the northern Goya coast. Their Capital City of Brinstan on the Island of Umin in the Goyodan Chain of Islands in the Northern Shallow Sea.
Immor-Onn	Large city on the western coast of the Twilight Lands. Home of the Bailian Empire.
Idonian Philosophy	Avion belief that humans are a scourge on the Annigan and should be wiped out. It is the driving belief of the Idonian Cabal of Avion House Pyre and Solas.
Innaca Deep	Giant whirlpool in the Northwestern Ocean of Lumina. It is the location of one of the

	largest Flavian Portal. Its ripples extend out hundreds of miles.
Innaca Run	Final test for admittance to the elite Brightstar Sailors. It comprises making a tight circle around the turbulent seas around the Banok Atoll without being pulled into the giant Flavian Portal there.
Ironmark	Brutal enforcers serving the Quartermasters in the Goyan Islands of Lumina. Each island chain has their own Ironmark, which specializes in a specific form of torture.
Itori	Shamans found throughout the agricultural western Goyan Islands to control mostly locust. They can control any insect and are immune to all insect poisons and stings.
Jangwa	These are elite desert commandos used by the two civilized oases in the Dark Waste Desert to defend the outer parameter of the oasis. They choose Jangwa from the ranks of the Oasis Guards, which show promise. Capable of traveling under the sand and rapidly over the surface of the desert, they make frequent scouting missions to the untamed Qua-Raman oasis and the Buried City of Nof-Saloom.
Kaefom	An Amarenian breeding ritual overseen by the Darek Witches.

Kan	Period of the day in the Goyan Islands when thick sea fogs rise. It is an effect caused by geothermal activities only found in the Goyan Islands and Shallow Sea. Citizens mostly use this time to sleep.
Kel	Flying lizards bred and tended by Avions for food and as beasts of burden.
Kharry Institute	Tiikeri medical facility in Hai-Darr specializing in the crossbreeding of Mawl races to produce Mongrels for specific duties. It is run by the brilliant and ruthless Dr. Met-Ge. The Institute is responsible for the Cheepas &. Ves-Lari.
Kinjuto Dominator	Sex mage specializing in BDSM techniques.
Konaleeta	Called the Island of the Lost. The entire island is caught in a permanent Flavian Loop. It bounces around from location to location across any of the planes of the Middle Realms, never staying in anyone place too long.
Kusars	Mawl bandits of the Dasos region in the Land of Mists.
Kvara	Fourth of the ten Quinte Grand Cycle, summer.
Ky-Awat	Sentient rat creatures of the Dark Waste Desert. They have bred them up from the Cul-Ta and are larger and more aggressive, but no smarter. Various factions use

	them as cannon fodder. They breed quickly and are plentiful, especially around the three main oases.
Land of Mists	This is the largest land mass in Nocturn. It is so named because the combination of cold temperatures in the air combined with the warmth of the ground results in a uniform constant low hanging fog over the entire continent.
	Three distinct landscapes cover the surface of the land, separated by the Kel-Raku Mountain range and dimly illuminated by bioluminescence, outcroppings of Etheria crystals and the moon and stars.
	The thick rainforest of Arboro lies to the north, and the vast savannah of Rovina runs to the south. They're connected by the Bor-Kaa Pass. The dense jungles and swamps of Dasos lie to the east.
Landagar Group	Research and development division of the Valdurian Air Service. It is in the balloon city of Landagar situated high in the mountains of the Valdurian home island of Atar.
Larimar	Etheria crystal used for communication. It is milky white with blue striations. When in

	proximity of the gem all parties hear what the other is saying in their head.
Learned Sister	The title given to Amarenian teachers, scribes & academics.
Lideri	Regional governess of Amarenia. There are eleven, one for each province or Dor. They act as a high council to the Amarenian queen.
Lor-Danta Oasis	The eastern most and sparsely populated major oasis in the Dark Waste Desert. The large obsidian field stretching from its shore contains six Tanum Charts of the skies used by the Arron-Nin Astrologers who dwell there.
Lumina	Half of the world in constant sunlight.
Luna	Term used for the lunar cycle by every culture in the Annigan except the humans in the Goyan Islands who cannot see the moon.
Luroh	Bolo/sash weapon used by the city guards of Mostas the Mahilia. The sash contains the person's rank and record. At either end are two metal balls which when twirled become an effective weapon.
Magitech	Fusion of magic and technology. This mostly refers to the use of Etheria Crystals and specific mechanical items (i.e., airship engines).

Mahilia	Amarenian Capital City of Mostar city guards.
Makari	Inter-dimensional race of sentient spiders from the Pasture Plain of the Middle Realms. They seeded the Cevot race in the Os'Tor Mountains in the Land of Mists. The males resemble hairy wolf spiders, the females resemble black widows. The females are always alluring to any male of any race. She will then feel the compulsion to kill them after sex.
Malachite	Light green Etheria crystal, which absorbs energy.
Marassa	Professor at the University of Marassa in Zor.
Masha	Amarenian for master.
Maudo Grass	Tall grass with a bright blue flowering tuft growing in the Land of Mists. The flowers are a favorite intoxicant for Mawls and especially coveted by the Tiikeri.
Mawl	Overall name for the humanoid cat races of the Land of Mists. It is also the term used for the common language they share.
Medikua	Medical officer aboard Calden naval vessels.
Merve	Eighth of the ten Quinte Grand Cycle, autumn.
Middle Realms	Constantly shifting inter-dimensional plane between

	worlds. Sometimes referred to as the Fairy or dream realms.
Mongrel	These are the product of cross breeding between the Mawl races. Pure breeds mostly shun them. The Tiikeri use them for slave labor. They can be found all over the Land of Mists.
Moonfall	Period of the cycle when Nocturn's main illuminating body the moon, dips below the horizon issuing in the Moonless
Moonless	Period of the cycle when Nocturn's main illuminating body the moon, orbits around to the Lumina side of the Annigan (night).
Mora	Term used for teacher or master in the Whovian Sword Schools of Rohina Takki.
Morasian Puff Boy	Male prostitute from the port City of Moras on Goya's west coast. Known for their distinctly feminine demeanor.
Mostas	Capital City of the Amarenian Empire on the western shore of Amarenia.
Najuka	Amarenian emasculation ritual performed on all males except those used for breeding purposes in the Kaefom Ritual.
Na-Kab	One of the three insectoid groups that live below the Land of Mists. They occupy the eastern most hive closest to Mount Natal and have a fire make-up under their

	exoskeleton. Their tail has a penis shaped stinger that can impregnate anything anyplace they sting.
Namesake	Term used for spouse when they share a bespoke last name.
Narrows, The	These are the slums of the Hidden City of Toriss in Otomoria. They are the remnants of an old iron mine.
Nocturn	Half the world in constant night
Nolton Boat	Ships made of Ukko wood in a secret shipyard on the island of Zer and mostly used by Brightstar sailors. They hover less than an inch above the water. Their rudder is also Ukko, so it guides and propels. The specific construction of the hull makes the boat unsinkable.
Noma	Poison from the Noma Viper.
Nurian Edicts	EEtah rules of conduct set down by House Nur which are the basis for all Sunal laws. The various Sunals can and do add their own individual laws to this baseline for all Sunals.
Nyanja	Large seahorses ridden as sea cavalry by the Calden Navy.
Obsidian	Black Etheria crystal which holds psychic energy.
Ol'daEE	Person able to cast spells while having sex under the influence of Oldust.
Oldust	Hallucinogenic powder derived from the spores of the rare Impia

	Mushroom. It increases magical abilities and can allow travel to the Middle Realms.
Onay	Humanoid wolf men of the Barrens. They band together their various packs in three distinct hordes.
On' Dara	Sentient horse creatures living on the Plains of Taka-Vir in the southeastern Twilight Lands. They raise and train horses, which they sell to the rest of the Annigan. They also trade for silk with the Cevot Spiders.
ooD	Shell worn on the back of the male Otick warriors as armor. They mark the warrior's rank and house on the outside of the shell and inscribe the inside with a record of their deeds. They place the ooD over the entrance to their home, which is a hole in the sand.
Oracle of the River	A demigod who dwells in the cypress swamp at the end of the western fork of the Otoman River. It appears as a giant catfish partially submerged. Its many whiskers are sunken into the water. Through them it perceives anything that happens in, on or around the waterway. It has been around for thousands of grands,
Orad	Air goddess of death and predominate deity of the assassin's guild, the Hand of the Wind.

Orad Dex	Initiates to the Orad priesthood. Street/entry level assassins.
Orad Con	(Taker of the divine wind) These are full priests of Orad. Their special skills are the kiss of death, the poison breath, and the Phantom Dagger.
Orad Sto	(Giver of the Divine Wind) High priests of Orad who can also restore life.
Otick	Humanoid crab people that inhabit the Shallow Sea. These are the first sentient creatures to rise from the ocean floor and are a proud, deeply spiritual and noble race. Goya's volcanic warmed waters provide home to the Otick's prolific oyster beds littering the floor of The Shallow Sea. From these beds arose the five great Pearl Avatars, creation gods whose songs brought life and sentience to Lumina. Otick society is organized into a highly structured caste system, Worker Class, Warrior Class and Mother Class. Otick society is organized in two main categories domestic and military. The three Otick Great Houses are known as the Shelled Triad. Each house tends their own oyster beds and competes for the birthplace of the next Avatar.

Otick Great Houses:	
House Awa	Home of the last two avatars. Located in the Tellasian Chain, in the capital city of Hidet on the Island of Zod. Mother Class specialization.
House Pewa	Located in the Goyodan Chain, in the capital city of Oniack, on the Island of Zak. Worker Class specialization.
House Sensu	Located in the Otoman Group, in the capital city of Sunico, on the Island of Lakia. Warrior Class specialization.
Otomoria	Large Island continent in the western Goyan Islands. One of the main agricultural islands producing grain.
Outer Clan EEtah	Shark creatures smaller in stature than regular EEtahs cast out from the three great EEtah Houses from the hatchery. The ones that survive banded together into loose clans. the contract themselves out as deck hands and lately have been volunteering in the Valdurian Marines.
Padi	Regional demi-god of water worshiped in and around the High Holy City of Zor, associated with the peace and calming effect of water and represented by a calm pond.
Palu EEtah	Rare hammerhead EEtahs. They are as big as outer clan EEtah but

	extremely intelligent. They tend to be reclusive loners.
Pappia	Members of the child street gangs of the Hidden City of Toriss. They live in the slum section of the city called The Narrows.
Pa-Waga	Lawful evil god of greed worshiped mostly by the Tiikeri. Its clerics practice binary blood rune magic comprising "X" and "I."
Peace Babies	Children born of a union between any of the five major human houses.
Peto	Fifth of the ten Quinte Grand Cycle, summer.
Piceans	Humanoid fish people of Lumina. They have the capability of breathing above and below the water and are impervious to the ocean's depths. Their gill flaps are large enough to fold over their ears. When the sound waves of the voice pass through the membrane, it translates it. This makes them valuable translators in all seaports of the Goyan Islands.
Piety Watch	Militant, religious police faction of the Pa-Waga church. They roam the city arresting anyone who is caught begging, idle, or not being productive. Minor offences are punished by beating with thin cane rods.

The Fate of Tomorrow

	They wear black capes with high pointed collars that resemble cat ears and red shirts.
Pisar	Bailian title for a scholar.
Pomaku	Humanoid leopard people (Mawl) native to the Arboro region in the Land of Mists, Nocturn.
Protocol 13	Code phrase used by EEtah House Nur requesting a meeting between an intelligence asset and their Handler.
PSI	Short for psychic energy. It is the underlying force which powers all magic in the Annigan.
Qua-Raman Oasis	Oasis in the central Dark Waste Desert. Because its location is just south of the Tur-Qua Pass, it is a major trading post with the gems harvested in the Barrens to the north.
Quartermaster	Collector of taxes and tariffs in the Goyan Islands. They use the Ironmark for enforcing their rule.
Quinte	Time period equivalent to a month.
Ramu	This gambling dismemberment game has been banned throughout the entire Goyan Islands. The Free City of Tannimore is the only place that permits it.
Rayth	Pirate faction of the Amarenian people in open revolt and attempting to form their own nation.

Rod-Ema Trench	Massive abysmal fissure running the equator in the western ocean floor in Nocturn. At its head is the Agar Goyot. On its north wall dipping into the depths is the Black Mural.
Rohina Takii	Sword school originating on the island of Wou. Its distinctive characteristic is the strike while drawing technique.
Salar Winds	The turbulent winds surrounding the peak of Mount Goya which must be navigated to enter the Avion City of Darmont on the mountain's northwestern face. Avion term of exasperation, "By the mighty winds of Salar!"
Secor	Street name for the Imperial Gold Ingot equivalent to ten struck gold coins.
Sesto	Sixth of the ten Quinte Grand Cycle, autumn.
Si	The term for Mr. in the Common Tongue spoken in the Goyan Islands.
Shrouding Stone	A hybrid Etheria crystals (Magitech) consisting of Howlite for glamour, and Planchite, which connects to air magic. When powered with PSI it bends the light around the being or object attached to, rendering it invisible. The invisible object still has substance and can be collided with or struck. It is ineffective on

	creatures that have sonic or infrared capabilities.
Sikari	Female Singa hunter/killer squads. They travel in groups of two or more. They have crossed bandoleros on their chests filled with sickle shaped throwing blades.
Silent Partner	Organized crime families in the Goyan islands. There are seven cabals, each organized by local.
Simikort	Round engraved coin which acts as an Amarenian noble's calling card.
Singa	Humanoid lion people (Mawl) that inhabit the southern Rovina area of the land of Mists.
Skirting the Upwinds	Dangerous maneuver practiced by only a few airship pilots. It involves taking the airship up to the edge of the atmosphere, then down to your destination. Allowing long distance travel in a short period.
Society of Whispers	Term used for the general intelligence communities of the five human Noble Houses.
Spice Rat	Smugglers that operate mostly in the Spice Islands chains (Zerian Reef Chain and Outer Zerians) and occasionally in the entire western side of the Goyan Islands.
Spooks	Street term for spies and operatives in the Society of Whispers.

Strasta	Ancient prophet in the folklore of the Cevot spider people of the Os-Ani Mountains.
Sunal	EEtah war college specializing in a martial skill.
Szoldos mercenaries	One of several small private armies for hire on the Goyan continent.
Taking it Upstairs	Airship pilot slang for Skirting the Upwinds
Tanum Charts	Six maps of Nocturn's night sky. The Arron-Nin Astrologers use them for divination and sometimes the opening of Flavian Portals.
Teine	Second of the ten Quinte Grand Cycle, spring.
Ten - Fifty	Cliche phrase in the Goyan Islands referring to the ten cycles in the cluster (week) and fifty decis of the cycle. The equivalent of 24/7.
Tenable Sister	Title given to Amarenian lawyers
Tiikeri	Sentient Tiger creatures of the Dasos region in the eastern Land of Mists.
Tisa	Ninth of the ten Quinte Grand Cycle, winter.
Tisina, Code of,	Mobster code of silence in the city of Zor. Because no organized crime is allowed, the various independent criminals adopted a complete "no cooperation" rule with the city guards. The smallest violation is punishable by death.

Trinilic	Orange Etheria crystal, which connects with fire magic.
Turine	Tidal clocks used in the Goyan Islands.
Ukkonite	Bronze Etheria crystal with natural repellant properties. It is the crystal equivalent to Ukko wood found only in Nocturn.
Ukko wood	Magical wood from the world tree harvested only on the island of Zer in the eastern Goyan Islands. It has natural repellant properties. This makes it perfect for shields. They also use it as currency and to make Brightstar Nolton Boats.
Ulana	Chaotic Evil goddess of the sea worshiped by a small sect of Amarenian Rayth in the province of Durik-Dor.
Unification War	Conflict started by House Eldor in 2 P.A. against the eastern agricultural islands of House Valdur. It ended as quickly as it began when House Aramos forced them to the negotiating table by threatening to freeze both houses' accounts in the Imperial Bank.
Valorous Sister	Amarenian title for heroic acts which affected the realm.
Vedette	Small fast Nolton Boats crewed by a single ex-Brightstar sailor. They use them for fast, anonymous travel around the oceans of Lumina.

Velocomite	Etheria Crystal, Pale blue w/ red bands, which increases or decreases an objects speed in which it's travelling.
Veros Pearls	Highest quality pearl cultivated in the sacred Otick oyster beds. They can hold a magical charge.
Ves-Lari	Mawl mongrels bred by the Tiikeri for rowing and poling. They are a combination of Pomaku (leopard) and Duma (Cheetah). Crews can pole or row for hundreds of miles at a time without stopping. They keep crews together to promote unity but switch them out after long trips for rest.
Virago	Amarenian title for a female warlord.
Wraith	Deep cover agents for House Aramos. They are drawn from the elite Black Talons unit.
Yagur	Humanoid jaguars (Mawl) from the Arboro region of the Land of Mists. They are seers, healers and shamans, and serve all the various Mawl races.
Yudon	Harpoon and standard weapon of every Sunal EEtah. They rifle the shaft for accuracy in throwing.
Yupik	Also called Ice Clans, these are one hundred and sixty-five humanoid clans of Eskimo like people. They divide into 3 major groups. The nomadic wanderers of the western flows always in

	competition for food and resources. They are constantly being harassed from the Ash-Ta as prey. The largest group inhabits the vast eastern flows and has semi-permanent settlements all surrounding the Ice City of Mos-Agar'.
Zadim	Lapidaries which operate in the three large oasis of the Dark Waste Desert.
Zerian Rangers	Woodsmen fighters who belong to any of nine different clans which occupy the forests of the Island continent of Zer in the Goyan Islands.
Zorian Monetary Council	A ruling body controlling all banking located in the High Holy City of Zor. They regulate all exchanges of money, goods and services, including the collecting of taxes and tariffs through the Quartermasters Guild.

R.W. Marcus

MAPS

The Fate of Tomorrow

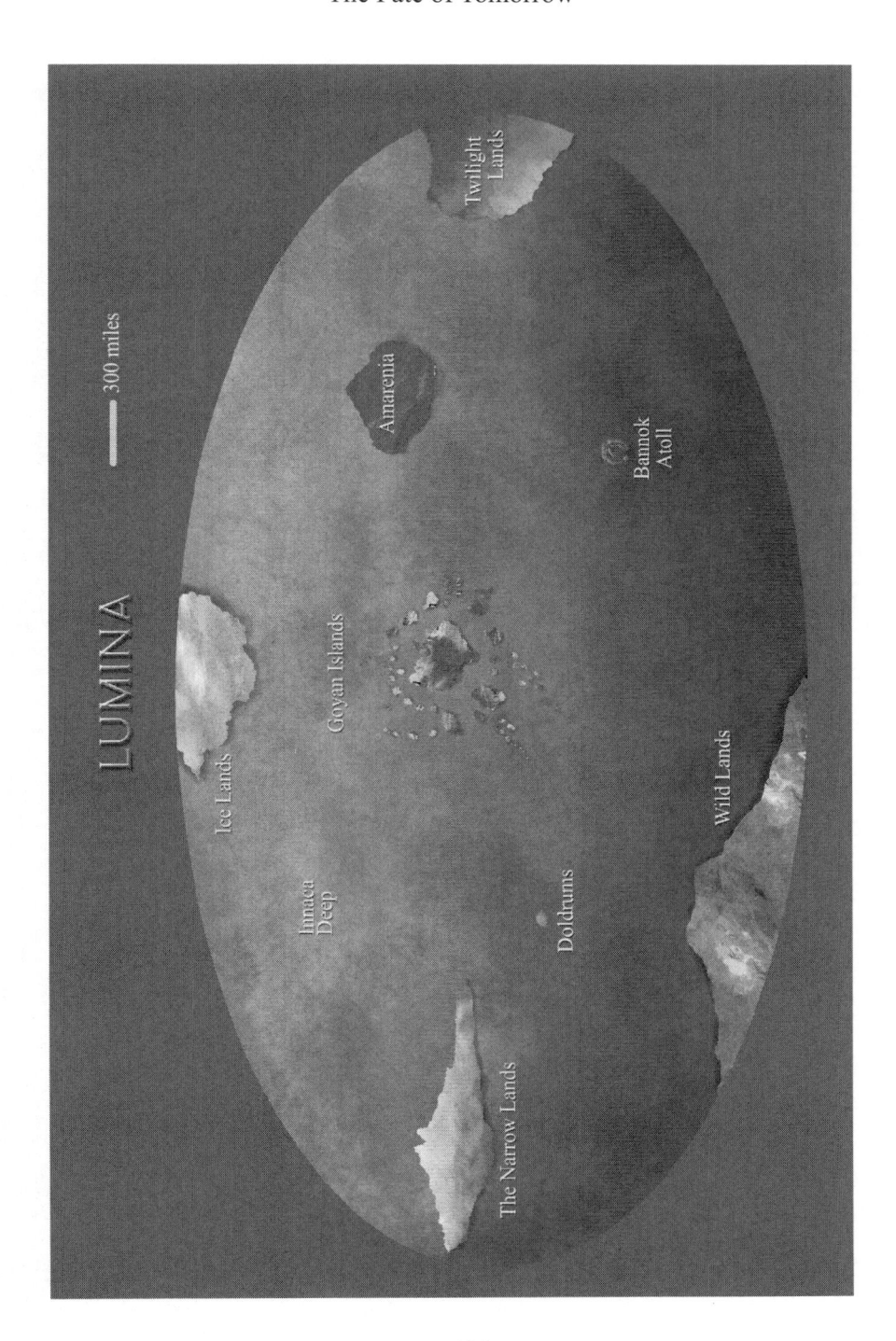

LUMINA

— 300 miles

Twilight Lands

Amarenia

Bannok Atoll

Ice Lands

Goyan Islands

Inmaea Deep

Doldrums

Wild Lands

The Narrow Lands

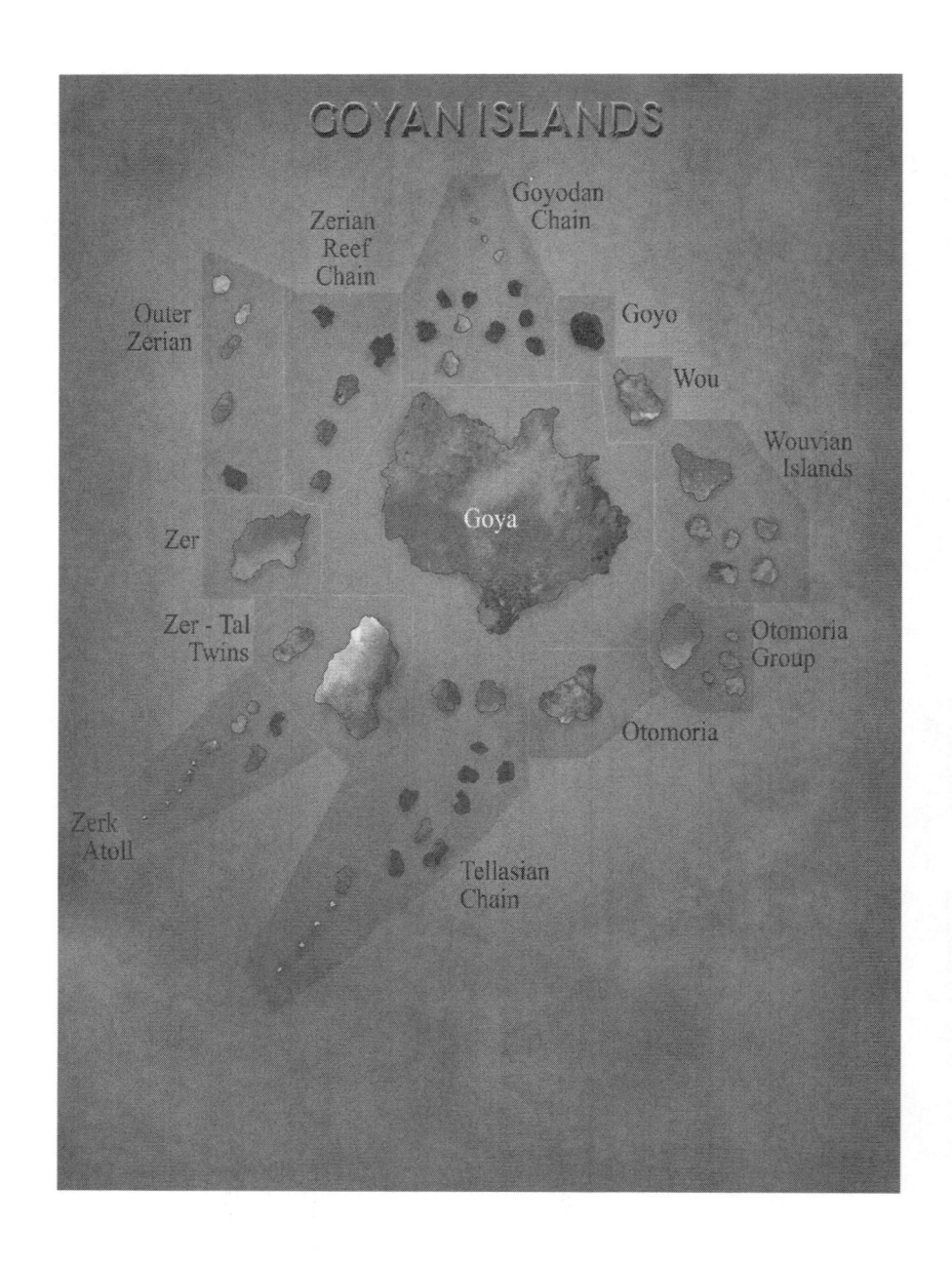

GOYAN ISLANDS

- Goyodan Chain
- Zerian Reef Chain
- Outer Zerian
- Goyo
- Wou
- Wouvian Islands
- Zer
- Goya
- Zer - Tal Twins
- Otomoria Group
- Otomoria
- Zerk Atoll
- Tellasian Chain

The Fate of Tomorrow

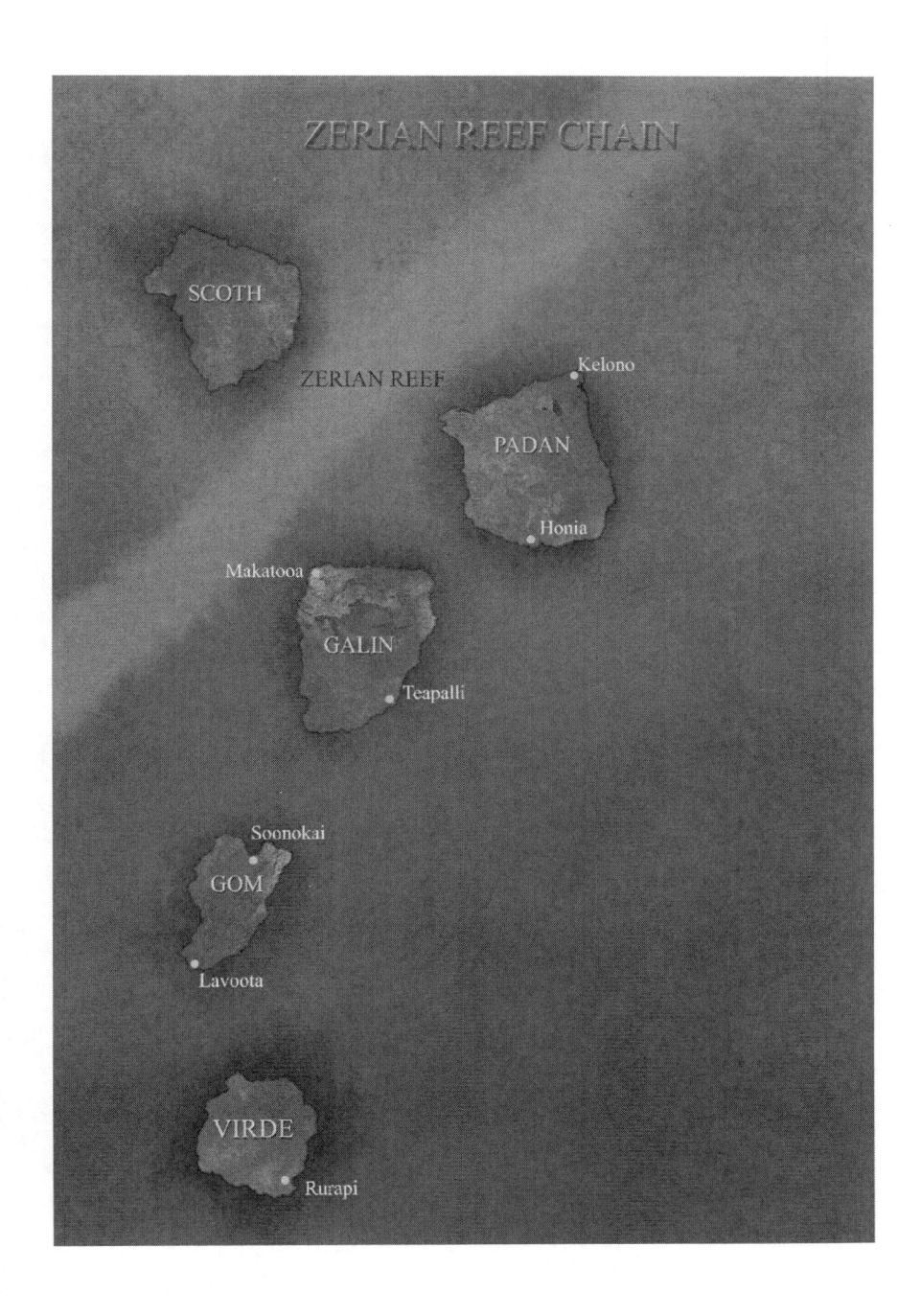

ZERIAN REEF CHAIN

SCOTH

ZERIAN REEF

Kelono

PADAN

Honia

Makatooa

GALIN

Teapalli

Soonokai

GOM

Lavoota

VIRDE

Rurapi

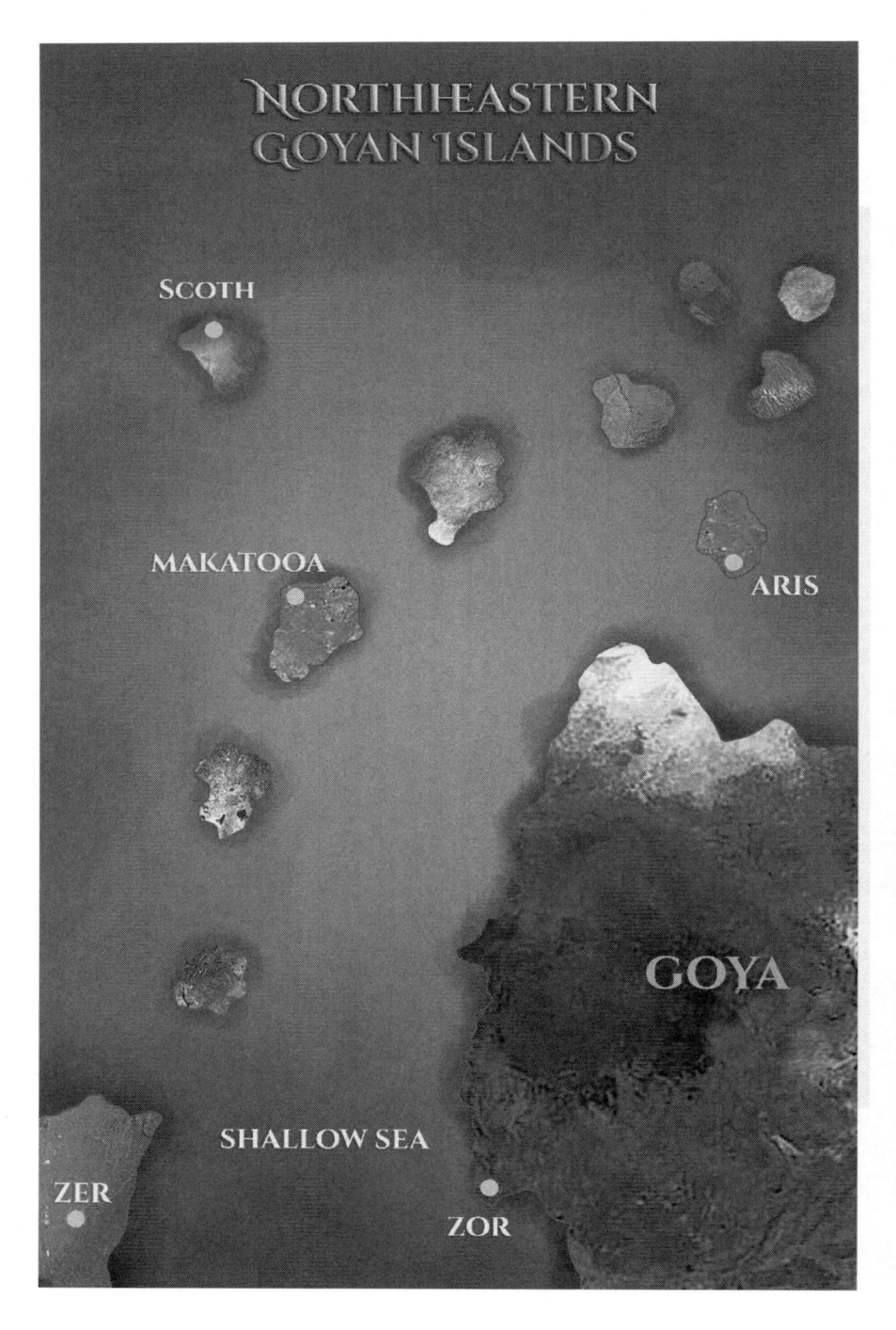

R.W. Marcus

NORTHEASTERN GOYAN ISLANDS

Scoth

Makatooa

Aris

Goya

Shallow Sea

Zer

Zor

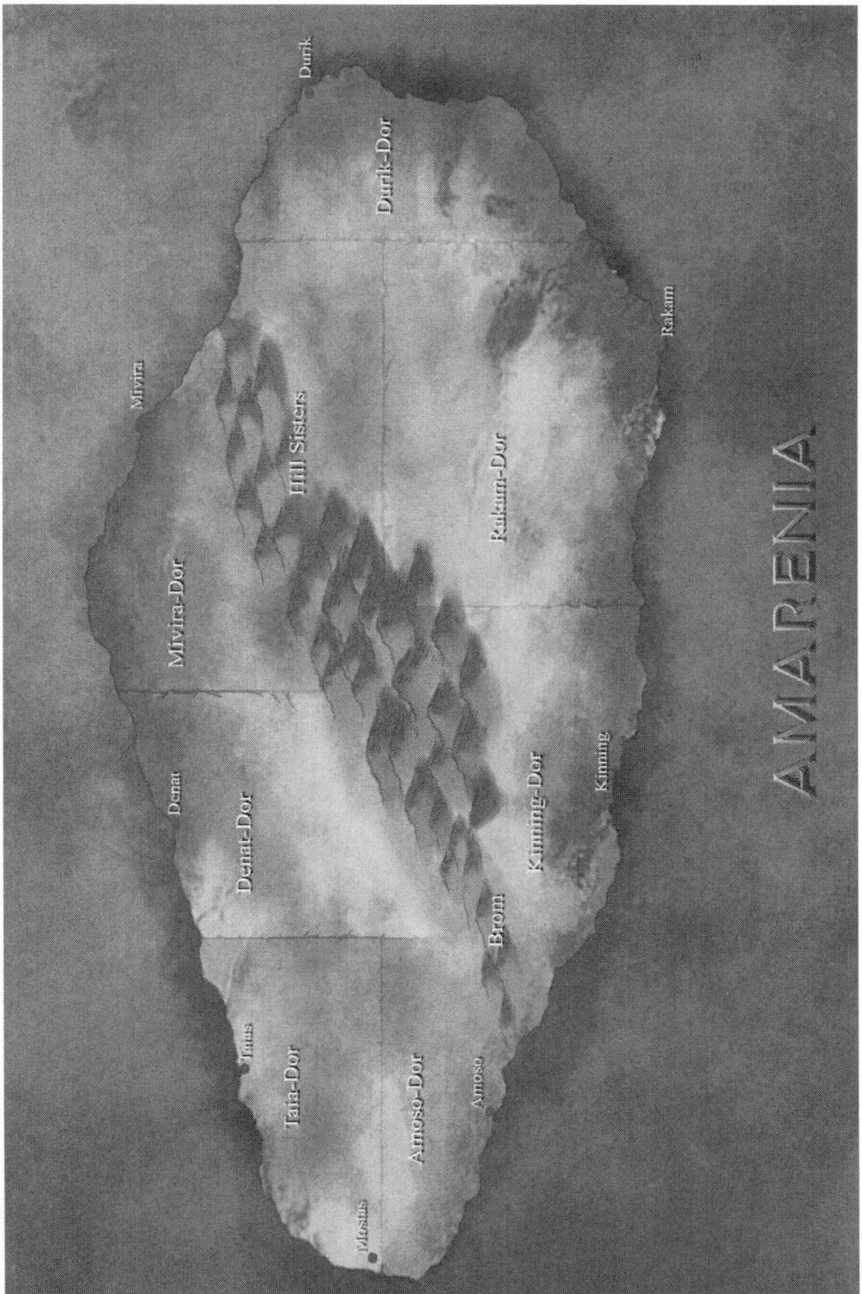
AMARENIA
Durik
Durik-Dor
Rakam
Mivira
Hill Sisters
Rakam-Dor
Mivira-Dor
Denat
Denat-Dor
Kinning
Kinning-Dor
Brom
Taia-Dor
Amoso-Dor
Amoso

ABOUT THE AUTHOR

R.W. Marcus spent most of his life selling books. Along the way he managed to become a Falconer, 3rd Dan Black Belt in Yoshukai Karate, Freemason, Freelance Photographer, Ad Copywriter and WMNF Radio Disc Jockey. Marcus' radio commercials and freelance photography won numerous awards, including Best of Shows and Best of the Bay Addy Awards for work with Creative Keys and Laughing Bird Productions. R.W. Marcus was also Founder and Creative Director of United Game Masters, where he cowrote the UGM Universal Gaming System which he used to create and playtest a role-playing game based in the world of the Annigan Cycle. He formally held the title of Director of Incunabula at Griffon's Medieval Manuscripts, where he penned his first nonfiction title, *The Ship of Fools to 1500*, which Amazon called "an authoritative guide to one of the most popular works of secular writing." Now retired, he has created a new genre of fiction - Pulp Fantasy Noir - to exorcise the darker side of his good nature. He currently resides in Tallahassee, Florida.

CONNECT

WEBSITE: https://AnniganCycle.com
FACEBOOK: https://www.facebook.com/noirrwmarcus/
TWITTER: @NoirRWMarcus
EMAIL: RWMarcus@yahoo.com

SHADOW of the TWILIGHT LANDS
TALES OF THE ANNIGAN CYCLE:
BOOK TWO
AVAILABLE FROM LAUGHING BIRD PUBLISHING

Made in the USA
Columbia, SC
07 February 2023